Highland Treasure

By Lynsay Sands

Lynsay Sands

Highland Treasure

AVONBOOKS

An Imprint of HarperCollinsPublishers

Excerpt from *Meant to Be Immortal* copyright © 2021 by Lynsay Sands.

First Avon Books mass market printing: February 2021
First Avon Books hardcover printing: January 2021

Print Edition ISBN: 978-0-06-305884-2
Digital Edition ISBN: 978-0-06-285541-1

FIRST EDITION

21 22 23 24 25   LSC   10 9 8 7 6 5 4 3 2 1

Highland Treasure

Prologue

THE SOFT JINGLE OF KEYS STIRRED ELYSANDE FROM A FITFUL sleep. Curled up on the damp, dirt floor, and facing the stone wall, she couldn't see who was approaching, but didn't particularly care. It would either be de Buci or one of his men, come to drag her up into the great hall to beat her again. Or perhaps to do something worse this time, since the beating hadn't worked to get the information he was looking for.

Thoughts of those worse things made her fingers tighten around the corners of the smelly, ragged blanket she'd dragged around herself to ward off the chill in the cold dungeon. De Buci had threatened several tortures for their next meeting as he'd had his men drag her away: rape, cutting off a hand or a foot, marking her face with a hot iron so none would look upon her without horror. He'd listed other threats but she hadn't heard them since his voice had become a muted growl from behind her as she was dragged down into the bowels of hell that was the dungeon of Kynardersley.

Elysande had never much considered whether she was a brave woman or not, but this experience had taught her that she wasn't. Because had she the answer the man was looking for, she would have given it to him about halfway through the earlier beatings. But she didn't know the answer to his repeated and insistent roar of *"Where is it?"*

"What?" she'd cried just as often, desperate to end the abuse, only to be told, *"You know what! Where is it?"*

But Elysande hadn't known. That morning, she'd woken happy

and cheerful in her bed, in the home she'd grown up in, with loving parents and a castle full of servants and soldiers who she considered family. Now . . .

The sound of the key in the lock finally had her lifting her head off the floor to look over her shoulder. Elysande stared blankly at her mother's maid, who now stood at the door to her cell, and then she sat up with surprise. The abrupt movement immediately sent pain rushing through her body, but she ignored it and rasped out a confused, "Betty?"

The maid's eyes widened with alarm. She put a finger to her mouth in the sign to hush, then peered anxiously to the sleeping guard slumped in the chair by the table outside Elysande's cell. When the man continued to snore loudly, Betty turned her attention back to the keys she held. Pulling out the one presently in the lock, she tried the next on the ring of half a dozen large keys.

Elysande watched silently, half-afraid she was dreaming. Then the third key worked and Betty eased the door open. They both winced at the squeal of the hinges, their gazes moving to the guard. But he continued snoring loudly.

"Can ye get up?" Betty whispered.

Elysande shifted her gaze back to the maid, a little startled to find the woman now standing right in front of her. She hadn't seen her move. Rather than answer, Elysande released her hold on one corner of the ratty blanket to reach out to the girl. She wanted to touch her, to be sure she was real, but the maid must have thought it a silent request for help, because she immediately took her arm and began to pull upward.

Steeling herself against the pain, Elysande managed to stagger to her feet with the maid's help, but it was an effort that left her sweaty and swaying as she fought the pain and dizziness that assailed her.

"Can ye walk, m'lady?" Betty whispered anxiously, looking close to tears as she clutched her arm to steady her.

Elysande swallowed the bile rising in her throat and nodded grimly. She would walk if it killed her.

Betty pulled Elysande's arm over her shoulders and helped her shuffle out of the cell. It was a slow, laborious effort, but once she had her out of the cell, Betty urged her to grasp the smooth bars to help her stay upright, then rushed to the end of the small hall and snatched up a bag by the wall. Elysande frowned slightly, but didn't ask questions; she merely watched her pull a gown from the bag and quickly begin to stuff it with the fetid straw that covered the hall floor. The maid filled the bag itself last and then hurried into the cell, and arranged her creation under the ratty blanket. Only when Betty straightened to examine her handiwork did Elysande understand what she was doing. She'd managed to make it look like a huddled figure curled against the back wall of the cell. Like she was still there, Elysande realized as the maid rushed back and closed the cell door.

They both stiffened and glanced warily to the guard when the action set up another protesting squeal. But the man remained asleep.

Elysande released a relieved breath, and drew in another, only to hold that one when Betty moved cautiously over to the man to set the keys carefully on the table in front of him, where she'd apparently got them. Despite the maid's caution, they made the faintest clanking noises as she set them down. Still, the man didn't stir.

Releasing a shaky little sigh, Betty moved quickly back to her side and took her arm over her shoulders again.

"This way," she whispered, and led her to the end of the hall where the bag had been.

"Mother?" Elysande asked in a soft voice when the girl pushed and turned the correct stone to open the secret passage.

"Aye. She told me how to open it," Betty admitted.

It wasn't what Elysande had been asking. She wanted to know how her mother was, but as the wall swung open to reveal what seemed like a million stairs stretching upward, she decided that her mother must be all right to have given the girl directions. So she saved her breath and moved into the hidden passage.

Hewn into the stone and disappearing up into darkness,

the stairs were too narrow for them to move side by side. Betty couldn't help her here. She would have to manage them on her own. And she would, Elysande told herself firmly, even if she had to drag herself up them on her belly. And she very nearly did. Elysande was on her hands and knees by the time they reached the top of the stairwell.

Gasping with relief as she made it off the last step, Elysande collapsed to the cold stone passage, every muscle in her body trembling with exhaustion.

"M'lady?"

Elysande sighed at that whisper from Betty. She wanted to just lie there and die, but she couldn't. Her mother . . .

The brush of cool cloth across her arm and cheek made her open her eyes. She couldn't see in this stygian darkness, but guessed that Betty was stepping carefully over her to stand by her head in the narrow passage and it was the maid's skirts she'd felt.

"M'lady? It isn't much farther now." The girl's whisper was accompanied by her hands clasping Elysande's shoulders. The maid was going to try to help her to her feet.

Ignoring her aches and pains, Elysande ground her teeth together and pushed herself up onto her knees. She then braced one hand against the stone wall, grabbed the girl's arm with the other and managed to drag herself to her feet.

"Are you all right?" Betty whispered with concern.

"I am fine," Elysande said, panting, and then took a deep breath to steady herself. "Let us go. I would see Mother."

She sensed rather than saw the girl move away. Elysande took another deep breath and then braced her hands against the cool stone walls on either side of her and shuffled forward, following. She didn't realize how far behind she'd fallen until Betty opened the secret entrance to her mother's room and light spilled into the passage from a good ten feet ahead.

Straightening her shoulders, Elysande tried to move more quickly. It still seemed like forever before she reached the opening and then she was blinded by the light in the room. There were only two small candles there to chase away the night's gloom, but after her time in the dark dungeon, those candles were like staring directly into the sun. Elysande had to close her eyes to protect them. Fortunately, Betty recognized the problem at once and took her arm to lead her across the room to her mother's bed.

Much to her relief, Elysande had adjusted enough by then that she could at least see, though she was still squinting against the light when she dropped to her knees next to the bed. Her strained eyes slid over her mother's frail form and swollen face and Elysande could have wept at the bruises covering every inch of Mairghread de Valance that wasn't covered by the furs on the bed.

"Mother?" she breathed, clasping the hand closest to her and then quickly releasing it when she felt how swollen they were. Only then did she recall that they had been broken.

"Oh, Mama," she moaned, resting her forehead on the bed with despair.

"Ellie."

That broken whisper made her lift her head at once. "Yes, I am here."

"The Buchanans," she managed, her voice so faint Elysande wasn't sure she'd heard her right.

"The Buchanans?" she asked with confusion. Elysande was tired and achy, her mind such a clutter with worry, pain and fear that she couldn't imagine why her mother would bring up the clan.

"The Buchanan healer is in England. You must go to him. He can take you to my sister."

"Nay. I will not leave you," Elysande said at once, and her mother's eyes shot open full of fire and determination.

"You must," her mother ordered, and then spoke quickly, telling her what to do.

Chapter 1

"Damn me, Buchanan," Ralph FitzBaderon, Baron of Monmouth, said cheerfully as he reached for his ale. "I thought I was done for, but you worked a miracle and saved my life. I still cannot fathom it. Are you sure you are not part English?"

"Nay," Rory answered distractedly, his gaze flying over the message his brother Alick had just handed him.

"Well," the baron said with a shake of the head. "I think you must have some English in you somewhere."

"Why is that?" Alick asked beside him, and Rory almost sighed to himself, knowing his brother wouldn't like the answer any more than he had the hundred or so times he'd heard it over the last two weeks.

"Because Scots are ignorant heathens," Baron Monmouth informed him. "Hardly capable of a mastery over healing such as your brother has. Nay. There must be English in your family history somewhere."

"And yet, there is no'," Rory said easily as he felt Alick stiffen beside him. Rerolling the message he'd finished reading, he tucked it inside his plaid and stood to leave the trestle table. "Time to go, Alick."

"Aye," the younger man growled, rising at once and falling into step beside him. "And thank God fer that."

"Here now!" Baron Monmouth protested, scurrying to his feet to chase after them as Rory led Alick toward the large keep doors. "What of FitzAlan? I told you he had a complaint he wanted you to look at."

"I had no agreement with FitzAlan," Rory said with unconcern as he yanked the keep door open and strode out into the biting wind. It felt more like January or February than late November and he could smell the promise of snow in the air. It seemed winter was coming early this year.

"But I paid you a small fortune!" Baron Monmouth charged after him down the stairs. "The least you can do is see the man. He should be along soon. He—"

"Ye paid me to get ye well and I did that," Rory pointed out mildly, drawing the top of his plaid around his shoulders as he crossed the bailey in long, quick strides. "Ye're well, the deal is complete and we're leaving."

"Praise God," Alick muttered beside him with a combination of relief and disgust that Rory understood fully. This had not been his first visit to England, but he was determined it would be his last. He hadn't really wanted to come in the first place, but Monmouth had offered him a king's ransom to travel down into this godforsaken land and heal him. However, two weeks in England was two weeks too many, and even the fortune he'd just made wasn't worth putting up with the constant sneering insults to his homeland and countrymen that he, Alick and their men had been served.

Monmouth's words just now had been kind in comparison to those of his soldiers over the last weeks. After two days of that nonsense, and the three fights it had caused between the English soldiers and the Scottish warriors who had accompanied them on this journey, Rory had told Alick to take their men and camp in the woods outside the walls of Monmouth. They'd been waiting patiently there for him to finish his work and leave.

"FitzAlan will pay you to tend him!" Monmouth cried. The man was still trailing behind them, but couldn't keep up and was beginning to huff and puff for air as he fell behind.

"Go back inside, m'lord," Rory said firmly without bothering to glance around. "Ye're on the mend, but no' yet strong enough to be running about, especially in this cold."

"FitzAlan will pay you whatever you want," Monmouth insisted, gasping for breath now.

Rory stopped.

"God, no, brother," Alick hissed beside him, alarm in his voice. Rory ignored him and turned back to face the baron.

"Whatever you want," Monmouth repeated in a raspy voice, bending to brace his hands on his knees as he tried to catch his breath.

"Baron, there is no' enough coin in all o' Christendom to make me stay in England another night," he said quietly. "Now get ye back inside before ye make yerself ill again. Fer I'll no' be staying to mend ye anew."

Alick's relief was plain to see when Rory swung back to continue to the stables where their horses were even now being led out.

Baron Monmouth didn't try to follow them farther.

"I was afraid the coin would tempt ye and ye'd agree to stay to see this FitzAlan."

Rory shook his head at Alick's words. "Never. I'm ready to be heading home. I've had enough o' this godforsaken country."

"Aye," Alick muttered, scowling around the bailey at the people coming and going.

Thanking the boy who had saddled and led out his horse, Rory quickly mounted and then waited for Alick to gain his saddle before saying, "Besides, we have something else we must do."

Alick gathered his reins and glanced to him with surprise. "What's that?"

"Collect a treasure and take it to Sinclair."

"The message?" Alick asked, his eyes narrowing.

Nodding, Rory clucked his tongue, and urged his horse to move.

"What is this treasure?" Alick called.

When Rory ignored the question and urged his horse to put on speed, Alick cursed and rode after him. Not wanting to speak of it until they were well away from Monmouth, Rory rode at a fast trot until he'd crossed the drawbridge, and then set his beast to gallop across the frost-tipped grass of the open area outside the castle walls.

He heard Alick whistle behind him, and saw the four warriors their brother Aulay had sent with them appear ahead at the edge of the woods on their mounts. Rory immediately turned in their direction at once and rode to meet them.

"Ye've broken camp and are ready to head home?" he asked, reining in before them, and wasn't surprised by their silent nods. Since they carried little when traveling and slept rolled up in their plaids, there wasn't much to breaking up camp besides putting out whatever fire had remained by morning.

"What were ye talking about back there? What treasure?" Alick asked as he drew his mount to a halt beside him. "And who was that message from that ye received this morn?"

Rory raised an eyebrow in surprise at the second question. "Did the messenger no' tell ye when he gave it to ye?"

"Nay," Alick said grimly. "And he did no' stay long enough to be questioned either. Just rode up, tossed it at Conn, said to get it to Rory Buchanan and rode off ere anyone could even move. Since I was coming to check and be sure we were still leaving today, I brought it in to ye fer him."

Rory grunted at this news, but before he could comment, Conn suddenly tilted his head to the side and stiffened.

"Riders," Alick muttered after a moment.

They all looked toward the opposite side of the clearing, but no one was yet visible through the trees. Even so, Rory urged his horse farther along the trail so that they would be hidden from view. The others followed suit and they sat their mounts, silent and still in the cover of the woods, to see who was approaching. It wasn't long before a large contingent of soldiers charged out of the trees on the other end of the clearing, riding for Monmouth's gates.

"Think you 'tis FitzAlan?" Alick asked.

"Nay," Rory said with a frown. "There are no nobles among that rabble. They are soldiers every one." He watched silently as half a dozen men broke off from the group and crossed the drawbridge, leaving the remaining men waiting outside. Rory then turned his horse and spurred him into a gallop again. He had a feeling the men had something to do with the message he'd received and that it would be a good idea to find the treasure mentioned in it and head north as quickly as possible. With that thought in mind, he kept up the pace for the half hour it took before they reached the point of the trail where the river ran over it. Rory crossed the shallow flow of water and then stopped and glanced around, searching the trees on either side of the path.

He wasn't surprised when Alick immediately moved up beside him again. To forestall the questions he knew were on the tip of his brother's tongue, he said, "The message ye brought me was from Lady Mairghread de Valance, Baroness of Kynardersley. She is Lady Sinclair's sister."

"Jo's sister?" Alick asked with surprise.

Lady Jo Sinclair was their sister Saidh's dear friend, wife to Laird Campbell Sinclair and the only Lady Sinclair they'd met.

"Nay. Lady Bearnas Sinclair. Cam's mother," Rory answered, his tone distracted as he scanned the woods around them, searching for the sign the message had mentioned.

"Oh," Alick muttered. "So the message was from Cam's aunt, and she wants you to collect a treasure and take it to Sinclair," Alick reasoned out, and when Rory didn't comment, he asked, "What are ye looking fer?"

"There is supposed to be"—Rory paused and smiled—"a ribbon."

"A ribbon?" Alick asked, moving up beside him. "I do no' see—"

His words died when Rory pointed out the thin, white ribbon tied around the trunk of a tree on their left. There was a narrow trail next to it, leading deeper into the woods that would have been easily missed without the ribbon to mark the way.

"I do no' recall Cam mentioning an aunt, but even so, what would she be doing in England?" Alick asked, shifting uncomfortably on his mount. "Mayhap 'tis a trick or a trap."

"Mayhap," Rory agreed, aware of the way the suggestion made

the other warriors all now sit up in their saddles, eyes alert as they searched the surrounding area for signs of trouble.

They were all silent for a minute, listening to the bitter wind whistling through the trees, and then Rory turned in his seat to eye the four men with them. "Fearghas and Donnghail, you two stay here and keep an eye out. Fetch us if ye catch wind o' trouble."

He waited long enough to see the men nod, and then added, "The rest with me."

Rory urged his horse down the new path, but his hand moved to his sword, ready to draw it at the first sign of trouble. The narrow trail, if it even could be called that, forced them to ride single file. They took it at a walk, Rory leading the way, Alick behind him and Conn and Inan following to guard their backs. No one spoke and they all eyed the surrounding forest warily until Rory came to the edge of a small clearing where a cart sat unattended. The moment he stopped, Alick moved up on his right to get a better look.

"Where's the horse?" Conn asked in a rumble. The warrior had urged his mount up on Rory's left, leaving Inan to guard their back.

Rory's narrowed gaze swept the area. A horse must have been used to bring the cart here, but there was no sign of one now.

"What exactly did Sinclair's aunt say in her message?" Alick asked, his voice grim and eyes sharp as he awaited the answer.

"That she had heard we were in the area, and knew from her sister's correspondence that the Buchanans were dear friends to the Sinclairs. As such, she begged our help. A great treasure waited at the end of a trail we would find by a white ribbon tied around the trunk of a tree just past the river in the woods outside Monmouth, and she would be forever grateful if we saw that treasure safely delivered to Sinclair."

"Forever grateful, eh?" Alick muttered, twisting his head to check the trail behind them. "No mention of a reward?"

"Nay."

"Well, if 'twas a trap, they'd probably mention a reward as a lure," Alick pointed out.

"Aye," Rory murmured, and then gesturing for Conn and Inan to wait in the cover of the trees, he urged his mount cautiously out of the woods and crossed the small clearing until he could look down into the cart. There was something in the bottom, a lumpy bundle covered by a large fur. Rory hesitated, and then took another look around the woods before leaning down to snatch up a corner of the fur and tug it aside.

"What is it?" Alick asked, urging his own mount up next to the cart.

Rory didn't bother to answer. His brother was already close enough to see. He grabbed one of the four lumpy bags that had been hidden by the fur. His eyebrows rose slightly at the lack of weight to the item. It wasn't light as a feather, but not heavy enough to carry any kind of jewels or gold. Cloth of some sort was his guess, proved true when he opened the bag and peered inside. Blue velvet lay at the top, concealing the cloth beneath it. Rory took a moment to feel the bottom of the bag to see if there was anything solid inside, but all he felt was more cloth.

Pulling the strings to close the sack, Rory hung it from his saddle to keep it out of the way as he swiped up another bag. Like the first, it was light, carrying mostly cloth and something he would guess was a brush by the shape of it when he squeezed the bottom.

"Clothing?" Alick guessed, eyeing the bag he held, and when Rory grunted in the affirmative, he asked, "Then where is the treasure we are to transport?"

Rory opened his mouth about to admit he had no idea when movement drew his gaze to the opposite edge of the clearing. They watched in silence as two men on horseback moved out of the woods. They were English soldiers and moving at a snail's pace so that a full minute seemed to pass before they were fully out of the trees and a third horse appeared behind them. This one carried a woman, though they could see none of her beyond the fur-lined silver-blue cloak and matching coif and veil she wore.

Rory's eyebrows rose at the sight. While he'd seen many a

woman in a headdress and veil, the veil usually hung below the face. This one completely covered the face so that she must be having trouble seeing them. He certainly couldn't make out any of her features.

"Lady de Valance?" he guessed, thinking the woman had come herself to deliver the treasure into their hands.

"Aye."

Her voice was a soft whisper and he found himself leaning forward over his horse's neck to better hear her if she spoke again.

"I am Rory Buchanan and this is me brother Alick," he announced when she said nothing more. "Ye requested our aid in getting a treasure to Sinclair?"

"Nay." Despite his leaning, Rory barely heard the word, but then she cleared her throat and said with a little more volume, "'Twas my mother, Lady Mairghread de Valance, who wrote to you. I am Elysande de Valance. 'Tis me she wanted you to see to Sinclair."

Rory sat back as her words rushed over him. Lady Mairghread de Valance's greatest treasure was her daughter and she wanted him to escort Elysande north to Sinclair.

A glance at Alick showed that he was not the only one stunned by this news. While he was still digesting this information, she added, "I felt sure that Tom and Simon here would be enough to escort me north. We could ride fast as a small party. However, Mother seemed to think it would be better to have Scots with us. She said the English are not well liked in the Highlands and 'twould be safer to have Scots for escort as well."

When Rory was slow to respond, she shifted slightly and added, "Mother also said, as a friend to our kin the Sinclairs, you may be willing to aid us. Howbeit, I understand if you do not wish the trouble. We will do fine on our own."

"Nay," Rory said abruptly when she began to gather her reins as if to leave at once. "The Sinclairs are good friends. We would be pleased to see ye to them."

Rory noted the way her shoulders seemed to ease a bit at his agreement, but she offered no gratitude, merely gave a stiff nod and said, "Then shall we?"

Rory hesitated the briefest moment, pondering the fact that it apparently hadn't even occurred to her that there might be some reason he could not leave at once. For surely there was no way she could know that he'd planned to leave this morning anyway. But more important to him was the fact that she offered no explanation for this journey and he knew there must be an interesting one. Usually a simple trip to visit relatives would have included a large retinue of soldiers and servants, along with wagons to carry tents and such for the lady's comfort. It definitely would have included other women to accompany her. But she was alone with two soldiers.

Before he could ask any of the questions now rushing through his mind, a sharp whistle drew his attention to where he'd left Conn and Inan at the edge of the woods. Their number had doubled. Fearghas and Donnghail were now with them and the foursome was moving into the clearing to approach.

Eyebrows rising, Rory rode to meet them, knowing that only trouble would have made Donnghail and Fearghas follow them when they had been ordered to stand guard.

"Riders," Fearghas announced once Rory was close enough to hear. "A large group. At least twenty riders, but I'd guess more from the noise they're making. I'm thinking 'tis the soldiers we saw approach Monmouth as we left."

Rory frowned and then glanced back to the woman and her two men to see that one of the soldiers was grabbing up the last two bags and the fur from the cart. He passed the fur to the other man to roll up and tie to his saddle, while he hung the bags from his own. It made Rory realize that he still held the second bag he'd picked up. Hooking the tie to his own saddle with the first, Rory considered the situation. He had no idea if the contingent of soldiers they'd seen approach Monmouth were looking for the lass, but it didn't matter. He'd rather avoid them either way. Soldiers en masse could be trouble on the road and something he'd like to avoid when they had a lady in their midst.

"We'll stay away from the main road and travel as fast as we dare through the woods," he decided as he straightened in the saddle. He didn't wait for agreement, but led them to the English trio to tell them of his decision. The grim expressions of the soldiers and the way the woman stiffened at the news of a troop of soldiers approaching told him they were expecting trouble, but he didn't question them. There was no time now. He could get the answers he needed later, Rory decided, and got them moving at once.

"ARE YOU ALL RIGHT, M'LADY? DO YOU NEED A REST?"

Realizing she had begun to slouch and sway a bit in the saddle, Elysande straightened abruptly and scowled despite knowing Tom couldn't see her expression through her veil. Or perhaps only because he couldn't. She knew the soldier only asked the question out of concern and she surely would have appreciated it if it didn't simply make her focus on the pain she had been trying to ignore for the last several hours of travel.

The truth was, Elysande was not all right. In fact, she was weary and in agony and there was nothing she wanted more than to stop and rest. But they could not stop. She would not be safe until they reached Sinclair. She could rest then—and even sleep for a week if she wished.

But dear God, she was racked with such agony right now that all she wanted to do was lie down and die. And the pain was not all just physical. Her mother and father—

Elysande cut off her thoughts lest they lead to tears, and forced herself to stiffen her spine. She would not die. At least, not without one hell of a fight. She would survive her losses and this hellish ride, and get to Sinclair. It was the last thing she could do for her mother.

"I will tell Buchanan you need a rest."

Tom's voice drew her from her thoughts and she shook her head at once. "Nay. I'm fine. No stopping."

The soldier hesitated briefly, but then sat back in his saddle with a dissatisfied grunt. She wasn't surprised. Tom knew just how badly injured she was. He'd had to carry her from her mother's bedchamber, using the secret passage to deliver her down to the cart and horses he and Simon had waiting in the woods outside the castle walls. He'd laid her gently in the cart and then they'd been away, and while she'd tried, she hadn't been able to wholly stifle her moans and cries of pain as she was shaken and jolted about on the ride to Monmouth.

They'd arrived a couple of hours before dawn and Elysande had rested until the sun rose, only mounting her mare after Simon had returned from delivering her mother's message to Rory Buchanan. The two men had both protested the move, insisting she should travel in the cart, but Elysande had been equally insistent that she would ride. She had not wanted to meet the Buchanans on her back. She hadn't wanted them to know that she was injured, nor suffer the humiliation of their seeing her men helping her mount. Tom and Simon had pretty much had to place her in the saddle. She hadn't been able to manage it on her own, but once seated she'd actually felt a little better. The cart had shaken and jolted horribly on the journey to Monmouth, causing her constant agony. But seated upright on the saddle she'd felt better. At least, she had until they'd started to ride. Now it was nearly as bad as the ride in the cart had been. At least there she hadn't had to use her trembling muscles to keep her seat.

Tom suddenly dropping back behind her again drew her attention to the trail ahead to see that it was narrowing once more, forcing them to ride single file. If it could be called a trail, Elysande thought. Half the time the lead Scot seemed to be beating a path through the woods. But then perhaps that was normal. She had no way of knowing; Elysande had never traveled beyond the forest around Kynardersley castle until now, while the Buchanans were from Scotland and surely knew their way home.

That thought drew her gaze to the man riding in front of her as her eyes slid over the dark plaid he wore. Rory Buchanan. She'd been a bit startled when he'd appeared in the clearing. The man was much larger than Tom and Simon. He was also wearing a scandalous outfit that left his knees and lower thighs bare between the tops of his boots and the bottom of the skirt he wore. Elysande had blinked at the sight and then forced herself to keep her eyes on his face for propriety's sake. Not that that had been a hardship. Even through her veil she'd been able to see the man was handsome with a nice face, bright green eyes and long dark hair shot through with red. He was also large and muscled, but not overly bulky with it, and apparently that was a shape she quite liked. Although for some reason that same shape on the other Buchanan brother hadn't affected her quite the same way. Alick, she recalled, and guessed by the way he deferred to Rory that he was the younger of the two Buchanan brothers. He actually looked very like the older, with the same auburn hair and green eyes. They were both handsome, but Rory Buchanan had an air of confidence about him that was missing with the younger man. Perhaps that was why she found him more attractive.

As if her thoughts had drawn him forward, the younger brother suddenly rode past her as the path widened again. She watched with curiosity as he moved his horse up beside his brother's and began to speak. She could hear the soft rumble of his voice, but couldn't make out his words. Elysande knew it must be about her, however, when Rory Buchanan suddenly glanced back at her.

She immediately forced herself to sit up a little straighter, realizing only then that she'd started to slump in the saddle once more. Ignoring the way her muscles and her very skin cried out at the action, Elysande held herself stiff in the saddle and raised her chin. She would not show weakness. She could manage this. Besides, it must be nearly midday by now, she reassured herself. They would stop soon if only to eat and relieve themselves. She hoped.

RORY LET HIS GAZE SLIDE OVER THE VEILED FIGURE BEHIND them. Lady Elysande had been riding slouched in the saddle when he first glanced back, but had straightened when she realized he was looking. There was little to see but the headdress and veil that hid her hair and face from him, and the rich, warm cloak she clutched closed against the cold with one gloved hand while handling the reins with her other. In truth, she could have been a corpse or a man under the outfit, but there was nothing alarming in the way she sat her mare.

"She looks fine," Rory said finally as he shifted his attention forward once more.

"Aye. Now she does," Alick said with irritation. "But I am telling ye there is something wrong. She was slumped and swaying slightly in the saddle until ye looked back."

Rory looked back again, but she was still sitting upright, seeming perfectly fine.

"Why do ye think she wears the veil like that?" Alick asked suddenly.

Rory just shrugged. He had no idea.

"Think ye she is so ugly her mother feared we would refuse to escort her did we see her face?"

That brought a startled laugh from his mouth, and Rory raised his eyebrows at his brother. "What difference would her face make? We are doing this as a favor to the Sinclairs, not because of what the woman looks like."

"Aye," Alick agreed on a sigh. "Still, it seems fair strange that she would cover herself wholly like that. It must make it hard for her to see where she is leading her mount."

"All she needs do is follow me," Rory pointed out with unconcern. "The veil obviously does no' blind her so much she canno' do that."

"Hmm." Alick shifted unhappily in his saddle. "We do no' even ken why she needs our escort. Why has she not a large retinue with soldiers and servants to see to her well-being? She has no' even a maidservant to act as chaperone."

Rory grunted at the comment, for it was something he'd pondered himself and had no answer to. There had been no time to ask back in the clearing once he'd realized soldiers were headed their way. He knew the soldiers would have continued on the

northeast road from Monmouth while their party was now heading northwest. He'd decided they would use the less traveled
route to Scotland. It would reduce the likelihood of encountering
the soldiers who may or may not cause trouble, and also remove
the risk of bandits as well since such ruffians preferred to ply
their trade on the busier routes where there were more travelers
to attack.

"Why do ye think— Damn," Alick interrupted himself, and
slowed his horse, allowing it to fall back behind Rory's and drawing his attention to the fact that the path was narrowing again.
It was also growing steep, he noted, slowing his mount to avoid
bumping into Inan's as he and Conn reduced speed in front of
him to manage the steep descent.

The path was taking them down into a valley with an ascent
nearly as steep on the other side, Rory saw, and decided they would
stop in the dale to eat and let the horses rest before continuing up
the incline on the other side. It would give him a chance to ask
Lady Elysande those questions that had been tumbling through
his mind since the clearing. It might even give him a chance to
see the woman's face. Surely she'd have to remove her veil to eat?

Thinking to tell her his plans, and perhaps discover if Alick
was right and she was struggling to maintain the pace he'd set for
this ride, Rory urged his horse off the path to allow Alick's mount
to pass and waited for Lady Elysande to reach him. It was the
only reason that he noted her trouble and was able to grab her up
before she tumbled out of the saddle and to the ground.

Chapter 2

"M'LADY!"

It was a wonder Rory heard that shout over Lady Elysande's scream of pain as he pulled her into his lap, but he did. Glancing around to see the English soldier trying to maneuver around the riderless mare to reach them, Rory barked, "Get her horse!" even as Lady Elysande went limp in his arms.

Much to his relief the man obeyed at once, pausing to gather the reins of his mistress's horse, though his expression was dissatisfied and anxious as he did.

Rory lowered his gaze to the woman lying unmoving in his arms. Her veil had shifted, revealing half of one cheek, and the swollen skin there, black with bruising. Mouth tightening he shifted her to a more stable position in his arms and urged his horse to continue down the steep pass into the valley. He would have to wait until they reached the valley floor to examine her and he now wanted to get there as quickly as he could. Someone had beaten the lass. She needed tending.

It was a good twenty minutes before they reached the valley floor and stopped. Elysande was beginning to stir by then, but hadn't woken fully. She was moaning though, a low, pained moan between gasps for air that he knew spoke of agony. Rory didn't understand what was paining her until Tom and Simon leapt from their horses and rushed to his side to take Elysande from him. It was the way they handled her that told him it was more than her face that was injured. They were careful to grasp her from each side, holding her upright by her upper arms as if she was walking, though she hadn't yet regained consciousness. They carried her to an open area like that and set her slowly and cautiously down on her left side. To him that meant there was something wrong with her back, or perhaps her right side, or both.

Cursing, Rory dismounted.

"Let me see her," he growled as he reached them. "I'm a healer. I can help."

Much to his surprise, Lady de Valance struggled to sit up, saying, "I do not need a healer."

Rory stopped at her feet and stared down at the top of her coif at that soft growl. She was awake.

"Ye've bruising on yer face," he said finally when not one of them looked up at him. Tom and Simon were crouching on either side of their lady, both eyeing her with concern as she stared down at the hands she held clenched in her lap. Regaining her composure was his guess, or waiting for pain to end. He'd seen it often enough with the wounded. The utter stillness, almost not breathing, as they waited for their agony to ease.

Rory guessed that the worst of it had finally passed when she sighed and seemed to sag a bit where she sat. After a moment, she raised her head, peered at him through the filmy veil and said wryly, "I have bruises everywhere. But there is naught you can do about bruising, is there? Besides, 'tis not your healing I need, my lord, but your escort and your sword arm if there is trouble."

Rory blinked at the words. He wasn't used to being needed for anything other than his healing abilities. In fact, he could not recall ever having someone require something else from him, especially not a strong sword arm. It wasn't that he was not good in a battle. These last few years his brothers had insisted on his training with them in the practice field. Considering all the trouble his clan had encountered of late, he'd seen the wisdom of the suggestion and had set himself to the task. The activity had increased his bulk and he was now nearly as good as Aulay with the sword. He was just not used to anyone having a need of that new skill. It left him feeling a little taken aback, and yet he felt his chest puff up a bit at the same time. She needed his escort and protection.

"Right," he muttered aloud with a nod, then shifted uncertainly on his feet, before adding, "Ye're probably hungry. I'll fetch ye an oatcake to—"

"We have food," she interrupted, and then turned toward Tom and instructed, "Fetch the sack with the chicken and cheese. We shall share it with the Buchanans."

THERE WAS MORE THAN CHICKEN AND CHEESE IN LADY ELYsande's sack. It held two roast chickens, cheese, bread and apples. Enough for all of them to eat well for the one meal at least. There was even a little left over when they finished and remounted.

Rory watched with a frown as the English soldiers argued briefly with their lady about how to go about getting her in the saddle before she finally gave in to the necessity of allowing them to lift her onto it. He wanted to offer to have her ride with him, but suspected she wouldn't appreciate the offer, so held his tongue.

"Will she be all right?" Alick asked softly beside him as they waited for the two English soldiers to mount up and follow their mistress to them.

Rory shook his head, not sure of the answer himself. If her back had been abused as badly as her face had appeared to be in the glimpse he'd got, riding could not be comfortable.

"We'll go slowly," he decided, but Elysande heard him as she approached on her mount and shook her head.

"Nay. Do not slow for me. I want to reach Sinclair as quickly as possible," she said firmly.

Rory scowled slightly, thinking that would be a mistake, but didn't voice his concern. Shifting his gaze to Conn, he shrugged and said, "Ye heard her."

Nodding, Conn took the lead out of the small clearing. Inan immediately followed, but this time Rory had the lass and her men fall in next so that he and Alick rode behind with Fearghas and Donnghail. He wanted to keep an eye on Elysande to judge for himself how she fared. If she showed signs of having trouble keeping up the grueling pace, he would signal Conn to slow. Or take her on his horse whether she liked it or not. Although, Rory supposed, sitting leaning back against him would not be comfortable for her either if her back was paining her.

He contemplated that problem over the next two hours as they galloped through the early afternoon. It had been cold when they left Monmouth, but was growing colder still as the day drew on. It was quite frigid by midafternoon when Lady de Valance began to sway in her saddle again. Rory whistled to signal for Conn to stop and urged his horse up past the English soldiers to reach the mare's side.

"Ye're wearying," he said without preamble when Elysande drew her mount to a halt and turned to peer at him.

"I am fine," she assured him, sitting up a little straighter. "There is no need to stop for the night so early. I will manage."

"Ye're no' fine," Rory argued. "Ye've done well, but ye're beginning to struggle and I'd rather no' have to sew up a head wound, or bury ye do ye break yer neck falling from yer horse."

He couldn't see her expression, but the way one hand clenched around the cloak she was holding closed and the other on her reins told him she wasn't pleased. "I do not wish to stop so early. I want to get as far from—"

"I was no' suggesting stopping," he interrupted, and when she stilled and tilted her head, Rory said, "Ye can ride with me."

He watched the veil billow slightly as she heaved a sigh and shook her head. "Riding with you at my back would be more painful than riding alone."

"Aye. I thought it might," he admitted. "But what if *ye* rode at *my* back? Would that pain ye too?"

She seemed to still at that, and he could sense the uncertainty rolling off her. "At your back?"

"Aye, behind me with yer arms around me waist. Ye could lean on me back, and we can tie yer hands together to keep ye in place should ye fall asleep."

A moment of silence passed and then she said, "Aye."

Rory nodded and leaned to the side to retrieve the small length of rope he kept with the medicinals in a sack that hung from his saddle. By the time he straightened with the rope in hand, her soldiers had dismounted and moved up to help her from her horse to his. Rory waited and watched, ready to offer assistance if it was needed, but unwilling to touch her without permission.

From his position he was able to see that Elysande had been sitting astride her mare rather than sidesaddle. He'd suspected as much, but the thick, voluminous fur-lined cloak had draped down either side of the horse, hiding her well enough to make him unsure. Now, as her cloak flapped open, he saw that aside from her unconventional choice in riding position, she also wore unconventional clothes. Lady de Valance had men's breeks under her gown, the skirts of which had been hitched up to allow her to sit astride the animal. The knowledge made him think of his sister, Saidh, who had absolutely no qualms about wearing men's clothing when she wanted to. It made him wonder about this woman's character. Was she bold and daring like Saidh? Or had it only been necessity that had made her don the breeks?

Rory didn't know. Hell, he didn't know anything about her except her name and that she was the half-English cousin of Campbell Sinclair. He hadn't asked his questions of her while they ate their meal as he'd intended. Her posture had been so exhausted and stiff as they'd sat on a fallen tree partaking of the food her men had presented that he'd left her to cope with her pains and consume her meal, which she had managed to do with the veil on. She'd simply slipped the food under the cloth and up to her mouth. But he really needed to ask some of those questions swarming around inside his head soon. How had she come by the bruising she admitted to? Why was she traveling with only two men rather than a large contingent? Why was she going to Sinclair at all?

Rory was distracted from his thoughts when Lady de Valance was finally settled on the saddle behind him and he felt her arms slide around his waist. He glanced down at her hands in her fur gloves. Despite the fact that her chest brushed his back, her hands barely met, the tips of her mitts merely reaching each other. Hoping that was because she was petite and not a sign that he'd gained weight during his stay in England, Rory tied one end of the rope to one wrist over the gloves and then tied the other to her second wrist, leaving a little slack so it didn't pull on her while they rode.

"Is that all right? It's no' too tight?" he asked once he was done.

"Nay. 'Tis fine," she assured him quietly.

"Sleep if ye wish," Rory suggested. "I'll ensure ye stay in the saddle." When Elysande didn't respond and remained stiff and upright behind him, he glanced around to be sure someone had the reins of her mare. Seeing that the soldier named Tom had taken on that chore, he whistled to Conn to let him know they were ready, then urged his horse to follow when Conn, Inan and Alick headed out before him.

They rode like that until near dark. At first, Lady de Valance remained stiff and upright behind him, but gradually she began to relax and lean into him. When she finally slumped against his back, he knew she'd either fainted or fallen asleep. Either way, it was for the best. She was right—there was no healing for bruises except the passage of time, and sleep could only help with it.

Elysande didn't wake up right away when Rory finally called a halt to their journey. Not even when he untied the rope around her wrists. It wasn't until her men had lifted her from his saddle and had her halfway to the ground that she woke and then it was with an agonized cry that she quickly cut off. She remained stoically silent after that as they set her down, but he suspected the movement was causing her great pain and wished he could see her face to know just how much. He also wished he could examine the bruises to see how much damage she'd suffered, but suspected that wasn't likely to happen. The woman was covered from head to toe and her complete refusal of his help earlier made it obvious she would not willingly reveal her injuries to him. That being the case there was little he could do except perhaps offer her a tincture to help her sleep through the pain.

That last thought had Rory grabbing his bag of medicinals

the moment he'd dismounted and opening it to see if he had the weeds needed to make such a tincture. Much to his relief he did have them. He also had the metal chalice he carried with him to mix such tinctures in. All he needed was water. His gaze slid to the river that sided one end of the clearing they'd stopped in. It was narrow, and ice was forming along the sides, but the center was bubbling with moving water. It would be cold, but would do.

Rory glanced around for Lady Elysande then. She was moving stiffly away into the woods, no doubt to find a private spot to relieve herself and manage personal issues. He'd have the tincture mixed and waiting when she returned, he decided, and walked to the river's edge to scoop up water with the chalice. She'd be asleep within minutes after drinking the tincture he planned to make for her and that would be a good thing.

Every step Elysande took seemed to jar. Her muscles screamed at the movement and her skin would have wept if it could have. So would she, but she'd cried herself dry hours ago, grateful for the veil that hid her body's response to her pain. Elysande wasn't one who usually cried, but she hadn't been able to stop and hadn't tried. It wasn't just the physical pain that brought the tears on. She was grieving too, and knew those tears must flow at some point. Better to let them out while she was on horseback and no one was likely to hear, than to be sobbing when she was surrounded by the men.

Elysande made herself walk a good distance from the clearing before she decided she'd gone far enough to ensure privacy while she took care of her personal needs. She then leaned her good shoulder wearily against a tree, giving herself a moment to gather strength before she bent to the effort of pushing her breeches down, hiking her skirts up and squatting to relieve herself. It was all hard work for her at this point, but pulling up her breeches and straightening was even harder and for one moment she feared she'd have to suffer the humiliation of calling for help to rise. But the idea of the pity on the men's faces was enough to force her upright despite the screaming agony it caused.

Elysande paused again to rest, leaning her face and chest against the tree as she waited for her breathing to slow. Dear God, her life had become some sort of hell, and so quickly. She'd never suffered such pain in her life. Not like this. Feeling depression and grief pressing down on her, she shook off her thoughts for now. She couldn't let herself weaken. She needed to remain strong. At least until she reached Sinclair.

She had no idea how long the journey was, but surely they could be there within a week at the speed they were traveling? Then she could collapse and let her aunt and cousin deal with everything while she healed. One week. Seven days. She could bear anything for seven days, Elysande assured herself. She would just take one day at a time.

Sighing, she lifted her head and straightened. She was turning to head back to the men when she heard the sound of bubbling water. On impulse, Elysande moved toward the sound until she broke out of the trees onto the edge of a fast-moving river. This was the sound she'd heard, the water rushing downstream, splashing over and around the rocks and boulders in the riverbed.

Elysande stared at it for a minute, noting the ice forming on the sides where outcroppings forestalled movement and the water was still. It would be bitter cold, she knew, but cold was supposed to be good for bruising, wasn't it? At least her mother had always told her that it helped. Usually that was directly after an injury though, and it had been a couple days since she'd suffered hers. On the other hand, the cold might numb her pain a little.

At this point Elysande was willing to try anything, including a dip in the shallow icy river. Except that she didn't trust herself to be able to get in and out with her body as weak and pained as it was now. But perhaps she could dip the tunic she wore into the water and then put it back on. That might help a bit, numb her back and ease the pain enough to let her fall asleep. Sleep was her only escape from it at the moment.

Aye, she'd try it, Elysande decided grimly, and reached up to undo the clasp that held her cloak together.

RORY USED A SMALL BRANCH HE'D FOUND TO AGAIN STIR THE tincture he'd made, and then glanced toward the spot where Elysande had disappeared into the trees. She was taking an extremely long time about her business. Long enough, in fact, that he was starting to worry. He wasn't the only one. He'd noticed the way Tom and Simon were watching the woods and talking quietly, concerned expressions on their faces.

Alick's arrival at his side drew his attention from the men and he glanced at his brother as he settled on the log next to him. "She's been gone awhile."

Rory grimaced. Alick was the least observant of his brothers. If he thought it had been a while, it had been much longer than he'd realized.

Cursing under his breath, Rory handed the full chalice to Alick, muttered, "Hold this," and then stood. He would just go check on her and make sure she hadn't fainted or run into difficulties of some sort, Rory told himself as he headed for the woods. He wasn't at all surprised when the two Englishmen hurried to follow him.

None of them spoke as they moved into the trees. Rory didn't because he was listening for any noise that might lead him to the lady. He supposed that was also why the other two men were silent. They'd gone quite a distance when Tom suddenly grabbed his arm and pointed ahead and to the left a bit.

Rory stopped to look, but didn't at first see what had caught the soldier's attention until movement caught his eye close to the ground. It was a lighter brown amid the dark brown tree trunks about forty feet ahead, and he watched it briefly before he recognized what he was seeing. Lady de Valance was kneeling on the cold hard ground in nothing but a pair of breeks and a light-brown tunic that was partially obscured by the long, silky black hair now flowing freely down her back.

Grunting acknowledgment that he'd seen her, Rory started slowly forward again, thinking that he would just ensure himself she was all right, and then retreat if she wished it.

He was just ten feet away when a splash of silver blue drew his gaze to the clothing lying in a pile next to her, but then movement drew his gaze back to Elysande. She had straightened and was now removing the tunic she wore, pulling it slowly up to tug it off over her head. Rory jerked to a stop, stifling a startled mutter when Tom didn't stop fast enough and bumped into his shoulder. They all stood silent then, watching as Lady Elysande's back slowly came into view, revealing inch by painful inch of the mottled red and black color that covered most of her back and her right side, leaving only a strip of pale unblemished white skin on her left side.

In all of his years of healing, Rory had only seen damage that extreme once. It had been on a village woman whose husband had beat and kicked her for hours. She'd been barely alive when she was brought to him, and had died shortly afterward from what he'd suspected was inner damage he hadn't been able to see or heal. As he recalled, she had been in so much pain she had prayed for death before it came, and welcomed it with relief as the life left her eyes.

Rory had almost forgotten the men were with him when Tom murmured, "I knew she was badly beaten, but . . ."

"Aye," Simon breathed when the other man fell silent. "How the devil has she sat the horse at all?"

Rory didn't respond to the man's question. It was something he was wondering himself.

"What is she doing?" Simon asked as they watched Lady Elysande lean forward to lower and lift the tunic she now held in her hands. It was only when she raised it that he realized she was kneeling at the river's edge. They all watched silently as she wrung out the now dripping cloth and then covered her face with the cold damp material. It was only then he recalled the bruising he'd seen on her face when her veil had moved a bit.

"What happened to her?" he asked grimly, keeping his voice low.

There was a moment of silence and then Tom said, "Baron de Buci had one of his men take his fists and boots to her."

"And her father allowed this? Is de Buci her husband?" Rory asked at once, for only husbands and fathers could get away with such abuse.

"Nay. De Buci is no relation at all. He was a friend to our lord and lady ere all this happened," he added grimly.

"What is 'all this'?" Rory asked as he watched Elysande remove the cloth from her face and bend to dip it in the water again.

A moment of silence passed and he could almost feel Tom and Simon exchanging glances behind him to ask each other how much they should reveal, and then Tom finally said, "We are not sure. We were on a task for our lord, Robert de Valance. Gone near a week and then returned to find everything in chaos. We were told that de Buci's men guarded the keep, that our lord as well as most of the Kynardersley soldiers were dead and that our lady was abed, fighting for her life while Lady Elysande lay beaten and broken in the dungeons."

"We no doubt would have been killed too if we'd ridden up to the castle," Simon put in. "But several servants had fled the keep during the chaos and were hiding in the woods. They stopped us and told us what was happening. Warned us against approaching."

Tom took up the tale again. "We were going to ride to our closest neighbor, Lord Grenville, and request his aid for Lady Mairghread and Lady Elysande, but thought it best to take a message from Lady Mairghread to convince Grenville to act quickly. So we sent one of the escaped servants, a kitchen boy named Eldon, into the keep to try to get to Lady Mairghread for such a message."

"He was gone for hours," Simon told him when Tom paused. "We were just starting to think he had failed and been captured when Lady Mairghread's maid, Betty, found us. The boy had succeeded at his task and reached Lady Mairghread. Our lady had sent Betty out to find us. She had a message, but not for Grenville, for you. We were to smuggle Lady Elysande out of the keep and take her to you. Which we did."

"But this is the first time we have seen the extent of Lady Elysande's injuries," Tom said solemnly as they watched Elysande wring out the tunic again. This time she didn't press it to her face when she was done, but began to pull it on over her head in slow, torturous moves.

Rory instinctively started forward again, intending to stop her, but paused after only one step. Putting on a cold, wet tunic in this chill weather was a bit risky. Falling ill to a lung complaint was the last thing she needed. On the other hand, it would dry quickly against her body and if it eased her pain it was worth the risk. He would just have to make sure she was kept warm tonight, he thought, and then realized Tom was talking again.

"She's been mostly silent since we left Kynardersley," Tom said, eyeing the woman with pity as she tugged her gown on over the tunic and breeches in slow, methodical movements. "I think her spirit has broken. 'Tis a shame that. She was always a happy girl ere this. Always smiling and laughing, kind to everyone. She treated us all like family—servants and soldiers alike. I worry she will not recover from this."

Rory didn't comment. He'd have been amazed if something like this didn't change the lass. But he agreed it was a shame. In his mind he was thinking of Saidh, and how she might have been affected by such events. She might have bounced back, but she also might have pulled into herself and become altogether different. Harder, perhaps, or bitter.

Rory watched Lady Elysande finish with the gown and reach for the cloak next. The way she huddled into it and fumbled with the clasp under her chin told him how cold she must be. Giving up his position in the trees, he strode forward now, determined to help whether she liked it or not.

Chapter 3

$\mathcal{E}$LYSANDE'S HANDS WERE STIFF AND SHAKING SO WITH COLD that she couldn't fasten the clasp at her throat. She was just thinking to give it up when the sound of a snapping branch made her whirl on her feet. Her eyes widened when she saw Rory Buchanan step out of the trees with Tom and Simon at his back.

"Ye took so long we began to worry," the Scot said mildly as he approached.

Elysande stood stock-still, her heart suddenly hammering rapidly in her chest. She knew he was no threat to her, especially with her men there, but he was a huge man and with the memory of the beating she'd taken still fresh in her mind she was hard-pressed not to back instinctively away from him. Elysande was still struggling with the urge when he stopped before her and quickly fastened the clasp of her cloak. It was done so swiftly she didn't get to embarrass herself by pulling away or even stiffening in response before the task was done and he was bending to pick up something.

It was only when he straightened and held out her coif and veil that she realized her face was still uncovered. Taking the item from him, she quickly redonned it, a small sigh of relief slipping between her lips once she was hidden behind the veil again. Elysande had no idea how bad her face must look at the moment, but it felt lumpy and was swollen to the point that her skin hurt, so she feared she must look like a monster. She didn't mind that so much. She wasn't interested in looking pretty for him, but she'd hidden her face in the hopes of avoiding the pity and dismay she feared it would elicit from anyone who looked upon the damage. She'd also wanted to give the appearance of being strong and well, fearing that if the Buchanans had realized the shape she was in they might decide she was more trouble than they wished to take on and refuse to escort her to Sinclair.

But he'd seen her face now. Hopefully that wouldn't make him refuse her further escort. Elysande was just grateful he hadn't approached a few minutes earlier and seen her back. He'd probably mount up at once and leave them behind then.

"Are ye ready to return to camp?"

Elysande peered at him through the veil. As she'd noted earlier, Rory Buchanan was a handsome man, and built like a warrior. He was unmarred by the scars most warriors carried on their faces and bodies though, and that made her wonder about him.

"Aye," Elysande said finally when she realized he was waiting for an answer. She hesitated when he offered his arm, but then placed her hand on it and allowed him to lead her back toward the clearing where they were to camp, Tom and Simon trailing behind.

"I MADE YE A TINCTURE," RORY ANNOUNCED AS THEY STEPPED out of the trees. "I left it with Alick while I came to look fer ye."

"A tincture?" Elysande asked, her eyes seeking out the younger brother and finding him sitting on a log in the center of the clearing, a chalice in hand.

"Aye. 'Tis the best I can do at the moment. 'Twill make ye sleep deeply so the pain does no' bother ye," he explained.

Elysande shook her head. "Thank you, but I will not take your tincture."

The Buchanan stopped walking at once and faced her, his expression both surprised and concerned. "'Twould help ye sleep, m'lady."

"A deep, potion-induced sleep," she pointed out.

"Aye," he agreed solemnly. "But sleep is all I can offer to help ye through the pain."

"But I would be hard to waken if there was trouble," she said with concern.

"Should we expect trouble?" he asked at once.

Elysande hesitated and then started walking again, forcing him to walk with her as she admitted, "I am not sure."

That was the truth. Her mother had hoped that de Buci would think she'd head south to court. It was why she'd sent her north to Scotland. Her mother had wanted her to be safe at Sinclair. But the mention of the soldiers that had approached Monmouth while they were in the clearing made her worry that de Buci had somehow figured out they were traveling to Scotland and had sent men after her. If so, there would definitely be trouble.

"Ye need to tell me what this is all about so that my men and I can be prepared to handle the threat," Rory said quietly as they reached the fallen log where Alick sat.

Elysande peered up at his face made hazy through the veil, admitting to herself that he was right. In truth, she was surprised that it had taken him so long to demand answers. She steeled herself against the memories and put off the telling by moving in front of the log and slowly and carefully easing herself to perch on it next to Alick. She then waited for Rory to settle on her other side before lowering her head to stare at her slippers where they peeked out from her skirts and cloak.

"Three days ago my life was as it had always been," she began slowly. "It was calm, happy and peaceful. And then de Buci arrived at Kynardersley castle."

"Four," Tom said as he and Simon settled on the ground in front of her. "De Buci arrived at Kynardersley four days ago."

"You were three nights in the dungeon, m'lady," Simon informed her as the Buchanan warriors moved closer to hear. "The night de Buci arrived, and two nights after, before we took you away."

Elysande recognized the pity in Simon's voice and turned her gaze back to her slipper-clad feet again, murmuring, "I was unconscious by the time we reached the cells in Kynardersley's dungeon. I must have remained so for longer than I realized."

She didn't give them time to comment, but started over. "Very well, then, four days ago my life was as it had always been . . . and then de Buci arrived. He was a longtime friend of my parents. He had been to Kynardersley often over the years, but this time he arrived with a good-sized army at his back. That was unusual, but he explained that he was just stopping in on his way to court, and he left most of them to camp outside the walls. He brought only a dozen men into the bailey with him. His knights.

"Father welcomed him as always, and then informed him we were just about to sit down to our evening repast and invited him and his men to join us, saying he would send the stable master out to see to the horses. But de Buci told him not to bother the stable master and ordered his men to see to the horses themselves and then come inside to join us at table."

Elysande recalled the smiles and light chatter and laughter as they'd gone back into the great hall with this old family friend. Shaking her head, she carried on. "Everything seemed fine at first. We chatted lightly and then Father fell into a discussion with de Buci about politics or the king or something, and Mother waved a servant over. She was telling her to prepare the guest chamber when the keep doors opened and de Buci's men began to file in. No one paid them any attention, but I noticed that there seemed to be more of them than the dozen or so we left outside and that they were filing around the table, rather than each finding seats. I was just thinking that it was almost as if they were surrounding those of us seated at the trestle tables when Father suddenly cried out. When I looked his way it was to see him stumble back from the table, and then fall, a dagger in his chest. Before I could even grasp that he was dead, murdered by de Buci, that bastard was dragging my mother and me to our feet. As he shoved us over toward the hearth, he shouted to his men to 'kill them all.'"

Elysande could still hear the startled shouts and shrieks of the people around the trestle tables as the soldiers were murdered where they sat, along with any of the women brave or foolish enough to try to intervene. They were all caught so much by surprise that she didn't think one man had managed to draw a weapon to defend himself before being cut down. It had been a slaughter that had left the rushes soaked in a widening pool of blood. And the stench! She had tended to many ill and injured with her mother and knew death could be a messy ordeal, but nothing could have prepared her for what she witnessed.

Elysande swallowed as the little bit of food she'd had when they'd stopped to eat tried to crawl up her throat. Pushing the memories away, she cleared her throat. "My mother and I stood huddled together by the hearth when he released us to watch his men kill everyone. It could not have taken more than a minute before 'twas all done. Then de Buci ordered one of his men to watch us and told the others to search the castle before storming off to the small chamber where Father worked on the castle accounts. I presume he searched that room himself.

"Mother was in shock, I think. She kept saying everything would be fine. The guards on the wall would realize something was wrong and come to take care of these men, and then we could bind Father's wound and he would survive." Elysande squeezed her fingers tightly closed and shook her head. "But I could see he was dead already, and I knew that for so many of de Buci's men to have entered the castle, our own men on the wall and in the soldiers' barracks must already be dead too. I didn't tell her my suspicions at the time, but I later learned I was right. While de Buci had sat chatting and laughing with us, the dozen knights who had entered the bailey with him had gone around and quietly killed the men on the wall, and then had opened the portcullis to let the rest of his army in. The first thing they'd done was attack the men in the barracks, taking them enough by surprise that they put up little more of a fight than the ones who were at table with us. Only then had his men entered the keep and surrounded the trestle tables to finish off the remaining soldiers."

"God in heaven," Alick breathed at her side, and Elysande felt her lips twist with disgust. God had nothing to do with the slaughter of her people. And if He had been watching, He hadn't raised a finger to intervene.

"De Buci was not gone long," she continued, her voice sounding unnaturally calm to her own ears. "He immediately began questioning his men as to whether they'd found anything. When the last man returned from the ordered search and said no, he turned his attention to us."

Straightening her shoulders, Elysande tried to brace herself against the memories as she told them, "He started with Mother, tearing her from my arms and shaking her so violently I feared he would break her neck. The whole time he was yelling, *'Where is it? Where is it? Where is it?'*"

The words were like a chant in Elysande's head. It was all the man had said at first, shrieking it over and over again, spittle flying from his mouth as he roared that question.

"When he stopped to let her speak, some of Mother's shock seemed to have left her and emotion was setting in. Mostly terror. She cried that she did not know what he was looking for. If he would only tell her what it was he wanted, she would tell him where it was if she knew. But he just shook her again and snarled, *'Do not play that game with me, Mairghread! You must know. Tell me where it is!'*

"When that did not get the answer he wanted, he began to break her fingers one after the other. Pausing between each, he would demand, *'Where is it?'* and then break the next as she cried and begged him to stop or just tell her what *it* was."

Her mouth tightened as she recalled her mother's helplessness in the face of de Buci's strength. "I tried to stop him. I rushed forward, intending to hit him, or jump on his back, or something. But his soldier caught me around the waist, scooped me up and dragged me back. He then held me there, and all I could do was watch and scream and beg him to let her be, but he just continued, moving on to her other hand when he finished with the first. And then once he ran out of fingers he began to shake her again."

Elysande lowered her head unhappily. "I heard it when her neck broke, and saw her go limp in his hold. I feared she was dead, but then her eyes opened and she looked at me. But nothing else was moving. She no longer raised her hands to try to fend off his blows and she was not standing under her own power. He was holding her up like a child's doll as he punched her. She hardly seemed to even feel the blows anymore unless they were to her face. But in his rage he did not seem to notice.

"I thought it would go on forever, but finally he just let her drop to the ground, kicked her a couple of times with frustration and then stood glaring at her and panting heavily. But after a moment he followed her gaze to me and smiled nastily.

"'Perhaps if you will not tell me where 'tis to save yourself, you will to save your daughter,' he said, and I saw the fear enter my mother's eyes, along with helplessness and grief and apology. I knew then she really had no idea what he was looking for, and she could do nothing to stop him from doing to me what he'd done to her."

Lifting her head, Elysande turned to peer toward the blur that was Rory Buchanan and said, "I really thought that I would end up in the same shape as my mother then, and I was terrified. But he had managed to wear himself out beating her, and rather than grab me and start all over again, he threw himself into one of the chairs by the fire and ordered the soldier holding me to beat me instead. Fortunately, he did not seem to have the stomach for it."

"The hell he didn't," Rory growled, sounding furious. "I've seen . . . yer face," he finished after a slight hesitation that made her think he'd meant to say something other than her face.

Elysande briefly considered the possibility that Rory and her men had arrived sooner than she'd realized down at the riverbank, and had seen more than she'd thought. But since there was little she could do if they had, she pushed the worry away. "Aye. He beat me badly, but broke no bones. Not even a finger. I think he held back on his punches and kicks too. And while he punched me in the face several times, he avoided my temples and head. Also, when de Buci ordered him to throw me to the ground and kick me, he kept those kicks to my back, buttocks and legs. The only injury I took to my head was when he threw me to the ground. My head bounced off the floor, but that was probably an accident. He never hit my head himself."

Elysande had been grateful for that. She'd curled into a ball on the floor, her hands over her head to try to protect it. But it hadn't been necessary. He'd never once kicked her in the head.

Smiling wryly to herself that she would feel gratitude for a man who had beat her so badly, Elysande lowered her gaze to the tips of her slippers again. "De Buci eventually grew tired of watching. Or perhaps he was just impatient that it was getting no results. My mother had lain weeping throughout, and eventually I became so insensate that I could not feel the blows anymore and stopped screaming. I was very close to unconsciousness when he called a halt to the proceedings and ordered me to be thrown into the dungeon. Even so I heard the threats he yelled at my mother as I was dragged away. He would give her time to consider what he might do to the both of us next if she did not tell him where it was. Perhaps he'd let his men rape us, or start cutting off limbs, or burn my face so no man would look upon me . . ."

After a brief pause, Elysande shrugged. "Several other rather nasty options followed before I was so far from the great hall that I could not hear him anymore. Or perhaps I just lost consciousness. I do not recall being carried into the cell they kept me in. The next time I woke was the day Betty came for me. She managed to sneak the keys from the guard and get me out of there without waking him. I still do not know how."

"Lady Mairghread had her take your guard his food and put a sleeping potion in his drink," Tom explained.

"Oh," Elysande breathed, thinking she wished she'd known that at the time. It would have been less stressful to her. She'd spent the entire time terrified the man would wake and catch them. Shrugging, she continued. "Betty helped me to the secret passage and up to my parents' chamber. Mother was in bed." She paused as the image of her mother flashed through her mind, alive still, but so pale and weak. She'd been unable to move anything below the neck, but was still able to talk, though she appeared to be having trouble with her breathing and swallowing. Elysande had known, or at least feared, she wouldn't last long.

"Mother's first words to me after greeting me were 'the Buchanans,'" she admitted, glancing from Alick to Rory and then keeping her gaze on the older brother as she told him, "She said you were a healer, and a friend to our kin the Sinclairs. She wanted me to come to you for aid getting to them. She then told me that Simon and Tom were still alive and outside the wall. She'd had Betty pack clothes, coin and food for our journey before the maid had rescued me from the dungeon, then sent her to fetch the men. But while we waited for them, she needed me to write messages for her to both you and the Sinclair."

Elysande paused then to peer curiously at Simon and Tom when they released small "ahs" of sound as if she'd just explained something they'd wondered about. Supposing they'd wondered about the written messages when her fingers were broken, she explained, "Mother dictated the messages and I sealed them with her ring. She then insisted I change into a boy's breeches and tunic and don a fresh dress over them for the journey. I was in a lot of pain, and moving about just increased it. I managed the task, but only just, before collapsing beside the bed."

That last part was a lie. Or at least a lie of omission. She'd left out that she'd argued with her mother the entire time, trying to convince her to come with them, pointing out that if this Rory Buchanan was such a grand healer, perhaps he could help her. But her mother had refused to even consider it.

"No one can help me, love, and you know that," she'd said. *"'Tis fine. I am going to be with your father. You are the only reason I still live. I must see to your safety ere I can rest."*

Sighing, Elysande continued. "I woke when Tom arrived and picked me up. And I'm afraid I caused a bit of a kerfuffle that could have got us caught." She paused and turned her face toward the two English soldiers with an apologetic expression they couldn't possibly see through the veil. Tom had stifled her cries with a hand over her mouth. If he hadn't, and the guard she suspected was in the hall had heard . . .

"I am sorry for that," she said finally. "But I could not leave my mother there so weak and defenseless. De Buci had left her alone because she had been feigning unconsciousness since that first night. He had apparently tried to rouse her several times each day with blows to her stomach and such, but Mother said she could not feel the blows, and so continued to feign unconsciousness by merely keeping her eyes closed. She worried he was growing impatient, however, and she did not think he would leave me be in the dungeons for much longer. She feared he would take those frustrations out on me soon and I needed to go or I would be dead right next to her."

Elysande lowered her eyes to her slippers again. "I knew she was right. Still, I could not just leave her." She breathed out slowly. "Apparently she had feared as much and had prepared ahead of time for it. When I refused to leave, she told Betty she was thirsty and it was time for her drink. Only after Mother had emptied the chalice Betty held to her mouth did she admit to me that it had held poison."

Elysande's throat constricted and she had to swallow several times before continuing. "I was horrified. 'Tis a sin to take your own life. But she assured me that she felt God would understand. She had done it to save me and she was dying anyway, and had just sped it along. She then said that if she was wrong about God's thoughts on the matter, and was banished to purgatory for the act, then she considered it worth the sacrifice so long as it got me away from de Buci. She wanted me to leave at once, find you, stay alive and get to Sinclair. She said it was the last thing I could do for her as a daughter: to live, marry and have children to love and treasure as much as she loved and treasured me."

Elysande broke off then, fighting the tears that were trying to swamp her.

"Lady Mairghread died minutes later," Simon continued for her. "And Tom scooped up Lady Elysande again and we slipped into the secret passage, using it to get back out beyond the wall. We thought we would be taking her on one of our horses, but Betty and Eldon had managed to arrange for her mare to be hooked to a cart and brought out."

"How the devil did they manage that?" Rory asked with surprise beside her.

There was a moment of silence before anyone spoke, and this time it was Tom who answered. "The blood-soaked rushes in the great hall were apparently starting to stink and at dinner that night de Buci had finally had enough of the stench. He ordered them taken out beyond the wall and burned at once. It took several trips to haul it away. The servants had been working on it since the evening meal and were still working on it at that late hour, so Betty and Eldon had one of the carts lined with fresh hay, attached Lady Elysande's mare to it and then filled it with the dirty rushes and the boy rode it out along with the others. He went with them to where the dirty rushes were to be burned, but rather than return inside the walls with the others, he broke off from the line of carts and took it to where our horses waited instead. Fortunately, it was a moonless night and his defection seemed to go unnoticed, so we placed Lady Elysande and our bags and furs in the cart and headed to Monmouth."

"And you know the rest," Elysande said into the silence that fell. "Simon took you the message my mother dictated, you came to meet us and now we are on the way to Sinclair." Swallowing, she added, "But to answer your earlier question, I do not know if we should expect trouble. Mother expected de Buci to think we would be headed for court and the king, 'tis why she sent us north instead. She hoped I could remain safely at Sinclair while a message about all of this was delivered to court," she explained, and then frowned and added, "But I am troubled by the soldiers you said arrived at Monmouth as you were leaving."

"Does de Buci ken ye're related to the Sinclairs and might go to them?" Alick asked, drawing her gaze his way.

Elysande considered the question and then shook her head helplessly. "I do not know. As I said, he used to be a friend to us. My mother or father or even I might have mentioned our Scottish relations at some time." She paused briefly and then admitted, "But I worry about Betty and Eldon. I tried to convince them to come with us, but Betty insisted she would stay and see Mother buried properly first, and young Eldon decided to stay in the woods to keep an eye out for her and be sure she got away. He determined he would use the secret passages to get her out if there was trouble." Elysande bit her lip unhappily. "But what if de Buci figured out that my guard in the dungeon was drugged and found out that Betty was the one to take the meal to him? He would know she was involved in my escape. And if he started taking his fists and boots to her as he did my mother . . ."

"She might have told him all," Tom said worriedly.

"He would have had to beat her horribly to get the information," Elysande said miserably. "I should have insisted she come with us. Both of them. I should have *made* them come," Elysande muttered, angry at herself that she hadn't. Betty had been a good and faithful maid to her mother for many years. More like family than a servant. She should have made her and Eldon leave with them, ordered the pair to, but she'd been so tired and weak . . .

"The soldiers we saw might not be de Buci's," Rory said now. "But whether they are or no', by continuing on this trail to Scotland we should be able to avoid them."

"Aye," Alick agreed. "Those soldiers, whoever they are, will most like continue on the main road. This path is much less used."

A moment of silence passed and then Rory stood. "We should eat and bed down for the night. Tomorrow is another long day for us if we wish to reach Scotland ere we stop."

"I am not really hungry," Elysande said quietly, bringing the men to a halt.

She thought Rory Buchanan was frowning at this, but his voice was gentle when he said, "Ye really should eat. Ye need yer strength fer healing."

"Aye, but . . ." Elysande grimaced. The truth was that recounting all that had happened had stolen any appetite she might have had and she feared she might be ill if she tried to eat now. But she simply said, "I will eat when I wake up."

When Rory didn't argue further, Tom stood and offered his

hand to help her up. Glancing to Simon, he said, "Lay out the fur for her to sleep on."

Elysande accepted the help, and was grateful for it when her abused muscles protested their use as she got to her feet. Her movements were slow and stiff, and Simon had the fur unrolled and laid out by the time they reached him. Elysande then grasped Tom's hand tightly and used his strength as she lowered herself to the fur. She lay down on her uninjured side, tugged the cloak around herself and pulled a corner up to cover her face. It had been cold all day, but was growing colder still as night fell.

The damp tunic she wore beneath her dress was not helping. It had soothed her bruises at first, but was now merely warm and damp against her skin. She knew it would dry eventually, but couldn't imagine being able to sleep like this. In truth, damp tunic or not, she suspected she would have trouble sleeping. Elysande had never slept outside of her own chamber at Kynardersley where a nice fire and several furs kept her warm the night through in her bed. At this moment, she would have given a lot to be back in that bed, with her mother and father safely tucked away in the next chamber. She was still having trouble accepting that her life had changed so drastically and so quickly. It was like a nightmare, and she felt very cold and alone inside.

That thought had barely slipped through her mind when something pressed up against her front. Stiffening, she tugged the cloak away from her face and blinked at the figure in front of her. It was growing dark enough that she couldn't be sure, but she thought it was Rory Buchanan who had settled on his side in front of her with his back to her chest. He was close enough that she could feel his warmth through his plaid and her cloak, and smell the woodsy scent she recognized from riding with him.

Movement at her back distracted her, and she glanced over her shoulder to see Tom settling himself down behind her, leaving a couple inches between himself and her sore back, but close enough that she could enjoy his warmth too.

"Sleep, m'lady. We will guard you well," the soldier said solemnly when he saw her looking.

Having no idea what to say, Elysande merely nodded, then glanced around at the other men as they lay down around them. Simon was settling himself lengthwise at her feet so that her toes pointed at his chest. She could tell that it was he by his silhouette. He was the only one besides Tom not wearing a skirt. She tilted her head upward then as another man lay lengthwise above her head, and recognized Alick Buchanan's voice when he whispered, "Good sleep," as he curled up in his plaid. Three of the other Scottish warriors were arranging themselves around the other men, doubling the barrier between herself and anyone who might approach from the sides or above. But she could see the last man had moved to sit on the log they had just left. To keep watch, she guessed, and supposed the men would take turns at sitting watch, each of them doing so for a couple hours before waking someone to replace them.

"Cuddle closer if ye're cold, m'lady. The last thing we need is fer ye to fall ill during this journey."

Elysande lowered her head to peer at Rory Buchanan's back at those words. She was very tempted to do just that, slip her arms around his waist and lean her face against his back as she had on the horse. But it wouldn't be proper, so she merely pulled her cloak back over her face to keep it warm and tried to relax. She was positive she wouldn't sleep, but at least she was warming up, Elysande thought just before drifting off.

RORY WOKE UP ON HIS BACK, HIS FACE COLD BUT WITH A WARM weight on his shoulder, chest and legs. Not the sort to take women to his bed for a night, he blinked his eyes open with confusion, and started to turn his head, but froze when his lips brushed against Lady Elysande's coif. The contact made him stiffen and then he pulled back slightly to stare at the sleeping woman now draped over his body. Her head rested on his shoulder, her chest half on his with her arm and cloak wrapped around him. She had also cast one of her legs over both of his. They were as entwined as lovers, and he couldn't say he minded, but suspected she would when she woke.

Unsure how to extricate himself without disturbing or inad-
vertently hurting her, he glanced around the clearing and grimaced when he saw that he and Elysande were the only ones still
sleeping. The other men were all up and about, going about the
business of starting a fire and tending the horses, even the two
English soldiers. Although he noticed that Tom and Simon kept
casting worried glances to where he and Elysande slept, as if unsure what to think or do about their cozy sleeping position.

It was completely improper, of course, Rory acknowledged. But
then little about this journey was proper. The lady was traveling
alone with eight men due to circumstances beyond anyone's control. Besides, it wasn't like he'd deliberately arranged this. The last
thing he remembered was falling asleep on his side in front of the
woman. He had no idea how he'd ended up on his back with her
snuggling into his chest like a sleepy kitten. The fact that he quite
liked waking to find her there was a bit disturbing though.

That thought was enough to make Rory decide he should try
to ease out from under her. He was tensing in preparation of attempting just that when she murmured in her sleep and shifted
her leg, sliding it up his thighs to rest over his groin. A most unfortunate event, Rory decided grimly when his cock stirred with
immediate interest.

Rory was lying as still as death, taking deep breaths to try to
calm his body so he wouldn't embarrass himself when he did
manage to get out from under her, when she shifted again. This
time her hand slid across his chest under the cloak, even as her leg
moved down a bit and then up again, rubbing against his growing erection.

Oh, this was bad, Rory thought, and then tilted his head to look
down at Elysande, when she suddenly stiffened against him. For
a moment he wasn't sure if she was waking up to their situation,
or merely suffering a nightmare. He got his answer when she
suddenly gasped and pushed herself upward, then cried out and
flopped back onto him, panting for breath as she fought against
the pain her abrupt action had obviously caused her.

"Breathe," Rory instructed, his voice rough from sleep as he clasped her upper arms to keep her from moving again too quickly and causing herself more pain.

Elysande whimpered in response, but then released the breath she'd been holding and took in a fresh one.

"What can we do to help?"

Rory glanced up to find Tom and Simon standing over them, concern on their faces as they watched their lady struggle with her pain. Alick and the other warriors were right behind them. It seemed that while he had only noticed the two Englishmen glancing their way, the others had been just as aware of them the whole time. Now they were all there, wishing to help.

The hell of it was, they couldn't. Even he couldn't. He had nothing to take away her pain except that sleeping draft she'd refused to take.

"Lift me up, please."

Rory glanced down at that muffled request from Lady Elysande, realizing only then that when she'd dropped back down, her face had landed in the curve of his neck. He could feel her warm breath through the veil there, and the way her lips had moved the cloth against his skin as she spoke had been quite nice. Rolling his eyes at his own thoughts, he shifted his attention to Tom and Simon as they moved up on either side of him and bent to clasp her upper arms.

"Brace yourself, m'lady," Tom said gently, and then glanced to Simon and said, "On three."

The man then counted out the numbers aloud and they both lifted her by the arms at three.

Elysande did not cry out, moan or make any sound at all as they lifted her. But once on her feet Rory saw that her headdress was askew, leaving a bit of the undamaged side of her face on view. One look at the gray tone to her skin told him that she was definitely in agony and probably biting her lip to keep any pained sounds in.

Mouth tightening, he got quickly to his feet and then bent to retrieve the fur they'd lain on. He took his time rolling it up, and only after he finished the chore did he risk looking at her again. Much to his relief her skin tone was a little better already. Some color was leeching back into the visible bit of cheek.

"I need to . . ." Lady Elysande didn't finish that sentence, but headed into the trees, carefully raising her hands to straighten her coif and veil as she went.

They all watched her go with concern, knowing she no doubt needed to relieve herself, but every one of them, he suspected, worried over whether she could manage the task on her own. She was walking like an old woman, her movements stiff, one hand at her lower back, and her spine slightly bent backward as if her muscles or skin could not bear to be stretched to get her fully upright. But she would not welcome aid with this task, and they all knew it.

When she disappeared from view, Rory finally turned away and handed the fur to Tom as he said, "Today is market day in Carlisle, I think, and we should reach there by late afternoon. If I can find some wolfsbane at market I will make a liniment from it that should ease her aches and pains."

"That would be good. Thank you," Tom said, and Rory noted the other men were nodding in agreement. None of them enjoyed seeing her suffer the way she was. It left a man feeling helpless and useless. Rory would rather suffer the pain for her, but since that wasn't possible, he would do what he could to ease it for her.

Chapter 4

ELYSANDE SUPPOSED SHE SHOULD BE MORTIFIED AT WAKING UP plastered to Rory Buchanan's chest, but she wasn't. Well, she was a little embarrassed, Elysande acknowledged, but it wasn't as if she'd done it on purpose. She must have rolled toward him in her sleep or something. And the man had made a very comfortable and warm bed, much nicer than the cold hard ground, even with the fur beneath her. She had slept better last night than she had since this whole horrible chapter of her life had begun. She hadn't suffered pain, or nightmares, or wept in her sleep with grief as she had in the dungeon and then in the cart on the way to Monmouth. Also, for one moment when she'd first woken up, she hadn't felt quite so alone as she had since de Buci had torn everyone she loved away from her. It had been nice.

Of course, then she'd woken up fully, recalled where she was, inhaled Rory's woodsy scent and realized whom she was sleeping on. That was when she'd tensed and tried to get up. Her body had immediately reminded her of her injuries.

It was something she would try not to forget in the future, Elysande decided as she finally removed her gloves and turned her attention to her reason for being out in the woods. Much to her relief, the distance she'd walked while thinking had helped to work out some of the stiffness that had set into her back and legs while she'd slept. She even managed to take care of her personal needs without crying out in agony.

Hoping it was a sign that her injuries were improving, Elysande headed back to camp, arriving to find most of the men already mounted. Only Tom, Simon and Rory Buchanan were still on the ground.

"Are ye all right to ride, lass?" Rory asked with concern as she approached the three men standing by her horse.

A bit startled by the familiar address, Elysande flushed slightly, but didn't comment on it. She merely nodded in response to his question as she paused before them.

Simon and Tom worked together to place her in the saddle. It was done quickly and efficiently, the men now quite adept at the chore. Still, she was embarrassed by the need for it and gave a start when a round, flat bread-type thing that she'd never seen the likes of before suddenly appeared by her mare's mane.

Elysande blinked at it and then glanced to Rory in question as he held it up to her.

"'Tis an oatcake," he explained gently. "To break yer fast."

"Oh." Managing a smile, she finally took it from him, noting that it was as hard as a biscuit. "Thank you."

Rory nodded. "If ye tire or yer back pains ye and ye wish to ride with me again, give a shout."

He waited for her to nod before moving away to mount his own horse.

The moment Rory's back was turned, Elysande raised the oat-cake to her nose to give it a sniff through her veil. It didn't really have much of a scent. Curious, she slipped it under the veil and took a small cautious bite. It was a very hard, rather tasteless bread. But she supposed it would fill her stomach.

Glancing up to see that the men were all waiting on her, amusement on their faces, Elysande stuck the oatcake in her mouth to hold between her teeth, and quickly gathered her reins. She thought Conn grinned at her before turning his horse to head out of the clearing, but couldn't be sure with the veil obstructing her vision as it was. She did know it was Inan who followed him with Alick behind them. Elysande then urged her own horse to follow when Rory waved her forward. Once she had passed him and was following the other horses, Elysande shifted the reins to her right hand and reached her left under the veil to pluck the oatcake from her mouth.

"Do ye no' like oatcakes, Lady Elysande?" Alick teased, dropping back to ride beside her.

"I— 'Tis fine," she said weakly, not wishing to insult anyone.

Apparently taking pity on her, Alick merely said, "They may be tasteless, but will give ye strength and fill yer belly so ye're no' hungry."

He didn't wait for a response, but urged his horse up in front of hers again so they all rode single file once more. Sighing, Elysande peered down at the oatcake in her hand and then took another bite. The flavor of it wasn't offensive, just rather bland. But as Alick had pointed out, it would give her strength and fill her belly, so she'd eat it. But she had to wonder if they were always this hard, or the oatcake had traveled all the way from Scotland with them and was now stale after being weeks in some sack.

"Carlisle ahead!"

Elysande lifted her head from where it rested against Rory's back, and glanced around at that shout. Sitting behind him as she was, she couldn't see anything. Not until she lifted her veil to toss it over her headdress and leaned to the side to look around his arm. Then she saw what Rory was shouting about. Despite the driving snow that had been pelting them for hours, she could make out what looked like a church spire and a bunch of buildings that appeared almost to grow out of the wall that surrounded them. They were merely a dark silhouette against a gray and black sky, but it was a welcome sight nonetheless, Elysande decided as she tugged her veil back into place.

The snow had started falling while they were still only halfway up out of the valley where they'd camped. Elysande hadn't been worried then; she'd even thought it was pretty. But the moment they'd crested the hill, the wind had slapped at them, and those pretty, soft little flakes fluttering to the ground in the valley had quickly become icy needles stabbing at her neck and the side of her face where the wind blew her veil aside.

It had made for a cold and bitter ride through the morning, and she'd been relieved when they'd stopped to rest, huddled together in the shelter of a group of close-growing trees to eat another oatcake each. The shelter had spared them from the wind at least, but it had still been bitterly cold, the kind that settled in your bones and left your teeth chattering.

Elysande had chewed methodically on her tasteless oatcake and listened dully when Rory mentioned his intention to stop at Carlisle because he wished to visit the weekly market. But when he added that they would hopefully find someplace to warm up and purchase a hot meal as well before continuing on their journey, her interest had been engaged, and she had been as eager as the others to cut short their rest and set out again. But an hour later, the light snowfall had become a blinding deluge. Where the earlier snow had been more wind than snow, barely peppering the ground, this was equal parts of both. The trail had quickly become buried under a blanket of white that had grown deeper by the minute and their party had been forced to slow down both to avoid wandering off the trail, and because the snow had become so deep the horses were having trouble galloping through it.

Still, they'd pushed on. They'd had no choice. Stopping could be deadly in this kind of weather. But late afternoon had passed without their reaching Carlisle as they'd expected when they'd set out that morning. Now the sun had disappeared beyond the horizon and they were traveling through a grim, gray world as the last fingers of light drifted away. Elysande knew they would not make it across the border into Scotland this night, and was quite sure the weekly market Rory had hoped to visit would now be done and the vendors gone in search of a warm bed too. But they were alive, and soon to be somewhere warm. She hoped.

Elysande grimaced at her own thoughts. She was actually much warmer now than she had been before Rory had stopped and had Tom and Simon help her from her horse onto his. She'd done well, lasting much longer on her own horse than she had the day before, but about an hour ago she'd been exhausted to the point that she'd feared tumbling from her mare. Riding behind her, Rory had obviously noted that she was having difficulties. She'd heard his whistle that had called the party to a stop, and had felt only relief when he'd announced she would ride with him from there.

Elysande had felt even more relieved to share his heat as she'd settled on his mount behind him. It had made her wonder how the men were faring. Tom and Simon should be fine. They were wearing layers of clothing along with their capes and gloves, but the Buchanans and their warriors only had their tunics and plaids. Although she'd noticed they'd lowered the skirt of their plaids to cover them to the tops of their boots, and each man had wrapped the top part of the heavy woolen cloth around them like a cape. They also all had gloves on now. And this time as she'd ridden with Rory she'd noticed that the cloth of his plaid was oiled and wondered if it helped keep the cold out, because the man's back was like a furnace against her chest, warming her through.

A shout caught her ear then, and Elysande leaned to the side to look ahead again. She could have wept when she saw that Conn, still at the head of their group, had reached the city gate and was shouting to the men on the wall. Even as she watched, the portcullis was being raised for them to enter. Soon she would be enjoying that hot meal and warm fire Rory had promised.

The gale force winds that had pummeled them for most of the day died considerably once they rode through the gate, the wall and buildings acting as a buffer. But the snow was still falling rapidly.

Elysande glanced around with curiosity as their party slowed to a walk. There wasn't much to see in the gloom but wooden buildings all stacked together. The streets of the small northern English city were eerily silent and empty with no sign of its inhabitants, or that it had held a market that day. The only sign of life was the soft glow of candles or firelight that was escaping around the furs used to cover the windows they passed, an effort to keep out the cold. Elysande frowned when she noted that many of the windows were dark and uncovered. But then she recalled her mother and father talking about how the cities had been affected by the Black Death years ago. Some cities had lost half their inhabitants or more to the disease, and still struggled to regrow their population. She was guessing Carlisle was one of them.

Her attention was drawn from their surroundings when Conn, who had remained in the lead, suddenly turned back to approach them. Inan and Alick stopped at once and urged their horses to the side so he could pass.

"Alehouse or inn?" he asked Rory, and she felt him tense with indecision under the arms she had around his waist.

"I've no' stopped here before," Rory admitted finally. "Do ye ken an inn that will take us all?"

"Nay. They do no' much like Scots here," Conn said with a grimace. "But there's an alehouse at the end o' the next street that'll feed us and give us a place to lay our heads for a small king's ransom."

She could feel the sigh that slid through Rory at this news and then he said, "The alehouse, 'tis, then."

Nodding, Conn took the lead again.

"Why do they not like Scots here?" Elysande asked with curiosity when Rory urged his mount to start moving.

"Because Scots are no' English," Rory said with disgust, and then shook his head and admitted, "And because of the reivers."

"Reivers?" Elysande asked with interest.

"Groups o' Scots who raid them and steal their animals and such. It's happened along the border for years. 'Tis just desperate and hungry men looking to survive, but it makes it hard for the people trying to make an honest living, and makes them hate harder. O' course, the English forget that there are Anglos raiding the Scots on the other side as well and just blame it on we heathen Scots with our stealing ways."

Elysande considered that silently. Her mother hadn't mentioned that when she'd spoken of her kin, but then the Sinclairs were Highlanders who lived far to the north—too far away to be involved in reiving from the English.

"But while that makes the English refuse to rent a room to a Scot, ye're English," Rory pointed out now. "We could probably find an inn that would take ye and yer men, and then we could hopefully find someplace nearby to—"

"Nay," Elysande interrupted him. "We will stay with you."

"Are ye sure?" he asked, and she could hear the frown in his voice. "Ye'd no doubt find more comfortable lodging in an inn, and with yer back paining ye—"

"Ye ferget I'm half-Scottish meself, laddie," she said with a very bad attempt to mimic his accent. "I'll no' stay where me kind are no' welcome."

"Lass?" Rory said, a smile now in his voice.

"Aye?"

"Stick to yer English. Ye're a muckle mess as a Scot."

"Oh!" Elysande gasped on a laugh, and smacked his stomach where her hands rested. "I thought it was a very good attempt at mimicking you."

"Ye thought wrong," he assured her.

Elysande merely squeezed her arms around him briefly and remained silent, listening to him chuckle. It was a nice sound, and the first time she'd heard it from him. Besides, she'd got what she wanted. He'd forgotten about her pitiful state, and wasn't going to leave her at some inn while he and his men went somewhere else where he might decide she was too much trouble and should be left behind here in Carlisle while he made his way home.

Not that she really thought he might do that, Elysande assured herself. After all, he could have simply refused the chore back in the clearing outside Monmouth and hadn't.

But then he hadn't known that she was injured and might slow them down, her mind argued, and Elysande grimaced as she admitted to herself that it was a concern to her. She'd lost so much the last few days, and feared losing his escort on top of it all. And that couldn't happen. She felt safe with Rory Buchanan. And his brother and the other men too, of course. She added that last as an afterthought, but it was true. Tom and Simon were fine soldiers, but these Scots . . . There was something strong and wild about them that made her feel that they would stand firm in the face of any challenge and see her safely through it.

THE ALEHOUSE LOOKED LIKE EVERY OTHER BUILDING ON THE street except for the sign over the door—a rooster sitting on a bull and holding a foamy stein of ale. There was no writing on the sign, but then most people couldn't read, so businesses had to depend on images to advertise themselves.

"The Cock and Bull Alehouse?" Elysande asked.

"That'd be my guess," Rory said, his words reminding her that this establishment had been Conn's choice.

"You told Conn you had never stopped here before. So this is the first time you have been to Carlisle?" Elysande asked with curiosity as they followed Conn, Inan and Alick up a tiny alley-way between the alehouse and the building next to it.

"Nay," he said. "But 'tis the first time I've stopped here fer the night."

"But Conn has stayed the night here before?" Elysande asked. It was the only explanation she could come up with for why the man had known of a place to stay while Rory hadn't.

"Aye." Rory nodded. "Conn has traveled this way half a dozen times or more with one o' me brothers or another. But I don't travel much to England."

"Really?" she asked, a bit startled at the admission, although she wasn't sure why. She'd never even left Kynardersley, so why should she expect Rory to leave not only his home but his country on a regular basis?

"Aye," he assured her. "When younger I traveled a lot to speak to healers who were said to know much, but few of them were in England."

"Where did you travel to speak to these healers?" Elysande asked with interest as they reached a small courtyard behind the alehouse where a stable waited.

"France, Gascony, Aragon, Castille . . ." He brought the horse to a halt, and then tugged off his gloves and placed them in her hands while he set to work on the rope at her wrists that had kept her arms around his waist without her needing to hold on.

While she waited, Elysande noted that the last two Scots—Fearghas and Donnghail, she thought their names were—were following Tom and Simon and her riderless mare into the courtyard. It made her realize that she hadn't even thought to check to be sure they were still behind them when they'd ridden through the city gates.

"There ye are, lass," Rory said as he finished freeing her.

"Thank you," Elysande murmured, reluctantly retrieving her arms from around his waist after he took back his gloves. She'd enjoyed sharing their body heat, but now sat back and pulled her cloak closed as she waited for Tom and Simon to come help her down.

"There now. How many horses have ye?"

Elysande peered down to see a round-bellied, bowlegged little man scurrying toward them, clutching a ratty old blanket around his shoulders.

"Nine," Rory answered. "And we'll be needing food and drink and a place to sleep fer the night."

The man's eyes fairly glowed with avarice at this news. "It'll cost ye, but we've got plenty of pottage and ye're welcome to bed down in the stable."

"The stable is fine for us, but the lady'll need somewhere warmer," Rory said at once, and Elysande stilled as the man's greedy eyes found her.

"Well, now, we sometimes let travelers bed down in the kitchen and I wouldn't mind if she did, but I'm thinking me wife won't be happy letting her sort sleep there."

Elysande felt Rory stiffen at the words, and wasn't surprised when he growled, "And what sort is that?"

"A woman what travels so freely and alone with men. And some of 'em Scots," the man answered as if it should be obvious, and Elysande supposed it was, at least the traveling alone with men part. That was not how a lady was expected to travel. She should have servants and at least one older kinswoman or maid for propriety's sake. Unfortunately, the situation hadn't allowed for that.

Aware that Rory was almost vibrating with fury, Elysande touched his arm gently and said, "The stable is fine. I would rather be with the rest of you in case we need to leave quickly."

As the little man nodded and hurried toward the stable, Rory jerked around to peer at her with surprise. "We should be fine," he assured her. "The soldiers took the other route north. And we do no' even ken if they were de Buci's men."

Elysande shrugged. "But they could be, and they could also easily have split up later and sent half the men the way we came when they did not encounter us on that other route."

When he looked dubious, she said, "I can see you doubt me, but you did not witness de Buci's actions at Kynardersley. I have known him all my life and never seen him act like that. He was mad with desperation. If those men at Monmouth were his, or even if they were not and he has discovered I am missing, he will search high and low for me and will not stop," she assured him grimly. "I will not be safe until I reach Sinclair, and even then I would not put it past him to attack my aunt and uncle's holding. His very life depends upon it and de Buci knows it."

Rory's mouth spread into a smile at the suggestion. "He would no' even make it to Sinclair with an army, lass. Scots like the English as little as the English like us. No clan would let a horde o' English soldiers cross their land and there are a lot o' clans between here and Sinclair. Once we're in Scotland, ye'll be safe."

"Then I look forward to reaching Scotland," Elysande said, though she didn't really think what he said was true. She wouldn't feel safe until de Buci was taken care of. While she hadn't known what he was searching for that night at Kynardersley and why her mother and father along with most of their faithful soldiers had died, she had found out afterward. And that knowledge told her that de Buci would kill anyone and everyone who got in his way.

He had to, for it was his own life he was fighting for. What he was searching for would put his neck on the block if he didn't retrieve it before it reached the king.

RORY GROUND HIS TEETH TOGETHER AS HE HANDED OVER PAY-ment to the alewife for stabling their horses, being able to bed down in there with them and nine bowls of pottage along with nine mugs of ale. The amount she'd demanded was outrageous, enough to cover nine rooms as well as meals at an inn if any had been willing to take them. But there wasn't much choice in the matter. The woman had them at a disadvantage and knew it.

Leaving the alewife chortling happily as she counted his coin, Rory made his way to the long table the others had settled at in front of the large fireplace. Elysande sat on one side with Tom, Simon, Conn and Inan, while Alick, Fearghas and Donnghail filled the other, leaving the spot across from Elysande open. Rory dropped into it with a sigh and glanced around at his companions.

Everyone looked tired, he noted, and their cheeks were wind-burned; at least the men's were. Elysande still wore her coif and veil and he couldn't tell if she was windburned too, but at a quick glance everyone seemed well enough, and that was something. The last part of the journey that day had been bad enough that he'd worried about frostbite setting in, or a horse losing its footing in the snow and taking a tumble with its rider, or— Well, the list of what could have gone wrong was endless, but they'd made it here relatively unscathed and he decided he'd take that as a win.

It was the only win of the day. He'd missed the weekly market so didn't have the wolfsbane to make the potion he'd hoped would ease Elysande's pain, and they hadn't reached Scotland before nightfall as he'd planned, which meant—

"Another night in bloody England," Conn growled suddenly, as if reading his thoughts.

Rory smiled faintly and shook his head. "It could be worse."

"What could be worse than having to stay in England?" Inan asked morosely.

"Death," he answered promptly, and they all laughed.

All except for Elysande and her soldiers, Rory noted, and realizing he was insulting their country, he cleared his throat before saying, "Do no' mind us. 'Tis been a long day."

"Nay. 'Tis fine," she said quietly. "I do not blame you for disliking England if our countrymen all treat you as the alewife and her husband did."

Tom scowled toward the door to the kitchens where the alewife was hopefully collecting their dinner. "The husband threw out insults like he thought you were too deaf or dumb to understand them, and the wife overcharged you shamefully for our pitiful lodging. Made me embarrassed to be English."

Simon grunted in agreement, and Rory relaxed somewhat but said, "Aye, well, there are many in Scotland who are just as rude to the English."

The moment the words were out of his mouth, he realized how true they were. Once they crossed the border, Elysande and her men might encounter the same rude treatment he and the others had experienced the last several weeks in England. The idea was a troubling one.

And apparently not only to himself, he thought when Conn shifted suddenly and said, "The last time I was here there was a draper's shop a street over that carried the occasional lengths of plaid cloth. If he's still there and open tomorrow we might see what he has and get some for our English friends here."

Inan nodded. "'Twould make them less noticeable once we reach Scotland if they were dressed like us."

"Oh, nay!" Tom said with horror. "I'm not running around with naked knees! 'Tis indecent."

"Aye," Simon agreed. "And in this weather we'd freeze our bollocks off in those skirts of yours. Sorry, m'lady," he added as he apparently realized what he'd just said.

Rory couldn't see Elysande's expression, but was guessing she was blushing under her veil. She did emit a slightly choked sound as she waved away the apology. "'Tis fine."

Clearing her throat then, she said, "But it may be a good idea for us to dress more like Scots. If de Buci did catch wind that we traveled this way, he will be looking for a group that includes an Englishwoman and two English soldiers. Dressing like Scots might help keep him and his men off our trail."

Tom and Simon stared at her blankly for a minute and then looked at each other before Tom grimaced at his comrade and reluctantly pointed out, "She's right about that."

"Aye," Simon agreed on a sigh, and then lowered his head and muttered, "There go our bollocks."

Rory and the other men were still laughing at that when the alewife and her husband appeared with trenchers of pottage. They passed around the food and then moved off to fetch ale for them before disappearing back into the kitchen, leaving them alone. The moment they were gone everyone began to eat.

Pottage was a stew of boiled vegetables, grain and sometimes meat. But this one was lacking any meat as far as he could tell. It was also a bit thin, as if the alewife had watered it down to make it stretch for all of them, but it was hot and tasty enough, Rory supposed, and then glanced to Elysande when she gave up trying to eat with her veil on, and tossed it over her head.

Rory's gaze automatically ran over her face, examining the bruising that covered all of one side, as if it had been slammed into a wall repeatedly. Much to his relief, it wasn't as swollen as it had been when he'd first seen it. The bruising also wasn't as dark, the almost black cast it had originally been was fading more to a reddish-purple color. It was healing. In a week or so it would be mostly gone, and it would be wholly gone by the time they reached Sinclair.

A soft curse drew his gaze to Alick to see that he was staring at Elysande's face with dismay. He wasn't the only one. Every man at the table was taking in what had been done to her—even her own soldiers who had already seen it—and every man there was wearing an expression of dismay mixed with disgust that anyone would abuse a woman so.

Rory glanced quickly back to Elysande, hoping she hadn't noticed the attention focused on her. Though she was staring steadfastly down at her pottage, there was a tinge of pink in the cheek on the undamaged side of her face that told him she was very aware of it, and embarrassed.

Mouth tightening, Rory cleared his throat to get the attention of the others and then scowled at them in a silent order to stop their gawking. They got the message and immediately dropped their gazes down to their food. Satisfied, he glanced back to Elysande to find her looking at him with a somewhat wry smile.

"I do not mind their looking," she said quietly. "I would stare too if I were them."

"I assumed ye wore yer veil to avoid being stared at," he said solemnly.

Elysande shook her head. "I wore the veil because I did not want any of you to feel sorry for me, or think I was weak."

Rory's eyebrows rose at the admission. "M'lady, I canno' imagine anyone thinking fer a moment that ye're weak. The verra fact that ye've sat a horse fer the better part o' the last two days with yer back and side as black bruised as yer face fair boggles me mind. I've tended grown men, *warriors*, who did naught but lay about and moan for days after suffering less damage than was done to ye. Ye're no' weak," he assured her.

"Her back and side are as badly damaged too?" Alick asked with dismay. While they'd all heard her tell of the beating she'd taken, Rory recalled then that only he, Tom and Simon had seen the damage done, and then they'd only seen part of it. He suspected that black bruising that covered her back and side ran down over her buttocks and at least the upper backs of her legs too. Perhaps even her shins.

"Aye," he sighed, and then turned back to Elysande and paused at the narrow-eyed gaze she was giving him.

"So you did come upon me in the woods earlier than you let me think," she accused quietly.

"Er . . ." Rory muttered, his gaze shifting to Tom and Simon, who were looking about as dismayed as he felt. And he was feeling like a boy caught sneaking a peek at the maids at their bath. Any minute he expected his mother to come box his ears.

"And you saw me naked."

Rory shifted his eyes quickly back to her with alarm. "Half-naked. Ye still had yer breeks on," he pointed out.

"Breeks?" she asked with bewilderment.

"We call them breeches," Tom explained to Rory, and then told Elysande, "And it is not his fault that he saw you, m'lady. We were all quite concerned when you were gone so long from camp, and the three of us set off together to look for you. Me, Simon and Lord Buchanan."

"It was too much to hope you'd leave me out of it, wasn't it?" Simon muttered under his breath with disgust.

"Well, you were there too," Tom pointed out with exasperation.

"Aye, but she didn't know that," Simon countered.

A small burst of laughter broke up their bickering and they all turned to peer at Elysande. Rory was surprised to see her eyes dancing with amusement.

"'Tis fine," she told her men at once. "I am not angry, Simon. I suspected you may have arrived sooner than you let it be known anyway. I was just teasing."

The soldiers looked relieved, and then Tom assured her, "All we saw was your back, m'lady, and God's truth I was so focused on the bruising 'twas all I saw."

When Elysande merely nodded and began to eat again, the rest of them continued eating as well, and it wasn't until everyone had finished before anyone said anything more. This time it was Tom who asked, "How long should it take us to get to Sinclair?"

"Better than two weeks," Rory said.

"Two weeks?" Elysande asked with dismay.

"Aye," he said slowly when she continued to stare at him with horror. "Sinclair is nearly as far north as ye can go in Scotland. We have to cross the whole o' it to get there, and after two days' travel we are no' even out o' England yet." He paused briefly, and then added, "We could do it more quickly had we each a spare horse to switch to halfway through the day, but as we do no', 'twill take better than two weeks to get there," he explained, this time stressing the "better than" part.

"And that is only do we no' end up snowed in here or somewhere else until the spring," Alick added.

"Nay! We cannot be snowed in here or anywhere else. The spring will be too late to warn him. I must—" She stopped talking suddenly and snapped her mouth closed. Rory cast a questioning glance at Tom and Simon, but the two men looked as bewildered as he was by her upset.

His gaze slid sharply back to Elysande when she stood abruptly.

"I need to think. I mean, sleep," she muttered, and left the table. They all watched silently as she turned away and hurried from the room. But the moment she disappeared down the hall, Tom and Simon stood to follow.

"WHO DO YOU THINK SHE WAS TALKING ABOUT WHEN SHE SAID spring would be too late to warn him?" Alick asked.

"And what does she need to warn whoever it is of?" Donnghail asked.

"I'm thinking it has something to do with what that de Buci bastard was looking for," Conn said slowly.

Rory glanced at him sharply. "Ye think she knew what de Buci was after the whole time and allowed her mother—"

"Nay," Conn interrupted, shaking his head firmly. "No daughter would see her mother beaten and not give whatever she must to save her. Neither do I think her mother could ha'e stood by and watched her beaten without speaking up either."

Rory relaxed back on the bench at those words, relieved that Conn thought that way, because he did too. There was no way he would believe that Elysande or her mother had known what de Buci was after.

"But," Conn added now, "'tis possible the bastard said something during those times he tried to rouse Lady Elysande's mother when she was feigning sleep. Or perhaps the guard in the dungeon said something to Elysande that gave away what the man was looking for."

"Aye," Rory murmured, remembering what Elysande had said while trying to convince him that de Buci was a threat. She had said that she feared de Buci might even attack her aunt and uncle's holdings to get to her. *That his life depended on it.* What he should have wondered at the time was how she knew de Buci's life depended on his finding whatever he was searching for if she didn't know what it was? That hadn't occurred to him then though. He'd been more interested in, and even amused by, the idea that any Englishman could march an army to Sinclair without every clan south of it getting up in arms and eager to kill the arrogant bastard.

Standing abruptly, Rory headed for the door, saying, "Stay here and finish yer drinks. I need a word with Lady Elysande."

Chapter 5

"Nay," Elysande said firmly.

"But, m'lady, 'tis warmer in the loft and there is fresh hay there for sleeping," Tom argued with frustration as she gathered her cloak around her in preparation of easing herself down onto the hay of the only empty stall left in the stables.

"That may be so," she admitted wearily. "But I cannot climb that ladder in the state I am in, and you certainly cannot carry me up it. So I fear I am sleeping down here."

"If Simon and I worked together," Tom began soothingly, "surely we can get you up there, m'lady."

"How?" Elysande asked with exasperation. "I am bruised from my shoulders all the way down to my calves. Will you lift me by my ankles?"

"All the way down to your calves?" Tom echoed with dismay, and then turned toward the stable door as it swung open. She saw him reach for his sword, only to relax when Rory entered.

"Go back inside and finish your ale, lads. I'll help your lady up to the loft."

Elysande stared at the man. His words suggested he'd heard their conversation as he approached, but it was his demeanor that had caught her attention. He seemed different somehow. Stiffer, almost stilted. By her guess, he was angry about something.

Tom considered him silently for a moment, and then straightened and said, "We will stay in case you need help."

Rory wasn't impressed. "Nay, ye'll no'. I need a word with Lady Elysande," he said firmly, and then eyed her grimly as he said,

"About why de Buci's life might depend on his getting what he is looking for."

Elysande's eyes widened at the words. She recognized them as her own from a previous conversation, though somewhat rearranged, and realized the mistake she'd made. Nodding that she understood, Elysande told Tom and Simon, "Go ahead. He is right. We must talk."

Tom hesitated, his concerned gaze shifting between her solemn expression and Rory's grim one, but then a determined glint entered his eyes and he shook his head. "It would not be proper for you to be alone with him."

"'Tis not proper for me to be alone with all three of you either," she pointed out sharply, and then relented. "He is our protector, Tom. My mother trusted him with our lives. I think my virtue is safe." And then smiling wryly, she added, "Besides, 'tis not likely he could want to seduce me the way I look now, is it?"

Elysande suspected she should be insulted by the way Tom and Simon both nodded and relaxed at those words. But she was just glad they finally obeyed her and headed out of the stables. Sighing as the door closed behind them, she turned toward Rory and then gasped in shock when she found his shoulder lodged in her lower stomach and herself being lifted into the air and nearly tumbling over his back before he caught her by the ankles to steady her. She'd slipped enough that her bottom was in the air and her groin rather than her stomach was resting on his shoulder now with her legs hanging in front and her chest down his back.

"Do no' move," he growled, carting her to the back of the stables in that undignified position.

Elysande didn't respond. She couldn't. He'd knocked the air out of her and she was still struggling to regain it when he released his hold on her ankles and began to climb the ladder with her hanging over his shoulder unanchored. More than a little panicked when the floor became farther and farther away and her upper body began to sway back and forth with his movement, Elysande grabbed at the back of his plaid for something to hold on to, and pulled. Instead of steadying her as a pair of breeches would have done, the cloth pulled upward and she found herself cheek to cheek with his bare bottom. At least temporarily, before her bobbing and swinging about had her sliding away and back.

"I suddenly feel a draft," Rory said, and Elysande was sure she heard laughter in his voice rather than the embarrassment she was experiencing. It so annoyed her that she was tempted to bite the soft, white skin in front of her face when she swung the other way like the pendulum she'd become.

Common sense prevailed at the last moment, however, and she dropped the plaid, and threw her arms around him instead. It was a desperate attempt to stop herself from swinging, as well as to be sure she didn't drop to the ground like a stone. It was not a well-thought-out maneuver. Elysande realized that when her hand slammed into his groin.

Mid-step, Rory let out a hiss of pain and instinctively hunched forward and lost his footing. For one heart-stopping moment, she was sure they would plummet to the ground, but then his foot caught on the next rung down on the ladder and they jerked to a stop.

Elysande groaned as his shoulder jammed into her groin. By the time her groan ended, he'd scooted up the last couple of steps and was setting her down on her feet in the loft. She immediately stumbled back several steps, casting him a baleful glare as she went.

"You are not taking me down the same way in the morning," she growled, clenching her fists to keep from rubbing her pelvic bone. Dear God, he'd probably given her another bruise, she thought with dismay.

"We'll find another way to get ye down," he assured her, but his back was to her now and he'd lifted the front of his plaid, she presumed, to examine himself in the light that reached them from the torches below.

Sighing as guilt claimed her for unintentionally smacking him in the groin, Elysande glanced around the loft. It was quite large.

Certainly big enough for all of them to sleep in, especially if they slept as close together as they had the night before. There was also lots of hay, bushels of it, that they could spread around if they wanted, and considering what they'd paid for sleeping there, she decided she wanted to. And Tom had been right; it was warmer than the lower level of the stables.

"Ye ken what de Buci was looking for."

Elysande turned from her inspection and eyed Rory warily. He'd dropped his plaid and was facing her again. After the briefest hesitation, she nodded.

Apparently Rory wasn't expecting that, because he simply stared at her, seeming unsure how to proceed.

"WHAT WAS IT?" HE ASKED FINALLY.

"A letter," she answered without hesitation.

"A letter," he echoed with disbelief. "He killed yer father and all of his men, beat yer mother to death's door and then verra nearly beat ye there as well fer a letter?"

"Well." Elysande shrugged helplessly. "'Twas an important letter."

Rory shook his head mildly, and then sighed. "I think ye'd best be explaining it, lass."

She nodded solemnly, but then walked to the edge of the loft to peer down and make sure no one was below before moving to perch on a bale of hay.

"De Buci is a powerful lord," she began slowly. "But he is impatient, and too fond of coin and power. He dislikes anything that he feels gets between he and that."

When she paused briefly, Rory nodded and settled on a bale of hay across from her. "Many lords are like that."

"Aye," she murmured. "Well, he's long been a critic of the king. He feels he takes too much in taxes and wastes it on . . ." She waved away the explanation and simply said, "He just dislikes him. Mostly because he could not worm his way into being one of his favorites, I think."

Rory nodded again.

"We all knew this. Father even teased him for it, but none of us imagined that he would decide to do something about it. Except his wife," Elysande said heavily. "While we thought he was all talk, she knew it was more than that. But then, I suspect he was more circumspect with us and was perhaps just talking to feel Father out to see if he was of a like mind."

"But he was no'," Rory guessed.

"My father was loyal to our king," she said firmly, and when Rory nodded, she continued. "So was Lady de Buci."

"Was?" Rory queried.

"I suspect she too is dead," Elysande admitted on a sigh. "As I said, she apparently suspected he might be moved to do something. I gather she noted certain lords visiting more often, other lords of a like mind to her husband. He would send her away to the solar and have meetings with them. In her letter she said she tried to slip out to hear what they spoke of, but de Buci would post a guard outside the solar who would suggest she stay put and he would fetch whatever she needed. She felt like a prisoner in her own keep at those times and it only made her more certain he was up to something. But two weeks ago a messenger arrived while de Buci was away on a hunt. She accepted the message and opened it."

Pausing, she met his gaze before saying, "It was a most incriminating letter. De Buci and several lords have contrived a plot to kill the king and his young son and replace him on the throne with his brother, who they feel will be grateful for their efforts and reward them accordingly. Because the lords have been careful never to meet all together at once so as to avoid suspicion, Lord Wykeman was writing to confirm the entire plot. It mentioned names, the time and place of the planned murders and who was expected to do what."

"Damn," Rory breathed.

"Aye." Elysande stood and walked over to peer into the empty lower floor again before continuing. "Lady de Buci was horrified.

She needed to get the message to the king, to warn him, but her husband was in total control of his men. Every last one was faithful to him. She could not send a message with any of them. But the servants and villagers were faithful to her. However, none of them could have got the message all the way to court and to the king. So she wrote a letter to my mother explaining everything, rolled up Wykeman's damning scroll inside her own message begging her to get her letter and the one she had opened to the king. She then gave it to the blacksmith along with coin and had him take it to a spice merchant who had visited the castle that day and whom she knew was still in the village. He was to give the coin and the message to the spice merchant and have him deliver it to my mother when he stopped in at Kynardersley."

It was not an unusual occurrence; messages were often delivered by the slow-moving traveling merchants if they were not urgent. This message had been urgent, but Lady de Buci had felt she had no choice but to send it the slower route.

"What happened to the spice merchant?" Rory asked, drawing her back to their conversation.

Elysande stared blindly toward the stable doors, the tops of which were just visible where she sat and said, "He did not make it to Kynardersley before de Buci did. So none of us knew or understood anything that was happening when de Buci arrived. He must have asked Father about the message from his wife at the table, and demanded he hand it over. Father would have said, quite honestly, that he had no knowledge of a message from his lady wife, and de Buci, thinking he lied, killed him."

A sudden image of her father rising from the table and stumbling back to fall dead to the floor with the dagger protruding from his chest flashed through her mind, and Elysande firmed her lips and continued.

"The spice merchant arrived shortly after Simon and Tom returned, and like them he was stopped by the servants hiding in the woods and warned against continuing on to the keep. Apparently he was trying to decide what to do about the message

Lady de Buci had paid him to deliver when he heard Tom and Simon charge Eldon with the task of getting word to my mother of their presence in the woods. The spice merchant saw this as his opportunity to complete his task and gave Eldon Lady de Buci's message and a coin and told him to deliver that to her as well."

"Ah." Rory almost sighed the word, and when she turned to peer at him, he said, "That is why it took hours fer Tom and Simon to hear anything. Yer mother had to read the letters and decide what to do."

"Aye. That is part of the reason," Elysande murmured. "When Eldon said the message was from Lady de Buci, Mother knew at once that it must have something to do with what was happening at Kynardersley. She immediately had Betty open both scrolls and hold them up for her to read, and then she—" Elysande paused abruptly. Her mother had admitted to her that she'd cursed Lady de Buci and her husband to hell in that moment of realization and then had wept for all she'd lost and the troubles they were in through no fault of their own.

Leaving that out, Elysande simply said, "She started to plan then. She had Betty take Eldon down to the kitchens using the secret passages, and while he gathered food for our journey, she prepared the dungeon guard's evening meal, dosing his ale with a sleeping potion as she did, and then delivered it. She then returned to the kitchens, collected Eldon and snuck him back up to the master chamber with the food for us. Then they had to wait for the sleeping potion to take effect. Once they felt enough time had passed, Eldon waited with Mother while Betty came down to the dungeon to free me. And then she took Eldon out to the woods with her when she went to speak to Tom and Simon."

"And while they were fetching Tom and Simon, yer mother told ye about Lady de Buci's message and dictated her own messages to Sinclair and meself," Rory finished for her solemnly.

Elysande merely nodded. There was nothing else to say. He knew everything now.

"Ye should ha'e told me this, lass, when ye told me the rest," Rory said.

That made her sigh unhappily. "I would have told you, but Mother cautioned me not to. She said 'twould put your life even more at risk than your escorting me would. She said that would be a poor thank-you for your aid."

Rory's eyebrows rose and a smile tugged at his lips at that. "I suspect just aiding ye puts me life and everyone else's at risk. Kenning the danger involved could only help us, lass."

Elysande didn't comment. She didn't know if he was right or not. Not knowing was the only reason she herself was alive. Had Lady de Buci's letter arrived before Lord de Buci had shown up, and had they handed it over, she was quite sure he would have immediately killed them all anyway. He wouldn't have been able to risk anyone who knew about the letter carrying word of it to the king.

"So the letter to Sinclair has the other letters inside it?" Rory asked suddenly.

Elysande's mouth curved into a half smile. "Actually, it has three messages inside it. The original letter Lady de Buci opened, Lady de Buci's letter to my mother about it and my mother's letter to the king about Lady de Buci's letter and the other."

"Ye have them somewhere safe?" he asked.

"Aye," she assured him, but didn't tell him that the bulky scroll was in a small sack that Betty had quickly sewn into the lining of her skirts.

"So ye need to get news to the king ere the attempt is made on his life," he said slowly.

Elysande nodded unhappily. "The plan is set for late December, before the New Year. Even if we are not snowed in somewhere until spring, 'better than two weeks' from here to Sinclair means most like another five weeks for a messenger to get all the way down to court to warn him." Pausing, she shook her head and then fretted, "I do not know why Mother did not think of that when she insisted I travel to Sinclair first."

"Has she been home since she traveled to England to marry yer father?" Rory asked.

"To Scotland?" she asked. Quite sure that's what he meant,

but she found it odd to think of Scotland as her mother's home. Their home had been Kynardersley her entire life.

"Aye. Has she traveled back and forth to Scotland at all since her marriage?"

"Not that I know of," she said slowly, scanning her mind for any mention of such a trip, and then she added, "Definitely not since I was born."

"Then she probably just did no' recall how long a journey 'twas to get from one place to the other," Rory reasoned, then pointed out gently, "And she was verra ill at the time she made these plans. It is no' surprising that a few details may have been fuzzy fer her, or slipped her mind altogether."

"Aye." Elysande nodded agreement. That made perfect sense. "But it does cause problems. I must get Mother's message to the king ere the end of December. Mayhap I should not go to Sinclair at all. Mayhap Tom, Simon and I should head to court to give the king Mother's message."

"Nay," Rory said at once. "Ye could ride right into de Buci, or he could ha'e men watching the roads fer ye." He shook his head. "Nay. Yer mother sent ye to me to see ye safe to Sinclair, and that's what I'm going to do."

When she opened her mouth to protest, he added, "But I'll think on a way to deliver her message to the king that will get it there faster," he assured her, standing and moving toward the ladder. Pausing there, he looked thoughtful and murmured, "Perhaps if we had the messenger travel by sea part of the way."

Elysande's eyes widened slightly at the suggestion. Traveling by sea would be much quicker, she was sure. The idea at least gave her new hope that they might accomplish the task in time, after all, something she'd begun to seriously doubt when she'd learned how long it would take to reach Sinclair.

"Anyway, that's enough talk fer now. Ye need yer rest. We all do if we hope to leave tomorrow if we're able," Rory said as he began to descend the ladder. "You go ahead and get settled. I'm just going to fetch the men and let them ken they can join us now."

Elysande waited until he was out of sight, and then moved to the edge of the loft to watch him walk out of the stable. She couldn't help noticing how the light from the torches caught the red in his hair. Most of the time his hair just looked a rich, dark brown but there was actually red among the brown.

And wasn't she pathetic for even noticing? Elysande thought with disgust. She was acting like she'd never seen a handsome man before when there were plenty of fine-looking men at Kynardersley. Or there had been, she corrected herself solemnly. They were all dead now.

Suddenly wearied by the realization, Elysande turned to survey the loft. The fur she'd slept on the night before was lying in a corner with the bags that held her clothes. Tom and Simon had obviously put them up here earlier, probably when they'd tended the horses with the other men, though Elysande had been here and hadn't noticed at the time. She'd probably been too busy watching Rory brush down his mount, she admitted to herself. She did find her eye drawn to him more and more the longer she knew him, which made her feel rather guilty. Her father had been murdered and her mother too, along with every man under them except for Tom and Simon. She should be grieving too much to notice that any man was attractive. Shouldn't she?

Elysande didn't know. She'd never been through anything like this before. And where was the numbness that had claimed her directly after those horrible events? It had cloaked her for the journey to Monmouth, and even for the beginning of her journey with the Buchanans, but it had been fading ever since she'd told Rory and Alick and their men what had happened at Kynardersley. It was as if talking about it had stolen the protective numbness from her. Or perhaps it was the tears she'd shed on her horse. Whatever the case, she missed that numbness. Elysande didn't know how she should behave or feel, or what was appropriate. She felt like she should be numb still over such a great loss. Instead, she was feeling attraction for a complete stranger and it felt wrong.

Elysande fretted over all of that as she spread some hay around and then fetched and unrolled the fur in the middle of the loft. She then gathered her cloak around her and eased herself down to lay on the bed she'd made, resting on her good side and using one of the sacks of clothing as a pillow. It was surprisingly comfortable, and actually warmer than she'd expected. It would be warmer still when the men arrived, she thought, and as if drawn by her thoughts, she heard the stable door open and the soft murmur of the men's voices as they entered.

Their soft speech died off as they neared the back of the stables. Elysande supposed they were being quiet in case she was sleeping. The possibility made her close her eyes and feign sleep. Confused as she was, she didn't feel like talking anyway. So she lay still and breathed steadily as she listened to the quiet movements around her as the men climbed up into the loft one after another and bedded down.

Elysande felt someone bump against her hands where they rested in front of her before moving away, and was sure she recognized Rory's scent. But she could hear the others settling in around her. Someone was at her back, someone by her feet, someone above her head again, just like last night, and she guessed they were all taking up the same positions they had then, surrounding her protectively. It made her feel safe, and she sent up a silent prayer of thanks that Tom and Simon had survived to bring her to the Buchanans.

Chapter 6

$\mathcal{R}$ORY WOKE SLOWLY, HIS MIND RELUCTANT TO LEAVE THE warm comfort of sleep, but his body telling him there was something missing. It was the warm weight of Elysande curled into his body, he realized. Rory had woken up in the middle of the night to find himself in the same position he'd been in when he woke the first morning of this journey—on his back with Elysande's head on his shoulder and her body half on him, her arm and leg thrown over him with abandon. He'd lain there for the longest time trying to decide what to do about it, but in the end he'd just settled back, enjoying the heat from her body and inhaling her scent and wondering what it would be like to wake up every morning like this, with this woman in his arms.

Oddly enough, he'd quite liked the idea and that had kept him awake for hours as he'd pondered why that would be. He didn't really know the woman and at the moment she wasn't much to look at with half her face battered and bruised. Of course, the other half of her face was mostly undamaged and attractive enough, and the one eye that wasn't swollen closed was large and a lovely gray blue. But his attraction definitely wasn't lust based. Most of the time she had that veil covering her face so he couldn't see her at all. Nay, it was definitely something other than her looks he was attracted to.

She did feel good in his arms, soft and warm . . . and she smelled good too. But he admired her for her courage. She was so damned brave, and showed a quiet strength that was truly impressive. Elysande had lost everything. Most women would have been weeping and wailing over what had happened to them, but not Elysande. If she cried, she did it silently behind her veil. And while he knew that her every movement, and even just sitting a horse, must cause her agony, the woman never complained. She'd kept up with the men despite the grueling pace he'd set and ridden until she was tumbling from the mount rather than beg them to slow down or stop for rest. And her composure when she'd told them what had happened . . . The pain and horror of all she'd witnessed had been there in her eyes, but she'd remained strong, never giving in to hysterics.

Then there was the most telling moment of all for him. When it had been suggested that her mother's maid, Betty, might have given up her mother's plans to de Buci under duress, Elysande hadn't been angry at the betrayal. She'd been worried about the maid and angry at herself for not taking better care of her, for not insisting she accompany them.

Aye, she was brave, and strong, and he admired her greatly. If he were in the market for a wife, she would definitely be one worth considering. He wasn't, of course. At least, Rory didn't think he wanted a wife yet. Otherwise, he wouldn't be so annoyed by his family's efforts to find him a bride. Still, Elysande was quite a woman, and any man would consider himself lucky to have a wife he not only enjoyed holding in his arms, but could depend upon through life's trials.

Thinking of the "enjoying holding her in his arms" part reminded him that she wasn't there now and Rory opened his eyes. Not only was she gone, but so were the men. He was alone in the loft.

Rory was suddenly wide awake and on his feet, moving toward the ladder. Once there though, he paused when he spotted Fearghas and Donnghail sitting in an empty stall below, talking quietly.

"So ye've finally decided to wake up, ha'e ye?" Fearghas asked, not even glancing his way. He hadn't been quiet about getting up and wasn't surprised the man had heard him.

"Where is everyone?" Rory asked as he started down the ladder.

"Gone to the shops," Fearghas answered easily.

"What?" Rory whipped his head around with shock.

Donnghail stood and leaned against the stall to grin at him. "We wanted to wake ye, but the lass insisted we let ye sleep. Said ye must need it," he added with a twinkle in his eyes. "And then she announced she needed to find the cloth shop and get plaid for her and her men, and off she went with the rest o' the men trailing her like eager pups."

"Donnghail and I stayed to let ye ken where they were when ye woke," Fearghas added, standing up now as well.

Rory grunted at that and then continued down the ladder to the stable floor. He had some shopping to do himself. He'd missed the market yesterday, but if there was an apothecary in Carlisle he might find some wolfsbane there and still be able to make a liniment for Elysande. "How long ago did they leave?"

"After convincing the alewife to give us bread, cheese and watered-down ale to break our fast," Fearghas said.

Rory's mouth twisted with disgust. "That must have cost us a muckle load of coins."

"Nay," Donnghail said solemnly. "The alewife gave it up fer free."

Rory blinked at this news. "How did Elysande manage that miracle?"

"I'm no' sure exactly. When we went into the alehouse to break our fast, the alewife was no' pleased to see us. Said as we should clear off now that 'twas morn and then stomped off into the kitchen. We all started to turn back to the door, but Elysande told us to sit, removed her headdress and veil, set them on the table and sailed into the kitchen after the woman like a queen pursuing an ornery servant."

"Aye. Just like a queen, she was," Donnghail said with a small smile of admiration that matched Fearghas's. "Shoulders back, head up and following her nose like she was on the trail o' a terrible stench." He shook his head, his smile widening as he described it. "I was expecting a flaming row—screaming, banging pots, the crash o' things breaking. Thought sure we'd have to rush in to rescue the lass. Or maybe the alewife," he added with a wry twist to his lips.

"I think we all thought that," Fearghas admitted with amusement. "We were all tense as cats, ready to leap up and run in at the first sound o' trouble."

Donnghail nodded. "But there was no trouble. No noise at all except the murmur o' voices. It went on fer a long time too, and then just when Conn stood up like he was going to check on them, Lady Elysande and the alewife came hurrying out the door of the kitchen, chatty as old friends, bearing trays with bread, cheese and ale fer all o' us."

"'Tis true," Fearghas assured him when Rory's eyebrows rose. "And the alewife was like a different woman—smiling and pleasant, e'en to us. Saying as how the food and drink was included in what we'd paid to stay, and apologizing that she had nothing better to offer us. She even sent bread, cheese and watered-down ale out fer ye to have when ye wake."

Fearghas bent out of sight behind the stall's half wall and then popped up again to hold out the food and drink in question.

"I wonder what Elysande said to her," Rory muttered as he accepted the offering.

"We do no' ken," Donnghail repeated almost apologetically. "Lady Elysande went back into the kitchen with the alewife after helping her hand out food and drink, and didn't return till just as we finished eating. Then she announced she was off to the shops and headed for the door. There was a mad scramble as it was decided the rest o' the men would go with her while Fearghas and I stayed to wait fer ye to wake, and they were gone."

"One o' them may have got it out o' her on their visit to the shops," Fearghas suggested. "I guess ye'll have to ask when they return."

"Which should be soon," Donnghail pointed out. "'Tis nearly the nooning hour."

Rory stiffened, his head jerking up, eyes wide with shock. "'Tis that late?"

"Aye." Donnghail smirked. "I've never kenned ye to sleep so long. Ye did no' even rouse when Tom and Simon lifted the lady off where she was tangled up with ye again. Well, one part o' ye was awake, but ye still slept."

Rory closed his eyes briefly at the teasing, knowing exactly what part of him had been awake. No doubt he'd been tenting his plaid in response to her body pressed up against his. Especially if she'd been shifting her leg over his groin in her sleep as she had the first morning. He only hoped Elysande hadn't noticed. He wouldn't want her embarrassed or uncomfortable around him.

Sighing, he downed his ale and headed for the stable doors.

"Where are we going?" Fearghas asked at once, hopping over the stall and falling into step beside him.

"I need to ask the alewife if there's an apothecary nearby. I might yet be able to get some wolfsbane to make a liniment for Elysande's bruises," Rory answered around a bite of bread.

"There is," Donnghail announced from his other side, and when Rory glanced to him in question, he explained, "Lady Elysande asked after one while they were passing out the bread and cheese. The alewife told her where to find it."

"Aye. We may run into them there," Fearghas commented.

Rory merely grunted at the suggestion as he led them out into the courtyard. He ate the bread and cheese quickly, and was just swallowing the last of it as he entered the back door of the alehouse. A good thing too, or he might have choked on it when they reached the main room and he saw Tom and Simon both in plaids so short he was surprised he couldn't see their bollocks hanging out the bottom.

"Are you sure this is right?" Simon was tugging at the bottom of the plaid. "Yours aren't this short."

"We told ye," Alick said patiently. "The plaid'll drop lower by the sup. Do ye put it any lower now, ye'll be tripping on it when it does drop and we'll have to start all over."

"Alick," Rory growled the warning, and then crossed his arms over his chest to scowl at his brother, as well as Conn and Inan for this trickery. "Quit messing about and fix the plaids fer them."

"Ah, Rory," Alick complained. "Did ye have to ruin the first bit o' fun we've managed to find since leaving Scotland?"

Rory felt a moment's guilt at the words, because Alick and the men had camped outside Monmouth for two weeks, sleeping on the cold hard ground and hunting their own food while he'd been in the keep.

But that guilt quickly died when he thought of Elysande seeing her men like this, and he scowled again. "Would ye have the lass see them like this and be embarrassed? Speaking o' which, where is she?"

"In the kitchen, making a liniment for her pains," Conn said solemnly.

"A liniment for her pains?" Rory echoed blankly.

"Aye, with the wolfsbane, willow bark and several other weeds she purchased from the apothecary this morn," Tom said almost apologetically.

"She is making *my* liniment?" Rory asked with dismay.

"Ah. Well, most like 'tis a recipe Lady Mairghread taught her," Tom said with a grimace, and then explained, "I fear I may have forgot to mention that our lady was a somewhat renowned healer in England, and that she trained Lady Elysande in all she knew."

Rory gaped at the man, his mind in an uproar. He'd wanted to make Elysande a liniment for her pains. It was his one skill, healing. Or at least the one skill he was known and valued for. Any man could wield a sword. Hell, every man at Buchanan did. But healing was the one thing about him that was special. It made him much in demand. Monmouth was not the first man who had paid him a small fortune to travel to heal them. He was just the latest, and with the money the English lord had given him, he now had enough to build his own keep on the plot of land his parents had left him. That was how sought after he was; he'd earned a fortune any man would envy.

Not that Rory made everyone pay or even asked for payment in return for his skills. He became a healer because he couldn't stand by and watch another person die as he'd been forced to watch happen with his mother. But almost every patient tried to give him something to show their gratitude, whether it was coin, or livestock, or something else. Even the poorest patient he'd healed had gone picking wild herbs and medicinals they hoped would come in handy in his healing capacity. But wealthy lords who lived far away and feared he would need an inducement to travel to them often offered coin. And because it was an inconvenience to travel long distances and be away from home and family, and because they could afford it, he accepted the payment.

But with Elysande it had been different. He'd wanted desperately to use his skills to help her. He'd wanted to be the hero and take away her pain. He'd wanted . . . He'd wanted her to see him as special, he realized. Instead, she was in the kitchen making a potion herself. One her mother had taught her. Using wolfsbane, an extremely poisonous plant that had to be handled with extreme caution to prevent accidental poisoning and death.

Concern rushing through him now, Rory turned on his heel and headed for the kitchen door, growling, "Fix their plaids."

Ignoring Alick's groan and Tom and Simon's irritated demands that the men fix their "bleedin' skirts," Rory started to push through the kitchen door and then froze halfway into the room as his mind processed what his eyes were seeing.

Lady Elysande, completely naked, was lying on her stomach on top of a linen laid over the kitchen table, her head pillowed on her folded arms. It left her naked back and bottom on view as the alewife smoothed liniment gently over the bruises on her back.

"How is that, then, m'lady?" the alewife asked. "Is it helping any?"

"Aye, thank you, Mildrede," Elysande breathed the words with obvious relief. "Really, thank you so much for offering to do this. I was planning to do it myself, but you were right, I could not have done my back alone."

"Nay, you could not have," the alewife said firmly, and then her tone turning apologetic, she admitted, "In truth, I only made the offer to get a look at your back and see if 'twas as bad as yer face. But seeing it . . ." She clucked under her breath and shook her head as she scooped more liniment out of a bowl next to Elysande's hip and continued her work before murmuring sympathetically, "How ye must have been suffering, m'lady. I do not know how ye bore it," she said with amazement, her hands now moving lower over her buttocks.

"You can stop now if you like, Mildrede," Elysande said gently. "I can reach everything else. 'Twas just my back I could not do myself and I certainly appreciate you doing it for me."

"Oh, nonsense, m'lady," the alewife said as her hands made quick work of the chore. "I'm pleased to help you, and it will only take another minute. Besides," she added, a wry twist to her lips as she moved onto the backs of her legs, "my hand is numb already from the cream. Might as well save you numbing your own hand. You'll have enough parts going numb as 'tis," she pointed out with a chuckle.

Rory could hear the amusement in Elysande's voice when she agreed. "Aye, but better that than the pain."

"Aye." The alewife's smile faded then and she shook her head. "'Tis a wonder to me that you're able to walk let alone sit a saddle. You're a brave one, m'lady."

"Nay, not brave," Elysande assured her quietly. "Just terribly frightened that was I too much trouble they might leave us behind somewhere."

"Oh, surely not," Mildrede said with a frown.

"Nay," Elysande agreed. "I realize that now, but I did not at the start. I did not know then that these Scots were such good, kind and honorable men."

"Nay. I suppose not. I surely wouldn't have expected it of a Scot." The woman sighed. "You got lucky with this group, m'lady. I venture there are few Scots who would act so honorably as to trouble themselves to save a young maiden in such a nasty predicament."

"Aye," Elysande breathed the word. "Is life not funny that way?"

"How is that, m'lady?"

"Well, I was just thinking . . . Truly, the murder of my mother, father and all of our soldiers was the most unfortunate event of my life. But encountering our new Scottish friends was, I think, the most fortunate. And both happened one behind the other."

"The best and worst of life all rolled into one incident," Mildrede said sadly. "Life never seems to be able to give you one without the other."

"Aye," Elysande murmured solemnly.

They were both silent for a minute, and then the alewife backed away from the table, wiping her hands on a cloth that hung from her waist. "There. All done."

"Thank you," Elysande said, easing into a sitting position with her back to Rory. "'Twas very kind of you to help me."

"Nonsense," the alewife said firmly. "But ye must give me the recipe. 'Twould come in handy when my bones are hurting if it can get that deep. Sometimes they ache so bad I just want to sit down and weep."

"Of course. But remember that wolfsbane is poisonous, so you must be careful while handling—"

Rory didn't hear anymore. He'd backed out of the room and eased the door closed for fear one of the women would look over and catch him standing there gawking. But he'd heard enough. Elysande obviously knew how dangerous wolfsbane could be, and must have used the correct amount in her liniment, because there was enough cream slathered on her that she'd already be dead if she'd got it wrong. And, God in heaven, that would have been a crime. Elysande had a beautiful body, all soft curves and pale pink skin where she wasn't bruised.

"That's better. I knew 'twas too short before."

Rory turned at Tom's grim words to see that the men had finished fixing his plaid and were now working on Simon's. Tom's plaid now reached almost to his knees, as it should. Although he didn't seem all that much more happy with it, Rory noted. Tom kept bending to look at his knees and frowning. It would take him a while to get used to it, Rory supposed.

"It seems the lady did no' need yer healing skills."

Rory grimaced at that comment from Conn as the man moved up beside him. "Nay. She has those skills herself."

"Aye," Conn murmured, but there was sympathy in his eyes, as if he knew how disappointed he was.

Rory tried to shrug it off. "'Tis fine. It gives me a break from tending to everyone's wounds."

"She's an interesting lass, is Lady Elysande," Conn commented. "Brave as our Lady Saidh, skilled at healing like Laird Sinclair's wife, Lady Jo, and kind as all yer brothers' wives. I think she'll be lovely like all o' them too once she heals," he added. "In fact, at one point this morn while visiting the shops, she briefly forgot her sorrows and smiled and laughed and I saw a hint o' the beauty the bruises are shadowing."

Rory immediately felt envy twitch at him a bit. He would like to see the lass smile and laugh.

"Oh, you're up."

Rory turned toward the door to the kitchen to see the alewife peering out. Offering her a smile, he said, "Aye. Good morn, madam. Thank ye fer the bread, cheese and ale. 'Twas appreciated."

"Well, I could hardly let ye go hungry after Lady Elysande explained ye'd sat up all night to guard her and your men against those nasty villains who attacked her."

Rory blinked at the words and glanced to Conn, who was nodding solemnly, a twinkle in his eyes. Apparently he was aware of the lie Elysande had told to cover for his sleeping in. One that made him look better than he deserved, he thought as the woman began to speak again.

"And 'tis handy you're here, because we need some help with the plaid," the alewife said with a slight frown. "I've done me best, but m'lady suggested I fetch you if you were up, or your brother if you were not."

"I'd be pleased to help," Rory said, and moved toward the door when she gestured for him to follow.

When he entered the kitchen this time, Elysande was fully dressed in not just her own gown, probably her breeks and tunic still under, but now she also had a strip of plaid over it and belted around her waist with a bit of rope. The hem though was a bit lopsided, the pleats uneven and the part above the rope at her waist had just been pulled around her shoulders like the blanket it was.

"I fear while I've seen a Scottish lady or two wearing the plaid over their gowns, I wasn't sure how they managed it," the alewife said fretfully. "I couldn't seem to get the pleats right and—"

"Actually, ye did well fer yer first try," Rory assured her kindly.

"I told you, Mildrede," Elysande said at once, smiling at the woman. "It just needs a tweak or two."

Rory stared at her blankly, losing his train of thought at the sight of her smile. Elysande was at a slight angle to him with the bruised side turned away and when she smiled kindly at the alewife, or Mildrede as she called her, he was stunned to see just how pretty she was under all that damage.

"Is that not right, my lord?" Elysande prompted him, making him realize he was just standing there gaping at her.

"Aye," he said finally, his voice gruff, and moved forward to perform those tweaks.

"I still don't know why ye think you and yer men need to wear Scottish dress," Mildrede commented as she watched him work.

"Because if de Buci forced my mother's maid to tell him what she knew, he and his men will be looking for an English lady and her two soldiers traveling with Scots. Not a Scottish lady and her men."

Rory had just knelt to straighten her pleats, but leapt up in horror at her words. "Ye told her about de Buci?"

Elysande's eyes widened slightly at his reaction, but then she patted his arm soothingly. "Aye, but 'tis fine. Did you not see the portrait of our king in the great room where we ate last night? Mildrede is a loyal subject who would not see our king murdered either. She is more than happy to help us now she knows the importance of our mission."

"Aye," Mildrede said firmly. "Why our king is a saint. Much better than his father, Edward II, or that Mortimer, who basically ruled and bankrupted the treasury while our king was a child. Only Satan's henchmen would wish to see our king and his son dead so they could place his brother on the throne. Nay, we do not need that happening."

Rory had some difficulty with anyone calling Edward III a saint. He knew the man had done some good things, like an overhaul of the government and such, and unlike his father he wasn't trying to take over Scotland. At the moment. But that was only because he had his hands full with France.

Still, the woman seemed sincere in her loyalty to her king. Besides, with the roads unpassable there was no worry that she could send a messenger to de Buci to betray them for coin, and he intended they would leave the moment the roads were passable, so he supposed it mattered little if she knew.

Sighing, he merely nodded and turned his attention back to straightening the plaid, and quickly had the skirts fixed.

"I need a pin to clasp the top," he muttered after pulling the material up and around her throat. "If we pin it here, ye can leave the remainder to lie, or pull it up o'er yer head like a cloak hood."

"I have a pin," Mildrede said, and rushed from the room.

"You are upset that I told Mildrede," Elysande said quietly once they were alone.

Rory grimaced, but acknowledged, "Well, s'truth I'd rather ye had no'. She likes her coin, the alewife. Do ye no' recall the ridiculous sum she demanded to let us sleep in the stable?"

"Aye. I remember. But 'twas only because you are Scottish," she said defensively.

Rory frowned at the words. "What's that to do with—"

"You said yourself that the people here do not like the Scottish. They see you as the source of all their hardships. Why, English children are raised being told to behave or the Scots will drop from the trees and get them."

"Were ye told that as a child?" he asked with dismay.

"Nay, of course not. My mother was Scottish. She said we are a strong, brave people determined to hold on to our independence."

Rory smiled, liking the way she included herself as a Scot despite being half-English.

"The point is," Elysande continued firmly, "Mildrede is naturally afraid of Scots. Still, she was too kind to see us out in the cold on such a horrible night even though we are naturally something of an enemy. So, she let us stay, but made you pay a lot so that she could salve her conscience and keep her neighbors from thinking poorly of her by being able to claim, rightfully so, that she had made us pay dearly just to sleep in the stable."

Rory stared at her silently, thinking she was the sweetest, most naive woman he'd ever met.

"Besides, she gave us food to break our fast with for no charge. She let me use her kitchen to make my liniment and helped me with it, and is including a fine meal tonight too to make up for it now she knows everything."

"The liniment," Rory said now, latching on to that bit and letting the rest go. "Ye were careful with the wolfsbane? 'Tis—"

"Poisonous," she finished for him with amusement. "Aye. I know. I was most careful in the handling of it and in the amount used."

Rory nodded, and then asked, "Is it working?"

"Aye. I am feeling much better. Numb most places, which feels odd, but . . ." She shrugged fatalistically.

"'Tis better than the pain," he finished the unspoken thought for her.

"Aye," she whispered, and then glanced past him to the door when it swung open.

"Here. You can use this one," Mildrede announced bustling into the room and holding out a fine cameo brooch.

"Oh, nay, Mildrede," Elysande protested. "'Tis too fine. I cannot take that."

"I want you to," Mildrede assured her, and then ran one finger over the brooch. "'Twas my mother's. She received it from a lord she found injured in the woods and helped as a young woman. He had no money on him and gave her the brooch as a thank-you. She gave it to me when I married."

"Then I definitely cannot take it from you, Mildrede," Elysande said firmly.

"Well." Mildrede frowned briefly. "You could borrow it, then. Once you've warned the king and he's taken care of that de Buci bastard and his friends, you can come back for a nice visit, tell me of all your adventures and return the pin. I'd like that I would. To see that you were all right and learn how you're faring."

Elysande smiled at the suggestion, obviously touched by it, but then frowned. "But what if de Buci captures and kills me? The pin would be lost forever. Nay, I cannot."

Rory saw the way Mildrede paled at those words, and fully understood her response. He felt a little weak and sick at the suggestion himself. More so by the way Elysande said it so cavalierly, as if it was a good possibility and one she was not only aware of, but had accepted.

"De Buci will not have ye," he said firmly. "Me men and I will keep ye safe. Me whole clan will once we reach Scotland, and I've brothers and a sister with their own clans and armies all across Scotland that will help. Between them and the Sinclairs, we will get ye through this alive, lass. And warn yer king too."

Mildrede seemed to start breathing again then, and even cast a smile his way. "There, you see? He and his men will keep you alive. So you can borrow this."

"Aye, we will," Rory said firmly. Taking the pin, he used it to fasten the plaid around her neck, saying, "But only for a short while. We'll go out at once, purchase a much less expensive brooch for her to use, find our lunch at one o' the inns and then return yours when we get back."

When Mildrede opened her mouth as if to protest, he added gently, "'Tis a lovely piece and might draw notice, which is the last thing we want until this ordeal is over. Something less expensive would serve us better."

"Oh, aye. I suppose it might," the alewife relented.

"And I promise I will see Lady Elysande here myself for a visit once this is all over."

She rallied at that, and gave him another smile. "Well, that's fine, then."

Nodding, Rory took Elysande's arm and urged her toward the door. "Then we'll be off and let ye get about yer business."

"Aye," Mildrede said. "But make sure you're back for the sup. I sent my Albert out to find some meat so I could make you a fine stew tonight. Nothing fancy mind, but a hearty pottage to fill yer bellies and build up yer strength for the trials ahead."

"We shall look forward to it," Elysande assured her as Rory whisked her out of the kitchen. He was moving her so quickly now they were several steps into the ale room before she got her head turned forward again, and then she drew to an abrupt halt as her gaze settled on Tom and Simon in their new finery.

Chapter 7

"M'LADY?" TOM SAID UNCOMFORTABLY WHEN ELYSANDE merely gaped at them.

"Are you displeased, m'lady?" Simon added, glancing from her to Tom and back, and then he asked almost hopefully, "Should we change back into our own—"

"Nay!" she blurted, starting forward again and smiling now. "You look like Scots, and that is what we wanted."

And it was true. They did look like Scots. Just a little shorter and a little less brawny than the real Scots they traveled with, Elysande thought as her gaze slid over them. Tom and Simon had looked much larger in their hauberks, chain mail and padded tunics. Now they didn't seem very threatening at all. At least not next to the Buchanans, each of whom were a couple inches to half a foot taller, and most definitely wider with much larger upper arms. Even Rory, who was supposed to be renowned for his healing rather than his sword work, had huge upper arms. But Tom and Simon were two of her father's youngest men. It was why they'd been away delivering a message when de Buci arrived and hadn't returned home until after the slaughter was over. Still, it was shocking to her to see how much smaller they appeared in the Scottish gear.

"Ye look lovely in yer arisaidh, Lady Elysande," Conn said in his quiet voice. "Like a true Scots lass."

Elysande flushed with pleasure at the compliment until she recalled the damage on one side of her face and that she couldn't possibly look lovely. The man was just being kind. Taking it in the manner it had been intended, she smiled at the man, drew the sides of her plaid skirts out a bit and quickly dipped into a curtsy.

Popping back up, she smiled widely and tried to mimic their Scottish accents. "Thank ye, kind sir. 'Tis pleased I am to be a Scottish lass."

The horror on the Buchanan men's faces told her they were no more impressed than Rory had been with the effort. Rolling her eyes, Elysande spun on her heel and headed for the door. She pulled the top of the plaid over her head, drawing it across the damaged side of her face as she went, adding in that accent they so abhorred, "Come alon', then, laddies. Apparently, we're off to the shops again and then on to find our noonin' meal somewhere."

"Ye'll have them weeping do ye keep that up, lass," Rory said with amusement as he appeared at her side to open the door for her.

"'Tis nae tha' bad," she protested as they left the alehouse.

"Aye. 'Tis," he assured her with a grin as he took her arm.

Elysande merely gave an annoyed sniff and kept walking.

"Why are we heading back to the shops?" Alick asked as he and the other men moved out around them.

"Lady Elysande needs a pin fer her arisaidh," Rory answered.

"But she's wearing a pin," Alick pointed out, leaning his upper body forward to peer around Rory at the pin fastening Elysande's arisaidh at her neck.

"'Tis the alewife's," Rory explained. "Just borrowed until we can find her another to replace it."

"Ah," Alick said with understanding.

"Conn, do ye ken o' a shop where we could find what we need?" Rory asked.

"Aye."

"Lead the way, then," Rory suggested, and the man moved out in front of them to do just that.

They walked the next few minutes in silence until Rory asked her, "What do ye think o' the city, lass?"

Elysande glanced to him and then around at the busy street, managing not to grimace. It had been beautiful this morning when they'd first left the alehouse. The air had been cold and crisp, the street almost empty and the ground covered with fresh, clean snow. But by the time they'd returned to the alehouse they'd had to pass through a very different scene. The city had been teaming by then, the air had reeked of offal and the street had been a mixture of slush, mud and the contents of the chamber pots that had been emptied out the windows of the upper floors of the buildings.

In truth, she found the city disgusting and felt sorry for the people who had to live here. She was also grateful she had grown up in a castle far away from the cesspits of such a city. But instead of saying that, she asked, "Are all cities like this?"

"Some are bigger, some smaller, but aye. Otherwise, they are all much the same," he answered, glancing around.

Elysande wrinkled her nose at this news, but simply said, "Well, 'tis nice to have the shops available, and not have to wait for the various merchants to roll up to the castle."

"Aye. 'Tis an advantage," Rory said, and then grimaced. "But the smell."

"Aye," Elysande gasped, and tugged the hood of her tartan over her nose as they passed through a particularly putrid area. "And it cannot be healthful to be walking about with this kind of filth in the streets. 'Tis no wonder the Black Plague hit the cities so much harder than everywhere else."

"Aye," Rory said grimly, and then pressed her closer to the building they were passing, and rushed her along as they heard a shutter open overhead. They were just quick enough that none of their party got splashed by the contents of the chamber pot that someone tossed out.

"Where do the children play?" Elysande asked with sudden concern.

"What?" Rory asked with surprise.

"At Kynardersley the servants' children played in the bailey when they were not helping their parents. But where do they play here? I have not noticed any children about."

Rory glanced around now as if in search of them. "Mayhap the cold keeps them inside today. But I have no idea where they would play on nice days."

They were both silent as they followed Conn down another street. Elysande glanced around to see the men beside and behind them. Alick was on the other side of Rory, while Inan was beside her and the rest of the men were behind them, but all of them were alert, their eyes scanning the people in the streets, on the lookout for trouble. Elysande supposed Rory had told them to keep an eye out for de Buci's men.

Not wanting to think about that just now, Elysande sought her mind for something to say and asked, "What was it like growing up with so many brothers and a sister?"

Rory looked surprised by that question, and then he smiled crookedly and shrugged. "I've never really thought about it. I guess 'twas noisy, busy and sometimes a pain in the arse."

"Why a pain in the arse?" she asked with curiosity. She'd always wanted brothers and sisters. It had never occurred to her that it would be anything but wonderful.

"Because o' the pranks we pulled on each other," Rory said with a fond smile of remembrance. "After my mother died, I always had me nose in any book on healing I could find, and they were fond o' teasing me o'er it, or snatching them away and making me give chase." He shrugged wryly. "Although, to be fair, they ne'er picked on me as much as each other."

"What kind of pranks did they play on each other?" Elysande asked with interest.

"Oh, well, shaving each other's heads if they were fool enough to drink too deep and lose consciousness. Putting crushed rose hip in their beds to make them itchy."

"Putting pigs in their beds while they slept, or carting their beds out to the bullpen while they were still sleeping in them," Alick put in, joining the conversation. Leaning around Rory he met her gaze and explained, "Those last two were when we were older and the brothers we did it to were in their cups."

"Aye," Rory agreed. "But I think the worst was when we were younger. One o' our brothers carefully cut out the stem o' a pear, hollowed it out and filled it with beetles, then put the stem back and waited to see what would happen."

"What happened?" Elysande asked, her eyes wide.

"Saidh started to eat the pear, got a mouth full o' beetles and started choking." He grimaced at the memory. "That was probably the nastiest. We only figured out how 'twas done because the stem popped out when she dropped it." He shook his head at the memory. "We ne'er found out who the culprit was, and no one confessed."

"Aye," Alick said grimly. "No doubt whoe'er did it was afraid o' the retribution should they be discovered. We were all upset by it. Anyone o' us could have picked that pear, and Saidh near choked to death. She was only ten."

"Dear heavens," Elysande breathed, and then shook her head. "I always wished I had brothers and sisters, but now think I must have been lucky not to. Who knew children could be so cruel?"

"Ye were an only child, then?" Rory asked solemnly, and when she nodded, he admitted, "I'd assumed as much, but did no' ask fer fear o' bringing up a painful memory."

"Mother was with child several times ere I was born," she said quietly. "And several more after. But I was the only one to survive more than a few days past birth. 'Twas a source of terrible sadness for her. She had always wanted several children."

"Which is why you were her treasure," Rory murmured.

"Aye." She smiled faintly. "She used to call me that all the time."

Rory nodded with understanding and opened his mouth as if to comment, but then paused and glanced around with surprise when he bumped into Conn, who had stopped.

"We're here," the warrior said, gesturing to the shop he'd stopped in front of. "The pinner should have what ye need, or be able to make one."

"Oh. Right." Rory smiled wryly, and then ushered Elysande inside. "Ye men wait here, we'll no' be a minute, and then we'll find somewhere for our nooning meal."

Elysande glanced around the shop with interest as Rory explained what they wanted to the shopkeeper. She'd never been in a pinner's shop before and was surprised at the array of goods available. There were pins for headdresses and clothing in wood, iron, bronze, silver and even gold. She'd never seen this kind of selection from the traveling merchants. It was really quite wondrous to her. Despite the selection, however, he didn't have exactly what they were looking for. Plain pins were popular because they were less expensive and he claimed he'd sold his last one just before they'd arrived. But he was planning to make more that afternoon if they'd like to return later in the day.

Once Rory described what was needed, Elysande gave the man a coin to be sure he didn't sell it to someone else before they returned and they thanked him and went out to rejoin the men.

They left there to find an inn willing to feed them and filled up on sausages and lese fryes, a sweet cheese tart that was quite good. With time to kill, they dawdled over their meal, and then visited several more shops they came across. They stopped at a glover's where Conn and Rory purchased new leather gloves to keep warm on the ride, a girdler's where Elysande purchased a belt to replace the rope Mildrede had used to secure the plaid around her waist, a souter's where Simon had a hole in the bottom of one of his boots repaired and then a potter's with beautiful bowls and pots.

Even with all their stops, the brooch wasn't quite ready when they got back to the pinner's shop, and they had to wait a bit while it was polished. By the time Rory had approved it and she'd paid, it was getting late. They returned to the alehouse to find Mildrede had their dinner ready for them.

This meal was much different than the night before. Tonight they were served fresh bread for trenchers and a hearty stew with mutton in it. Albert and Mildrede even joined them, Mildrede blushing and pleased while her husband flushed with pride at the many loud compliments the men all gave her on the meal.

Afterward, they sat over their ales and talked of this and that. Elysande was enjoying the company and talk at first, but as the night wore on and the numbness in her back began to fade, she began to stiffen in her seat. She finally had to excuse herself and leave the table. Tom and Simon immediately started to rise, but she waved them back to their seats. Murmuring that she was just going to fetch something, she slid out of the room and headed for the stables.

What she needed to fetch was her liniment, and only to put more on. She did not need witnesses for that.

Climbing up the ladder to the loft wasn't the trial it would have been the night before after riding all day, but it was bad enough that she would have been grateful for Rory's carrying her up again. Her legs and arms were trembling and there was sweat on her forehead by the time she stumbled into the loft. Elysande re-trieved her liniment. Not wanting to go to the effort of removing and redonning the plaid, she only removed her breeches, yanked up the back of her skirts and quickly applied the salve to her legs and bottom. She then pulled the breeches back on, and removed the pin to let the top of the plaid fall away, before working herself out of the top of the gown and tunic. Leaving them to hang down at her waist, Elysande proceeded to apply some liniment to as much of her back as she could reach. Which wasn't much, she was realizing when she heard the stable door open.

A squeak of alarm slipping from her lips, Elysande scrambled to pull her gown up to cover herself, but paused when Mildrede called out, "M'lady?"

"Aye?" she responded with relief.

"I thought mayhap you could use some help putting on more liniment ere sleeping?"

"Oh." Elysande sighed the word, and then said, "Aye, if you do not mind?"

"Nay. 'Tis why I came out," Mildrede said, her voice growing closer as she mounted the ladder. "It did not occur to me at first, else I would have come with you when you excused yourself. But then I got thinking on how you had gone quiet as the evening progressed and realized the liniment must be wearing off."

"And you were right," Elysande said with a smile as she watched the older woman pull herself up into the loft. "I already did my legs and bottom, but was struggling with my back when I heard the stable door open," she admitted.

"'Twill be quick work, then," Mildrede said lightly as she approached. "Lay yourself down."

Elysande lay down on the fur, letting the top of her tunic and gown drop as she did. "Thank you, Mildrede."

"My pleasure," Mildrede murmured as she collected the ceramic pot from where Elysande had set it. Pausing, she examined it and then picked up the lid that went with it. "This is interesting. Where did you get it, m'lady?"

"'Twas Rory's idea," she said, turning her head to glance at the small pot with a faint smile. "We came across a potter's while waiting for my pin to be ready. He was making cups and Rory asked him to make one without the handle and with a lid. He offered to pay him extra did he have it done by end of day and he did. The lid comes off easily though, so 'twill have to be wrapped with cloth or something while we travel."

"'Tis very clever," Mildrede said as she knelt on the fur next to her.

"Aye," Elysande agreed, and then fell silent for the few minutes it took Mildrede to smooth the liniment over her back.

"There you are," Mildrede said, putting the lid back on the pot as she straightened.

"Thank you." Elysande sat up and quickly redonned her tunic and pulled the top of her gown back into place. Once finished with the task, she stood and met Mildrede's gaze as she added, "For everything."

"You're welcome, m'lady," she said quietly as she handed over the pot. "I heard the men mention the snow was melting as quick as it fell and you'd most like leave tomorrow."

"Aye." Elysande had heard them say that as well.

"I know you need to if you're going to warn the king in time, but I'll still be sorry to see ye go. I enjoyed sitting and chatting with ye today and tonight," Mildrede said gruffly, looking embarrassed at the admission.

"Even though it meant putting up with a bunch of Scots at your table?" Elysande teased.

"Aye." She smiled crookedly and then grudgingly admitted, "They're not a bad group of lads for Scots. They all look after you real fine and watch you with concern. Especially that Rory. He rarely takes his eyes off ye. I know he'll keep ye safe like he promised."

"Aye. I think he will do his best," Elysande agreed, and meant it. Though she wasn't at all certain he could succeed at the task. There was nothing more dangerous than a desperate man, and de Buci was as desperate as a man could be.

"I'll say good sleep, then, and let ye be. I have some baking to do tonight ere I find my bed, but I'll be sure to get up early. Don't you leave without saying farewell to me first."

"I will not," Elysande assured her as they walked to the ladder.

"Good night, then," the woman said before hurrying down to the stable floor.

Elysande watched until she'd bustled out of the stable, and then packed the bowl of liniment away in one of her bags. She considered going back into the alehouse to sit with the men, but then decided that if they were leaving on the morrow, she should probably get as much sleep as she could. While the liniment did a lot to ease her pains, it was still going to be a long day in the saddle.

She was just trying to decide if she should wrap herself in the tartan she wore as the men did, or leave it be and use the cloak as a cover, when she heard the stable door open again. Deciding to use the cloak as a cover so she wouldn't have to struggle with the pleats in the morning, Elysande grabbed it from where she'd left it lying across a bale of hay and pulled it around herself, then quickly dropped to lie on the fur on her good side. She then closed her eyes. It just seemed easier to feign sleep and let the men settle rather than face the embarrassment of sleeping as they were. After a lifetime of sleeping alone in her own bed, she still found it a bit discomfiting to be sleeping surrounded by so many men. It didn't help that she kept waking up plastered to Rory's chest like she had a right to be there. The fact that it happened in her sleep, and that she couldn't be held fully responsible, didn't make it any less embarrassing for her when she woke up there. Elysande was just glad nobody had commented on it when they were awake. Tom and Simon had merely lifted her up off the man both times to save her back, and then gone about their business without comment or even a look to shame her.

"I ken ye canno' be asleep, lass. Mildrede just left."

Recognizing Rory's voice, Elysande opened her eyes, and then pulled her head back slightly with surprise when he dropped to lie down next to her, but facing her rather than with his back to her as usual.

"How is yer back?" he asked, pillowing his head on his arm so he could look at her in the faint light cast by the torches below.

"Much better now. Mildrede helped me put on more liniment," she admitted.

"Aye. I suspected it was paining ye after the sup," he admitted, and when she raised her eyebrows in question, he explained, "Ye'd gone unnatural quiet and pale ere ye excused yerself."

"Oh." She grimaced. "'Tis good for hours after the salve is put on, but then the benefits fade. I should have thought to reapply it ere the sup."

"Hmm," he murmured, and then they fell silent, and stared at each other for a moment. Just when Elysande was starting to feel uncomfortable and considering rolling away from him, he said, "The swelling is gone on yer face and the bruising is more red than black now, with a bit o' green around the edges. 'Tis healing."

"Is it?" she asked with interest. She had no mirror here to check her face, and couldn't see her back. She had managed to get a glimpse of her bottom and the backs of her legs by twisting about, but just enough of a glimpse to see that it seemed a little better. Her muscles were still sore from the beating she'd taken and had protested at the movement.

"Aye. Another few days and the worst o' it should be done," he assured her.

"'Twill be at least another week or more before 'tis gone completely though," she said wryly.

Her words made him smile. "Ye *do* have healing knowledge. Yer men mentioned ye were skilled at it," he told her.

"And you doubted it?" she asked, for his comment had sounded surprised.

"Nay. No' exactly," he said slowly, and then smiled wryly as he admitted, "I am just used to being the healer in most situations."

"Ah. Mother did mention that you had earned quite a reputation for it," she admitted.

Rory arched an eyebrow at that. "And how did she ken that?"

"Her sister," Elysande said at once. "Aunt Bearnas wrote Mother often. In fact, that is how she knew you were at Monmouth. She said your sister—Saidh?" she queried, and when he nodded, she continued. "Saidh mentioned in a letter to my cousin Cam's wife, Jo, that you were heading to Monmouth to tend the baron in exchange for a small fortune. And Jo told my aunt."

"Who told yer mother in a letter," Rory finished for her, and grinned. "I had no idea my goings-on were o' such interest."

Elysande shrugged awkwardly where she lay. "Your sister is proud of you. Aunt Bearnas often sent tidbits of news about your family in her letters."

"Such as?" he queried with interest.

"Oh, let me think," she murmured, searching her mind, and then smiled. "The first mention of your family was when she wrote to tell us that Cam had finally taken a wife. She told us all about his bride, Jo, and then a rather gripping tale of how one of the lasses she'd invited to the castle to meet him tried to kill his new bride, Jo, but that all had ended well and Jo had become good friends with many of the other girls, including one Saidh Buchanan, when they helped save her life."

When he nodded, she continued. "The next mention was when Jo gave birth to their first child. Your sister and some of the other friends she'd made apparently attended the birth."

"Aye," Rory agreed. "'Tis how our Saidh ended up marrying Greer MacDonnell. She was traveling with one o' the other lasses and their brother on leaving Sinclair. The company she rode with stopped at MacDonnell on the return journey. Our cousin Fenella was married to the laird there. But he had died, and Saidh stayed to comfort Fenella and ended up marrying Greer, who had arrived to take o'er as laird. Fenella and her husband had no children, so Greer was the next in line," he explained.

Elysande nodded, and tried to recall the next mention her aunt had made of the Buchanans. There had been a lot of them over the years. "I think the next time your family was mentioned was something to do with one of your brothers and the lass who saved Jo in the first letter. Murine?" she asked, unsure she was getting the name right.

"Aye. Murine. She is married to me brother Dougall now. He and some o' me other brothers rescued her from her brother, who wanted to use her for his own gain. Dougall married her, but her brother caused trouble later and tried to steal her back. Cam brought his army to join ours and a couple others who showed up to help resolve the situation."

Elysande nodded. Aunt Bearnas had mentioned that in her letter. She'd revealed a lot about the Buchanans in her letters, so much that Elysande had almost felt like she knew them despite never having met them. Perhaps that was why she'd felt so comfortable with Rory so quickly, she thought. "The next mention was when another one of the ladies from the group who had befriended Jo had married another of your brothers. I think she said 'twas Edith? And that you had gone there to try to heal her from something?"

Rory's mouth tightened. "Aye. Saidh was most concerned about her. She'd received a letter from Edith mentioning she was feeling unwell, but weeks had passed since then and Saidh hadn't heard from her again, despite having written to her several times to ask how she was faring. Saidh was growing worried to the point that she had determined to travel to her home to check on her fer herself, which was giving Greer fits because Saidh was heavy with child. The only way we could convince her no' to go was if I went to check in her place. Niels, Geordie and Alick accompanied me."

"Was she well?" Elysande asked with curiosity. Her aunt hadn't mentioned any of this in her letter.

"Nay. She was being poisoned and would have died had we no' been there," Rory said grimly.

"Oh," Elysande murmured, eyes wide.

"She recovered once we discovered what was going on, and Niels ended up marrying the lass."

Elysande nodded, and then said, "The next mention was when your oldest brother got married. Aulay?"

"Aye. Aulay married Jetta."

When that was all he said, she decided their courtship must have followed more traditional lines, and went on. "And then she wrote to tell us that Conran had been kidnapped and, of all things, married the lady who had kidnapped him?" Elysande finished the sentence as a question, because she still had trouble believing that one.

"His kidnapping was purely by accident," Rory assured her. "Evina meant to kidnap me, but mistook Conran fer me and took him instead."

"What?" she squawked, shocked at the thought that Rory might have been kidnapped if not for a mistake. "Why the devil would your brother marry a woman who had kidnapped him? Aunt Bearnas never explained that so we thought she must have been mistaken."

"Oh, aye, he was kidnapped," Rory assured her. "Naked, unconscious and tied o'er the back o' a horse. But Evina only did it because she was desperate. Her father was ailing, ye see. She originally came to Buchanan to ask me to tend him, but something went wrong, and rather than ask she ended up kidnapping Conran. The wrong brother. Fortunately, Conran had assisted me more than a few times dealing with the sick and was able to cure the man who then ended up becoming his father-in-law."

Elysande stared at him blankly, her only thought that if not for that mistake Rory might have been married to this Evina and not here in England when she'd needed him most.

"Did she write about our Geordie and his Dwyn too?" Rory prompted when she continued to stare at him with dismay.

Elysande blinked away her own concerns, and nodded slightly. "She said your sister and the other wives copied her idea and gathered a bunch of eligible ladies together at Buchanan who could offer you and your still-single brothers advantageous marriages. The hope was that you would each find one you liked. She said you and Alick had not met anyone you wished to marry, but Geordie settled on Dwyn."

"I would no' say Geordie settled on her. He and Dwyn are quite in love . . . and as per usual with my family, their courtship was no' as smooth as yer aunt's letter apparently made it sound. But aye, they are married and he is laird o' Innes now."

Elysande pondered that, wondering how the courtship had not been smooth, but before she could ask, Rory said, "So, Lady Bearnas wrote to yer mother, and ye say she read her letters to you and your father by the fire at night?"

"Aye. Aunt Bearnas's letters were always entertaining. Especially when she wrote about your family."

"So, ye have the advantage," he said, and when she looked uncertain, he pointed out, "In a way ye knew me before we ever met, whereas I had never even heard of you."

"Mayhap," she agreed with a faint smile. "But the last letter was quite a while ago. We have all been waiting patiently to see which brother would marry next. Have you or Alick married, or are the women in your family still trying to find you wives?"

Oddly enough, Elysande found herself a bit tense as she waited for his answer. It had never occurred to her that Rory might have a wife back in Scotland, awaiting his return, but now that it had, she found the idea distressing.

"Nay. Alick and I are no' married," Rory said.

Elysande released the breath she hadn't realized she'd been holding.

"But aye, the women in our family are doing their best to change that," Rory added, his mouth twisting slightly with disgruntlement. "Every time Alick and I return home we find the place packed full o' prospective brides. 'Tis becoming tiresome."

"Oh," she murmured, but her lips twitched at his put-upon air.

"What?" he asked, his eyes narrowing on her expression.

"Nothing," she assured him quickly, but then couldn't resist saying, "I mean, I do understand. It must be terrible having so many people who love you and put themselves out to try to see you happily settled in an advantageous marriage."

"Well, when ye put it like that, lass," Rory said with a wry smile, and then his smile faded. "It must have been lonely growing up without any brothers or sisters."

Elysande lowered her gaze to the fur. It *had* been lonely. Growing up, she'd often wished she had a sister to play with, or share secrets with, but she was only now realizing what else she'd missed out on by being an only child. Unlike Rory, she didn't have any siblings who cared and wished to see her happily settled in marriage. She would have liked that, but merely said, "'Tis for the best that I did not have any brothers or sisters. De Buci would have just killed or abused them too, and 'tis doubtful we would have escaped if there had been more than just myself."

"Aye," Rory said with a frown, examining her face solemnly.

Elysande withstood it for as long as she could and then shrugged. "I am sure whomever I marry will have them though, and perhaps can share them with me. Well, if I marry," she added with uncertainty.

"Why would ye no' marry?" Rory asked at once, and then added, "Why are ye no' married already, lass? Ye're old enough to be wed. And surely yer father arranged a betrothal contract fer ye when ye were a child?"

"Aye, he did," she assured him. "But the boy I was to marry died when I was eleven."

"And yer father did no' arrange another marriage contract?" Rory asked with surprise.

"He was going to, but said most of the good prospects were

already contracted to others." She grimaced. "And then too, what he wanted for a husband for me had changed by then."

"In what way?" Rory asked.

"Well, when he made the first contract, I was just a bairn. He chose the eldest son of a wealthy lord who had his own castle to leave him. Father had assumed he would have a son someday to take over Kynardersley," she pointed out. "But by the time my betrothed died when I was eleven, he was resigned to the fact that I would be his only heir. He no longer wanted a titled lord with his own castle. He said he needed a special man, someone without his own estates to distract him, but with the skills to keep Kynardersley safe and prosperous, and who would also treat me well." Elysande smiled wryly. "Apparently that was not an easy man to find. He was still looking."

"I see," Rory murmured thoughtfully.

Elysande shrugged. "I suppose the king will have to arrange my marriage now. Or assign another lord to the task." She grimaced and muttered, "Which is unfortunate."

"Why is that?" Rory asked.

"Because I doubt the king or anyone he saddles with the duty will be as concerned as my father was that any prospective husband would treat me well," she pointed out quietly.

Rory's eyes widened slightly with realization at her words, and then his mouth turned down. "Elysande—" he began, and then broke off as they heard the stable door open. In the next moment, he'd leapt to his feet and moved to look down into the stables. It was only when his shoulders relaxed and the hand holding his sword dropped to his side that she realized he'd grabbed it from the floor where it had lain while they'd been talking.

"'Tis fine. 'Tis the men," Rory assured her, and moved to the ladder to greet them as they began to climb up.

Elysande didn't comment, merely closed her eyes and tried to relax, hoping sleep would come. Her last thought as the men began to settle around her was to wonder what Rory had been going to say before the men had arrived.

Rory was the last to lie down after the men returned. This time he settled with his back to Elysande as he usually did. The men's presence wouldn't allow for a continuation of their conversation. Probably a good thing, Rory thought. Because he'd been about to say something utterly ridiculous. He'd been about to suggest that she marry him. The idea had struck him out of the blue. A response from his gut to the idea of her being married off to someone who wouldn't treat her well. Elysande was smart, sweet, caring and brave. She deserved a man who would care for her and treat her well. But he doubted the king would concern himself much with that consideration, despite her present efforts to save his life.

Still, offering to marry her was a ridiculous sacrifice to make for a lass he barely knew, Rory acknowledged. Good Lord, he didn't even know if she would be married off to someone cruel or careless. The English king might choose a good, kind and honorable man for her to marry, Rory told himself. Which, oddly enough, didn't comfort him much as he drifted off to sleep.

Chapter 8

"M'lady. Psst. M'lady."

Elysande opened her eyes sleepily and blinked around, trying to understand where the sound was coming from.

"From below, lass," Conn's deep voice said from somewhere over her head. He sounded very alert, and since she knew none of the men stood guard at night here, she suspected he'd woken at the sound of the stable doors opening and shifted into immediate wakefulness.

"Thank you," Elysande mumbled to the man, and then, still half-asleep, she planted her hands and started to push herself up only to cry out and drop back down again as pain shot through her back. Her cry was joined by Rory's as she apparently did him some injury and it was only then she realized she was lying on the man again as she had been every morning since the Buchanans had agreed to escort her to Sinclair.

"M'lady?"

"She's comin'," someone whispered down to the woman just before Elysande found herself grasped under the arms and lifted off Rory . . . by Conn, she realized when a torch suddenly burst to life in the lower part of the stable. The big warrior smiled at her bemused expression and then twisted his upper body to set her down away from the other men now stirring and starting to sit up.

"Thank you," Elysande managed through gritted teeth as she rode the wave of pain still pulsing through her. She started to turn then toward the ladder, only to find Rory in her way. He was wincing and standing funny, but the wince was replaced with a frown as he took in her expression.

"Sit," he said firmly, urging her to one of the bales at the side of the loft. Pushing her onto it, Rory then walked to the ladder.

"Can ye come up?" he asked in a low rumble. "Her back is painin' her this morn."

"Oh, aye, of course. The liniment will have worn off," their landlady said at once in a hushed voice, and Elysande heard the ladder shake a bit as she started up.

By the time Mildrede reached the loft, every man was awake and on his feet at the opposite end of the loft from Elysande, as if to offer them the chance to talk in private. And despite her waking them, the men all greeted the alewife with quiet good morns and curious expressions that only became worried when they noted her pallor and distress.

"What is it, Mildrede?" Elysande asked with concern, catching the older woman's elbow and drawing her to sit on the bale next to her when she rushed to her side. The woman was still wearing her nightclothes under the blanket she'd pulled around her shoulders, her hair was standing up every which way and she was clutching a bag to her chest. She'd obviously been roused from her own sleep by something, and it had been distressing enough that she hadn't even dressed before hurrying out to them.

"English soldiers," Mildrede gasped anxiously, a little breathless from her rush to reach them.

"Where?" Rory asked sharply, giving up any pretense of allowing them privacy and moving to stand in front of them. The rest of the men were right behind him, faces grim.

"In the taproom," Mildrede moaned, and then shook her head. "Elizabeth came ahead to warn us, but we were up so late, and didn't hear her pounding at the door. She had the devil of a time waking us, and finally just barged in and ran up to our room. Scared the life right out of me to wake to her shaking me arm."

"Oh, dear," Elysande murmured sympathetically.

Rory was more concerned with the soldiers. "What are the soldiers doing in the taproom?"

"Drinking ale by now, I should think. Albert was fetching it for them when I slipped out to warn you."

All the men blinked at this news, and then Rory said slowly, "So a bunch of English soldiers are drinking ale in yer taproom?"

"Aye."

When he looked a bit bewildered as to what to make of that, Mildrede shifted impatiently. "They're looking for you lot. Well, for Lady Elysande, really. But—"

"How do ye ken that?" Rory interrupted with alarm.

"Because the first thing they did when my Albert answered to their banging was ask if he'd seen an English lady traveling with two English soldiers, and possibly some Scottish warriors as well," Mildrede explained with exasperation. "It must be you lot."

"What did Albert say?" Rory asked at once.

"He said nay," Mildrede assured him with a frown for even asking. "Said 'twas a shame though because we could use the coin and would have overcharged ye horribly if ye'd come to us."

Rory didn't comment on the fact that they'd done just that. After all, Mildrede and Albert had more than made up for it by feeding them and allowing them to stay a second night free of charge. "Right. So he said nay . . . and then invited them in fer ale?" His voice rose a bit at the end with his upset.

"I told him to," Mildrede informed him with some dignity. "I figured it was better we know where they are if we're to get you all out without encountering them. So I said to him, 'Albert, you say nay if they ask do we have Lady Elysande or any Scots here, and then say as how they must be fair cold and thirsty if they just rode in, and offer them ale on the house they can drink by the fire to warm up, and then keep 'em here as long as ye can so I can get Lady Elysande and those men away.' Then I slipped into the kitchen, grabbed some things and hurried out here to wake and warn ye."

"Oh, Mildrede, that was brilliant," Elysande praised when Rory just gaped at her.

Shoulders slumping, Mildrede managed a worried smile. "I

thought so, but now I'm worrying that if they stay too long, they'll want to put their horses in the stables rather than leave them out front as they are now. The man standing out there with them will surely want some ale and to warm up too."

That suggestion had a galvanizing effect. The men were suddenly moving for the ladder and hurrying down it one behind the other, even as Rory caught Elysande's elbow and urged her to her feet. "Time to go, lass."

"Aye, I—" Her words ended on a gasp of surprise as they reached the ladder and, rather than urging her to climb down, Rory suddenly picked her up and dangled her over the side by her upper arms. Before she could squawk in alarm, she felt hands at her hips, clasping her and taking her weight when Rory released her.

"Thank you," Elysande whispered as Conn set her down on the stable floor, and then turned at a startled sound from Mildrede to see Rory handing her down the same way and Inan there to take the alewife.

"Oh, my," Mildrede breathed, looking a little stunned as Inan set her down next to Elysande.

"English soldiers," Alick growled as he worked to saddle the horse in the stall next to where Elysande and Mildrede were standing. "They must have arrived at Carlisle ere we did and been staying at the inn the whole time. Somehow they must have got word that an English lady was spotted walking about with two English soldiers and a bunch of Scots yesterday, and decided to start the search early this morn and catch us abed."

"Nay," Mildrede said, appearing surprised at the suggestion. "They only arrived this morning with the dawn. Did I not mention that?"

"Nay," Elysande assured her. "You left that bit out."

"Oh. Well, Elizabeth said she'd only been awake for minutes and was emptying her chamber pot out the window when she saw the portcullis was being opened to let someone in. The minute she saw it was English soldiers and that they'd stopped to ask questions of the men at the gate, she worried this would be trouble for ye. So, she sent her young Jimmy down to see what he could hear. He came back saying they was asking after an English lady and two English soldiers what might be traveling with Scots. She knew then it must be de Buci's men here about you and came to warn ye. She said she would have rushed straight to the stables, but she was afraid the Scots might be quick with their swords and kill her ere she could explain the problem."

Elysande bit her lip as she noticed the way Rory's men all stiffened at that suggestion.

Rory, however, didn't seem to care about that. He was looking amazed as he asked, "How did this Elizabeth woman ken it must be about Elysande? Who is she?"

"The draper's wife," Elysande explained, and he whirled on her with shock.

"Ye told the draper's wife about de Buci when ye stopped there fer plaids?" he asked with disbelief.

"She was very kind," Elysande said apologetically. "And very upset about my face. She assumed your men had done it, and I could not have her thinking that when you are all risking yourselves to aid me."

"So ye told her everything?" he asked, his voice raising.

"Elizabeth is a faithful subject to our king," Elysande said firmly, aware that Mildrede was nodding in agreement beside her. "She has a portrait of him in her shop for all to see. And," she added firmly when he opened his mouth as if to respond, "she has proven she is loyal by coming to warn us, has she not?"

Rory blinked at that, and then scowled, tossed the rolled-up fur to Simon and stomped into his horse's stall to quickly saddle his horse. As he then hooked her bags to his pommel, he asked, "Did she mention if they kept the portcullis up, or closed it again, Mildrede?"

"She said they left it up," Mildrede said at once. "She said the snow has melted enough that the roads are clear and they expect a lot of people coming and going so didn't bother closing it."

"Good," Rory said grimly as he finished saddling his mount.

"Why is that good?" Elysande asked as she watched him.

"Because with the soldier out in front of the alehouse, we are going to have to charge out of here at speed and straight out the gates." He grimaced and then added, "And pray to God they've been riding all night, have exhausted their horses and our well-rested horses can outrun them and leave them behind quickly."

"But Robbie should be along any minute to lead you out the back gate so you needn't risk the front," Mildrede said with a frown.

Rory froze at those words and turned narrowed eyes on Mildrede. "Who's Robbie?"

Mildrede took a nervous step back from the fury in his gaze, but said, "The blacksmith."

Rory nodded slowly, repeatedly, and then whirled on Elysande and snapped, "Is there anyone in this godforsaken city that ye've no' told about de Buci?"

When Elysande's jaw dropped at his show of temper, it was Conn who stepped forward and pointed out quietly, "She could not have told the blacksmith. We have not gone to the blacksmith's since reaching Carlisle, and she has not been out of my sight since we arrived."

When Rory merely closed his eyes and dropped his head briefly, muttering, "Right," Elysande snapped her mouth closed and glared at him.

It was Mildrede who stepped forward and said, "I'm the one who told the blacksmith. In fact, I told several shop owners that I considered trustworthy about *Lady Elysande's* situation." She emphasized Lady Elysande as if to say he had no right to be angry about it. Chin lifting, she added, "And I did so because I was worried about just such a situation as this. I thought it might be best to have some people watching out for any English soldiers who might arrive looking for her, and it appears I was right to be worried. Thank goodness Elizabeth spotted them and came to warn me. Had the soldiers arrived first and not been able to rouse us from our beds, they would not have simply come inside and shaken me awake as Elizabeth did. I'm sure they would have simply walked around back to check the stables for horses ere moving on to the next alehouse or inn. And had they done that, they'd have caught you all sleeping."

Rory stood silent for a moment, and then nodded and raised his head. "Ye're right, o' course. I beg yer pardon fer snapping." His gaze slid to Elysande as if to include her in the apology. When she continued to glare at him unappeased, he shifted uncomfortably, and then turned back to Mildrede with a sigh. "Ye mentioned this Robbie coming to fetch us to take us out the back gate?" he asked. "Is it behind the stables?"

When Mildrede appeared confused by the question, Rory suggested, "If so, mayhap we should wait fer him there. Just in case the soldiers decide to bring their horses back here and stable them while they search on foot," he added.

"Nay." Mildrede shook her head and said, "I mean, aye, there is a gate to the alley behind the stables. But Robbie is to lead ye to the gate at the back o' the city using the back streets. 'Tis just before the castle."

Elysande noted the way Rory glanced to Conn, who frowned briefly before admitting, "I've ne'er heard o' such a gate."

"Well, 'tis hardly information we bandy about," Mildrede said dryly. "And we'd certainly not be telling Scots, when 'tis there for the women and children to slip out through should the Scots invade. In fact, Robbie and the others were reluctant to let you know about it now, but I convinced them 'twas for the greater good if it saved the king. And I assured him that Lady Elysande would not let you reveal it to anyone else," she added, and then clutching Elysande's hand she asked anxiously, "You'll make sure they don't tell anyone, won't you?"

Before Elysande could respond, Rory said, "We vow on our lives that none o' us here today will reveal the presence of a back gate to Carlisle."

When Mildrede nodded, but still looked anxious, Elysande suggested, "If 'twould make you more comfortable, we could always have Rory and his men go out the front while Robbie leads Tom, Simon and I out the back. De Buci's men should not be interested in a group of Scots on their own. 'Tis me they are looking for," she pointed out. "And once outside the wall we could wait for them in the woods and go from there."

"Oh." Mildrede brightened at the suggestion. "That would be perfect."

"Nay," Rory said at once, scowling at Elysande for the suggestion. "How can I guard ye if I'm no' with ye?"

Elysande scowled right back, but did say, "Fine, then the others can leave Carlisle through the front gate, and you can come with us. Blindfolded."

Rory's mouth opened, closed, and then he growled, "I canno' guard ye blind either."

Elysande nodded easily, but asked, "Are there hidden gates or secret passages into Buchanan castle?"

Rory stiffened, his chin jerking up and mouth compressing.

"See," she said when his mouth stayed tightly closed. "You will not even admit to having one. How can you expect these people to happily show you theirs?"

"She's got a point," Alick said with amusement.

"Fine," Rory growled. "Then Conn, Inan and I will go through the back gate blindfolded and with Tom, Simon and Elysande leading us. Alick, you take Fearghas and Donnghail out the front gate. Wait for us just inside the woods to the north."

Relieved he understood, or at least was willing to cooperate, Elysande moved past him to his horse and removed one of the bags.

"What are ye looking for?" Rory grumbled, moving to join her.

"The leftover plaid," she said, opening the sack and digging around inside. "We can use it to make blindfolds."

"Right," Rory muttered, sounding pretty grumpy. Elysande decided to ignore him. She was a bit put out with him and the way he'd snapped at her anyway.

It didn't take long to find the plaid and quickly slice off three strips to use as blindfolds. Mildrede then peeked out the door to be sure the courtyard was empty, before waving them out and hurrying around behind the stables to a stone wall with a gate in the center of it. While Elysande and the others followed, walking their horses, she opened the gate and peered out, then waved them through.

"M'lady." Mildrede rushed to her side as Elysande prepared to mount in the alley.

"Aye?" she asked, pausing.

"Here." Mildrede thrust out the bag she'd been clutching. "Fruit pasties to break yer fast. 'Tis why I was so hard to wake—I was up late baking them. I wanted to give you all a fine treat to break your fast before you left," she admitted, and then added, "And there's cheese and bread in there too to eat later, and a bladder of ale as well. Hopefully there's enough for everyone."

"Oh, Mildrede," Elysande murmured, accepting the bag and then hugging her impulsively. "Thank you. That was kind and I know the men will appreciate it. I certainly do."

Mildrede was flushed and smiling shyly when Elysande released her, but her smile fled under wariness when Rory joined them.

Elysande was a little wary herself until Rory took the woman's hand, and said solemnly, "Mildrede, I apologize fer snapping earlier. Ye've been a fine host and a good friend to us helping us this way. In fact, ye've saved us all this day with yer cleverness in enlisting yer friends to help us. Thank ye." He then bent and kissed her hand, bringing a bright-red blush to the woman's face and a flustered look to her eyes.

"Oh, well, that's . . . you just keep her safe," she finished finally as he released her hand. "Lady Elysande is a fine woman, with a most important mission."

"Aye, she is," he agreed solemnly. "And I vow I will keep her safe, and I'll bring her back to visit when 'tis all over as I promised," Rory assured her.

"Oh, good." Mildrede beamed at him, and then glanced past Rory and sighed with relief. "There is Robbie now. He's been out telling the others what to do."

"The others?" Rory asked with a wince.

"Aye. The other shop owners who know about Lady Elysande," she explained. "He and Elizabeth have been visiting them all to warn them de Buci's soldiers are here so they know that, when asked, to tell them they did see an Englishwoman and two soldiers here or there, but always on the streets closest to the front gate. I thought it best to keep de Buci's men busy running in circles far away from where Robbie is taking ye."

A startled laugh slipped from Rory, and then he grasped Mildrede by the shoulders, lifted her off her feet and gave her a loud smacking kiss on the cheek. "Ye're a wonder, Mildrede," he said with appreciation as he set her down.

Her hand pressed to the cheek he'd just kissed, Mildrede breathed, "Oh, my," and then hurried off to consult with Robbie the blacksmith.

Rory watched her briefly and then moved over to talk to Conn. It seemed like he'd barely left when Mildrede led Robbie over to her.

"Thank you for your assistance," she said before either of them could speak.

"My pleasure," the blacksmith rumbled, nodding his head politely. He frowned as he took in the damaged side of her face. "Ye should maybe cover that, m'lady. We don't want anyone taking note of ye and mentioning to de Buci's soldiers that they saw a woman what looked like she was beaten passing through."

"Oh, aye." Elysande felt herself flush with embarrassment and quickly pulled the top of her plaid over her head and around to cover the bruised side of her face. "Better?"

"Much," he said, and then glanced around at the men waiting. "Mildrede said three of the Scots are going out the front gate and the other three will come with us blindfolded?"

"Aye." Elysande nodded. "The Buchanans did not wish to leave us completely unguarded so agreed to blindfolds. My men and I will lead them." Offering him the strips of plaid, she said, "We will use these to cover their eyes."

Robbie took one and held it over his eyes, then grunted with satisfaction and relaxed a little. "That's fine, then," he said as he handed back the strip of plaid. "Which are your men?"

"Tom and Simon there are English soldiers from my father's castle," she said, pointing them out.

Robbie nodded as he glanced at them and then shifted his gaze over the Scots, before saying, "The others can ride with us for the first couple of lanes, but when we turn toward the castle, they should head the opposite way toward the gates. The three men coming with us don't have to put on blindfolds until we reach the church."

"All right," Elysande murmured.

Grunting, the blacksmith started back the way he'd come.

Elysande stared after him blankly, and then glanced to Mildrede uncertainly, unsure if she was to follow or not.

"Robbie's a man of few words," Mildrede said with a reassuring smile. "But he'll get ye safely out of Carlisle, m'lady."

"I am sure he will," she said, managing what she hoped was a convincing smile in return.

"Ye'd best go," Mildrede added gently when she still stood there. "I'll be praying for ye."

"Thank you." Swallowing a sudden thickness in her throat, Elysande gave her another quick hug, and then grabbed her mare's reins and started reluctantly away. She was actually unhappy to leave Mildrede behind. The alewife had reminded her of her mother in some ways, and Elysande had enjoyed working and talking with her. She'd even found herself smiling on occasion since arriving in Carlisle and now felt as if she was leaving that behind.

"Are ye all right, lass?" Rory asked as he fell into step beside her, leading his own mount.

"Aye," she said sadly, and then cleared her throat and told him,

"Robbie said Alick and the others should go with us until we turn toward the castle."

"I heard. So did Alick and the others," Rory assured her, and then they both fell silent and kept their attention on Robbie, watching for any signal that there might be trouble ahead, or that they should hurry. But after a moment, he said, "I truly am sorry fer snapping at ye, lass. I was just a bit overset by waking to the news that the English were here. I ken ye've been worried this verra thing might happen, but I was sure we'd avoided them by using this route. And the knowledge that I put ye at risk with me arrogance upset me."

"You have not put me at risk, my lord," Elysande said quietly. "If anything, I have put you at risk by requesting your escort." She briefly fell silent, and then because she didn't want him to ever feel guilty should they fail at their escape, she added, "And I want you to know that, should the worst happen, and de Buci does catch or kill me, I do not hold you responsible. This game was weighted in his favor from the start and just grows more so by the day."

"Elysande, I'll no' have ye talking like that. Ye sound like ye're already resigned to being captured, but I'll no' fail ye. I'll— Wait," he interrupted himself suddenly, and caught her arm to stop her. "What mean ye the game grows more weighted in his favor by the day?"

Elysande shrugged. "I just mean that by now de Buci has no doubt sent messages to the other lords involved in his murderous plot, and they too will be desperate to kill me. There are probably now several armies presently scouring England and Scotland in search of me."

"Good Christ," he breathed with realization.

"Robbie's wanting your attention, m'lady," Tom said suddenly from behind her, distracting them both.

Elysande glanced toward the blacksmith, and then started walking again, moving more quickly as Robbie waved them forward.

"This way. Try to keep up," the man added, leading them down another street.

They followed, making sure to stay close behind him this time until he stopped at the corner and gestured for them to wait as he walked forward and surveyed the next area. They all tensed a little when a man rushed up and held a brief conversation with Robbie, glancing repeatedly toward them as he did.

"Is that no' the potter who made the handleless cup fer us?" Rory asked with a slight frown.

"Aye," Elysande said as she returned the nod the potter sent their way before he hurried off. "He must be one of the shop owners Mildrede talked to who are helping to keep the English busy. Mayhap he had news to aid Robbie."

"Hmm," Rory murmured, and then took her elbow to urge her to move again when Robbie waved them forward once more, but took them down a different road.

"Damn, I can hardly believe it," Rory said with wonder after the fourth such incident where someone rushed up to talk to Robbie and their path was changed.

"What?" Elysande asked with a faint smile. "That so many English would work together to help us?"

"They're helping you, lass. And yer men, perhaps. They're only suffering us as a necessary evil," Rory assured her, and then said, "But what is hard to believe is that Mildrede could put together a small army o' shopkeepers and others to work as a unit to get us out o' here. She should have been a man."

"Aye, she'd have made a fine warrior," Conn agreed from behind them.

Elysande smiled at the words, and told herself to remember them so that she could tell Mildrede if she survived this. She was sure the woman would get a hearty laugh from it.

Shortly after that, Robbie announced it was time for the group to split up. Rory nodded and asked Elysande to hold his mount's reins as he had a brief word with his brother. She waited patiently as the four men grouped together briefly, and then they broke apart and Rory watched Alick, Fearghas and Donnghail ride off before returning to Elysande's side and taking back the reins to his horse.

"They'll be fine," he assured her, but she knew he was the one who was worried.

"They *will* be fine," she responded. "They are three men alone. De Buci's men will not bother them."

"Aye," Rory muttered, and ushered her after Robbie as the blacksmith led them in the direction of the castle.

They were all silent after that, but Elysande didn't miss how often Rory glanced over his shoulder, and suspected the other men were doing the same thing. They were all tense, and obviously worried about someone coming up behind them. Elysande was a little less so, but only because she was looking forward and noted many of the people they passed were standing about doing nothing but watching the road behind them, and nodding reassuringly at her as if to say all was well. She had no doubt they were more of Mildrede's army, keeping an eye out to see they made it safely away.

"The church." It was all Robbie said as they walked along the wall next to a building that looked more like a cathedral to her. But she understood his meaning and pulled out the three strips of plaid she'd tucked up the sleeve of her gown and handed them to Rory, Conn and Inan.

Chapter 9

"HOW ARE WE GOING TO DO THIS?" CONN ASKED, ACCEPTING his blindfold, and then warned, "I'm no' holding Tom's or Simon's hand."

Elysande bit her lip at the consternation on the man's face as he said that, and then suggested, "I can lead you."

Conn relaxed at that and nodded, but now Rory was scowling. "Nay. I was going to have ye lead me."

"I have two hands, I can lead you both," she said with exasperation. "But Tom will have to take the reins of my horse. You will both have to hold on to the reins of your own mounts though."

"And I'm left to hold Simon's hand," Inan said with disgust.

"Well, 'twill be no picnic for me either," Simon snapped with irritation.

"I can lead him."

Elysande glanced around with surprise as the draper's wife rushed up, a little out of breath as she made that offer.

"Elizabeth," she said, smiling at the woman and reaching out to clasp her hand and squeeze it gently. "Thank you so much for warning Mildrede about the English soldiers. You have saved us all."

"My pleasure, m'lady. We all must do our part to help ye save the king," she assured her, squeezing her hand back. "I was just coming to let you know the other men made it out through the front gates just fine. The English paid them no attention at all."

"Oh, good. Thank you for letting us know," Elysande said.

"I thought 'twould ease your minds," she said, grinning, and then glanced to Inan and added, "But now I'm here, I'd be pleased to walk this young fellow to the gate if 'twill help."

"Aye. I believe it just might. Thank you, again," Elysande said with amusement as Inan nodded fervently and moved to the older woman's side.

"I thank ye too," Inan assured her. "'Tis always a pleasure to walk with an attractive woman, and definitely preferable to holding hands with that ugly sod."

"Ugly sod?" her soldier protested, and then rolled his eyes. "I'll remember you said that the next time you need my help sneaking out of an English city."

Inan smirked at the words. "Since we'll be in Scotland shortly, that will no' be an issue."

A sharp whistle from Robbie silenced the two men and drew their attention to the blacksmith.

"Blindfolds," he growled, glancing anxiously around. "They cannot keep the soldiers busy forever."

"Of course," Elysande murmured, and handed her mare's reins to Tom before turning expectantly to Rory, Conn and Inan.

"Will wearing blindfolds no' draw attention to us?" Inan grumbled even as he tied his on.

"'Tis fine," Elizabeth assured him. "Most people know what's going on, and the rest think Scots are strange anyway. 'Twill be fine."

Elysande had to bite back a laugh at Rory's, Conn's and Inan's disgruntled expressions at the suggestion they were thought strange. Although she suspected Rory's countenance had more to do with the increasing number of people who knew about them and what was happening than with the insult. It did seem to trouble him a great deal.

Shrugging that worry away, she took the reins to both Conn's and Rory's mounts to free their hands even as Elizabeth took Inan's reins. They both waited patiently as the men quickly donned their blindfolds, and then returned their reins. Elysande then grasped Conn and Rory each by an arm, and urged them to follow Elizabeth and Inan and his horse when they moved toward Robbie. She did check to be sure Tom and Simon were following with their horses and her mare first, but after that, Elysande kept her gaze forward, and concentrated on steering Conn and Rory in the right direction, which was surprisingly difficult to do. Neither man seemed capable of walking in a straight line, but kept veering away or, alternately, toward her, so that she was always having to tug them back, or steer them away to keep them going.

"I do no' like this," Conn muttered suddenly.

"Aye," Rory agreed grimly. "I feel helpless as a babe without me sight. How much farther is it?"

"Not far." Elizabeth answered the question with a quick glance over her shoulder at them, and Elysande was grateful for the response. Partly because she hadn't known the answer to the question, but also because she wasn't caring for this herself. The muscles in her back and arms, already painful before this, were now screaming from the strain that directing the men was putting on her muscles. She would be glad to reach the gate.

"How are we going to ride blindfolded?" Conn asked suddenly.

"You will all just have to sit on your horses and let Tom, Simon and I take the reins of a horse apiece to lead you out," Elysande said, her jaw a little tight as she fought the pain.

"Are ye all right, lass?" Rory asked. "Yer back's paining ye, is it no'?"

Elysande glanced at him with surprise that he'd picked up on that, but then sighed and admitted, "You are both showing a distressing tendency to weave about like a pair of drunken fools without your sight, and 'tis a bit of a strain on my back and arms."

"Oh." Rory hesitated, and then asked, "Would it help if we held yer hand instead of ye trying to steer us by our arms? That way, ye could just squeeze our fingers and move our hands in the direction ye wanted us to go. It may be less o' a strain fer ye."

"That's what I thought the plan was to begin with," Conn commented, obviously having heard Rory's suggestion.

"Aye, it was, and it may help," Elysande agreed, and released first Rory's arm to clasp his hand instead, and then did the same with Conn. Both men had huge hands, she noted as her fingers stretched almost painfully wide to slide between theirs. But it actually was a little easier that way, it certainly hurt her back and arms less, she acknowledged as Robbie turned left and led them along the front of the church.

"Better?" Rory asked after several minutes.

"Aye. Thank you," she murmured, and then smiled with amusement and said, "Although I fancy it looks odd to anyone watching to see a woman walking down the street holding hands with two men."

"And the blindfolds do no' look odd?" he asked dryly, and then still in that dry tone added, "But then most people ken why we're blindfolded."

Elysande grimaced at the comment. She'd known he'd be irritated by Elizabeth's words about most people knowing what was happening. But she was just glad there were so many people willing to help. She only hoped everyone who knew was on their side and there wasn't a Judas among them who might approach the English soldiers to exchange the knowledge for coin. Elysande wasn't a fool and knew that was a possibility with so many holding the knowledge. But she also knew there was nothing she could do about it if it happened, so tried not to think about it. Her life was in God's hands at the moment.

"Is anyone following us?" Rory asked suddenly.

"Nay, I am sure— Oh," Elysande said with surprise when she looked over her shoulder. Actually, there were several people following them, and several more joining every moment. Mildrede had mentioned to her that Carlisle had a population of two thousand people. It looked to her like half of them were now following them to the gate. They seemed to be coming from everywhere and filling the road behind them, trailing them past the church. The street was full of children and adults both . . . and every single one smiled and nodded reassuringly when they saw her looking.

"What is it?" Rory asked tensely, his hand jerking in hers as if he would pull off his blindfold.

"Nothing." Elysande tightened her hold on his hand and flashed the crowd a smile before facing forward again. She was quite sure he wouldn't be happy knowing they had what looked to be almost half the city following them this last stretch to the gate. She wasn't sure she was either actually. Who was distracting the soldiers searching for her if half the city was following them to the gate? The other half of the city, she hoped.

Robbie turned right next, leading them down a slightly angled street with perhaps ten dwellings on the left and eleven on the right. Much to her relief she could see the city wall now at the other end, running at a slight angle to the street they were on. She thought the gate couldn't be far now.

"I ken ye only told Mildrede and Elizabeth about de Buci here and that they then spread the news far and wide, but once we're in Scotland, I suggest ye no' be so free with the tale o' de Buci, lass."

"Oh, nay, I will not be," she assured him firmly, glancing over her shoulder to see the crowd still following. When they all smiled and nodded, some waving, she smiled again before facing forward once more and adding, "I will not be telling anyone in Scotland. Not a single person."

"Good," he said, sounding relieved. "Then I'll say no more about it."

Elysande murmured agreeably to that, but her wide eyes were taking note of the people now coming out of the dwellings they were passing to watch them parade by.

"Why are ye no' going to tell anyone in Scotland?" Conn asked suddenly, curiosity filling his voice.

"Well, they are Scots, and I suspect most Scots would be pleased to see the English king die, or at least would not care if he lived, so would not be likely to help," she pointed out, and then added under her breath, "Besides, it appears information spreads like seeds on the wind."

"Oh, aye, it does," Rory assured her. "Just look at how many here know about de Buci already."

"Oh, I am," she muttered, glancing over her shoulder again.

ELYSANDE BREATHED A SIGH OF RELIEF WHEN THEY FINALLY reached the end of the street and she saw Robbie walking toward the wall. She was near enough now to see the gate. It was much smaller than the main gate, but big enough to walk the horses through without problem. They could even ride them through two apace.

"What is that noise behind us?" Rory asked, his voice tense, and Elysande glanced back to see the crowd had drawn closer to watch them leave.

"Just children playing," she said. She wasn't *really* lying—some of the children were playing as they followed. "We are approaching the gate now. Robbie is opening it." She didn't mention that another man was helping him.

"Thank God," Rory said, relief heavy in his voice. "I canno' wait to take this bloody blindfold off."

"Aye," Conn growled in agreement, and she almost felt guilty that they'd had to wear the blindfolds. Elysande did feel responsible. It had been at her suggestion, after all. But she hadn't wanted Mildrede and the others fretting over their secret gate being common knowledge to men whose countrymen they considered their enemy.

"Why are we stopping?" Rory asked a moment later as she drew them to a halt behind Inan's horse.

"We are at the gate," she explained, and glanced from Robbie to Elizabeth as they both suddenly looked to her as if for instructions on what should be done next. Realizing that was exactly what they were waiting for, she glanced around at the men and horses and then back to Elizabeth, still holding Inan's arm. She doubted the woman wanted to walk them out the gate, so . . .

"I guess we should get them on their mounts," she suggested to Robbie and Elizabeth.

When Robbie nodded and then moved to Elizabeth and Inan to help the warrior mount, Elysande glanced back toward her soldiers. "Tom, give Simon my mare and mount up. You will lead Inan's horse until we get to the woods."

"Should I help Conn and Rory mount first?" Tom asked as he passed her mare's reins to Simon.

"Nay," Rory said firmly. "Ye should help yer lady onto her mount. Conn and I can manage on our own."

Conn grunted his agreement to that and then both men looked expectantly in her direction. Elysande didn't realize what they were waiting for until Rory squeezed her hand gently.

"Oh," she gasped, and released their hands. She watched with interest as Rory and Conn then followed the reins they held to their mounts' heads, and felt their way along the horses' sides to their saddles. She was rather impressed when both men then felt for the stirrup, inserted a foot and mounted without any aid at all. Truly, it was as if they'd practiced the maneuver.

"M'lady?"

Elysande turned to find Tom and Simon waiting next to her with her mare and sighed with resignation. They were going to have to help her mount in front of all these people. Had she had the chance to reapply her liniment this morning, she might have managed with just a leg up from one of the men, but without it . . .

Setting her mouth, she nodded grimly and stepped up beside her mare. Tom and Simon immediately moved to either side of her, clasped her elbows and lifted her as high as they could, which was just high enough for her to place her foot in the stirrup. The minute she did that, Simon released her side closest to the mare, and slid quickly out of the way and around to the other side of her mare so that she could swivel her body with Tom's help and pretty much half throw and half drop herself sideways onto the saddle. At least that's how it usually went, but this time, self-conscious about so many people watching, Elysande misjudged and nearly toppled herself over the horse. Tom's hand tightened on her arm, and Simon immediately reached up to grab for her to keep her in the saddle, catching her with one hand at her lower back and one on her stomach. It was the hand at her back that was the problem. It sent a shaft of intense pain through her that had her arching her back, her face tipping skyward as she sucked in a gasping breath and struggled against the agony vibrating through her.

"Lass? What's happening?" Rory barked with sudden panic. Elysande saw him reaching for his blindfold out of the corner of her eye, but couldn't do a thing about it. She didn't have air to breathe let alone speak at the moment, and Tom and Simon were too busy trying to keep her from tumbling out of the saddle to pay attention to what he was doing.

Fortunately, Elizabeth rushed to his side, and grabbed his leg, saying, "All is well. One of her men just touched her back while trying to put her in the saddle. Give her a minute and she will tell you herself she is fine."

Elysande saw Rory's hand drop from his face, and then closed her eyes as Simon finally removed his hand from her back to grasp her elbow instead, and the frenzied agony in her back began to calm to a dull throb. Sagging with relief, she made herself take several deep breaths.

"M'lady?" Tom asked when her breathing normalized.

Nodding, Elysande opened her eyes and then paused. The people who had been following them had rushed forward and now surrounded the horses, those closest reaching up as if to help catch her if she fell. But it was the anxiety and horror on some of their faces that caught her attention most. It made Elysande realize the plaid had fallen away from her face, leaving the bruised side on view.

Unable to cover it up at the moment with both of her men holding her arms, Elysande sighed and carefully shifted on the saddle, lifting one leg over it to sit astride the mare. The move hiked her skirts up, briefly revealing the men's breeches she wore under her gown to everyone, before the cloak she'd pulled on over the plaid slid forward to cover it.

Once she was settled, Tom and Simon released her and only

then was Elysande able to quickly pull the top of the plaid back up over her head and around the one side of her face to conceal the damage de Buci had wrought.

When Tom then gathered her mare's reins for her and held them out, Elysande murmured, "Thank you," and took them before looking toward Rory.

He was stiff and still in his saddle, tension in his body and expression and she realized he must be aware there was a crowd around them. They were pressing up around all the horses on all sides. Elysande was surprised he wasn't commenting on it until she realized several of the people nearest him were giving him commentary.

"There, she's in the saddle now and quite recovered," an old crone was telling him soothingly at that moment.

"Aye, but gor, that de Buci fella sure did her face something awful," someone else said, and Elysande felt her face flush with embarrassment.

"That's not the worst of it," someone else said. "I heard the alewife was weeping when she was telling Mrs. Elizabeth what he done to her back, arse and legs. 'Tis no wonder she needed help getting on her horse. I'm amazed she can ride if 'tis as damaged as her face."

"M'lady?"

She glanced down at that soft voice to see Elizabeth holding out the reins to Rory's horse.

"They mean well," Elizabeth said quietly as Elysande took the offered reins. "But Mildrede *was* weeping when she told me. Bless these Scots for taking ye away to keep ye safe from him."

Elysande managed a smile but then startled with surprise when Robbie roared, "Away with ye. They're mounted and ready to go. Get out of the way and let 'em leave ere de Buci's men decide to come see what the to-do is back here."

Elysande glanced around then for the other men and saw that Simon was mounted and holding Conn's reins, and Tom was mounted and trying to move his horse through the crowd to reach Inan to take his reins from Robbie. A task that was made much easier after Robbie's irritated bark, as the people began to back away to give them space.

"Good luck and Godspeed, m'lady," Elizabeth said, moving to the side to get out of the way. The sentiment was repeated by many others as their party finally started moving. Tom led the way. After glancing back to receive a nod from her, he urged his horse through the gate, pulling Inan's mount behind. Elysande was next, leading Rory and Simon, and Conn brought up the rear. Tom kept them at a sedate walk until they heard the gate close behind them and then urged his horse to a trot. This obviously wasn't a much-used path. Actually, there was no path to follow that she could see, and there was still snow on the ground here, but it was melting, the ground soft beneath it. She supposed that combined with the fact that the men were blindfolded was why Tom didn't immediately break into a gallop.

"Are ye all right, lass?"

Elysande glanced around at that question from Rory to see that his face was still tense and concerned.

"Aye," she assured him, and then offered, "A few more minutes and you should be able to remove your blindfold."

He didn't comment at first and then asked, "Do ye see anyone on this side o' the wall?"

Elysande glanced around, realizing only then that it should have been the first thing she'd done. They had no idea if the English soldiers who had arrived in the city were all of them, or if some of de Buci's men had waited outside the wall as they had done at Kynardersley. She was relieved to note that there was nothing but snow-covered ground as far as the eye could see. There was no sign of a camp, or soldiers. But they were leaving a trail of hoofprints from the gate, she saw, and hoped that wouldn't prove to be a problem.

"Nay. 'Tis only us," she told him.

Rory nodded, and then cleared his throat. "There sounded to be a lot o' people at the gate when we left."

"Aye. A few," she said with a grimace.

"More than a few, I'd say," he responded, his tone dry.

Elysande sighed with resignation, sure she was about to receive another lecture on telling people about de Buci, but he surprised her.

"'Twas obvious they were all eager to help," was all he said, and she relaxed a little.

They rode in silence after that until they reached the trees. Tom started to slow then but didn't stop for a few minutes. Until they couldn't see the wall anymore for the trees, she realized when he brought the party to a halt and she glanced back.

"Can I take off the blindfold now?"

Rory's question brought her head back around to see that Tom and Simon were looking at her, waiting for her answer. "Aye. Remove your blindfolds," she said loudly enough for Conn and Inan to hear as well.

The men couldn't get them off quickly enough, and only after doing so and looking around did the three Scots relax.

"I wonder where Alick and the others got to?" Simon commented.

"They'll be farther along the path," Rory answered. "I told him no' to stop until he was a good distance into the wood." When Elysande glanced at him in question, he shrugged. "That way they could no' see where we came out o' the wall. There's little sense in our being blindfolded if they could tell where the gate was, and I did no' want to put any o' them in the position to have to choose between keeping their word to the English, or serving their country with such valuable information if there is another war."

Elysande felt her mouth slide into a smile and murmured, "You are a good man, Rory Buchanan."

He smiled, but looked a little embarrassed by the compliment and then shifted his attention to the men. "Conn and Simon take the lead. Tom and Inan, follow behind Elysande and me. Let's find the others."

Her smile widened at the words as she noted he was pairing her men off with his own. She felt it was a good sign, though she couldn't have said why exactly.

"We'll stop as soon as we meet up with Alick, Donnghail and Fearghas so ye can apply more liniment," Rory said as they fell into line behind Conn and Tom.

Elysande appreciated the thought, but shook her head. "I would rather wait until we cross into Scotland."

"Are ye sure?" Rory asked with a small frown.

"Aye," she assured him on a regretful sigh, for truly the idea of applying the numbing cream was an attractive one, but . . . "I would rather not stop with de Buci's men so close. They might finish their search and follow us at any time. Or . . ." She hesitated, and then admitted, "A good many people knew about our being there and our leaving. If even one of them is tempted by coin to talk . . ." She shrugged. "I would rather not tempt fate and hang about. Let us just get to Scotland and then worry about it."

To give him credit, Rory didn't say I told you so, or point out that was what he'd been worried about when it came to her telling Mildrede and Elizabeth about de Buci. He merely nodded and let the subject drop.

They sped up to a gallop after that, and Elysande ground her teeth and resigned herself to at least a couple of hours of constant pain before they would stop for a break and she could apply the liniment.

Alick and the other two men had done as Rory had asked and it was a good quarter hour later when they met up with them. They stopped just long enough for greetings and for Elysande to pass out the pear-filled pasties Mildrede had packed in the bag she'd given her. They then set off again, breaking their fast in the saddle as they rode.

"Remind me to tell Mildrede she is a fine cook when we visit her after this is all over," Rory said as he finished off his pasty.

Elysande smiled and nodded at the suggestion, but in her heart she didn't think that visit would ever come about. At least not with Rory taking her. If she survived all of this, she would no doubt return to England and Kynardersley, or what was left of it. And she would try to make sure whoever escorted her back allowed her to stop in Carlisle to see Mildrede and the others. But once he got her to Sinclair, Rory wasn't likely to stick around for the weeks and possibly months it would take to resolve this situation. Rory had a family and a life, and people who required his healing skills. Nay. She suspected that, despite his promise to Mildrede, he would be long gone by the time she made her way back into England again.

Chapter 10

"WILL SHE BE ABLE TO APPLY THE LINIMENT ON HER OWN?" Rory tore his gaze away from where Elysande was disappearing into the woods with the container of liniment and glanced at Tom. It had been what he'd been worrying about just now too.

"Probably no'," he admitted unhappily.

"Well?" the man said when Rory just stood there.

"Well what?" he asked with confusion.

"Well, should you not go help her, then? You're the healer," he pointed out with exasperation.

"Oh, aye," Rory said with surprise, and headed into the woods after Elysande. It was only then he realized he hadn't been thinking like a healer. He'd been thinking like a man . . . who had no right to be looking on her naked back and buttocks and smoothing his hands over all that soft, warm flesh.

"Healer," he muttered, blinking his inappropriate thoughts away. "She needs yer help, no' yer lusty thoughts." And much to Rory's surprise, his thoughts were quite lusty where the lass was concerned. It was sleeping with her half on top of him that had done it, he supposed. Waking every morning to her scent in his nose, her warm body nestled against him, her leg rubbing over him . . . Aye, he didn't feel much like a healer at those times. But that's what he was and what she needed, so Rory tried to adjust his thinking now as he hurried to catch up to her. She was just another ailing lass who needed his care. He would spread the liniment on her back, bottom and legs as quickly and adeptly as he would any other patient and then leave her to dress in privacy.

"Oh!" Elysande's startled gasp drew his attention to the fact that she'd glanced back to see him following and stopped.

Pausing as well, Rory nodded and tried for the usual calm attitude he used when healing others. "Ye'll need help applying the liniment, lass, so I've come in my capacity as healer to help ye. Because I'm a healer. And 'tis my job. To heal ye. And put on liniment fer ye."

The way Elysande blinked and then peered at him a little oddly told him that he might have overstated his case. Sighing, Rory swung around so his back was to her. "I'll give ye privacy to undress. Let me ken when ye're ready."

There was a moment of utter stillness where he suspected she was going to protest, but then he heard her give a small sigh. It was followed by the rustle of clothing that told him she was moving . . . or undressing. Probably undressing, he told himself as he listened to the sounds. He hoped she was undressing. Purely because it meant she trusted him to tend her, he told himself, though in his mind he was recalling her laid out on Mildrede's kitchen table, her naked body on display, and his hands flexed at the thought of smoothing over all those rounded curves.

"I am ready."

Rory gave a start at the soft call, and spun around, disappointment claiming him when he saw she was lying on her cloak, with only her bare back on display. She was covered from the waist down by the plaid, her gown and probably her breeks. She'd merely slid her arms out of her gown and removed her tunic, and then lain down.

"I will no' be able to spread the liniment everywhere ye need it like that," he muttered, not moving closer.

"I can get my legs and bottom myself. 'Tis only my back I need help with," Elysande said. Her voice sounded unconcerned, but her face, the undamaged side he could see since she'd rested her forehead on her hands with the bruised side of her face down, was bright pink with a blush.

"Oh. Aye," Rory said, and then realized how disappointed he

sounded, and gave himself a mental shake as he moved forward. Healer, he repeated to himself firmly. Think like a healer, not the man who's held her in his arms each morning.

Elysande had unwrapped the container holding the liniment. It sat on the fur next to her hip, so he knelt beside her and let his gaze slide over her back as he scooped out some liniment. Like her face, her back and side were more purple than black now, with red and then green toward the edges. She was healing, but it still looked damned painful. It made him feel bad for not insisting they stop sooner.

With the path a boggy mess from the melting snow, they hadn't traveled as quickly as Rory had hoped and it had taken longer to cross the border into Scotland than he'd expected. Then they'd ridden for a while before finding somewhere to stop that wasn't a swamp of mud and wet snow. Which meant they'd had to wait until they reached higher ground. It was well past the nooning now.

"What are you doing?"

Rory blinked at the question, and then explained, "I'm warming the liniment between my hands so the cold does no' shock ye."

"Oh. That is very kind," she murmured, relaxing a little on the fur.

"I'm a kind maun," he responded, and then actually winced at how pompous and ridiculous he sounded. Good Lord, the lass chased his good sense away by just being near. Sighing, he leaned forward and began to smooth the liniment over her back.

Rory started out just spreading it, but when she sighed with pleasure, he began massaging it into the damaged muscles.

"Oh, that is lovely," Elysande breathed, seeming to melt into the fur under his touch.

"I'm no' hurting ye?" Rory asked with concern. He knew it shouldn't hurt—his hands were already numb from the cream so the skin on her back should be as well—but he wasn't as sure that the muscles underneath her skin wouldn't be paining her under his touch.

"A little, but 'tis nice too," she said, and then gave a small laugh and admitted, "Which probably makes no sense, but when you knead the muscle like that it hurts a bit, but when you move on to another muscle, the first feels better than it did ere you pressed on it."

"Because it encourages fresh blood to come to the area, which is supposed to help with healing," he explained, watching his rough hands move over her soft skin.

"Really? Mother never told me that. Where did you learn it?"

"Ibn al-Nafis."

"Where is that?" she asked with curiosity.

"No' where, but who," he said with amusement. "He was a physician in Egypt during the last century. A fascinating man who dissected the dead and wrote over a hundred volumes on what he discovered about blood and its circulation through the body. Aulay gave me one of his books fer Christmas some years back, though I do no' ken how he got his hands on it. It was probably brought back this way by a crusader in the last century and Aulay bought it from a trader or perhaps another lord who had ended up with it." He shrugged. "I do no' ken, but 'twas fascinating reading."

"It sounds it," Elysande murmured, sounding almost sleepy now, and then she stirred herself to ask, "The church allowed this healer Ibn to dissect the dead?"

He wasn't surprised by the question. That kind of thing was prohibited by the church. Even reading about his work would probably be frowned on by the church, but Rory had learned a lot from it. "They follow a different religion in Egypt. I presume 'twas allowed there or he would no' have been able to write about his work."

"I suppose, aye," she agreed. "Do you think—" Whatever she'd been about to ask ended on a gasp and she went still beneath his touch.

Rory had moved on to working on her side, and his hand had brushed along the edge of her breast, startling her. She wasn't the only one who reacted to it either. His body quite liked the unintended caress and wanted him to do it again. Actually, it would prefer he slide his hand under and cup the soft globe his fingers had just brushed against. Repeating the word *healer* in his mind, Rory resisted that urge and moved his hands lower to massage her waist briefly and then pulled his hands back and straightened.

"All done," he said abruptly, and stood. He had intended to offer to apply the cream to her bottom and the backs of her legs again, but that no longer seemed like a good idea. If just brushing the edge of her breast was enough to have his mind run off on a tangent of other things he would like to do to her, he did not wish to know what actually cupping the round curves of her bottom might spur him to do.

"I'll return to the others and let ye dress and apply liniment to yer legs and . . ." Nay, he wasn't even going to mention her bottom, Rory decided, and simply turned and strode back through the trees to the safety of the other men.

Rory briefly considered that it might be best if he didn't sleep beside her tonight when they stopped for the evening. Waking up with her in his arms was apparently giving him ideas. But he knew Elysande cuddled up to him in her sleep and was embarrassed when she woke up to find herself on his chest as she had each morning. That being the case, she'd probably do the same with whatever man took his place next to her, and the idea of her cuddling up to another . . . Well, Rory just wasn't having that.

He was still irritated at the very thought of that happening when he stepped out of the woods and joined the others in the small clearing.

"Everything all right?" Tom asked, approaching him the moment he appeared from the trees.

"Aye. I applied the liniment to her back. She is just taking care o' the other areas and then will join us," he said grimly.

Tom raised his eyebrows at his grumpy tone, but merely nodded. "Good. Then riding should be much easier for her for the rest of the day."

"Aye," Rory agreed, relaxing a little at the thought. He'd finally been able to do something to help her, even if it was only applying the liniment she'd made. Of course, that meant he probably wouldn't get to enjoy having her ride at his back with her arms around his waist later today. The thought made him grumpy again.

IT WAS PAIN IN HER BACK AS SOMETHING PRESSED AGAINST HER that woke Elysande from a dead sleep. Instinctively shifting forward to escape the pain, she pressed up against Rory's back and glanced over her shoulder. She was just able to make out Tom's outline in the faint light cast by the embers of the fire they'd enjoyed before retiring. He'd rolled toward her in his sleep, bumping her back. It made her wonder if that wasn't the reason she'd ended up on top of Rory each morning, an effort to escape Tom bumping and paining her back.

Sighing, she lay there for a minute, debating what to do. Her back had still been fine when they'd stopped for the night. She'd considered applying some more liniment anyway before going to sleep, but then Rory had suggested it, and she'd known he would insist on doing her back for her, so she'd said it was fine and lay down to sleep. She hadn't wanted his help . . . not when he was so grumpy, and she was still confused about the feelings his helping her the first time had caused her.

Even now, Elysande could almost feel the warm tingling that had raced through her when his hand had moved along her side and brushed against her breast. She'd never experienced anything like it before and had been shocked, but she'd also liked it and the excitement it had aroused in her.

Elysande had held still after that, hoping he would do it again, but he'd quickly spread the liniment over the rest of her side, and then headed back to camp as if nothing had happened. That made her suppose the touch had just been a part of his spreading the liniment and he hadn't experienced any of the tingles and excitement she had. He'd also been short-tempered by the time she returned to camp, and had stayed that way the rest of the day. So, when they'd stopped and he'd suggested more liniment should be applied, she'd shook her head and said, no, she was fine.

She was paying for it now though, and the question became, did she really want to crawl from her warm spot on the fur and traipse through the cold to apply more liniment? Especially when she couldn't reach the better part of her back?

Aye, Elysande decided when Tom shifted and nudged her again. Fortunately, it was the undamaged side of her back he brushed against this time, but it might not be next time. Holding her breath, she eased up onto her elbow, trying to figure out how to escape the center of the nest without waking everyone.

"Is it yer back?"

Elysande glanced around to see that Rory was awake and peering over his shoulder at her. When she nodded, he was suddenly moving, and she couldn't help noticing that he didn't seem to have any trouble getting to his feet without disturbing anyone. But then it looked like Inan had left a good deal more space between himself and Rory than Tom and Rory had left her, Elysande thought before she had to bite back a startled yelp as she was suddenly caught by the upper arms and lifted to her feet.

Well, not exactly to her feet, she acknowledged as Rory stepped over Inan while holding her a good foot off the ground. He didn't set her down until they were outside the circle of bodies, and then he settled her on a log next to Donnghail, who was stirring the dying fire back to life.

"Wait here. I'll get yer liniment," Rory said in a low voice, and then headed off in the direction of the horses.

"Yer back's paining ye," Donnghail said quietly as he propped the stick he'd been using against the log and relaxed.

"Aye," she confessed with a little embarrassment. "I suppose I should have let Rory put some more on before going to sleep as he suggested."

"Grumpy as he was?" Donnghail asked with amusement and shook his head. "I would ha'e said nay too."

Elysande beamed at him, feeling justified in her earlier refusal, but she merely asked, "Do you know why he was so grumpy?"

"I was going to ask ye that verra question," Donnghail admitted. "He was fine when he chased off after ye into the woods, but came back like a man with a hot poker up his arse."

Elysande blinked with bewilderment at the description, and then guessed, "He was moving fast?"

"What?" he asked with confusion, and then frowned. "Nay, he was cranky."

"Oh. I see," she murmured, and then explained apologetically, "I just thought if he had a poker up his—well, he would be moving quickly. But most like toward the nearest river or loch to cool the poker so he could pull it out."

"He might," Donnghail allowed with amusement. "But he'd also be cranky."

"Aye," Elysande admitted, and then frowned and said, "I do not know why he returned cranky. Though I did not get the chance to thank him for applying the liniment as he left so quickly. Do you think it could be that?"

"I think 'tis more likely touching ye that made him cranky," Donnghail said.

"Really?" she asked with alarm. "But—" Pausing, she bit her lip and then said, "I am pretty sure he will think he should put it on again now. However, if 'tis such an unpleasant chore for him and makes him angry, I would rather he did not. Mayhap you could put it on for me instead," Elysande suggested, and then frowned and said, "Nay, I am sorry. If 'tis so unpleasant I should not even ask you."

"Ye definitely should no' ask me," Donnghail agreed with a soft laugh. "I suspect my putting liniment on ye would make him crankier still."

"Well, for heaven's sake! Why would he care so long as he does not have to do it?"

"Ye misunderstand, m'lady," Donnghail interrupted gently. "'Tis no' that he did no' like putting the liniment on ye. I suspect he got cranky because he liked it too much. He's attracted to ye," he added solemnly.

"Do you think so?" Elysande asked with surprise, and then shook her head before he could answer. "Nay. He cannot be. I look awful."

"Aye, ye do," he said honestly. "And yet, he does no' let ye out o' his sight. Worries about ye more than he's a right to, and wakes every morning with ye in his arms and a smile on his face."

Elysande considered that, and then waved it all away with one hand. "That means nothing. He is merely trying to fulfill my mother's dying request and see me safely to Sinclair."

"Seeing ye safely to Sinclair does no' explain the tent he makes with his plaid every morning after they lift ye away from him," Donnghail said dryly.

Elysande was blinking in confusion at that when Rory returned with the cloth-wrapped container of liniment. She let him help her up, grimacing at the pain it sent shooting through the muscles of her back, and then walked with him into the woods, but her mind was distracted with what Donnghail had said. She had no idea what he meant. She was usually too embarrassed at waking in his arms to look at anyone when the men lifted her up, especially Rory, so had never noticed him making anything with his plaid.

A soft curse from Rory made her glance around in question, only to blink as she realized she couldn't see him in the dark. She could hear him muttering under his breath right beside her though.

"What is it?" she asked with concern.

"The ground is too wet here fer ye to lie on," he said with exasperation, his voice starting down by her knees and then moving upward until it sounded like it was coming from a little above and beside her again. She realized then that he'd knelt to check the ground, and she'd been vaguely aware of his drawing her to a stop and releasing her elbow briefly a couple of times before this. From that and his words, she guessed that he'd been stopping every once in a while to check the ground while she had apparently stood lost in thought.

"We'll have to keep going," he said on a sigh, and caught her arm again to urge her forward, but Elysande resisted the tug.

"Nay. We can do it here," she said, suspecting they would not find dry ground anywhere. Even the patch of ground where they'd laid the fur had been more than a little damp.

"'Tis far too wet to—"

"Then I will not lie down," Elysande said simply.

"What? How— What are ye doing?" Rory asked, a frown in his voice as she began to swing her free arm around.

"Trying to find a tree," she explained, moving to her right and dragging him with her since he was holding her arm.

"What for?" he asked with bewilderment.

"To lay my clothes over," Elysande explained. "'Tis dark as sin here, my lord. So, I shall just strip off my clothes, hang them over a branch to keep them dry and then redon them after you apply the liniment."

"Oh," Rory said with a touch of surprise. "Aye, that should work."

"Aye," she agreed, and then gave a grunt of victory when her hand smacked what she was sure was a tree trunk.

"Find one?" he asked with what sounded suspiciously like amusement.

Elysande moved her hand over what she'd hit, smiling once she was sure it was the nice thick trunk of a tree with several sturdy branches low enough for her to lay her clothes over. "Aye."

"Verra well." Rory released her elbow. "Tell me when ye're ready."

Elysande nodded, quite forgetting he couldn't see it, and started undressing. She removed her cloak and laid it over a branch she thought might be high enough to keep it off the ground. The plaid quickly followed, but her gown was more of a struggle to get out of. Her back and muscles complained bitterly of the movement as well as the cloth shifting against her skin, and despite the chill in the air she was sweating when she finally accomplished it. But she did. Though apparently not without some telltale sounds that told Rory she'd run into difficulty.

"Are ye all right, lass?" he asked with concern.

"Aye." Elysande sighed the word and paused to lean against the tree trunk briefly. "'Twas a struggle getting out of my gown. I just have to remove my tunic and breeches now and I will be ready."

His responding, "Oh," sounded odd, but Elysande had straightened away from the tree and paid him little attention as she started the battle to remove her tunic.

"How are ye doing?" Rory asked several moments later, his voice almost raspy.

"Just the breeches to go," she said as she hung the tunic over the branch with the rest of her clothes.

"Just the breeches." Rory barely breathed the words beside her, but Elysande caught them just the same. She was cautiously bending to push the breeches down by then, however, stretching her back muscles as slowly as possible to minimize her pain, and didn't speak again until she had them off over her slippers.

"There," Elysande breathed with relief as she laid the breeches over the rest of her clothes, and then she peered around at the darkness surrounding her. "Where are you?"

"Here."

Elysande felt a slight breeze as if something was moving past her face and reached up quickly to grab at it. She missed at first but then he must have been moving his hand back and forth because she caught it a moment later.

"There ye are," Rory said with relief as she clasped his wrist. "Dear God, I canno' see a thing in these woods."

Elysande thought that was a good thing. She'd hardly be standing there naked if he could see her.

"This is my left shoulder," she announced, raising his hand and placing it against her skin. "I am just going to face the tree and brace myself against it so I do not lose it and lose my clothes," Elysande explained as she did just that, leaning forward slightly to brace her hands against the tree trunk with her back out toward him.

"Right," Rory breathed by her ear, and then hesitated. "I have to let ye go to scoop up some liniment. Do no' move or I might lose ye in this dark."

Elysande chuckled softly at the words, though they weren't really funny. They could easily lose each other in this black ink night. She heard movement a little behind and to the side and then he said, "I'm going to give ye the cloth that was around the pot."

She felt his hand and the cloth brush her shoulder and then he followed her arm up to where her hand was braced against the tree and waited for her to take the cloth from him. Elysande couldn't help thinking it was a similar operation to how he'd felt his way along his horse to mount it when he'd been blindfolded.

Rory didn't give her warning before starting; she just suddenly felt what she thought must be the back of his hand brush her shoulder and then it moved down, skimming lightly over the skin on the uninjured side of her back before it moved to the side and then shifted slightly and he was smoothing cool liniment over the injured side.

Elysande released a little sigh of relief as the numbness began to set in, taking away her aches and pains, and then he began to knead her back as he had the last time. She moaned with the pleasure of it as his hand moved up and down her back, her upper body sagging toward the tree as her muscles loosened. Elysande didn't realize she was moving her back away from him until he stepped forward to follow and she felt his plaid and something hard beneath it rub against her bottom.

"Nay, do not stop," she begged when Rory froze. "The kneading feels so good."

Much to her relief, his hand started to move again, working her muscles, but he also eased his feet back, so that she could no longer feel his plaid.

Elysande felt like a lump of dough when he finally paused to collect more liniment and moved on to spread it along her side. His fingers glided up from her waist, drifting over the edge of her breast again as it had the last time. The same excited tingle slid through her at the touch, but then his hand was gone, dropping back down to knead the muscles below her ribs. The next time he stopped to collect more liniment, Rory must have knelt as well because his hand didn't return to her back, but to the backs of her legs, skipping her bottom altogether. His oily fingers glided from the backs of her knees, slowly upward, and Elysande's eyes blinked open, as did her mouth a bit, and her breathing became a little shallow and erratic as he skimmed his way up toward her bottom.

She was fighting the urge to close her legs, or to shift them at least. They definitely wanted to move, but she forced herself to remain still as he slathered the oil on first one leg, and then the other, before he started to knead them just as he had her back.

Elysande could feel his warm breath on her lower bottom as he worked one leg, followed by the other, his breath moving from one side to the other, brushing across the apex in the center with each pass. Every one of those times that his breath hit her there, it sent a bevy of tingles through Elysande that drew a soft moan from her and had her shifting slightly despite her best efforts. With one movement she squeezed her legs together, with another she widened her stance and eased them apart. Her body didn't seem to know what it wanted to do, and then his hands dropped away again. A moment later she felt his plaid brush against the backs of her legs and bottom and guessed he had stood up again. Then his hands were sliding over the curves of her bottom, running circles around them briefly before squeezing gently once the liniment had begun to numb her.

"Straighten for me, love." His voice sounded gruff and raspy, and he squeezed her bottom a little more firmly as he made the request.

Elysande didn't even consider disobeying; she simply pushed her upper body away from the tree to stand upright. The moment she did he rewarded her with a kiss on the side of the neck that made her swallow and still.

"Lean back a little," Rory murmured, one hand leaving her bottom to travel up her injured side and glide across the side of her breast.

Elysande leaned back and he kissed her neck again and then nipped lightly and she moaned and tilted her head to the side to give him better access as he began to nibble and suckle the length of her throat. When he reached her jaw and began to follow it toward her chin, she instinctively turned her head to make it easier and then sighed when his mouth found hers with first just a brush of lips, and then his tongue skimmed across them before urging them open.

Elysande was more than a little startled when she let her lips open a bit and his tongue slid in to fill her. For one moment she froze, and then she tasted him, and his tongue moved, rasping against her own, and she liked it and opened wider for him. Rory immediately deepened the kiss and his hand left her side to cup the back of her head, twisting it toward him until she released the tree and rotated in his arms.

Rory let go of her bottom for her to do that, but immediately clasped the soft cheeks again once she'd finished the move. He then used his hold to press her lower body firmly against his as his tongue thrust in her mouth.

Elysande gasped and moaned, her hands clutching at his shoulders, trying to get as close to him as she could. Her nipples tingled where they pressed into his plaid, and liquid heat was pooling between her legs as if his squeezing her bottom was milking her, but it wasn't enough. She wanted more, and then he broke their kiss to blaze a trail of them down her throat, across her collarbone and down the slope of one breast until he found one of her aching nipples and drew it into his mouth. The lash of his tongue over the hard tip had her almost thrashing in his arms with need until she gasped, "Rory, please. I need . . ."

The feverish words merely made him suckle harder, and drove

her wild so that she began to moan, "Please, please, please," over and over until he finally let her nipple slip from his mouth and lifted his head to nip her ear and growl, "Please what, love? What do ye need?"

"I—I do not know," she admitted plaintively, and then turned her head to catch his mouth with her own. This time she kissed him. Elysande had no idea what she was doing, or if she was doing it right, and didn't care. But it got a wondrous response. Rory kissed her back just as violently, tilting his head to find a better angle, and then let his hands drop to the back of her thighs and urged her legs apart as one of his legs slid between hers.

Elysande cried out into his mouth as the top of his thigh rubbed over the center of her, her entire body quaking with the excitement it caused, and then he did it again. She clawed at his shoulders, feeling like cloth wound too tight and about to unravel, and then a branch snapped somewhere behind her and they both froze.

Chapter 11

THE SOUND OF THE BRANCH SNAPPING WAS LIKE A BUCKET OF icy water splashed over Rory, recalling him to where he was and with whom. Elysande was a complete innocent. Her utter lack of skill at kissing at first had told him that. She was also a treasure he was supposed to be seeing safely to Sinclair. He suspected her mother wouldn't consider what he was presently doing as seeing her safely anywhere.

Another branch snapped, closer this time, and Rory pulled his mouth from Elysande's and eased his leg from between hers. He then followed the tree trunk behind her until his hand brushed cloth. Grasping the material, he drew it off the branch and pulled it between them to press against Elysande's chest. She didn't need to be told what to do. The moment he eased back, she took the piece of clothing and began to turn it between them, no doubt trying to sort out what it was.

Breeches was his guess when she urged him farther back and he felt her head brush his arm, the soft strands of hair caressing his skin as she no doubt bent to pull them over one foot and then the other.

Rory gave her the space she needed, but no more. It was still pitch-black in the woods and he couldn't see her or anything else. It would be too easy to lose her out here. Besides, he hadn't brought his sword with him, and was very aware he would be a poor protector if whoever was moving through the woods attacked them. The best hope was that it was one of the men looking for someplace to relieve himself, he thought, and then moved closer to Elysande when he sensed her straightening.

Her arms brushed against him as she finished pulling up her pants, and then her hip bumped his as she retrieved more clothing. He left her to it, his ears straining to hear any more sounds, and his hand finding her body every once in a while to be sure she was still there and check her progress. With the liniment numbing her pain, she dressed much more quickly than she'd undressed, and soon she found his arm and squeezed.

Guessing that was the signal that she was finished, Rory turned in the direction he thought camp was and started to move cautiously that way. He hadn't heard any more snapping branches or other sounds, and supposed what they'd heard could have been an animal. A stag, perhaps, or some other woodland creature. Still, he moved slowly, making as little sound as he could.

When several moments passed without any sign of the campfire ahead, Rory was beginning to think he had led them in the wrong direction. But just as he was about to try a different direction, he caught a glimmer of light ahead. He realized then that in his search for a dry spot to apply Elysande's liniment, he'd led them much farther into the woods than he'd realized. Much farther than any of the men would have gone to relieve themselves too, he thought grimly as he began to move a little more quickly.

"Do you think the noise was one of the men, or just an animal?" Elysande asked as they neared the edge of the trees.

Her voice was anxious and he realized she was probably worried one of the men may have heard her moans of pleasure. It apparently also hadn't occurred to her that it might be someone other than one of their men. But he didn't want her worrying, so said, "Probably a rabbit," to soothe her.

It seemed to work. At least, she didn't say anything else.

Rory wasn't at all surprised to note that every man was there and accounted for when he ushered Elysande out of the woods and over to the fur. Donnghail still sat on the log, watching, and the rest of the men were curled up on or around the fur. Catching Elysande by the arm, he whispered, "I'll be right back," and then kissed her gently on the forehead before lifting her over Inan's body and onto the center spot where she slept.

He waited until she had lain down and curled inside her cloak before moving toward Donnghail. It wasn't until he saw the man's raised eyebrows that he realized what he'd just done. Rory turned back sharply then, but Elysande was already asleep, or at least her eyes were closed. He couldn't tell how she'd reacted to the automatic show of affection. He couldn't even tell how she was reacting to what had happened between them in the woods. Her face was expressionless, and other than a little extra color in her cheeks, and the fact that her hair was a little mussy, she didn't look any different. And her hair might have been mussy before they'd headed off into the woods since she'd just woken from sleep. He hadn't really noted it at the time.

Sighing, he continued on to Donnghail, his expression grim.

"Ye two took a while," Donnghail said mildly as Rory dropped onto the log next to him.

"It's dark as pitch in the woods, but I swear I took her halfway to Glasgow before I gave up looking for a spot dry enough for her to lie down. I ended up having to apply the liniment with her leaning against a tree." He shook his head. "And then it took so long before I saw the light of the fire, I thought I'd got us lost."

"She looked startled when ye kissed her forehead," Donnghail announced, and when Rory grimaced, he added, "But then she looked pleased."

"Did she?" he asked, a smile tugging at his lips before he recalled why he'd come to talk to Donnghail. Waving away whatever the man was about to respond with, he said, "We heard snapping branches near us just before we came back."

Donnghail's eyes narrowed, then scanned the woods around them. "Ye're thinking we have company?"

"I do no' ken," Rory admitted solemnly. "It could have been a stag or something, but . . ." He let the sentence hang, his lips compressed.

"But keep an eye out," Donnghail finished for him.

"And yer sword close," Rory suggested, and then stood and moved back to the fur. He stepped over Inan, and stretched out in front of Elysande, his back to her and his hand going automatically to the sword he'd left lying there when he'd gone into the woods. Grasping it in his hand, he closed his eyes, but knew he wasn't likely to fall asleep.

"Ye heard snapping branches?" Inan's soft voice brought his eyes open again. The man was awake.

"Aye," Rory murmured. "It might have been an animal."

"It might," Alick murmured from directly above his head. He lay crosswise to them, his head just above Rory's, his stomach above Elysande's head and his feet above Tom.

"Then again it might not," Conn commented, his head popping into view on the other side of Alick as he sat up. Voice a soft rumble, the big man stood up, saying, "I'll keep Donnghail company."

Rory watched the man go, debating whether he should stay up to stand watch too, but then Inan commented, "No sense all of us losing sleep. Especially since it could have been a harmless stag."

"Aye," Rory agreed, and saw Inan's eyes close, but noted the warrior's hand also gripped his sword now.

Sighing, Rory shifted onto his back and glanced toward Tom and Fearghas on the other side of Elysande. Both men's eyes were open and looking around the clearing suspiciously, and both had their hands on their swords. Rory turned his gaze to the dark night sky then. He suspected none of them were going to get any sleep that evening. While Conn and Donnghail sat up guarding them, and Elysande slept, he and the rest of the men would probably lie there awake until the sun began to rise. Just in case it wasn't a stag. He'd barely had that thought when Elysande murmured sleepily, shifted closer and cuddled up to his chest, her arm and leg snaking over his body possessively.

Glancing down, he stared at the top of her head and found himself smiling faintly. Sleep was valued too highly, he decided. Sometimes going without was worth it.

ELYSANDE WOKE TO A LOVELY ALMOST SPRINGLIKE MORNING, and eight grumpy men. Truly, the lot of them were all red eyed with weariness and cranky as her father on the rare morning after partaking of too much whiskey. They were also strangely reluctant to let her leave the clearing on her own.

"I do not need even one of you to accompany me, let alone three," she repeated with frustration for about the tenth time.

"We will no' look," Rory growled for the tenth time in response. "Tom, Simon and I will stand with our backs to ye while ye . . . attend to matters," he finished delicately.

The very idea of them standing around her while she squatted and watered the grass was unbearable even to consider. "Why?" she asked finally with desperation. "I have attended the matter on my own before without difficulty. Why are you insisting on my having a guard now?"

That brought about an exchange of glances among the three men confronting her. It made Elysande's eyes narrow. "What has happened?"

"Nothing," Rory responded sharply.

Tom rolled his eyes, and answered more honestly. "We are concerned about de Buci's men. They no doubt would have finished their search of Carlisle by midmorn yesterday—"

"Or sooner if someone gave us up for coin," Rory put in on a mutter.

"Either way," Tom continued, "they obviously know we are headed for Scotland and would have crossed the border shortly after us. If they rode past sunset, they could be close."

"But they only reached Carlisle at dawn," she pointed out. "Surely their horses would have needed rest and prevented their leaving again so quickly."

"They could have traded their mounts for fresh ones from the garrison in Carlisle," Tom said gently.

Elysande's eyes widened at the suggestion. She hadn't thought of that. But it still didn't explain why the men were suddenly so worried about her finding a spot to relieve herself alone. She pondered that briefly and then stilled and glanced sharply at Rory. "The sounds in the woods last night. You said a rabbit probably caused the breaking branches."

He flinched at her accusatory tone, but said defensively, "It may have been."

"I have yet to see a rabbit so big it would break a branch large enough to make loud snapping sounds like the ones we heard," Elysande said impatiently as she realized that truth. She must have been exhausted to have believed the line last night. Or still overset by the passion she'd experienced in his arms, she admitted to herself, and glanced worriedly toward the woods. "If they are out there, why are they not attacking?"

"It could have been a stag," Rory pointed out, and then admitted reluctantly, "Or it could be that the men have split up into smaller groups of two or three to search a wider area, with the plan to fetch the others to them if one of the groups came across us."

"We do not know if 'twas an animal or man," Tom added. "But 'tis better to be cautious, and if a couple of de Buci's men have found us and they catch you on your own . . ."

Shoulders sagging, Elysande turned to head into the woods, and this time didn't protest when the three men followed her.

Never having left Kynardersley with its privy chamber ere this trip, Elysande had found relieving herself in the woods something of an ordeal to begin with. But doing so with three men standing point around her had to be the most humiliating experience of her life to date. She'd never noticed it being a particularly loud maneuver before, but in the silent woods, with the men still and unspeaking around her, she was aware of every telltale sound she made, from the rustle of her clothing to the duty itself . . . and good Lord wasn't that loud, Elysande noted with dismay, feeling her face heat up with a blush.

By the time she had finished and put her clothes back in order, Elysande was as grumpy as the men.

"Let us go," she growled, moving past Rory to head for camp. "And you had best do what you can to lose our followers if we have any, because I am not doing that with an accompaniment of men next time," she warned.

Whether because of her words, or not, Elysande didn't know, but they rode hard through the first part of the morning. Then they slowed to a trot and veered off the trail to travel through the woods when they came to a thick stand of trees that offered cover. They traveled through it and onto another trail and then picked up speed again.

With the weather much warmer, the snow had completely melted away, leaving mud in its wake. Elysande hoped that didn't make it easy to follow them, but suspected it would. Perhaps that was why Rory didn't call a halt for the nooning meal. Instead, Alick dropped back briefly to pass out oatcakes to each of them that they ate in the saddle.

Determined not to have to relieve herself with a guard, Elysande refused to drink anything when they passed the ale skin around. Still, by midafternoon her "teeth were floating" as she'd once heard one of her father's soldiers say. Even worse though, the liniment was wearing off and her back was starting to pain her again.

Elysande did her best to ignore it, but was relieved beyond measure when Rory apparently noticed the way she was shifting repeatedly in the saddle trying to ease her discomfort, and called out to Conn to halt. She agreed at once when he rode up beside her to suggest he apply more liniment to her back, and Rory escorted her alone into the trees to perform the task. Unlike the night before, he was quick and efficient without the least hint of impropriety. Elysande didn't know whether to be relieved or disappointed at that. She was very aware that the men weren't far away, waiting, but she had enjoyed his kisses and would have liked more.

Despite what she'd said that morning, when Rory finished and suggested she take the opportunity to relieve herself while he stood guard, Elysande did. It was still embarrassing, but much less embarrassing than wetting herself in the saddle would have been.

The moment they returned to the men, they set off again. They rode through the afternoon and continued on even after the sun set this night. But the moon was high and the sky was clear, leaving the trail easy to see.

While Elysande suspected she was the only one who had got a proper night's sleep, she was the first to flag and actually began to nod off in the saddle. The first time was an hour or so after darkness fell, but she caught herself and sat up abruptly, giving her head a shake in an effort to make herself more alert. However, moments later Elysande found her eyes sliding closed again and her head lowering and then was startled awake when Rory caught her around the waist and drew her into his lap.

She heard him order someone to take the reins of her horse, and considered telling him she was fine and insisting he put her back on her mare, but was just too tired to bother. She was across his lap, her good side against his chest, and the liniment was still working so that his arm around her back wasn't bothering her, so Elysande simply gave in to the inevitable and curled up against his chest to sleep.

When next she opened her eyes, snow was falling and they were moving through a street lined with the dark hulking shapes of buildings. Blinking away a snowflake that had landed on her eyelashes, she sat up a little straighter to look around.

"Where are we?"

"Ayr," Rory answered.

Elysande nodded, but had no idea where that was, except that it was obviously somewhere in Scotland.

"I thought ye might enjoy a bath and a night in a bed rather than out in the cold."

"A bath?" She breathed with happy wonder and peered at him through the darkness, able to just make out his features enough to see the smile that spread his lips.

"I thought ye'd like that idea." Rory sounded amused.

"Very much." Elysande usually bathed every day or two depending on the time of year. It was something she'd done since childhood because her mother insisted it was good for her health. But she hadn't bathed since the night before de Buci had shown up at Kynardersley, and none of the men had bathed since joining ranks in the clearing at Monmouth. But there hadn't been a thing anyone could do about it, so she'd simply done her best to ignore their stench and her own.

"Aye, so will I," Rory said, his smile widening. "That is the one thing I dislike most about travel in the winter, no' being able to bathe every day."

"You bathe every day?" she asked with interest.

"I do in the summer when I can just walk down to the loch to take a dip. But usually only every other day or so in the winter. The loch is too cold then, and I do no' like to trouble the servants to heat the water and carry up the tub nightly."

Elysande smiled with understanding. "I usually bathe in the kitchens in the winter to save them the trouble."

Rory nodded, and then said, "'Twill be good for the men to be able to sleep the night through without worry of someone attacking too."

His words made her glance around at the other men. If they had been flagging while she slept, they were all alert and appeared happy at the moment. No doubt they too were looking forward to sleeping in a bed, if not the prospect of a bath.

Recalling the fact that they hadn't been able to stay at an inn in Carlisle, she asked with concern, "Will an inn take us?"

"O' course, lass. We're in Scotland now. They'd no' turn us away," he said with a grin.

"Aye, but what about Tom, Simon and I?" she asked with concern.

"Ye're all wearing the plaid, lass. They'll take ye," he assured her.

THEIR RECEPTION AT THE INN WAS NOTHING LIKE THEIR EXPERI-ence at the alehouse in Carlisle their first night. They'd obviously dragged the innkeeper from his bed, but once he heard they had nine horses that needed stabling, and wanted four rooms, as well as food and drink for nine, the man perked right up. Suddenly beaming and full of good cheer, he ushered them into a large front room with three long trestle tables in it. While they seated themselves at the center table, he rushed off, disappearing through a door at the back of the room, promising to return quickly.

Weary smiles were shared around the table as they heard the man bellowing for everyone to get up. "We have guests!"

"Definitely a friendlier reception than in Carlisle," Tom said with a wry smile.

"Aye," Elysande agreed, thinking this made her even more embarrassed by how Rory and his men had at first been treated in the English city.

Sighing, she glanced around at the men, and then stopped and looked them over again. "Where are Simon and Fearghas?"

"They waited with the horses for the stable lad to come take them," Rory answered. "They'll be along shortly."

"Oh." Elysande nodded and relaxed. Rory and Alick had ushered her inside with most of the men following. She hadn't noticed that anyone had remained behind, but should have realized they would.

The innkeeper returned then, followed by a young woman, both of them bearing ale and assuring them food would follow quickly. Surprisingly it wasn't long after that before food actually did start arriving: bread, cheese, sausages, pottage and even warmed-up cottage pie, followed by pear and custard tarts, gingerbread, crispels, which were round pastries basted with honey, as well as an almond-filled pastry baked in honey and wine that made Elysande moan when she tasted it.

"The sweets are the reason we come here," Rory said with amusement as he watched her try one after the other.

"I can see why. I think I should like to live here forever," she announced.

The men chuckled at the claim, but were too busy gobbling up the delicious desserts to comment.

As they were finishing their meal, the innkeeper appeared and moved to Rory to bend and whisper in his ear. Elysande heard him murmur his thanks and saw him slip the man a couple of coins and wondered what it was about. It wasn't long after that though that he asked if everyone had had their fill and was ready to retire. Elysande wasn't surprised by the round of ayes in answer. They'd ridden hard all day and part of the night, and now that they'd eaten, the men were no doubt beginning to feel their lack of sleep from the night before.

Rory escorted her from the room and up a set of stairs to the second floor. He stopped at the third door along the narrow hall, and opened it, announcing, "Fearghas and Donnghail, ye're in here."

Elysande glimpsed a double bed and a table with a water basin and ewer on it and then Rory urged her along as Fearghas and Donnghail went into their room.

The next room was for Conn and Inan, and Elysande watched them slip into the room with a small frown. There were only two rooms left and four men plus her still in need of a bed. Her frown only grew when Rory opened the third door and announced it was for Alick and Simon. But now Simon and Tom were frowning too.

"Er . . ." Elysande began, even as Simon asked with concern, "Where is my lady sleeping?"

"In the next room along the hall with Tom and I to guard her," Rory answered.

Simon relaxed, but now Elysande was scowling. "There is no need to guard me here, my lord. I am sure I will be fine. You and Tom should not have to give up your chance to sleep in a bed just to guard me."

"We'll be sleeping too," he assured her, urging her along the hall. "And I managed to convince the innkeeper to drag up his personal tub and have a bath prepared fer ye too, as I promised. 'Tis waiting."

"Oh, aye, a bath." She sighed the words, forgetting her worry about the men sleeping on a pallet for the moment at the thought of sinking into silky, hot water. "Oh!" She stopped and whirled suddenly to glance between Tom, who was a step behind her, and Simon, who was still loitering in the door to the room he was to share with Alick.

"My bags," she said. "I will need clean clothes after I bathe."

"I left them on the horse," Simon realized, and headed for the stairs, saying, "I will go fetch them and bring them to you, m'lady."

"Thank you," Elysande called out, and then turned to Rory and allowed him to walk her to the next door. Her mind was already on the pleasure of a hot bath to wash away her stench, as well as clean, fresh-smelling clothes to wear after and a warm, comfortable bed to sleep in. It all sounded like heaven after sleeping on the cold, hard ground and in a stable. Although, to be fair, the stable hadn't been that bad. The hay under the fur had made it quite comfortable, and with the body heat of the horses and men, it had actually been warm, or at least not cold.

Elysande's thoughts fled when Rory opened the door and urged her into her room. Not only was a large tub full of steaming water waiting, but there was a hearth in this room that she was sure she hadn't seen in the others, and a fire was burning merrily in it, making the room warm and cozy.

"Oh," she breathed, moving quickly to the fire and sticking her hands out to warm them.

"I thought ye'd like that," Rory said, and she could hear the smile in his voice. "'Tis the only bedchamber in the inn with its own hearth. It's above the hearth in the taproom below, so shares the chimney."

Elysande smiled and surveyed the room, noting that the bed was a little bigger than the ones she'd spotted through the doors of the other rooms, and the room itself seemed larger too. She suspected the bedchamber cost more than the others as well. And Rory had paid for it, she realized, as well as the other rooms.

"My mother sent coin with me. I can help pay for our stay here," she offered.

"I do no' need yer coin, lass," he assured her solemnly, and then moved to the tub to test the temperature. Nodding with satisfaction, he straightened and said, "Tom and I'll leave ye be to enjoy yer bath. We'll collect the bags from Simon when he brings them and I'll set them inside the door fer ye to fetch when ye're done. Enjoy."

Elysande was so eager to get in the bath that she was removing her cloak and plaid as Rory and Tom walked to the door. A bare moment after it closed behind them, the rest of her clothes lay in a haphazard mess on the floor and she was sinking into the tub. It wasn't as large and deep as her own tub at Kynardersley, but was still lovely and Elysande leaned her head back on the rim and closed her eyes for several minutes, just enjoying the warmth enveloping her before sitting up to reach for the soap and small scrap of linen that had been left on a chair near the tub. She set to work at cleaning her hair and body.

Once she got to work, Elysande was quick about it. Not because she wouldn't have liked to soak for a bit and let the water soothe her back muscles, but because she knew Rory and Tom were no doubt exhausted and desperate for sleep.

That thought made her glance around for the pallets they would need to sleep on, but she didn't see any and supposed one of them was probably collecting them while the other stood in the hall and guarded the door. That thought made her worry that Rory intended for he and Tom to sleep out there in the hall outside the door to guard her, which wouldn't do at all. They could sleep in front of the door if they liked, but it would be inside the room where they could at least enjoy the benefits of the fire.

Aye, Elysande decided. She would be most firm with them about that. It was bad enough they weren't going to get to sleep in a bed like the rest of the men and herself. She wouldn't have them out in the cold hall too.

Determined that she was going to have her way in this matter, Elysande finished her bath, dried off using the linen that had also been left on the chair and then just stood there uncertainly when she realized she had no clean clothes to put on. Rory had said he'd set them inside the door when Simon brought them, but that hadn't happened yet. She'd obviously been quicker about her bath than she'd realized, Elysande thought, and almost sank back into the tub to enjoy it a little longer. But that would mean drying off again, and—

Her thoughts died on an alarmed squeak, and she scrambled to cover herself with the linen when the door opened. She needn't have bothered. The door opened on the side opposite her, and only enough for Rory to slide the bags in.

"Yer bags, love," he said, and then pulled the door closed.

Still clutching the linen to her, Elysande hurried to collect the bags and set them on the bed. She found a clean tunic and pulled that on, and then donned clean breeches as well. She picked which dress she'd wear next, a white-and-blue creation she liked a great deal, but Elysande didn't put it on. She simply laid it over the chair the soap and linen had been on by the tub. It was terribly wrinkled from traveling in the bag and she was hoping they would fall out by morning. Besides, she was decently covered in the tunic and breeches, and it would be more comfortable for sleeping if she didn't have lengths of skirt beneath her.

Setting the bags on the floor against the wall beside the bedside table, she gathered her dirty clothes, folded them quickly and set them next to the bags to go through later. The coin and messages her mother had sent with her were still in pockets sewn into the lining of her skirts. She'd have to transfer them to the clean gown in the morning, Elysande thought as she picked up the brush she'd retrieved from the bag earlier and sat on the bed. Walking to the fire, she stood in front of it while she quickly brushed her hair to get the tangles out, and then set the brush on the bedside table and went to open the door.

Chapter 12

RORY WAS ALONE IN THE HALL, LEANING AGAINST THE WALL, when Elysande opened the door. He looked to her to be half-asleep, but straightened with a start when she asked, "Where is Tom?"

"He went below to have a drink with Simon. I'm to call him after I've applied the liniment to yer back."

"Oh, aye . . . the liniment," Elysande murmured, and backed into the room when he started forward. While he stopped to push it closed, Elysande kept backing up until her legs bumped up against the bed. She bit her lip and glanced toward the bed and then the bags where the liniment was. Instead of going to get it though, she blurted, "The bath seems to have eased my aches and pains. Mayhap I could do without the liniment tonight."

Rory tilted his head and eyed her with concern before saying, "Are ye afraid o' me, lass?"

"What?" she asked with surprise. "Nay, of course not. Why would you think that?"

"Because ye're wringing yer hands and looking like ye're ready to bolt fer the door the minute I move away from it," he said gently.

Elysande glanced down at her hands to see she was indeed wringing them, and immediately let them drop to her sides. "Nay. I just . . ." She paused to try to sort out why she was suddenly so skittish and then sighed as she realized it was the bedchamber. They were alone in a bedchamber, with a bed . . . which wasn't proper at all. And after what had happened in the woods the last time he'd put liniment on her . . .

A little shiver slid through her as Elysande recalled the pleasure she'd experienced before they'd been interrupted. And that was the problem, she realized. She had enjoyed it, and would like to enjoy it again, but it was so wrong. Circumstances may have forced her to travel alone with eight men who were neither related nor married to her, but there had seemed little choice in the matter. That would be accepted or not by people, but she, God and her mother knew it had been out of necessity. However, if he started kissing and touching her again and she gave in to it—and she would give in to it, Elysande knew—then that would be her shame to carry.

She couldn't say all of that to Rory though. At least, not without possibly dying of embarrassment, so she said, "I would rather not use the liniment tonight."

"Lass, dawn is no' far off. I'm tired and planning to sleep until the nooning tomorrow. I would rather no' be woken in the middle o' me sleep because ye refused to allow me to put liniment on now."

Elysande chewed her lip a bit more and then said, "Well, then mayhap we should have Tom up here while ye put the liniment on. 'Twould be more proper."

That had his eyes widening incredulously. "Tom up here seeing ye half-naked would be more proper?"

"Nay. Not to watch. He could keep his face to the wall while you did it, but his presence would ensure . . ."

When she paused, blushing, he narrowed his eyes and then scowled and finished for her, "To ensure I behave? Ye think I'd take advantage o'—"

"Nay. So I behave," Elysande countered quickly, and felt her face go up in flames. She'd only blurted the truth because he appeared to be taking offense and she hadn't meant for that to happen. But the moment the truth left her mouth, she wished she could call her words back.

"What?" Rory asked with a combination of wonder and the beginnings of a suspiciously pleased smile.

Since she'd already humiliated herself, Elysande gave up on saving her pride in favor of saving her virtue instead, but she wasn't happy doing it. In fact, she clucked her tongue with irritation before saying, "My lord, I am sure you are aware that you are a very handsome man. You are also a highly intelligent and an exceptionally skilled healer. But as skilled as you are there, you are even more skilled in the arts of the bedchamber of the woods."

"The bedchamber of the woods?" he queried with a crooked smile.

"I thought it sounded better than at the art of tossing up a lady's skirt in the woods," Elysande snapped, annoyed that he would tease her for her choice of words when she was admitting to something so embarrassing.

"Ye were no' wearing yer skirts, lass," Rory said, his voice husky. "As I recall, ye were no' wearing anything at all. There was no tossing up. Just darkness and yer warm body and soft cries."

Elysande's flush deepened and she was quite sure the room was growing overwarm from the fire, but she ignored that and struggled on. "The point, my lord, is that you are so damnably skilled in the arts of loving that were you to try them on me again here, I fear I would happily throw off my clothes and toss my maidenhead at you like flower petals before the king." She frowned at him as she said that because she was sure it was all his fault, and then she added accusatorially, "And you smell good even though you have not bathed since I met you, which is, frankly, just unfair."

When Rory bowed his head briefly, her gaze narrowed on him. Elysande was quite sure he did it to hide his amusement from her, because she'd spotted his lips twitching just as he lowered his head. However, she couldn't be sure, and when he lifted his head again, his expression was solemn.

"Lass, I am verra pleased ye find me attractive, like me smell and find me attentions pleasing, for I feel the same way about you," Rory assured her, and then scowled and said, "What?" when she rolled her eyes at the claim.

"My lord, only a blind man could be attracted to me at the moment with my face swollen and lumpy like a black mass is grow-ing out of it," she pointed out dryly.

"The swelling is gone, and the black has faded to red like a wine stain on yer cheek. It does no' hide that ye're a pretty lass," he said firmly. "Besides, there is more to ye than just yer pretty face. And do ye really think I'd have acted like such a rutting bull if I did no' find ye attractive?"

Elysande considered his words and then shrugged unhap-pily. "My mother did say there were men who so enjoyed mating they'd bed a sheep or old crone, 'twas all the same to them."

Rory's jaw dropped, and then he shook his head with disgust. "I am no' one o' those men," he assured her grimly. "I find ye at-tractive, lass, and usually smart and kind, though I do wish ye'd show yerself some o' that kindness now, fer I've never met a lass so cruel to herself."

When Elysande didn't say anything, he sighed wearily.

"Me point is this. Ye need no' fear tossing yer maidenhead at me, because while I find ye attractive I'm too damned tired right now to accept it," Rory assured her. "Now take yer tunic off and turn around so I can spread the liniment on and we can get some sleep."

Elysande didn't know if it was his irritation, his commanding attitude or the exhaustion now plain to see on his face, but she stopped arguing, and spun away to tug her tunic off.

"Where's the liniment?" Rory asked testily.

"In the middle bag against the wall," she answered without looking around, and heard him cross the room. A moment later he was stomping back to smear the cool liniment over her back.

"The bruising is red and green here too now," he said grudg-ingly as he worked.

She gave a half shrug. "It no longer hurts to touch, but my muscles still ache back there. I think de Buci's man damaged them."

"Most like," he muttered. "Damaged muscles can take weeks to heal with rest. Riding as we have been will just slow the healing."

"I can rest after we get to Sinclair and send the message to the king," she said, straightening her shoulders determinedly.

Rory merely grunted and then fell silent as he finished covering her back and side with the liniment, massaging it quickly and impersonally into the skin.

"Put yer tunic on and get in bed," he ordered when he'd finished.

Elysande heard him cross the room to replace the liniment as she shook out the tunic she'd been clutching and pulled it over her head. When her head popped through the neck hole and she opened her eyes, he was standing in front of her.

"Ye *are* beautiful," he said firmly, and then kissed her. It was a quick brushing of lips, followed by a slower melding that had her melting against him before he ended it. Easing her away then, Rory sighed and said, "Get into bed, lass. I'll go tell Tom he can come up."

Nodding, she just stood there and watched him leave the room, then turned and walked over to crawl under the furs on the bed. Elysande settled on her side in the middle of the bed, her fingers rubbing over lips that were warm, wet and swollen . . . and still tingling from contact with his.

RORY WOKE FEELING WARM, WELL RESTED AND REASONABLY content, but like something was missing again. It took him a full minute to realize that what was missing was the warm weight of Elysande on his shoulder, chest and legs. Blinking his eyes open, he glanced to the side, and then sat up abruptly when he realized he was the only one abed.

Rory frowned when he spotted Tom sitting in the chair beside the tub of bathwater from the night before. The English soldier was also eyeing him expectantly and a little resentfully.

"Where is she?" Rory growled in a voice raspy with sleep.

"Gone to the shops with Alick and Simon. She wouldn't let me go," Tom added, his tone testy. "She said she needed to get more of those weeds the two of you are so fond of. She said her liniment was running low."

"Aye." Rory ran a hand wearily over his face. "'Tis. I noticed last night when I was putting it on her."

When Tom gave a "hrrumph" of sound, Rory narrowed his eyes on the man. "What?"

"She was most upset when she woke this morning to find us all abed," Tom announced, before adding with satisfaction, "As I told you she would be."

"What?" he asked with a frown. "Why? We slept the same last night as we have every night since I agreed to escort ye to Sinclair, you at her back, and me in front of her. The only thing missing was Alick above her head and Simon at her feet."

"Aye," Tom agreed mildly. "Except we were in a bed."

Rory waved that away with irritation and slung his feet over the side of said bed to get up. "What difference does that make?"

Tom arched his eyebrows at the question. "We were in a bed, the three of us, in a bedchamber, in an inn where anyone, for instance a servant, might enter at any time." He let that sink in for a minute, and then added, "And did."

"What!" Rory stopped in the midst of pulling his boots on to look at him with horror. "A servant came in while we were sleeping?"

"Aye, the innkeeper's wife was wanting her tub back, and one of the maids came up to see if it was all right to take it," he explained.

Rory's gaze swiveled to the full tub still sitting there as he finished pulling on his boots.

"Lady Elysande scared the lass off with her shrieking when she woke to find herself abed with the both of us," Tom explained dryly. "She bellowed at me, called me Judas and then said if the lass returned to let her take the tub. Since her shrieking hadn't woken you, she did not think anything would. However, the maid has not returned."

"Hmm." Rory stared at the tub, and shrugged. "Elysande must have given her a good scare with her yelling."

Tom's mouth compressed with irritation. "Frankly, I am amazed that she did not wake up the whole inn. But you and your men appeared to have no trouble sleeping through it. Which is rather concerning since you are supposed to be helping us protect her," he added with an unimpressed look.

"It must've been an angry shrieking," Rory said with confidence. "No' one o' us would have slept through a frightened cry, but camp followers are always fighting among each other and shrieking angrily. We learned to sleep through that."

"Oh, aye," Tom said with a nod of sudden understanding. "I should have realized. I can usually sleep through angry shouting too," he admitted, and then added under his breath, "When someone isn't trampling over me to get out of bed at the ass crack of dawn, shrieking Judas at me."

Rory gave the man a sympathetic smile and suggested, "Why do ye no' crawl back into bed and get more rest? I have business to attend to here and we'll no' be leaving until the morrow."

Tom shook his head and stood up. "I went back to sleep after she left with Simon and Alick. I only woke up again a short while ago. I was just waiting for you to wake before going down to break my fast."

"That sounds like a good idea," Rory said, running his hands through his hair as he headed for the door.

They passed a maid coming up the stairs as they were going down, and Rory stopped to tell her the room was empty and the tub could be removed now. The way the girl barely nodded and scampered away made him think that she must have been the one who had come in search of the tub that morning. "Elysande must have really given the lass a fright with her shrieking this morning."

Tom shook his head. "I suspect it was the innkeeper giving her hell for waking us up at all that really has her on her back foot. He came up the hall as she backed out of the room to Elysande's shrieking and I think the innkeeper misunderstood what had upset Elysande. He promptly grabbed the girl by the hair, tugged the door closed, and we could hear him berating her all the way back down the hall. He was not pleased that she would trouble paying customers as *'fine as the Buchanans.'*" Tom arched his eyebrows as he said that.

"Aye, we come here a lot. No' just me, but other members o' me family too. As I told Elysande last night, the sweets keep bringing us back. But so does the service. They always find room fer us, and always treat us well. Probably because there are so many o' us and one o' us is often stopping in. Dougall used to stop in on his way to deliver the horses he bred, Niels used to stop in a lot on his way to deliver hunting dogs, or cloth from his sheep. I stop in on me way to or from tending the ill . . ." He shrugged. "Over the years we've given them a lot o' business."

Tom nodded, but didn't comment as they entered the taproom and settled at a table. Instead, he glanced around at a lone customer at another table, and noted, "They do not appear to be very busy."

"Angus said they just had a large party leave the morning ere we arrived." He gave a shrug and added, "The Gordons on their way north to marry a daughter off to Campbell's second son or some such thing. He said he was turning people away while they were here, and then as soon as they left, no one came until we showed up." Rory smiled at the English soldier. "Good luck fer us."

"Aye," Tom agreed with a faint smile.

"Ye said Alick and Simon went with Elysande?" Rory asked suddenly.

"Aye."

"Where are the other men?"

"Sleeping, last I knew," Tom said. "They'll probably wake soon and wander down."

Rory nodded as Angus rushed up to see what they'd like. They had just asked for drinks and a serving each of whatever the innkeeper's wife was offering for the nooning when the front door of the establishment crashed open. Both men glanced toward the doorway to the hall in time to see Alick rush past carrying a protesting Elysande in his arms.

Cursing, Rory leapt to his feet to hurry after them, aware that Tom was following on his heels. They rushed out into the hall together, nearly running over Simon as he closed the door and turned to follow Alick.

Pushing the English soldier aside, Rory hurried up the stairs, catching up to Alick in the upper hall between the second and third bedchamber.

"What happened?" he growled, trying to get a look at Elysande over his brother's shoulder.

Alick came to a halt in front of the third door and faced him with a flushed and exasperated Elysande in his arms.

"Nothing," Elysande snapped as Alick opened his mouth to answer.

"It was no' nothing!" Alick barked, his usual good cheer missing and a glare in its place that he directed at Elysande. "Nothing would no' scare the life out o' me!"

"What happened?" Rory repeated grimly, his gaze shifting to the side when the door Alick had stopped in front of opened and Fearghas and Donnghail stepped out. Even as he noted that, Conn and Inan's door opened and they came out into the hall to see what was going on too. They'd apparently woken the men with their raised voices.

Alick tore his glare from Elysande and shook his head as he admitted tersely, "I do no' ken. We were on our way back from the shops. I was walking in front, and Elysande was behind me with Simon at her back. I heard her cry out, and Simon shout, 'M'lady!' and I swung around in time to see her fall into the street in front o' a moving horse and cart." His face went pale with the memory. "I could no' catch her in time to stop her fall. I thought sure she was done fer. Fortunately, the horse reared, trying to avoid her, and she rolled away before it came back down, but . . ."

Alick didn't have to say more, the expression on his face told Rory his younger brother was feeling like he'd failed in protecting the lass, and had probably been mentally berating himself all the way back to the inn.

"I am fine," Elysande said on a sigh. "There was no need for you to scoop me up and run through the streets like a madman to get me back here."

"Ye're no' fine. Ye've sustained an injury," Alick said grimly. "And o' course I rushed ye back here. We needed to get ye somewhere safe ere something else happened. 'Tis obvious de Buci's men trailed us here."

"De Buci's men?" Elysande asked with surprise. "What have they to do with this?"

"It must have been one o' them who pushed ye into the street. No one else wants ye dead, do they?" Alick pointed out with exasperation, and then assured her apologetically, "I was keeping an eye out fer them, but one must have slipped past me to push ye."

Elysande was shaking her head before he'd finished speaking. "Nay, there were no Englishmen around us when it happened, just a group of drunken Scots weaving about. I am sure 'twas an accident. One of them probably lost their balance and accidentally bumped me into the road."

When Alick frowned, and looked uncertain, Rory turned to Simon. "Was she pushed or was she bumped by accident?"

"I did not see," the English soldier admitted unhappily. "I was watching for threats, looking for any sign of de Buci's men or Englishmen in general. Then, like Alick, I heard her cry out and looked down in time to see her fall into the street." He hesitated briefly, and then added, "But my lady is right, we were passing a group of drunken men when it happened."

"Aye. I'd just passed them before she cried out," Alick recalled, and then looked uncertain. "They were sailors and fair fou. Mayhap one o' them *did* stumble into her by accident."

"There, you see. 'Twas an accident. I am fine. All is well. Now put me down," Elysande demanded impatiently.

"I'm no' putting ye down till I have somewhere to put ye." Alick scowled at her. "It may have been just an accident, but ye were still hurt. We helped ye up, and ye promptly fell right back into the muck o' the road with a moan o' pain."

"I twisted my ankle when I fell," Elysande responded on a sigh. "When I put weight on it, it hurt and gave out, is all. But truly, I am sure 'tis fine now," she repeated, and then snapped, "My lord!" with outrage and lunged upright in Alick's arms to slap at Rory's hands when he lifted her skirts to peer at her lower legs.

"I have to examine it," he said firmly, but released her skirts and gestured toward the room they'd slept in last night. "Take her to our room and I'll examine her there."

"Nay!" Elysande squawked when Alick continued up the hall. "'Tis not proper to have a bunch of men in *my* bedchamber." She was glaring daggers over Alick's shoulder at Rory as she said that. Turning a kinder face to his brother, she added, "He may look at me in the taproom below where we can all have some food and drink. You did mention you were hungry just before the accident happened and now so am I. But I can walk," she added when he turned back toward the stairs. "Please put me down."

When Alick hesitated and glanced at him, Rory considered Elysande briefly and then nodded.

He didn't miss Elysande's little sigh of relief when Alick released her legs so she could stand on her own. He also didn't miss her gasp of pain and the way she wobbled when she tried to put weight on the injured ankle. Alick caught her arm at once and then stepped back when Rory scooped her up.

"Ye're injured," Rory said firmly when she opened her mouth in protest. "Stop being so bloody stubborn and accept help when 'tis offered."

"I am not stubborn," she said with irritation as he started down the stairs. "And I have been accepting help. Are you not escorting us to Sinclair? And did I not let you put liniment on my injuries?" She nodded grimly. "Aye, and just look where it has landed me. You took liberties, crawled into my bed, and now my reputation is in ruins," she complained.

"I did no' take liberties," Rory said with dismay, and then frowned as he realized that yes, he had . . . though not last night in the bed. Scowling at his own thoughts, he said defensively, "Tom was there last night too."

"Aye, the Judas," she growled, glaring over his shoulder, probably at Tom, he supposed. "And his being there just makes it look worse."

"Lass, ye've slept between us every night since we met in the wood outside Monmouth and I accepted the request to be yer escort," he said firmly.

"That was in the cold dark woods, my lord. We were all fully clothed and bundled in our own cloaks and plaids, not the bed of an inn."

"We were all still fully clothed last night, and ye were under the furs while Tom and I were above them," he pointed out, feeling righteous.

"You were not," she denied hotly. "You were under the furs with me."

"I was no'," Rory denied vehemently. He distinctly remembered curling up on top of the furs next to her. The first thing he'd done after returning to the room with Tom was take advantage of the still-warm bath and bathe himself. It had left him a bit chilled when he'd got out and he'd approached the bed thinking it would have been nice to crawl under the furs with her to warm up. But he hadn't. He'd curled up in his plaid on top of the furs and shivered himself to sleep.

A soft "ahem" made him pause on the bottom step and glance back. Tom was directly behind them with the other men filling the stairs behind him, Rory noted, and then tilted his head back to focus on Tom, who had one eyebrow raised. The man shook his head once their eyes met, and told him, "You were under the furs with her this morning and she was plastered to your chest as usual when the maid arrived."

"See! I told you," Elysande said at once, and then sighed unhappily. "Why could you not have slept on a pallet? Or just told me you planned to use the bed, then I could have used a pallet. Now I am ruined."

Rory frowned at her desolate tone and then heaved a sigh and stepped off the stairs and carried her into the taproom. Angus was standing by the table he and Tom had been seated at earlier, two drinks in hand and uncertainty on his face, but he brightened when he saw them returning and set down the drinks. "Yer food'll be right out."

"Good. Thank ye, Angus. I suspect Elysande and the others will be wanting food and drink now as well," he said. And when the innkeeper smiled widely and started to head back to the kitchens, Rory called out impulsively, "Angus?"

The innkeeper turned back at once, one eyebrow raised in question.

"We were so tired when we rode in last night, I do no' believe I introduced ye to me wife." He nodded to Elysande in his arms and said, "Lass, this is Angus, the finest innkeeper in Scotland. Angus, this is me wife, Lady Elysande Buchanan."

"Oh, ho!" A broad grin claimed Angus's face. "Finally found the right lass to settle down with, did ye?" he asked. "Lady Jetta and yer sister must be well pleased."

"Aye," Rory agreed as he squeezed Elysande in warning. She'd stiffened against him at his words, but now quickly changed her expression from shock to a poor attempt at a smile as Angus bowed to her.

"'Tis a pleasure, m'lady," the innkeeper said sincerely as he straightened. "Ye've a good man there. The finest healer in all of Scotland."

Rory was just puffing up a bit at the words when Elysande said, "So I have heard. However, I am more in need of his other talents, so let us hope they are just as fine."

Rory knew she was referring to his sword arm and escorting her safely to Sinclair, but Angus had no idea she would need either and his eyes twinkled with wicked merriment as he gave her a wink and said, "Well, I'm sure he'll no' let ye down there, m'lady. Now I'll fetch drinks fer the rest o' ye, and see about food as well, shall I?"

A chorus of ayes from the men was enough to send him on his way. The moment he was gone, Elysande asked Rory, "What talents did he think I was referring to? It was not your sword arm, was it? And why on earth did you tell him we were married?"

"To save your reputation," he answered the last question, happy to use it as an excuse to avoid the first two.

"How does claiming me as your wife save my reputation?" she asked with surprise as he set her down sideways on the bench, with her legs out.

"It excuses me presence in yer bed," he pointed out.

"Aye. But not Tom's," she pointed out with exasperation. "And besides, once he learns you lied— What are you doing?" she gasped, trying to snatch her legs away when he started to push her skirts up to her knees.

Rory grabbed her legs by the calves to hold them in place. "Settle. Ye're wearing breeks. 'Tis fine. Now, which ankle did ye hurt?" he asked, ignoring her outrage.

"The right one, but 'tis fine, I—" She broke off on a squawk when Rory took her foot in hand and pushed the bottom of her breeks up to get a look at her ankle. She fell silent though when she saw how swollen it was, and that it was beginning to bruise. When he pressed a thumb into the swelling, she drew in a hissing breath and clenched her hands.

Rory took his thumb away and noted the imprint left behind, and then glanced to Tom. "There should be strips of linen in my medicinals bag. Fetch them for me, please."

The man nodded and rushed away at once.

"You are going to bind it," Elysande guessed with a sigh.

"Aye. 'Twill help keep the swelling down," he murmured, twisting his head one way and then the other to see as much of the injury as he could. Once he was finished, he set her foot back on the bench and said, "Ye'll have to rest it and keep it elevated as much as possible."

"I can hardly rest it and keep it elevated on a horse, my lord," Elysande pointed out with irritation. "Resting it will have to wait until we reach Sinclair."

"Then 'tis a good thing we are staying another day so ye can at least rest it until then," Rory muttered, and then glanced to the doorway as he heard Tom pounding down the stairs. A moment later the Englishman was rushing into the room with the requested linen.

Rory bound Elysande's foot firmly, but not too tight. He didn't want to restrict the blood flow too much. By the time he'd finished, Angus had delivered drinks for everyone else at the table, and the food was now showing up. Elysande tried to twist around on the bench to sit properly to make room for the rest of the men to join them, but Rory held on to her foot, and reminded her, "Ye should keep it elevated."

"How can I keep it elevat—" Her voice died as he collected her other foot as well, shifted from straddling the bench to sit on it properly and then lifted both her legs and slid toward her on the bench, before setting them down in his lap. He knew it was awkward for her to sit like that, but Elysande didn't complain or try to remove her feet again; she merely twisted her upper body to face the table and began to eat when one of the maids set food in front of her. But she didn't join in the conversation he and the men had about the weather and how long they thought it would take to reach Sinclair while they ate.

"I need to go above stairs and make more liniment."

Rory glanced to Elysande at that announcement and then started to get out from under her feet, intending to pick her up, but she scowled and said, "I would rather go alone. I am guessing you have business to take care of here anyway, else we'd be leaving today."

Rory met her gaze, his own eyes slightly widened with surprise, but in the end he nodded as he stood. "Aye. I do. But I'll carry ye up first, and then Simon and Alick can guard the door," he added, his gaze sliding to his brother and the English soldier.

"I can stand guard with Simon," Tom said, getting up as well.

"Nay. Simon and Alick will do fine," Elysande said at once, scowling at the man. She was obviously still annoyed about the sleeping arrangements from the night before, Rory supposed, and gave him a sympathetic look as he bent to pick her up.

Elysande didn't protest, but crossed her arms and stared

straight ahead as he carried her upstairs. Rory tried to think of something to break the silence, or get her past her irritation with him, but nothing was coming to mind, so he simply carried her upstairs to the chamber, set her on the bed and headed out of the room to find Alick and Simon waiting in the hall.

"Do ye want us in the room or outside the door?" Alick asked as Rory pulled the door closed.

"Out here is fine. Ye can play dice or cards to pass the time as ye like," he suggested. "I'm taking Tom, Conn and Inan with me, but I'll tell Fearghas and Donnghail to replace ye in an hour or so if I'm no' back by then."

"Where are ye heading?" Alick asked.

"I want to go see about spare horses," Rory admitted. "'Twould speed up the journey if we had horses to switch to halfway through the day, and the sooner we get Elysande to Sinclair, the better. We need to get her mother's message to the king."

Alick nodded and said, "Good luck," as Rory headed for the stairs.

Chapter 13

$\mathcal{E}$LYSANDE WAITED A MOMENT AFTER RORY LEFT, AND THEN stood on her good foot and hopped to the bags against the wall. She dug through them until she came across the weeds for making the liniment, as well as the mortar and pestle she'd bought at the apothecary shop there. Once she had everything, she turned to glance around the room, and then called out to the men. She wasn't at all surprised when the door immediately opened and Alick stuck his head in.

"I need you two to help me," she admitted, and thought to herself, *See, I'm not too stubborn to accept help.*

"O' course." Alick pushed the door open and led Simon in. "What do ye need, m'lady?"

"Would you please move the bedside table and that chair over by the fire?" she asked, and as the men quickly moved to grab a piece of furniture each, she began hopping toward the fire with the items she'd gathered.

Cursing, Alick set down the table he'd just picked up and rushed over to grab her arm. "Ye should no' be on yer feet at all, but hopping around like that— If ye fell and hit yer head . . ." He shook his own head, and then scooped her up and set her down in the chair the moment Simon finished moving it.

Elysande bit her tongue on any protest. The man was trying to help, after all, so she remained silent and waited as Simon brought over the table.

"Thank you," she murmured the moment they were done, and then set her things on the tabletop as the men started to leave, only to blink at the items as she took them in and then squawk in alarm, "My bag!"

Alick and Simon stopped at once and turned back.

Elysande stared at them wide-eyed. "The wolfsbane and comfrey we went out to purchase. I must have dropped the bag when I fell. You rushed me away so quickly I did not realize."

The two men looked at each other, and then Alick sighed, and headed for the door.

"I'll go back and see if the bag is still there. If no', I'll purchase ye more wolfsbane and comfrey. I remember the quantities ye got the first time," he assured her, and then glanced to Simon. "I'll be as quick as I can. Stay and guard the door until I get back."

Simon nodded as he followed him out of the room.

Once they were gone, Elysande began to measure out the items she did have into the mortar. She had about half of the wolfsbane she needed, but no comfrey. She did have the willow bark and other weeds though. Once she'd added what she could to the mortar, Elysande stood on her good foot, picked up the pestle and began to grind the weeds into a fine powder. She hadn't been doing it long when she suddenly stopped and called out for Simon. The door opened at once and he stuck his head in.

"Aye, m'lady?"

Elysande smiled apologetically. "I need you to fetch a bucket of water from the well, and then see if you can borrow a pot about yea big"—she used her hands to show him what she needed—"from the kitchen. One with a handle I can hang over the fire."

Simon hesitated, and then pointed out, "I'm supposed to be guarding the door."

Elysande grimaced with irritation. "I will be perfectly fine for a few minutes, Simon. Even if de Buci's men did track us here to Ayr, they have no idea where we are staying, or what room I am in," she pointed out, and when he shifted uncertainly, she narrowed her gaze and reminded him, "I am your lady, Simon. Please do as I requested. You may tell them I ordered you to do it should Rory or anyone else find out. But I should like to get the water warming before Alick returns with the rest of the weeds."

Giving in, Simon nodded. "I'll be back as quick as I can," he said, and then warned a bit irritably, "But I will be blaming you if I get hell for this."

Elysande went back to her grinding as he pulled the door closed with a snap.

"SPARE HORSES WE COULD SWITCH TO HALFWAY THROUGH THE day would certainly speed our journey along," Tom commented with a nod, but then said solemnly, "But 'tis a large expense, and not to be indelicate, but I know you are not a first son, or even a second or third, and Lady de Valance did send coin with Lady Elysande. I think she should —"

"Ye can stop thinking," Rory interrupted solemnly. "I do have the coin fer it."

Tom's eyebrows rose slightly, but then he shrugged. "Very well, then. Do you need any help picking or collecting them?"

"Aye," Rory said, getting to his feet. "Tom, Conn and Inan with me. Fearghas and Donnghail will stay here to back up Simon and Alick." Turning to the men in question, he added, "Replace them in an hour if we are no' back by—" Rory's words died in his throat when a woman's scream rang out from the upper floor.

Rory recognized it as Elysande's voice and was moving before he quite realized it. Racing out into the hall, he charged up the stairs, vaguely aware that the men were hard on his heels. As he reached the top step, Rory spotted Simon just rushing into the bedchamber where he'd left Elysande. It was a couple of steps later that his brain recognized that the English soldier had carried a bucket and pot, one dangling from each hand by its handle, and water had been slopping out of one or the other as he'd hurried forward.

"M'lady!"

That alarmed shout from Simon made Rory's blood run cold, and while he was moving so fast that his feet seemed hardly to touch the floor, it still felt like it took forever for him to get to the room. He tripped over something inside the door as he rushed in, and glanced down to see the pot Simon had been carrying skitter away across the floor, and then his gaze found Elysande and everything else was forgotten. She lay splayed on the floor in much the same position he found her every morning—partially on her side, and partially on her stomach, her arm and leg thrown out as they usually rested over him—but he wasn't there and now her hand was in the ashes at the front of the fireplace. Even more alarming than that though was the blood seeping out from under Elysande's body.

Simon was kneeling next to Elysande. As Rory reached them, the soldier caught her shoulder and turned her onto her back, pulling her hand out of the fire. Rory wanted to look at her hand and see if she'd been burned, and if so, how badly, but as he squatted across her from Simon, his gaze was transfixed by the dagger sticking out of her chest and the wound bleeding freely on her forehead.

Rory's heart was pounding a wild tattoo in his chest. He was a healer, used to seeing the injured and the ill. He was usually the calm one when it came to such situations, but seeing Elysande like this, so helpless and pale, made his gorge rise up his throat.

"I was only gone for a minute," Simon muttered with what sounded like dismay. Shaking his head, he then asked anxiously, "Is she dead?"

The question galvanized Rory into action. Bending, he pressed his head to her chest briefly, and then picked her up.

"Is she dead?" Simon repeated, straightening to follow him.

"Not yet," Rory said grimly, and carried her to the bed, barking orders as he went. "I need water, clean linens and my medicinals. Now!"

Vaguely aware that the men were suddenly running every which way, Rory laid Elysande on the bed and then glanced around, his gaze landing on the open window shutters, before continuing on in search of his brother . . .

"Where is Alick?" he asked sharply.

"He went to get Lady Elysande's weeds," Simon answered, rushing forward with the bucket he'd left by the door. "She dropped them when she fell and only realized it when we got up here."

Rory's mouth tightened at this news, but his gaze lowered to the bucket the man was holding out. There was water in it, but not a lot. Rory was guessing there was more of it on the floor by the door than remained inside, but there was enough for him to at least start on washing away the blood, he thought, his gaze moving to the knife in Elysande's chest. He couldn't remove it until he had linens to staunch the bleeding with and—

Turning abruptly as his mind processed Simon's words and he recalled seeing him enter the room with the bucket and pot, he asked sharply, "Neither one o' ye was guarding the door?"

"She ordered me to fetch her water and a pot to make her liniment with. She *ordered* me," he repeated helplessly, still holding out the bucket.

Rory's mouth tightened, but he made a mental note to himself that if Elysande survived, he would make sure he left only his men to guard her in the future. Men she couldn't order away, he thought, and told him, "Set the bucket on the bedside table."

"Here." Tom was beside him, holding out fresh linens and Rory's medicinal bag.

"Thank ye," he muttered, accepting both. He set the bag on the table, but held on to the linens and bent over Elysande. Now that he had the cloth, Rory didn't hesitate but yanked the dagger from her chest and quickly pressed the linens over the open wound, applying pressure as he tossed the knife on the table. He waited then, watching to see how quickly the blood would soak the linen cloth, when what he really wanted to do was look at the wound itself. Unfortunately, he had to get the bleeding to stop, or at least slow down, before he would be able to examine the wound. But it seemed to him that it was actually in her breast, not as near the heart as he'd thought. There was something hard over her heart though. He could feel it against the back of his fingers through the linen. Rory had just noted that when the bedchamber door opened and Alick entered, only to stop abruptly on the threshold.

"What on earth is all over the floor? Is that wolfsbane? Christ, that's poisonous. What—" When Alick's question ended on a curse, Rory guessed he'd either spotted the blood by the hearth, or the men gathered around the bed, or both. But Rory was more concerned with what Alick had said, and glanced at the floor by the fireplace, noting only then that Elysande's mortar lay on the wood, its contents spilled in a wide starburst that now had boot prints all through it.

"Do no' come any farther into the room," he warned Alick, and then turned to Elysande, searching for any sign that the powder might have gotten in either of her wounds. If it had, she was as good as dead. Fortunately, he didn't see any of the powder on her face or the front of her dress. Thank God. She must have fallen just outside the starburst of powder.

Able to breathe now that he saw no sign of the poison on her, Rory glanced to his brother again. "Ye need to go get a broom. The wolfsbane needs to be swept up so we do no' traipse it throughout the inn."

Nodding, Alick backed out of the room at once and closed the door.

Rory shifted his attention to the men then, his gaze sliding over their footwear. "When he brings the broom back ye'll need to brush off the bottoms of yer boots, and do it well. Mayhap even go rinse them off outside too. Use a bucket and do it far from the horse trough or any other water source."

"Surely wolfsbane is not that poisonous?" Tom asked with concern.

"If ye take yer boots off, get any on yer hand and raise it to yer mouth without thinking and swallow some, ye'll die. Or if ye've a wound on yer hand and it gets into that, ye'll die too," he said grimly. "That's how poisonous it is. Ye want to make sure 'tis off yer boots ere ye touch them."

"Jesus," Tom breathed with dismay. "And Lady Elysande has been rubbing it on her bruises?"

"What she's been using is no' full strength," Rory explained, and then glanced to the door when it opened again. Much to his relief it was Alick back with a broom. "Give it to Simon, Alick, and go fetch some whiskey from Angus. I need to clean Elysande's wound before I sew it closed."

Alick was gone almost before he finished speaking, and Rory said to the other men, "I need the room. But ye canno' leave until Simon's brushed any wolfsbane from yer boots. I will no' have ye dragging this out into the hall and possibly poisoning one o' the maids or another guest." Shifting his gaze fully to Simon, he added, "Be thorough."

He waited long enough to see Simon nod and then turned his attention back to Elysande.

The head wound wasn't too bad, he noted. In fact, it had already stopped bleeding. The chest wound had him more concerned. Although now that he had pressure on it, the bleeding there had slowed a great deal as well. The linen was bloody where he pressed it to the wound, but hadn't leaked up through the bunched-up cloth to his fingers yet. That was good . . . and unexpected for such a serious injury. Daggers had to be driven deep for them to stay in. She really should be bleeding more, he thought, and then glanced toward the door, wishing Alick would hurry.

When his gaze landed on the men and he noted that half of them were already gone, he watched to be sure Simon was being careful to get the men's boots clean. He seemed to be, but he was also quick, Rory noted as he watched him clean off the bottoms of Conn's and Inan's boots. When he finished those last two men and started to set the broom aside, Rory ordered, "Yers too, Simon. Ye're leaving as well."

"Shouldn't I stay to help?" Simon asked with a frown.

"Nay. Tom can sweep up the floor and Alick will help me with Elysande when he returns. He's helped me before and kens what he's doing. Brush off yer boots and then go down to rinse them off. Then I need ye to get a bucket and mop and mop up the stairs and hall floor just in case any o' the powder was missed," he ordered.

Simon's gaze slid to Elysande and his mouth compressed, but he nodded and quickly brushed the bottoms of his boots. He even brushed off the top of one where a splotch of the powder marked it, before leaning the broom against the wall and leaving.

"How bad is it?" Tom asked grimly.

Rory lifted the linen slightly to check how badly Elysande was still bleeding, and frowned again when he saw how little blood there actually was.

"You're frowning. What does that mean?" Tom asked worriedly.

The door opened before Rory could answer and he glanced around to see Alick returning with the whiskey he'd sent him for.

"Avoid the powder on the floor, Alick," Rory reminded him, and then glanced to Tom and said, "Sweep up as much o' the powder as ye can while we attend to yer mistress. Ye'll have to brush the bottoms o' my boots too, and check Alick's as well, but his should be fine."

Tom hesitated, but then nodded and moved away as Alick stepped up to the bed.

"Set that on the bedside table, Alick, and then move around the bed and get yer knife out," Rory instructed when his brother stopped next to him.

"Her gown?" Alick asked as he set the whiskey down.

"Aye. We have to cut it away, straight down the middle. I do no' see any powder on her, but it may be on the side she was lying on, and might be on the bed furs. We'll have to remove both. I need a clear view o' the wound anyway."

They worked quickly and silently, Rory keeping pressure on the wound while Alick sliced away the gown to reveal a small lumpy sack that had been tucked between her breasts above the tunic and beneath the gown.

Alick grunted as he went to pick up the small cloth sack and coins spilled out of a tear in the center, falling over her chest. As he quickly gathered up the loose coins, Alick muttered, "It looks like her attacker's knife hit this and slid off into her breast rather than hit her heart."

"Aye. It may have saved her life, then," Rory said grimly, thinking Elysande had probably tucked the small pouch there to make the coins more easily accessible than they would have been in the small sack he knew was sewn into the inside of her skirts. She wouldn't have wanted to hitch up her skirts in the shops to pay.

Once Elysande's plaid, gown and tunic lay in strips around her, leaving her only in her breeks, Rory gave up applying pressure long enough to scoop her up so that Alick could roll the furs up and remove them from the bed, ruined clothes and all.

"Pull the top linen back," Rory requested when Alick straightened from laying the rolled-up fur and cloth out of the way on the floor. When his brother tugged the linen back, Rory laid Elysande down again. While Rory lifted the blood-soaked linen to check her wound, Alick moved back around the bed to the bedside table where the medicinals bag was and began digging through it for what he might need.

"Needle and thread, salve and linens. Anything else?" his brother questioned as he removed items.

"Nay. That's good," Rory assured him, glad his brother had assisted him a time or two before and knew enough about what he was doing to be helpful. "Hand me the whiskey."

"Were these shutters open when you brought Lady Elysande up?" Tom asked suddenly.

Rory took the whiskey from Alick and poured it over Elysande's wound as his brother glanced around and said, "Nay," with surprise as he noted the open shutters.

"It must be how her attacker got out, then," Tom muttered as he now closed them. They obviously weren't used much, for they squeaked loudly as he shut them. "We did not pass anyone in the hall or on the stairs as we rushed up."

"He must have got in the same way, then, because Simon was guarding the door," Alick said as Rory set the whiskey aside and began to stitch up Elysande's wound.

"Nay, he wasn't," Tom said grimly. "He was below getting water and a cooking pot for Lady Elysande."

"He left her alone?" Alick asked with shock.

"Aye," Rory growled, some of his fury seeping into his voice as he added another stitch to his work. It was only the second one, and all that was needed. The wound wasn't very big or deep. He should have realized that from the minimal bleeding, but the dagger had been sticking out of the wound when he'd first seen her, which usually meant a deep injury. Now he wondered if it hadn't gone through the coin bag partway before sliding to the side and stabbing out the other side into her breast. The coin bag itself might have been what had held the blade in place, because the depth of the wound wouldn't have done it. It hadn't gone in far enough to hold the weight there. Aye, it must have been the coin bag, Rory thought, and shook his head, marveling at how lucky she'd been.

"Simon said Lady Elysande ordered him to get the water and cooking pot," Tom pointed out unhappily. "As our lady he would have had to listen to her."

"Aye," Rory muttered as he tied off the thread and straightened to reach for the salve. "Which is why my men will be watching her from now on."

He half expected Tom to protest, so was surprised when the man nodded wearily. "That may be for the best."

A moment of silence passed and then Alick said thoughtfully, "So her attacker could ha'e come in the door and merely left through the window." Glancing from Rory to Tom, he asked, "Did ye see anyone go past the door to the taproom in the minutes ere it happened?"

"Nay," Rory said grimly. He didn't add that he hadn't even seen Alick leave. Believing Elysande was safe and guarded by Alick and Simon, Rory hadn't been watching the hall while talking to the men in the taproom. Something he berated himself for now as he smeared salve over the wound and then laid a strip of linen over it.

"No one took the stairs except Simon," Tom said with certainty. "I was watching. I would have seen." Tilting his head, he added, "I did not even see you leave."

"I took the back stairs and used the servants' entrance to leave. 'Tis closer to the stables," Alick explained, and then reasoned, "Her attacker could have come in that way. If so, he would not have had to pass the taproom."

Tom grunted at that, but then joined them by the bed and peered down at his lady with worry. "Will she live?"

Rory hesitated, his gaze shifting from Elysande to the shuttered window and then to the door as he thought. The truth was he thought she should be fine. She hadn't lost as much blood as he'd first feared, and the head wound appeared to be mild. He didn't say any of that, however. Instead, he said, "I do no' ken. She lost a lot o' blood, and head wounds can be tricky too. If she does no' catch a fever . . ." He shrugged, and then added, "The fact that she has no' woken up yet despite the pain we're causing her worries me though. 'Tis no' looking good."

Tom heaved an unhappy sigh at that, and turned to head for the door. "I'll go ask the servants if anyone saw a stranger enter from the kitchens," he decided.

"Brush yer boots off first," Rory reminded him as he reached for the linen wrappings. "And bring back a bucket of water and a mop. We'll need to clean the floor in here."

Nodding, Tom quickly brushed off the bottoms of his boots, and then tramped out.

"Help me sit her up," Rory requested, setting the linen wrappings on the side of the bed. He waited for Alick to crawl on the bed and kneel on the other side of Elysande, and then they lifted her up and Alick held her upright by the shoulders while Rory began to wrap the linen around her chest.

"Fer all the blood on the floor, it did no' look to me like the chest wound is verra deep," Alick commented after a moment.

"Nay, it is no'," Rory agreed.

"And the knife did no' hit any vital organs," he pointed out. When Rory grunted in acknowledgment, he added, "I've seen ye heal worse than this."

"Aye," Rory muttered as he worked.

"And ye're usually no' so pessimistic with family and friends," he pointed out. When Rory didn't comment, he asked, "Why are ye wanting Tom to think she's dying?"

Rory didn't respond for a long moment, and then admitted, "I do no' ken. Something's bothering me, but I ha'e no' had a chance to think what it is. I need to think about . . ." He let his words trail away as he worried over the thoughts running through his head.

"Something's bothering ye about what? Tom?" Alick asked with a frown.

"Nay." He shook his head firmly, quite sure Tom had nothing to do with what was troubling him. But something was tickling at the back of his mind. He just couldn't seem to grasp it yet and needed time to consider everything that had happened. Lifting his head, he met Alick's gaze and said, "I'm thinking 'tis best to let everyone think she's at death's door. If one o' de Buci's men is sniffing about and hears she's dying it might prevent another attempt and keep her safe until we can sort this out or get her to Buchanan."

"Buchanan?" Alick asked with surprise. "I thought we were headed to Sinclair?"

"Aye. Well, Buchanan is closer. A little more than two days' ride compared to more than two weeks to Sinclair," Rory pointed out grimly. Much as he hated to admit it, he feared he was going to fail at the task he'd promised to perform. Now, his main concern was keeping Elysande alive. "We'll never get her to Sinclair alive with de Buci's men hounding us. But we could take her to Buchanan and send a messenger to Sinclair. Then Cam could come to her at Buchanan, and take care of getting the message to the English king."

"Hmm." Alick considered that and then shook his head. "I suspect she'll fight ye on that. The lass is determined to fulfill her mother's last wish."

"Her mother wanted her safe," Rory countered firmly. "She would be safe at Buchanan."

"Aye, well, just do no' be surprised if Elysande leaves us behind to head fer Sinclair on her own," Alick warned, and then smiled wryly and added, "Or mayhap she'll head fer court instead, to deliver the warning to her king personally. But either way, I'm thinking she'll not sit idly by at Buchanan, safe or no'."

Rory didn't comment, but suspected his brother was right. Elysande would not be happy to simply go to Buchanan and wait safely there for Sinclair to come to her. Especially not when they were under such a tight time constraint to get the warning to the king. That meant he'd have to come up with another solution, Rory thought grimly as he finished binding her and eased her back on the bed.

He turned his attention to cleaning her head wound then, his mind preoccupied with the more immediate concern of keeping her safe while they were at the inn, and after a moment, he said, "I want either you, or I, with Elysande at all times from now on."

He was aware that Alick was watching him with a troubled glance, and wasn't surprised when he said, "None o' our men would hurt her."

"I ken that," Rory assured him.

"Well, neither would Simon or Tom," he added. "She would no' even be alive if no' fer them."

"I ken that too," Rory said. "But she can order Simon and Tom away as she did today, and while I trust all our men, I trust ye more."

Alick seemed to accept that and didn't question him further.

Rory finished cleaning the head wound, relieved to see that, as he'd suspected, it was more bluster than wound. Still, she had a bump and a cut from where she'd hit the edge of the stone hearth of the fireplace. Elysande would have a sore head when she woke up, and despite what he'd said to Tom, he was pretty sure she *would* wake up. While she hadn't woken as he'd sewn her up, she had twitched a couple times, as if struggling to wake.

"Does she really need her head wrapped?" Alick asked when Rory finished smearing salve on the wound and picked up the linens to start wrapping her head.

Rory shrugged. "'Tis best in case some of the powder did get on the bed and fell off the furs when ye folded them up. The bandage will keep it from her wound." He didn't add that it would make her look more poorly than he thought she really was, and he wanted that. He was hoping that if they let everyone think she was on the brink of dying, it would delay another attempt on her life long enough for him to figure out a way to either get her safely to Sinclair, and quickly, or alternately, get her safely to court to give the king her mother's messages.

Once he finished wrapping her head, Rory straightened to peer at Elysande. Alick had tugged the linens up to cover her bandaged chest, but she still looked pale and weak in the bed, her skin whiter than the off-white bandage and linens covering her head. After a minute, he glanced to Alick and said, "Ye did no' finish yer nooning meal before I ordered ye up here to guard the lass earlier. Go on down, rinse yer boots off and get something to eat. If the men ask how she is, just shake yer head and say it does no' look good."

Alick considered him briefly, and then nodded and headed for the door, promising to be quick.

Rory eyed Elysande for another moment, and then glanced around the room. She'd obviously been at the table by the fire, grinding the weeds, when she was attacked. Either she'd bumped the table trying to avoid being stabbed and that had knocked the mortar to the floor, or her hand or something else had hit it and sent it tumbling. He suspected she'd bumped it as she'd tried to get out of the way of the knife coming at her, because she'd fallen several steps past the table and spilled powder, and closer to the fire.

That made him recall her hand being in the ashes of the fireplace and Rory picked it up now to examine it, but the ash from the fire prevented his seeing much. Grabbing the damp linen he'd used to wash the blood from her head and chest, he rinsed it, wrung it out and then wiped the ash away from her hand and fingers. Much to his relief, her fingers were a little red and dry, but there was no blistering or scorching. She hadn't suffered more of a burn than one got by being out too long in the sun.

Sighing, he set her hand back and then glanced to the door when it opened. When Tom entered with a mop and bucket, he slid off the bed and walked over to move the table back to the other side of the bed. He then returned for the chair and carried it over to set up against the wall.

"No one was seen coming or going through the kitchens and the servants' stairs," Tom said glumly as he began to mop the floor.

Rory straightened from setting the chair down and then moved to the window and opened the shutters, wincing at the loud screech it made. He leaned out then to peer down. He could see the stables to his left, but the area directly below was open and unused. Unfortunately, while snow had been falling when they arrived the night before, it hadn't stuck around and there was nothing but grass below. No nice prints in mud or snow for him to follow. He'd take a closer look when he went down to rinse off his own boots though.

Rory closed the shutters, grimacing at the loud sound it made, and then paused briefly before opening them again, bringing about another squeal of protesting metal.

"He couldn't have come in the window. Lady Elysande would have heard him and been able to run out of the room before he climbed in," Tom commented, saying what Rory was thinking.

"Aye. But he could have escaped this way. We would no' ha'e heard their squeal below," Rory murmured, and closed the shutters again and then turned to survey the room thoughtfully.

"So," Tom said, dipping the mop in the bucket and then pulling it out to sweep it across the floor. "Her attacker came up either the front stairs or the servants' stairs unnoticed, attacked m'lady and then panicked and went out the window because she screamed and he knew we would come."

"Or he fled out the window when he heard us pounding up the stairs, or Simon running up the hall," Rory suggested, and paused to consider his own words.

"But how did he get up here without anyone in the kitchens or the taproom seeing?" Tom asked in a frustrated growl.

"Mayhap he was already above stairs," Rory suggested quietly.

Tom stopped shoving the mop around at that suggestion, his eyes widening and imagination taking over. "Aye, he could have come above stairs earlier, mayhap while you and I were still sleeping. He could have been hiding in one of the rooms, or in the servants' stairwell, just waiting for an opportunity, and then you brought Lady Elysande up here and left Alick and Simon to guard her, but Alick left and then Lady Elysande sent Simon for water. He saw his chance, slipped into the room and attacked."

"'Tis possible," Rory allowed.

Mouth tightening, Tom snapped, "Damn de Buci! If she dies and the king is never warned—" Pausing, he shook his head and growled, "Edward III is a good king. Better than the alternatives. No matter what, we have to warn him," he said firmly. "I'll take the damned messages meself if I have to."

Rory blinked at the words, and then nodded slowly as he turned them over in his head. His voice was considering when he said, "I'm thinking ye may just ha'e to do that."

When his words made Tom cast a stricken look at Elysande, Rory realized he'd misunderstood him, and almost explained that he hadn't meant the man would have to go because Elysande was near death. But then he changed his mind. He wanted people to think Elysande was at death's door, after all. This could only help. Still, it made him feel bad, but he pushed those feelings away and took the mop from him. "I'll finish this, ye go check on Simon and see if he's done washing the hall and stairs. If he is, tell him to go get some rest, and then find Conn and Inan and tell them the same thing. The three of them will be guarding Elysande tonight and I want them alert."

Tom hesitated, his gaze sliding to Elysande, and then he nodded and slipped from the room, pulling the door silently closed.

Rory started swishing the mop over the floor then, his mind only half on the job, as he considered the plan that had started forming in his mind since Tom had made the comment about delivering the warning to the king himself. The idea actually had merit and he considered it as he cleaned the floor.

Once he'd finished, Rory stuck the mop back in the bucket and strode to the rolled-up fur Alick had set beside the bed. He quickly unfurled it on the floor. The remains of Elysande's plaid, gown and tunic rolled out with it. His gaze slid over the bloodstains, and then he began to run his hand over the skirts until he found what he was looking for between the layers of cloth. Pausing, he began to shift the material until he found a long narrow pocket sewn to the inside of the skirt. Opening it, he plucked out the thick, stiff scroll inside and stared at the de Valance seal for a moment, imagining Elysande pressing her mother's ring into the wax. Then he slipped it into his plaid and rolled up the fur and cloth again.

Straightening, Rory then turned his mind to Elysande's attack, and walked to the window to open the shutters again.

The squeal of metal seemed loud in the room, but he hadn't heard it from below. Elysande would have heard it in here though. Her attacker definitely hadn't come in through the window. He peered down at the ground below for a moment, but then closed the shutters once more. Finally, he moved to the bed, and settled next to Elysande.

Leaning his back against the wall, Rory closed his eyes and tried to recall what the room had looked like when he'd entered, and then replayed everything that had happened from the time he heard the scream until now. Somewhere in there was a memory of something that had bothered him.

He was still going through his recollection of events when Alick entered the bedchamber, looking a bit upset.

"Tom told Simon, Conn and Inan that ye said they should go to bed and sleep. That they'd be standing guard tonight," he said, and then raising his eyebrows, he added, "I thought ye trusted only you and me fer the task?"

"Aye. Well, I trust only us in the room. But Conn, Inan and Simon can stand in the hall."

"Oh." Relaxing, Alick nodded and moved to the bedside to peer down at Elysande. "She has no' woken?"

"Nay." He peered at her solemnly, and then leaned down to feel her forehead. It was cool and dry, but that didn't really mean anything. It could take a full day and up to three for fever to set in. Straightening, he asked, "Are the men resting?"

"Aye," Alick said. "Well, they were going as soon as they finished their drinks. Which should be soon."

Rory nodded and then announced, "I need more linen. Between the lass's chest wound, head wound and my binding her ankle, I've used up nearly all o' mine. I'll need more to change her bandages later."

"Do ye want me to go to the shops and—"

"Nay," Rory interrupted, getting up off the bed. "I'll go. I need some more weeds anyway. I'm taking Tom, Fearghas and Donnghail with me. Do no' leave Elysande's side while I am gone. No' even for a moment. No' even if one o' the other men offers to stay with her. Understand?" He waited for Alick to nod before heading to the door, assuring him, "I'll be back as quick as I can."

"Rory?" Alick said as he reached and opened the door.

Rory paused, and glanced back in question.

"What are ye no' telling me, brother?"

He hesitated, and in the silence heard footsteps approaching up the hall. Rory didn't turn to see who it was, and spoke in normal tones when he said, "We obviously canno' leave tomorrow as I planned. I'll have to pay fer the extra time here. I'm thinking to send a couple o' the boys to Buchanan to fetch back some coin to cover our stay here just in case. Probably Donnghail and Fearghas, and maybe Tom too."

Alick blinked in surprise and opened his mouth, probably to protest that he couldn't possibly be out of coin. The Baron of Monmouth had paid him a small fortune, but Rory gave him a warning look that silenced him, and after a hesitation, Alick merely said, "That's probably a good idea."

"Aye. The lass could linger fer a while," he said grimly, and then repeated, "I'll be back as quick as I can," before pulling the door closed and turning in the hall to find Simon standing before him, a stricken look on his face. Conn and Inan were a couple of steps back, their own faces grim.

"You think she will die?" Simon asked, looking half-dismayed and half-guilty. "I never should have let her send me down to the kitchens."

Rory considered him briefly, and then moved past him, saying only, "I do no' ken. She's in God's hands now. Get yerselves to bed. I need ye to guard her later."

He left the men in the hall and headed down the stairs.

Chapter 14

*E*LYSANDE WOKE UP WITH A SPLITTING HEADACHE AND THAT was the only thing she was aware of when she first opened her eyes. Groaning as the light in the room added to her pain, she closed them at once and raised a hand toward her head, only to grimace and let it fall back to her side as moving her arm caused pain in her chest.

"Elysande?"

She frowned slightly at that voice, and then forced her eyes open again to find Alick Buchanan's face hovering over hers, his expression one of both worry and relief, which seemed an odd combination to her.

"Why are you looking at me like that?" she murmured groggily, and then squeezed her eyes closed and groaned, "And who kicked me in the head?"

"I think we were all hoping ye could tell us that," Alick said, and she could hear the wry tone in his voice, and then amusement entered it as well as he added, "And Rory is going to be verra angry that he was no' here when ye woke."

Elysande scowled at those words, oddly annoyed by the news that Rory wasn't there. Her head was pounding, her chest and back hurt and when she shifted her legs her ankle gave a twinge of pain to remind her it hurt too. Frankly, she was sick and tired of hurting. And for some reason, all she wanted in the world was to curl up against Rory and sleep. She always felt better when he was around.

"Where is he?" she asked testily.

"I'm no' sure," Alick admitted, and now there was an odd tone to his voice, almost troubled. "He said he needed more linens and weeds, but then he said he was sending Donnghail, Fearghas and Tom to Buchanan to bring back more coin to pay for the inn. I'm no' sure what he's up to. But I suspect he has an idea who stabbed ye and is—"

"I was stabbed?" Elysande squawked, blinking her eyes open with alarm, and then her mouth made an O as the memory returned to her.

"Do ye no'—" Alick broke off and stood abruptly, his hand going to his sword as the door opened, but he relaxed when Rory appeared.

Rory looked worried and exhausted, Elysande thought as she watched him enter. He carried a cloth sack in one hand, while his other was running down the back of his head and along his neck as if he was trying to rub away some stress that was troubling him. He let the hand drop away now to push the door closed and then turned to survey the room, his gaze finding Alick just as the younger man let his hand slip from his sword. She saw a smile tip his lips and then his gaze moved to her and he froze. As she watched, his eyes brightened and his lips split with delight and relief as he quickly crossed the room to the bed.

"Ye're awake," he said as he dropped the sack on the floor and sat on the edge of the bed.

"Aye. She just woke up a moment ago," Alick said when she didn't respond right away.

"How's yer head?" he asked solicitously, his gaze shifting between her eyes. Checking her pupils, she suspected.

"Sore," Elysande said, and then grimaced at how cranky she sounded. But then she *was* cranky. Being in constant pain did not make one cheerful.

"I'll make ye a tincture," he assured her, and stood up to begin fiddling with something on the bedside table that she couldn't be bothered to turn her head to look at. She was hoping if she held her head completely still, it would eventually stop pounding.

"Did ye get yer weeds and linen?" Alick asked, moving around the bed to Rory's side.

"Aye, and a new plaid fer Elysande," Rory answered absently as he worked.

"What happened to my other one?" Elysande asked with irritation. She'd liked the colors of the plaid she'd purchased in Carlisle.

"It got blood on it and needs washing," Rory explained as he settled on the edge of the bed next to her again. "I got one similar to it though. At least it has the same colors, deep blues and greens and red."

Elysande relaxed at that, touched that he'd bothered.

She saw Alick grab the bag and open it, but then was distracted when Rory eased her up to a sitting position so she could drink the tincture he was now pressing to her lips.

Elysande didn't refuse or argue and swallowed all of it one gulp after another. She closed her eyes with a small sigh when it was gone and he eased her back down to lie in bed.

"'Tis almost exactly the same as the one she had."

Elysande opened her eyes again at that comment from Alick, and saw the plaid he was holding up. He was right. It was almost exactly the same. Only there was a little more blue to it. She actually liked it better than the first, she decided, and smiled as she let her eyes slide closed. The men's voices drifted over her as she allowed the tincture to take effect and urge her toward sleep.

"I had to send Simon to bed just now," she heard Rory comment. "He was standing outside the door when I came up the stairs. Did he try to come inside? He did no' see Elysande is awake, did he?"

"Nay. He did no' come into the room. He came to offer to sit with me to help guard Elysande, but I told him to go back to bed. I told him I'd wake him when it was time fer him to stand guard. But Elysande was no' awake yet. If he saw her over me shoulder, all he saw was her bandaged head and closed eyes," Alick assured him. "He looked pretty rough though. I think he's feeling guilty that he left her alone to get attacked. I did point out that if she ordered him to go get her water, he had to obey and 'twasn't his fault. I do no' think it helped much though, and we'll probably find him hovering in the hall standing guard a lot."

Rory grunted what might have been an agreement.

"It was not his fault. I did order him to go fetch me water and a pot," Elysande admitted, and then explained, "He argued with me that he was supposed to be guarding me when I asked, so I ordered him to go." She smiled wryly, and added, "He got a bit huffy and said, fine, but he would blame me if he got in trouble for leaving his post."

Her eyes were still closed, but she could almost feel both men looking at her, and then Rory asked, "What happened then, lass?"

Elysande was silent for a minute, and then grimaced. "I went back to grinding the weeds, and several minutes later . . ." She hesitated before continuing. "I was distracted and do not recall hearing anything, but something made me stop and look behind me," she muttered, not wanting to admit that the hairs on the back of her neck had suddenly stood on end and made her whirl around. "There was a man right behind me and a knife coming at me. I think I screamed, but I know I jerked back into the table. I tried to move around it then to get out of the way of the knife, but my ankle gave out and I started to fall as I felt the knife strike me and . . ." She frowned. "I think I hit my head on something as I fell. I do not remember anything else."

"Ye hit yer head on the hearth," Rory explained solemnly. "Fortunately, while ye gained yerself a bump and broke the skin, I could no' feel any damage to yer skull. The headache should pass in a day or so, and ye'll be right as rain again. But I want ye to stay abed for the next day or two. I'll no' risk yer ankle giving out and yer hitting yer head again. Besides, the rest should do yer back and ankle good anyway."

"There is no time for resting," Elysande reminded him grimly. "I need to get to Sinclair quickly, because we need to sort out a way to get the warning to the king."

"Ye let me worry about that, lass," Rory said soothingly. "I think I've a plan to get yer king that warning more quickly."

Elysande tried to push her eyelids open to look at him and ask what plan, but they didn't seem to want to open, and she was losing her grasp on what she wanted to ask him anyway. The tincture was obviously taking effect, she realized, and allowed herself to drift off into sleep.

When Elysande woke without any pain for the first time in what seemed like forever, she thought she must still be asleep and dreaming. She even lay there for a minute, waiting for whatever came next in the dream. When nothing happened, she cautiously opened one eye, ready to blink it closed again at the first sign of pain, but there was none. No pounding headache, no screaming back pain, not even a twinge from her ankle when she moved it tentatively under the linens and furs covering her.

"Huh," she murmured, unsure what to make of that. She had woken up several times over the last two days since the attack, and each awakening had been accompanied by screaming headaches that had been bad enough that she hadn't fought Rory giving her the tincture that sent her back into blessed, pain-free sleep. But now that pain appeared to finally be over.

Elysande opened her other eye and glanced around the room. She recognized the bedchamber from the inn and realized they were still in Ayr, then shifted her gaze to the man in bed next to her.

Men, she corrected herself when she looked to her other side and spotted Alick there. Rory was on her left, and Alick on her right. Both men were sleeping above the furs, while she was under them. They had also left a good bit of space between themselves and her, which was the only reason she was able to wiggle her way out from under the furs and escape the bed.

It wasn't a fast or easy procedure to manage without waking either man, and it was while trying to do so that Elysande felt her first twinge of pain. It wasn't bad though, just enough to draw her attention to the bandages that ran across her chest and around her back, and make her realize that they and her breeches were her only covering.

She'd been stabbed, Elysande recalled, staring down at herself where she now sat in the bed, the fur only covering her from the hips down. Or maybe that had been a dream, because she felt sure a stab wound should cause more than just a twinge of pain. The thought had her moving a little more quickly to get out from under the fur, and within moments she was crawling down the center of the bed to the bottom, and then shifting to sit on the end of it with her feet on the floor.

Glancing over her shoulder, Elysande considered the two men still sleeping soundly, and then peered at her bandages again. She wanted to unwrap them and take a look at her wound, but that seemed a risky endeavor when Rory or Alick could wake up at any moment and catch her without the wrappings. They'd probably already seen her without them. At least, Rory probably had since she suspected he would have been the one to tend her wound and bandage her up, but that had been while she was unconscious. She was awake now.

Muttering irritably under her breath about the lack of privacy since encountering these Buchanans, Elysande got cautiously to her feet, half expecting her ankle to pain her, or suddenly give out. But it did neither. There was the faintest twinge when she put her full weight on it, but nothing more than that. Still, it was enough to make her walk slowly and cautiously as she made her way to the bags lined up against the wall.

A quick search produced a clean gown and a tunic. Elysande donned both, and then glanced around for her new plaid, but didn't see it anywhere. That was probably for the best though, she decided as she gave up on it. She wasn't at all sure she could have managed the plaid on her own anyway. She supposed she'd just have to do without it for now and hope the innkeeper and his wife were still nice to her, because she was not only starving, but she was so thirsty she couldn't even work up spit in her mouth.

The thought of food and drink urging her on, Elysande ran her hands through her hair as she walked to the door, doing her best to smooth out the worst of the tangles she could feel, and give it some sort of order. She gave up on her efforts though when she opened the door to find two large male backs in her way. Conn and Inan were standing side by side in front of the door, but both men glanced over their shoulders now, and then spun around and gaped at her like a pair of slack-jawed dalcops. It appeared her efforts to tame her hair had failed, she thought, but really didn't much care, and that was a testament to how hungry she was. Or how thirsty. She couldn't say which was worse at the moment.

Elysande smiled pleasantly back at the men, waiting for them to get over their shock at the state of her hair and move out of her way, but they were being rather slow about it and she was *so* thirsty. Finally, she said, "May I get past, please? I wish to go below and get something to eat and drink."

Both men's mouths snapped closed at once, and they were suddenly moving. But rather than getting out of her way, they moved toward her. Conn was the one who caught her by the shoulders and turned her around. He was also the one to march her back into the room, while Inan closed the door before rushing to the bed to shake Rory awake.

"Inan? 'Tis the middle o' the night," Rory muttered, blinking the sleep from his eyes and sitting up abruptly when he realized who was leaning over him. "What's about?"

"I was about to ask ye the same question," Inan said dryly, and then waved to where Elysande stood in front of Conn. "The lass whose death we've all been awaiting appears to have decided to live."

"Death?" Elysande squawked, stiffening with alarm. Eyeing Rory with dismay, she asked, "I was dying?"

"Nay," Rory assured her, and then glanced to Alick when his brother rolled over in bed and peered at their company. When the younger man then just flopped back on the bed, Rory sighed and started to climb to his feet as he explained, "I just wanted de Buci's man to think ye were so he'd no' try to kill ye again before I could get ye out o' here and on the *Mary Margaret*."

"De Buci's man?" Elysande asked with a frown, and then confusion covering her face, she asked, "And what is the Mary Margaret? Is that a horse?"

"Nay. 'Tis a cog. A ship," he added when she continued to look blank. "The *Mary Margaret* is a merchant ship that is setting sail from here the day after tomorrow, headed for New Aberdeen. The captain's agreed to drop us in Thurso on his way, which is half a day's ride from Sinclair. It will cut our trip by more than half, even with the few days we've had to wait fer the ship to sail."

"Oh," she breathed, a smile tugging at her lips. This was the plan he'd mentioned. The way he'd come up with to speed up their trip. They would sail to Sinclair, and then no doubt send a courier with her mother's messages on another ship going south afterward. They would be able to warn the king in time. "Oh," she repeated, and then impulsively rushed across the room to throw her arms around Rory and hug him tightly. "You brilliant man. You have saved the king."

"Aye, well, since 'tis the English king we're talking about, I'd appreciate it did ye no' mention that outside this room," Rory said dryly, his arms slipping around her waist.

Elysande laughed and hugged him again, but her stomach grumbled just then, reminding her of her original mission. Pulling back, she caught his hand and turned, intending to drag him out of the room in search of food, only to pull up short when she spotted Conn and Inan watching them with solemn expressions.

"Right," Rory sighed behind her, and then moved forward to face his men. "I let ye all think she was much more ill than she is because—" Pausing abruptly, he asked, "Where is Simon?"

"He went down to the stables fer something," Conn answered. "He should be back soon though."

Rory's mouth tightened, but he nodded. "Then one o' ye needs to stand by the door and keep an eye out for him."

Conn and Inan glanced at each other, and then Inan moved to crack the door open and keep an eye out.

The moment he was in position, Rory said, "Simon is the reason I let ye all think Elysande was dying. I suspect he is de Buci's

man, and did no' tell ye the truth because I did no' want ye slipping up and saying anything in front o' him that might make him
think she was well or recovering."

"Simon?" Elysande asked with amazement when she was finally able to speak past her shock.

"Aye." Rory took her hands and said apologetically, "I think
he's the one who stabbed ye."

"What?" she gasped with a half laugh of disbelief, and immediately began to shake her head. "Nay. Simon would never do that."

"Lass," Rory began patiently.

"Nay, Rory. You are wrong. Simon would not hurt me."

"Lass, he had powder on his boots, there was water only by the
door, I did no' hear him running up the hall after ye screamed
and I'm quite sure no one jumped out that window."

"I have no idea what any of that means," she admitted, feeling
perturbed at the very suggestion that her man might harm her,
and very angry at Rory for suggesting it.

"Ye remember the weeds ye were working on in the mortar ere
ye were attacked?" he asked.

"Aye, of course. I think it got knocked to the floor," she said, recalling the sound of the mortar thumping to the wooden planks.

"It did," he agreed. "And the men tramped through the fine
powder and had it on the bottom of their boots. I made them
brush it off ere they left the room, and then had it swept up and
the floor washed."

Elysande nodded solemnly at the precaution, knowing it was
necessary.

"But Simon did no' just have it on the bottom of his boots," he
told her now. "He had a spot of it on the top o' one o' his boots too,
just in front o' his ankle. That troubled me. Ye do no' get it on the
top o' yer boot by walking through it."

"But ye could were ye nearby when it hit the floor and flew in
every direction . . ." Conn said, his voice a rumble of realization.

Elysande scowled at the man for siding with Rory on this, and
said, "Mayhap he kicked it up while walking, or . . ." Her voice

trailed away as she realized that kicking it up would have got it on his toes, but not just a spot of it, and not by his ankle.

Rory eyed her sympathetically, and then added, "And another thing that troubled me was that when I crested the top o' the stairs, Simon was just disappearing into the room carrying a pot and a bucket with water slopping everywhere in his rush."

"I sent him for that," she said, not understanding.

"Aye, but the water was only spilled by the door, not all along the hall as it should have been if he'd hurried up the hall on hearing yer scream."

Elysande's mouth compressed with displeasure, but he wasn't done.

"And while we first assumed yer attacker had escaped out the window because we passed no one in the hall, I'm now quite sure that is no' true. I checked the ground outside our window, and the grass was verra wet from the melted snow, but there were no marks from someone leaping from a second-floor window and crushing the grass into the mud with his weight. Unless yer attacker could fly, he did no' leave through the window."

"I see," Elysande said quietly. "So you think Simon fetched the pot and bucket of water, set them outside the door, came into the chamber, stabbed me, opened the window and then rushed out to grab the bucket and pot to make it look like he was just arriving when you got upstairs?" she asked, trying to understand what he was suggesting.

Rory hesitated, and then admitted, "I canno' be certain, o' course, and I ha'e no proof, but that is what I think happened. It would explain away all o' those points I just mentioned, as well as how yer attacker got away without anyone seeing him."

"Mayhap, but there must be another explanation," Elysande said firmly.

"Well, when ye think o' one, let me ken, lass. In the meantime, 'tis better to be safe than sorry. So I intend to continue to let Simon think that ye're at death's door, so he does no' try to finish ye off." Meeting her gaze, he said firmly, "Ye got lucky the first time, lass.

I suspect he was in a panic when ye screamed. He knew we'd be coming and just thrust the blade in, opened the window and ran, no' noticing that what he gave ye was little more than a scratch. He did no' realize the knife hit yer sack o' coins and slid to the side and the coin sack then helped to hold it in place. Neither did I when I first saw ye. Aye, ye got lucky the first time." He paused briefly and then added, "If it was the first time."

Elysande glanced at him sharply. "What do you mean 'if it was the first time'?"

"I mean yer accident on the way back from the shops when ye were pushed in front o' a horse and cart."

"That was an accident, a bunch of drunken sailors were passing. One of them bumped me," she reminded him.

"Or was it Simon who pushed ye into the road as the sailors passed, kenning he could blame them for it?" he asked. "The man was at yer back, supposed to be watching ye. No one should ha'e been able to push ye into the street."

Elysande stared at him blankly, completely shocked by his words.

"Anyway," he said on a sigh. "As I said, ye've been lucky so far. But I suspect we'd no' be as lucky the next time and am unwilling to take the chance."

Elysande considered his words but she simply could not believe that Simon was her attacker. "I have known Simon for years, Rory. He trained at Kynardersley under Father from the time he was six years old. We grew up together. He is like family. I cannot believe he would betray me like that for whatever de Buci would offer. I just cannot."

"He may no' have been given a choice," Rory said solemnly. "De Buci may have threatened someone he cares fer. A parent or sister."

Elysande frowned at that possibility. Simon's parents and sisters had been to Kynardersley several times to visit over the years. His father had been friends with hers since they were boys, and had remained close. It was why Simon had trained under her father.

"But it matters little if ye believe or no', I did no' expect ye to anyway," Rory said now, drawing her from her thoughts. "However, yer mother tasked me with getting ye to Sinclair safe, and I plan to do that. I have no' accused Simon outright, but I'm keeping an eye on him. Ye'll no' be alone with him again. Either Alick or I . . ." he began, and then his gaze slid to Conn and Inan. When both men nodded, he added, "Or Conn or Inan will be with ye at all times." He waited a moment as if expecting a protest.

When Elysande didn't say anything, he added, "And I want ye to stay in this room until we leave the inn for the *Mary Margaret*. We ha'e to keep up the tale that ye're dying. 'Tis just one more day," he said quickly when she started to protest. "And necessary. By now there is probably a small army o' de Buci's soldiers in Ayr. They're biding their time because they think ye're dying, but if de Buci's as desperate as ye think, and learns ye're no' on death's door, he verra well might attack the inn during the night and slaughter everyone, or simply bar the doors and set it afire."

Elysande's eyes widened. It hadn't occurred to her that he might do something like that, but the man was desperate. He did not face a pleasant death if the king was warned. He would be found guilty of high treason for this plot. They would strap him to a hurdle, drag him through the streets to the place of execution so that people could hurl things at him along the way. Then he would be hanged, but not to death. He'd be cut down seconds before death could claim him and then he'd be unmanned and disemboweled, his organs and genitalia thrown in a fire in front of him so that it was the last thing his eyes saw. Then he would be quartered, and each part would be sent to decorate the four corners of the city as a warning to others not to follow in his footsteps.

Faced with all of that should he fail to stop her, Elysande supposed nothing would be beyond his capabilities at the moment. Even razing the city of Ayr itself, she suspected. Burning down the inn with all its occupants, including innocents, would matter little to him.

Shoulders slumping in defeat, Elysande nodded solemnly.

"Very well. I will remain in the room and even pretend to be dying if I must."

Relaxing a little, Rory nodded and then glanced to Conn and Inan. "Ye must be careful no' to reveal by word or deed that she is no' dying. If Simon even suspects she is recovering . . ."

"We'll be careful," Conn assured him.

"Aye," Inan agreed, tearing his gaze from the hallway briefly to make the promise.

"It'll no' be so bad," Alick said, speaking for the first time to address Elysande. "Ye'll ha'e Rory and I to entertain ye most o' the time."

Elysande smiled reluctantly at the promise, but said, "I'd rather have food and drink."

"That can be arranged," Rory assured her.

"But not a visit to the privy," she guessed grimly as she became aware of that need.

His gaze slid to a chamber pot on the bedside table, and Elysande barely held back a moan. But then she straightened her shoulders. "Fine. Then go out in the hall and talk to the men or something while I use it."

"Lass, I do no' think—" Rory began, but something in her expression must have made him realize he wasn't going to win that argument. He stopped speaking, hesitated and then nodded and headed for the door, gesturing for the others to follow.

Chapter 15

"So, WHAT BROUGHT ABOUT YOUR INTEREST IN HEALING?"

Rory started to glance around at that question from Elysande and then caught himself at the last moment. She was in the bath. Naked. And he was seated in the chair by the window with his back to her. He was not supposed to look, and frankly he didn't want to. It was torture enough imagining her in the bath without actually seeing it. He'd seen enough when he'd removed her wrappings to check her wounds. Both were healing nicely. The swelling was nearly gone from her head, and the cut had scabbed over, seeming smaller than the last time he'd checked it. As for the wound on her breast, it too was healing well. In truth, it was only a touch worse than a scratch. The knife hadn't gone in far at all. He probably hadn't needed to stitch it up. But on top of that, the bruising on her back and side had faded to a faint yellow and would be completely gone in a day or two. The same was probably true of the bruising on her bottom and legs, though he hadn't been able to come up with an excuse to see that.

"Rory?" Elysande prompted.

"Aye, sorry," he murmured, and then cleared his throat as he tried to remember what her question had been. When he couldn't recall, he said, "Mayhap we should no' talk while so far apart and with the shutters open."

He didn't point out that someone in the yard might hear her speaking and realize she wasn't close to death. He didn't have to. They'd been arguing about what she could and couldn't do for most of the night and day, including her desire to take a bath.

Rory had understood. He was a frequent bather himself and knew it must have been driving her crazy to have to go without. But arranging a bath for her meant Rory had to lie and claim he wanted a bath, and then they had to risk the servants carrying in the tub as well as bucket after bucket of water. He hadn't worried about one of them attacking her, but about her ability to feign unconsciousness until they left, and he felt it was important for them to continue this ruse until he could spirit her away from the inn.

The lass was one hell of a stubborn woman. She'd pestered him about the bath almost nonstop while they'd consumed the food and drink Conn had brought up after telling the innkeeper's wife it was for Rory and Alick. She'd continued her campaign through the games of dice, cards and chess that he and Alick had played with her to pass the time all day, and then again through the sup Conn and Inan had brought up for them to share with her. It was after the meal, when she'd threatened that if they would not arrange a bath for her, she'd just slip out and wash up at the horse trough once darkness fell. That was when Rory had given in. Partially because he wouldn't put it past the lass to try it, and partially because she was becoming more angry and frustrated with him every time he refused. Rory found he didn't like to disappoint and anger her.

So, he'd ordered her into bed, warning her not to open her eyes or change her expression in any way that might give away that she was awake, and arranged for the bath to be brought up. Now, he was sitting at the open window, peering out at the side yard and trying not to imagine Elysande reclining naked in the tub of water just feet away.

"Then close the shutters and come sit beside the tub so we might talk," Elysande said more quietly, and it sounded almost like an order. When Rory didn't respond at all except to freeze like a deer with a mad horseman pounding toward it, she confessed, "When we are not talking, my mind travels down dark paths. I think of my father's crying out and stumbling from the table with de Buci's dagger in his chest, and my mother screaming in agony as de Buci beat her, and my own helplessness in the face of their deaths and abuse as well as the beating I took. I—" Her voice broke, and he was sure that if he looked he would see tears in her eyes, but then she cleared her throat and said hoarsely, "When you talk, it all goes away, at least for a while."

Rory stood abruptly, closed the shutters and picked up the chair to carry it to the tub. He did not look at her. That was just asking too much. He kept his gaze on the chair as he set it down with its back almost against the tub, and then he sat in it, and cleared his throat before asking, "What do ye wish to talk about, lass?"

"You," she answered promptly, her voice lighter, though he suspected it was a forced lightness to cover the darkness her memories brought with them.

The chuckle he gave then was just as forced. "Well, I fear there is no' much o' interest about me. I spent most o' the last ten years training in healing. Reading any treatise on it I could find, and talking to any healers who would speak to me."

"Why?" she asked softly.

Rory blinked at the question, and then smiled faintly. No one had ever asked him that question. His brothers and Saidh already knew and understood the reason, and no one else had ever cared enough to ask why it had been so important to him. Until now.

"My mother," he answered solemnly.

"Was she a healer too? Did she train ye?"

"She was handy at healing, aye," he allowed. "But probably no' as skilled at it as yer own mother. And no, I did no' get my interest from her in that way and she never trained me."

"Then how did your mother raise your interest in healing?" Elysande asked, trying to understand.

"She became ill about ten years ago," he admitted. "Terrible ill. She had trained Saidh in what she knew about healing, and Saidh tried everything she'd taught her to try to mend her, but had no idea what to do. None o' us did. When it became obvious she was no' getting better, we sent fer the most skilled healers we knew of. But none o' them kenned what to do either and in the end we could do naught but watch her die. It was horrible. I felt so help-less. I imagine Saidh and me brothers did too, but—"

His throat was becoming constricted by a lump, or perhaps just a tightness there, and he had to stop and swallow to clear it, be-fore continuing. "I was verra close to me mother. We all were, and losing her was hard on all of us," he said, and thought it was prob-ably the largest understatement he'd ever uttered. His family had always been close, his parents loving and supportive. Losing their mother had been a crushing loss for all of them, equaled only by losing their father and brother.

"But I felt so useless just sitting there watching her struggle to live and not being able to do anything to help her," he said, his voice low and full of the torture he'd felt at the time. "My brothers handled it by practicing in the bailey, or beating each other to a pulp. Even Saidh did, but that gave me no peace or release, and I never wanted to feel that way again. I never wanted to watch a loved one just fade away and die in terrible pain and suffering, growing weaker even as their pain increased each day." He shook his head. "So, I determined to do something about it. I stopped training with me brothers and started learning all I could about healing."

"I understand the helplessness," Elysande murmured solemnly. "'Tis how I felt watching de Buci beat my mother. And I never want to feel that way again either," she admitted unhappily. "May-hap I should train in battle."

Rory gave a start and half turned around before catching him-self. "What? Why would ye?"

"Because if I'd had a dagger or some other weapon and had known how to use it, perhaps I would not have been so helpless. Perhaps I could have saved at least my mother from de Buci," she said sadly, and then asked, "Would you teach me how to wield a knife?"

"Aye," he said, though he doubted there was anything she could have done to save her mother. Any more than he, with all the knowledge he'd gained over the last ten years, would now know what to do for his mother were she here and ill as she had been ten years ago. He'd never again encountered an illness similar to hers, not in the writings he'd read or the patients he'd tended. Rory had come to suspect that sometimes there was just nothing you could do for the people you loved, no matter how much you wished you could. Sometimes there just wasn't enough knowledge, skill and love to save them. Otherwise, no one would ever die. But death was as natural and necessary as birth.

The sound of water sloshing made him still. It sounded like Elysande was getting out of the bath. He almost asked if she was, but then just waited.

"'Tis so nice not to be in constant pain anymore," Elysande said suddenly, apparently deciding a lighter subject was in order.

"I can imagine," he murmured, thinking that her voice sounded like it was coming from several feet higher than it had been. She *was* getting out of the bath. Forcing away the image that came to his mind of her standing up, and water sluicing away down her naked body in the light cast by the fire, he added, "I think surely ye've suffered a lifetime o' pain in the last two weeks."

"Two weeks?" she asked with alarm. "Surely it has not been that long?"

Rory did a swift calculation, and then assured her, "It has been about twelve days since de Buci attacked Kynardersley, so aye, nearly two weeks."

"It does not feel like it has been that long . . . and yet, at the same time it feels like a lifetime has passed since de Buci charged in destroying everything," she said sadly. "Is that not odd?"

Rory suspected it was a rhetorical question so didn't answer her, but he didn't think it was odd at all. In fact, he completely understood. For time had passed quickly for him too since her arrival in his life, and yet at the same time he felt like she had always been there.

He heard Elysande sigh and then the slap of her wet bare feet on the wooden planks of the floor as she stepped out of the tub. It was followed by the rustle of what he presumed was her drying herself with the linen the innkeeper had sent up for him to use. The bath was supposed to be for him, after all. And would be. He planned to use it once she fell asleep. He hadn't bathed since the night they'd arrived either and was no more happy about it than she had been.

"Are you going to use the bath now?" Elysande asked as if reading his mind. "I know you did the last time after I went to sleep, but if you plan to bathe you should do so while 'tis still hot. I promise not to look," she teased. "I am just going to sit by the fire and brush my hair."

Rory automatically started to turn toward her to answer, caught a glimpse of rosy pink flesh fresh from the hot water and quickly jerked his head back.

"Aye, mayhap I will," he answered, and closed his eyes when he heard how rough and husky his voice was. Just a glimpse of her generous curves had affected him. Having to live and sleep so close to her for more than a week did not help. Oddly enough, neither did talking with her, laughing with her or even arguing with her. All of it just increased his attraction to her. One that had started out as admiration for her courage and strength, but had quickly come to include lust. Elysande de Valance was one of those rare women a man could like, admire, respect and still want in his bed.

"I am sitting by the fire now. 'Tis safe for you to disrobe," Elysande said lightly.

Turning, he saw that she was indeed seated by the fire. She had donned her tunic, had wrapped her plaid around it under her arms, and was now curled up on the fur, brushing her hair in front of the flames. For a moment, Rory was tempted to join her and do the brushing for her, but instead he stood and removed his clothes, and then stepped into the bath.

"Will Tom and the others return from Buchanan in time to board the ship with us?"

Rory had just dropped to sit in the tub when Elysande asked that question. It was a small tub and he had to keep his knees up with the tops of his upper legs nearly flat against his stomach to fit in it, but the water was still hot and it felt damned good. He'd actually felt the tension seeping out of his body before Elysande had asked that question. It immediately made him tense again.

Rory didn't much care for lying, but when she'd asked about Tom, Donnghail and Fearghas earlier that day, and whether he'd tell them of his suspicions about Simon, he'd said he couldn't, that he'd sent them to Buchanan to fetch more coin to cover their prolonged stay at the inn. It was the lie he'd told the others, and was the one he was sticking to.

"Nay," he said finally. "'Tis at least a two-day journey to Buchanan from here. But I'll leave a message for them with the innkeeper." What he was really leaving was a note telling them where to find their horses. The ship he'd managed to get the men on going south had been fully loaded with cargo and had not had room for their mounts. They'd had to leave them behind and he'd given them coin to cover purchasing new ones when they reached Bristol. He'd then paid to have their mounts collected and stabled at an inn known never to take English guests. The innkeeper's wife had been raped and beaten to death by an Englishman some time ago and the man would sooner kill one as look at him. The innkeeper wouldn't be telling anyone with an English accent, or in English clothes, anything, let alone that he had Buchanan horses in his stables.

Fortunately, the horses weren't a worry for their own voyage. Having just unloaded its cargo, and carrying his group only so far as Thurso before continuing on to collect a fresh load in New Aberdeen, the *Mary Margaret* did have room for their mounts. So at least he wouldn't have to leave their horses behind and purchase new ones for the six of them when they reached their destination.

"Why did you send Tom with Fearghas and Donnghail?" she asked now, sounding troubled. "You do not suspect him too, do you?"

"Nay," he assured her quickly. "It just seemed better to have three to guard against attack by brigands or such, and I wanted at least two o' me men here to guard ye besides Alick and myself." That was almost the truth.

Afraid of what she might ask next, Rory prevented her from asking anything at all by telling her tales of the troubles he'd encountered on past travels as he rushed through his bath.

"MY, YOU HAVE TRAVELED A LOT AND HAD SOME ADVENTURES," Elysande commented, still laughing softly over a tale he'd told her about his party being attacked while he was bathing in a loch, and his rushing out to fight them naked, hampered by the need to cover himself with one hand for fear his adversary might lop off his manhood.

"Aye. I suppose I have," he agreed, sounding surprised at the realization.

Elysande hesitated and then asked, "Have you ever fallen in love during your travels?"

"Nay," he assured her with amusement. "No' until n—" He broke off abruptly, and then cleared his throat and said, "I was always too busy learning all I could about healing to pay much attention to the lasses."

Elysande was silent for a minute, considering what he'd said, and what she thought he might have been going to say. She was quite sure he had been about to say "not until now." At least, she hoped those were the words he'd cut off, because he made her feel loved and cared for and safe. The way he acted with her reminded her very much of how her father had been with her mother, and they had loved each other dearly. Her father had always been following her mother with his eyes, as Rory did with her. Had always been caring and solicitous, as Rory was with her. Even when disagreeing about something, her parents' love had been unmistakable.

And Mildrede had thought Rory cared for her. The alewife's comments about it were what had made Elysande notice his behavior toward her, and recognize her own growing feelings for him. Or at least acknowledge them. She supposed she'd been

aware of them on one level before that, but hadn't truly acknowledged them until Mildrede made her with a few comments. She
liked the man. She liked how he led the men with confidence and
ease. She respected him too, for both his healing skill and intel-
ligence. And she wanted him. Ever since those kisses and caresses
in the woods . . . well, they were never far from her mind. Nor was
the desire to experience them again. And perhaps more.

"What are ye thinking, lass?"

Rory's voice directly behind her made her start and glance over
her shoulder to find he was out of the bath, clad in his tunic and
plaid and settled on the fur behind her. She stared at him blankly,
vaguely aware that he was taking the brush from her hand, and
then she murmured, "That was fast."

"Aye. I found I wanted to help dry yer hair," he said with a
crooked smile, and then nudged her chin to get her to turn away
from him so that he could begin doing so. "Now tell me what ye
were thinking about."

"You," she admitted as he drew the brush through her hair in
long slow strokes.

"Oh?" She heard the smile in his voice. "And what were ye
thinking about me?"

"That I like you, and I like your kisses and would like for you
to kiss me again," Elysande said boldly, and was surprised when
Rory suddenly froze with the brush halfway through a stroke and
groaned miserably.

"Ah, lass," he sighed after a moment, and started brushing
again. "Ye ha'e no idea how much ye tempt me with such words.
But I canno'."

"Why?" she asked at once.

"Because ye're a temptation I find hard to resist, and the last time
I kissed ye I lost all control. Had we no' been interrupted by those
snapping branches in the woods, I might verra well have taken
yer innocence there up against that tree." When she didn't gasp
in shock or otherwise react to the comment, he added, "And if I
started kissing ye here, I'm quite sure I'd again no' be able to stop."

"Then do not stop," she said simply, and the brush stilled again.

"Lass," he said in warning.

Elysande turned to peer at him over her shoulder, and then shifted to face him properly and met his gaze. "When I left Kynardersley, I felt sure it would be the last time I would see it. I did not expect to survive to reach Sinclair, or warn the king. The odds were stacked against me, after all. One lass and a couple of young, newly knighted soldiers against up to six armies."

"Six?" he echoed with a frown. "De Buci has six co-conspirators?"

Elysande nodded, but left the subject behind to continue making her point. "As I say, I did not expect to survive, but you and your men make me feel safer. You even give me a little hope that I *might* survive or at least that my mother's messages will make it to Sinclair and the king. But most of me still does not expect to survive this journey."

Reaching out, she caressed his face gently, enjoying the feel of his newly shaved cheek against her fingers. "If there is even a chance that I might die, I should like very much to first experience your kisses and caresses again, and whatever follows should you lose control."

Rory caught her hand, stopping her from touching him anymore. "Lass, I ken ye fear ye'll no' survive and wish to enjoy what ye can while ye can, but I would no' do anything that ye might regret later."

"Why would I regret bedding a man I have come to love?" she asked, and the words were not at all hard to say. There was no hesitation, no blushing confession, no expectation that he should return her feelings and no fear that he would not. It was just a simple statement of fact, and Elysande felt that was as it should be. Love was a gift that should be given freely, and without the expectation of gaining anything in return. It was nothing to be ashamed of, nothing to be afraid of. It just was.

Rory stared at her for a long moment, and Elysande met his gaze unembarrassed, not trying to hide her feelings from him.

"Lass, I—" he began in a voice that rasped along her nerve

endings like a caress, and then he fell silent and she could see his honor battling with desire on his face.

Elysande wasn't interested in his honor, however. This might be her only chance to fully experience the pleasure he had given her a taste of in the woods. She was damned if she was dying without experiencing more of it. Elysande tugged her hand from his and reached up to untuck the plaid she'd wrapped around herself toga-style. Pulling the cloth free, she let the wool drop to pool around her waist and then began to undo the laces that ran down her chest to just above her breasts. Her hands were trembling now, but she managed the task, and then was able to push the wide neck off her shoulders, so that it too fell to pool around her waist. Raising her chin then, she smiled at him unashamed and said, "You introduced me to the innkeeper as your wife. Make love to me like a husband would."

The last word had barely left her lips when she found herself in Rory's arms, with his mouth on hers. A sigh of relief slipped from her as she parted her lips to him, welcoming him inside, overwhelmed by passion and need as he claimed what she offered.

By the end of the first kiss, Elysande was on her back on the fur, her arms tight around his shoulders, and her fingers buried in his hair as his hands began to move over her body. His touch was like fire, searing its way from her waist to her breast where it cupped and squeezed briefly before concentrating on the excited nipple there.

Elysande moaned into his mouth when he pinched and rolled the hard nub, her back arching eagerly into the caress. But the next moment she was groaning with disappointment as his hand glided away. But it was only leaving to examine other pastures, gliding over her shoulder, drifting along her collarbone, following her sternum to the valley between her breasts, before sliding left to claim the yet-untried one and palm and caress it now. All the while he was kissing her, his lips firm and demanding, his tongue thrusting and then rasping over hers until she thought she would burst into flames or die of the wanting. Instead, she kissed him back, unsure if she was doing it right, but emulating what he was doing and, if it felt good, doing it again.

Elysande thought she could go on kissing him until the end of time, so was most disappointed when his mouth left hers to sojourn across her cheek. That disappointment died when he reached her ear though. In a hundred years she never would have believed that his licking her ears and sucking the lobes into his mouth would be pleasurable, but it was and she found herself squirming, her hips rising in search of his, before dropping so that she could arch her back and press her breast into his caress.

When his mouth next made its way down her throat, nipping and sucking, she gasped and clutched at his hair. But when it trailed down to the breast he wasn't caressing, and closed over the hard, tingling nipple, Elysande had to release his hair and clasp her hand over her mouth to stifle the excited cry it brought out. It felt like he was drawing her soul out of her body through that hard nub, and filling her with flames at the same time. She was melting from the inside, liquid heat gathering in her lower stomach and then rolling down to pool between her legs where she suddenly felt swollen and achy with need.

As if sensing that need, Rory's meandering hand found its way down over her belly, and slid between her legs. His first brush against that most private juncture had her hips jerking, though she wasn't sure if it was from pleasure or shock, and then his fingers slid between her folds and found a spot she hadn't even realized existed; a button that swelled eagerly under his caress and began to pulse with shockwaves of mounting pleasure.

Almost frightened by the overwhelming passion now trying to claim her, Elysande gasped his name, and then his mouth left her breast and covered hers again, his tongue thrusting in a rhythm to match his caress. She was strung tight as a bow, her body almost vibrating when she felt something pushing inside of her even as he continued to caress her. The combination merely increased her pleasure and her fear as she became aware that her legs and hips were moving into the caress, wanting it, urging him on as he rimmed her entrance, slid deeper and then eased out to slide in again.

His mouth was still on hers, catching her cries when the dam burst and her body began to vibrate and convulse with the explosion of pleasure he'd brought on. Her legs closed instinctively around his hand, her mouth opening, unable to even pretend to kiss anymore as she lost control of her body.

Elysande thought he would stop then, or simply mount her and thrust into her body claiming her maidenhead, and she would have been perfectly happy to let him. It seemed a fair trade for the bliss he'd shown her. But he didn't. Rory didn't even stop caressing and kissing her, and before she could recover from the first wild ride, he was sending her on another.

By the third time he drove her to that pleasure again, Elysande was a mindless mass of trembling flesh on the furs, clutching at him as the only port in a storm. She hardly noticed when he shifted to rest between her thighs. She was aware though when he began to push into her, and noticed that what was entering her was much, much bigger, but her body stretched to welcome him, muscles she hadn't even realized she had tugging and pulling eagerly at him.

"Wrap yer legs around me, love."

Elysande heard that growled order, and automatically obeyed, curling her legs around his hips, her feet pressing eagerly at his bottom. Then Rory's mouth covered hers again and he thrust into her, breaking through her maidenhead and drawing a startled cry of pain from her before he froze, seeming to wait.

When he lifted his mouth from hers, she blinked her eyes open and peered up at his face in the light from the fireplace as she asked uncertainly, "Is it done?"

"The hard part is, love," he responded, and then lowered his head to kiss her again. This time it was a slow, sweet kiss that made her body slowly unclench. Once she relaxed, the tone of the kiss changed and he began to demand a response that she was happy to give now that the sharp sting was gone, and the earlier passion was returning.

When he began to move, Elysande was ready for it and moved with him, shifting her hips up into his thrusts even as she dug her heels into his bottom to urge him on. This time when she found her release and cried out into his mouth, he cried out with her, and it seemed the most perfect thing in the world to her that they found those heights together.

"A r e y e a l l r i g h t? D o e s a n y t h i n g h u r t?"

Elysande smiled at the question. Rory was on his back with her half on his chest, and his arms around her. One of her legs was thrown over his, and her fingers were skimming lightly over his chest, running through the coarse curls there.

"Nay," she said after a moment. "Nothing hurts, and I am more than all right. I am wonderful."

"Aye, ye are," he assured her, and she could hear the smile in his voice as his arm tightened around her briefly.

Elysande let her fingers drift down over his stomach, and asked, "Is it always like that?"

Rory hesitated, and then asked carefully, "Do ye mean will it always be like that between us? Or are ye asking would it be like that with another maun?"

"Both, I suppose," she said, rubbing her cheek against his chest. "I cannot believe that 'tis always like this for everyone, else no one would ever get out of bed."

Rory chuckled, and then said, "I can only tell ye that it has ne'er been like that fer me before. So I do no' think it would be like that with just any maun. As for whether it will always be like that between us . . . I hope so."

Elysande was considering that when he asked, "Shall we try again and see if 'tis just as good a second time?"

The question made her still, at least on the outside. But every nerve ending in her body seemed to jump at it. For an answer, she turned her face and pressed her lips to the almost flat nipple that had been resting under her cheek and sucked on it experimentally.

"Mmm," Rory murmured, his hand sweeping down to clasp her bottom and squeeze firmly. "Ye've an adventurous spirit. That's a good thing, lass. For I ha'e so many things I want to do with ye, I do no' ken where to start."

Elysande let his nipple slip from her mouth and glanced to his face with surprise. "There is more than what we already did?"

"Oh, aye," he growled, suddenly rising up and sliding over her. Holding his weight with his arms, he nestled his hips between her thighs and began to rub against her.

Elysande's eyes widened at this new caress. Moments ago, his shaft had been deflated and resting peacefully. Now it was hard as he pressed against her. Feeling her own excitement burst back to life within her, Elysande reached for him, wanting to draw him down for a kiss, but he eluded her hands by sliding farther down her body.

"No' this time, love, there are other lips I've a mind to kiss."

She was just stiffening at the suggestion that he might go find another lass to kiss when he clasped her thighs in hand, spread them and ducked in to press his lips to the center of her excitement. Elysande was reeling in shock from the bold move when he began to lash her with his tongue, showing her a whole other way of kissing. It was the first of many such lessons he taught her that night.

Chapter 16

"**Y**OU APPEAR TO BE WELL OVER THE ATTACK."

Elysande turned from watching Rory and the other men settle the horses about a third of the way up the *Mary Margaret*'s empty hold, and peered at Simon with a somewhat weary smile. She hadn't had much sleep the night before. Rory had kept her up well past the witching hour, showing her different ways of loving, and she had enjoyed every moment of it. But it had seemed to her that they'd barely, finally, drifted off to sleep before he was shaking her awake, kissing her cheek and urging her to dress because it was "time to go."

"Aye, I am feeling much better, Simon. Thank you," she murmured now, shifting her gaze back to Rory and the other men. While she was exhausted enough that she suspected she could drift off to sleep standing there on the deck of the cargo hold, leaning against the hull of the ship, Rory looked strong, and fit as ever. There wasn't even a hint of tiredness showing on his face while she knew she probably had dark circles under her eyes and was no doubt pale with lack of sleep. Life could be so unfair sometimes.

"The Buchanan gave us the impression that you were dying," Simon said now. "Yet you look fine."

"Aye. Well, head wounds can be tricky," she answered vaguely, wishing Rory would hurry and join her. She wasn't at all comfortable lying to Simon, but there was nothing else she could do.

After getting her up and dressed that morning, Rory had opened the door to the hall to find Alick on a pallet blocking the threshold. It was only then that Elysande had realized he should have been in the room with them. At least, the man had been sleeping in the bed with her and Rory when she'd woken up in the middle of that first night. He'd also spent the day in the room with them, playing cards and other games to help pass the time. It was only when the bath had been ready that he'd left and gone below to sit with the men in the taproom, leaving Rory to guard her alone. She had heard Rory promise to call him back up when she was done with her bath. But Rory had never called him back. Instead, he'd taken a bath after her and then . . .

Elysande bit her lip and switched her gaze to Alick as she wondered what he'd thought when Rory hadn't arrived to fetch him back to the room. Had he come up to see what was taking so long? If so, why hadn't he knocked?

The obvious answer seemed to be that he'd stopped at the door and heard something that had made him think an interruption would not be appreciated, so had gone to request a pallet from Angus, the innkeeper, and had settled down to sleep outside the door, probably hearing all their love talk, and her cries of passion. The very possibility of that having happened was enough to make Elysande go scarlet with embarrassment.

Not that Alick had said or done anything to cause her embarrassment when Rory had woken him. The younger man had merely risen, wished them both "good morn" and taken the pallet to wherever he'd got it. He'd then returned to help them gather the bags and carry them down to the stable. The brothers had then quickly saddled the horses, all six of them, before Alick had returned to the dark inn to wake and fetch the men.

While he was gone, Elysande had helped Rory hook the bags over the pommels of hers and Rory's saddles and then had mounted with no more than a leg up from him. That had been nice, she acknowledged now. It was really quite glorious to be without pain for a change.

Simon had been half-asleep and confused when Alick, Conn and Inan had led him out to the stables. He'd been complaining that it wasn't even dawn yet, and asking what they were about as he walked. But had fallen into a shocked silence when he'd spotted Elysande astride her mount beside Rory on his. He'd tried to rush to her side, but Rory had moved his horse in front of hers and ordered him to mount up or be left behind.

Simon had glanced from him to Elysande, but then had mounted. He'd tried several times to move his horse close to hers during the short trot through the dark, empty streets of the city. But Alick had taken up position on one side of her, and Rory on the other, and neither man had made way for him. Simon had started asking questions then, asking when she had woken, and where they were going, but Rory had hushed him and said he would explain all later. That they needed to move quietly did they wish to escape de Buci's men.

Simon had fallen silent as ordered, but he'd been practically vibrating with the questions he wanted answers to for the rest of the ride to the docks. And frankly, Elysande thought he deserved those answers. But he wasn't asking them anymore. At least, not ones she could answer. She could hardly tell him that she hadn't been badly hurt at all, but they had kept that from him because Rory suspected him of being her attacker. Besides, she *had* been unconscious for days, even if only because of the tincture Rory had given her and that she'd eagerly taken the first three mornings and evenings when she woke with her head pounding so violently she'd wanted to die. And she didn't regret it at all. The days of sleep had not only given her head a chance to heal so it no longer ached, but it had gone a long way toward healing her ankle and back as well. Other than feeling tired, she had not felt this good in weeks.

"Your head wound is nearly completely healed," Simon pointed out stiffly, drawing her attention back to him. "There is no swelling and it has scabbed over. It looks like it should have been little trouble at all."

Elysande reached up and touched her forehead, realizing only then that in their rush to dress and head for the *Mary Margaret*, they hadn't thought to replace the bandages on her head that she'd removed before her bath. Actually, they hadn't thought to replace any of her bandages, although her chest wound really didn't need it. In truth, none of her injuries needed it anymore. But they might have helped keep Simon from questioning her like an angry father.

"And I do not notice any stiffness in your movements, so can only presume your chest wound is not troubling you either," Simon said tightly.

"The chest wound was a trifle," Elysande said honestly. "'Twas really only the head wound that was a concern. However, the swelling went down, the pain eased and I woke yesterday morning."

"And yet the Buchanan didn't trouble himself to let the rest of us know?"

And that is where honesty gets you, Elysande thought grimly, but said, "In truth, he probably did not even think to tell you." That was definitely a truth, she thought. Rory wouldn't have even considered it because he suspected the man of being behind the attack. But she didn't say that: instead she told him, "He had a great many questions for me about the attack, and then had much to tell me about it as well, and then, of course, there were the preparations to make for this trip to Sinclair."

"Sinclair?" Simon asked sharply. "That is where we are going?"

"Of course. It is always where we were going," she pointed out.

"Aye, but I thought we would ride there," he muttered with a frown.

"So did I," she admitted. "But the boat will cut the length of our journey in half and we can get the warning to the king sent much sooner than if we had traveled by horse."

Simon looked away briefly, and then turned back to ask, "What about Tom? Rory said he sent him with Fearghas and Donnghail to Buchanan to fetch back coin to pay for the inn. Are we just going to leave without him?" he asked, and then added, "That's not right. We should get off this ship at once. We cannot leave Tom behind."

He grasped her elbow and tried to tug her toward the steps leading out of the cargo, but Elysande pulled free and scowled at him. Perhaps it was just that Rory had raised questions in her mind, but his behavior was making her very suspicious. "Tom will be fine. Rory left a message for him at the inn. He will follow us to Sinclair with Fearghas and Donnghail."

"But—"

"We are sailing for Sinclair, Simon. 'Twas our goal from the start. Get to Sinclair, give him my mother's messages and have him send them on to the king."

"I cannot guard you alone, m'lady," Simon said with frustration. "'Twas bad enough when it was just Tom and I, but now I alone stand between you and de Buci and I really think we should get off this ship and wait for Tom so that he can help me keep you safe."

"Simon," she said firmly. "You and Tom were only supposed to get me to Rory and his men and accompany us to Scotland. He is the one who is supposed to keep me safe and get me to Sinclair and he is doing that. I am not leaving this ship, and you should not want me to," she added grimly. "Not with de Buci's men somewhere in Ayr, waiting to kill me. We are safe on the *Mary Margaret* and we are staying on the *Mary Margaret*."

"But Tom—" Simon began almost desperately, only to snap his mouth shut when Rory appeared at Elysande's side and eyed him suspiciously.

"Are we leaving soon?" Elysande asked to draw his attention away from the English soldier.

"We already left," Rory said quietly. "The captain set sail the minute we finished moving the horses down here to the hold. We are under way."

"Oh," Elysande breathed, relaxing into him. She hadn't even realized they were moving, but then the harbor was calm, and they probably were not moving quickly.

"So that's the way of it," Simon said suddenly, his voice cold.

Elysande glanced to him with confusion, and then followed

his gaze to where Rory had automatically slid his arm around her waist and drawn her into his chest. After only one night as lovers, she'd already gotten so used to his touch and easy affection that she hadn't even noticed.

"The way of what?" Rory asked, his voice carrying a warning that Simon completely ignored.

"Why ye kept her locked in that bedchamber with you at the inn for three days and nights," Simon said sharply.

Rory narrowed his eyes, but his tone was mild when he said, "If there's something ye'd like to say, Simon, say it."

Simon glared at him briefly, but instead asked Elysande, "Are you still a maiden?"

Elysande gasped at the impertinent question, but it was Rory who answered, "That is none o' yer business. And unless ye're wanting me to throw ye off this ship, I'll thank ye no' to speak to me wife that way."

"Wife?" Simon barked with shock.

"Aye. I introduced her to the innkeeper as me wife, Lady Elysande Buchanan, if ye'll recall, and she answered to the name and title. In Scotland, that is consent and makes us married," he growled. "Now leave us, I would talk to me wife."

If Simon was shocked by this announcement, Elysande was no less so. Quite dazed, she stumbled over her own feet when Rory urged her away from Simon and toward the back of the cargo hold. Pausing then, he glanced back to be sure they had privacy, before looking her over with concern and asking, "Are ye all right, love?"

"Aye. Nay. I do not know," she finished finally, and then asked, "Are we really married by Scottish law?"

"Aye," he assured her. "Or as good as, but I'll no' hold ye to it do ye no' wish it. Though the truth is I'd like to," he admitted. "I'd like nothing better in this world than to take ye to Buchanan and marry ye good and proper in front o' a priest and with me sister and brothers and all their mates there as I claim ye as me own in front o' God and all."

"You would?" she asked, a smile of wonder claiming her lips.

"Aye. I love ye, lass. I should ha'e told ye that when ye told me o' yer feelings, but I had other things on me mind," he admitted with a grimace. "I'm telling ye now though. I love ye so much that I'd even move to that godforsaken country ye're from and help ye run Kynardersley. Though I'd really rather no'," he confessed.

While she was still blinking at that, Rory added, "And so ye ken, I'm no' just some seventh son without prospects. Me parents left me good fertile land here in Scotland, and I've earned enough coin with me healing to build a fine castle on it. But as I said, I love ye enough I'll move to England do ye wish it and—" Pausing abruptly, he glanced around with suddenly wild eyes, and then rushed to the corner where a bucket rested next to the wall. He had barely dropped to his knees before it when he began heaving up whatever he had in his stomach.

"Well, was no' that the most charming proposal ye've ever heard?" Alick asked cheerfully as he stopped beside her.

Elysande peered at him with disbelief.

"Well, except for the spewing," he added, and then told her, "That has nothing to do with you, lass. Or even with the idea o' living in England. Rory gets sick on the sea, is all."

"He does?" She eyed Rory with concern.

"Aye. Makes him terrible sick," Alick said with a shrug and complete lack of concern. "He'll be spewing all the way to Thurso."

"Oh, for heaven's sake," Elysande breathed with disbelief, and then asked, "Where is his bag of weeds?"

"On his mount still. Why?" Alick asked with surprise.

"Because I need it," she said dryly, and hurried to the horses with Alick on her heels.

"What're ye going to do?" Alick asked, lifting off the small leather bag for her before she could reach it.

"Make him a tincture to soothe his stomach," she muttered, opening the bag.

"Ye can do that?" Alick asked with interest.

"If he has the right weeds for it," she said, and then began to paw through the various items in the bag, murmuring the name of each she found that was needed, "Fennel, root of ginger, chamomile blossom . . ."

"I wonder why Rory has ne'er heard o' this tincture?" Alick muttered, taking the weeds she was passing him and holding them as she searched for the next.

Elysande shrugged as she continued pulling out items. "My mother and I learned it from the wife of one of our soldiers. She came from a coastal village and her father was a fisherman who suffered a sore stomach when he worked on the water. Which was rather inconvenient for a fisherman," she pointed out. "But she said this helped and I never forgot the ingredients she listed off. There," she finished with relief. "He has everything I need."

Closing the bag, she glanced around with a frown. "Is there somewhere to boil water on this ship?"

"O' course," Alick said with amusement. "They have to feed the men on voyages. Follow me."

"How do you feel now?"

Rory opened his eyes and peered at the angel hovering above him. Elysande. She'd made a tincture, and bullied him into drinking it, which he'd at first refused to do for fear of just giving his stomach something else to reject. Once she'd convinced him to down it though, she'd settled on the wooden deck and eased his head into her lap. They'd stayed that way for the last half hour, with her running her fingers soothingly over his forehead as they waited to see if he could keep the tincture down. It had been touch and go at first, but Rory hadn't tossed it back up, and now his stomach was actually settling, the queasiness almost completely gone.

"Better," he admitted. "Thank ye."

"You are welcome," she said, a relieved smile curving her lips. "Now, why do you not get some rest? You got little sleep last night and could only benefit from a nap."

"Aye." He turned his head in her lap to look for Simon and

spotted him sitting with the other men about halfway between where he and Elysande sat and the horses. Conn, Inan and Alick were playing cards with the English soldier. Rory watched Simon briefly, but then—deciding the men would keep an eye on him—he sat up and leaned to the side to grab the rolled-up fur that lay next to their bags. Standing, he spread it out on the floor, and then offered Elysande a hand to help her rise.

"What are we doing?" she asked as he urged her onto the fur.

"We're taking a nap," he announced. "Ye got no more sleep than I did last night and we would both benefit from a rest."

She didn't comment, but he noted the pink blush that crept up her face and knew she was recalling the reason for their lack of sleep. It made him think of the hours of loving they'd enjoyed too, and when his cock stirred under his plaid, Rory started wishing they had their own cabin. But the only cabin on this cog was the captain's and he hadn't been willing to give it up. Rory hadn't minded when he'd been negotiating this trip. He'd actually thought it was probably better for them all to stick together in the cargo hold. But now he was wondering how much coin it would take to convince the man to give up his cabin.

"Are you not going to lie down too?"

That question from Elysande drew him from his thoughts to the realization that she had lain down on the furs on her side with her head on her arm for a pillow. Leaving the possibility of a cabin for later, Rory stretched out on his side at her back, and then wrapped his arm around her and pulled her possessively back against his chest. When she released a little sigh, and wiggled her bottom back against his groin before settling down, Rory found himself smiling and pressing a kiss to her ear.

He had her safely on the ship. They'd reach Sinclair in a few days, and probably stay there until the English king dealt with his conspiring lords. It was the safest place for her until then and he had nothing pressing to drag him away from her. They could spend the time planning their future. Either working out what they would need to do to set Kynardersley back to rights, or design the castle he'd planned to build. He was hoping for the latter. Rory would live in England if he had to in order to have Elysande . . . despite disliking the country. But he didn't think it would be good for her. Kynardersley would never again be the happy childhood home where she'd grown up. Not after watching her parents die there, he thought. She would see that again in her mind every time she entered the great hall. He didn't want that for her. The shadows were only now starting to leave her eyes; he didn't want her to live somewhere that would bring those shadows back several times a day.

"I love you, Rory."

The words were so soft he barely heard them, but they were powerfully strong, sending a rush of warmth through him that made his arm tighten around her.

"I love ye too, lass," he growled, and pressed a kiss to her ear before closing his eyes and allowing himself to drift off to sleep.

ELYSANDE WAS MUTTERING TO HERSELF MOST UNHAPPILY AS SHE made her way to the steps out of the ship's heads. This was her first trip on a boat, and she was determined it would be her last.

There was no privy on the cog.

That had been a shock, but even more shocking had been what a person was expected to do to take care of such matters. Good Lord, traveling by horse was bad enough with its lack of amenities. But it was worse on the *Mary Margaret*. On the ship, everyone went to the foredeck and climbed down into an area they called the heads, which was under the bowsprit of the ship. There they either pissed through the slats, which were several inches apart, or sat on a plank hung over the side of the ship for their other business. Of course, that was how the men did it. She had to sit the plank for both, her bare bottom hanging out over the water far below.

Elysande found it nerve-racking, especially when the water was rough and the wind was high and the risk of tipping—or being blown—off the narrow plank and falling into the sea far below increased. But she also had the strangest thoughts while sitting there. She worried over whether sharks could jump high enough to bite her bare bottom. Nay, no more sailing for her. At least on land, you didn't risk your life every time you had to relieve yourself.

"M'lady."

Elysande stopped abruptly, her wary gaze rising to Simon as he stepped down into the heads, blocking her exit. It had been two days since they'd set sail, and nearly as long since she'd had to speak to the man thanks to Rory and the others running interference. But they were supposed to reach Thurso sometime on the morrow and she was very aware that if Simon was behind the stabbing, and even pushing her in front of the horse and cart, then he would want to finish the job before they reached Sinclair. He was running out of time.

"I wanted to have a word with you, but it has been hard to get you alone," Simon said pleasantly. "The Buchanan doesn't usually leave your side."

"Nay. He is very protective, but he was sleeping and I did not wish to disturb him," Elysande murmured. She hadn't wished to disturb Rory because she found it humiliating to be sitting there with her bare arse hanging out in the wind and him guarding her. He might have seen her naked, and touched nearly every part of her body the night before this journey on the *Mary Margaret*, but that was not the same as watching her perform such personal functions. So, when she'd woken up with a desperate need to relieve herself, Elysande had left him sleeping with the rest of the men and crept out of the cargo to make her way to the heads alone. It had never occurred to her that Simon might wake up and follow her. But then, it wasn't something she would have expected. No one followed her when she went to the heads except Rory. Even the sailors stayed away and allowed her privacy.

Simon was still moving slowly closer, and Elysande had nowhere to go unless she wished to sit or step back onto the plank, so she held up her hand in a silent order to stop. Much to her surprise, he did. Then they stood there for a minute just looking at each other. Elysande took in his grim and miserable expression, and noted that his hand was on his sword, clenching and unclenching as if he was waging an inner war, and she just knew that Rory had been right about everything. Simon was working for de Buci.

The realization was a depressing one. It also hurt her a great deal. She had lost her mother and father to de Buci's cruelty and perfidy, not to mention every soldier at Kynardersley but Tom and Simon. She could not understand how he could betray her to such a man. Had he cared so little for her parents, who had shown him nothing but kindness and caring? And what of the soldiers who had been his comrades?

Lifting her chin, she spoke in an empty voice. "Rory was right. You are the one who stabbed me."

Simon stiffened, dismay on his face, and for one minute she hoped she was wrong after all, until he said, "He knows?"

Elysande's shoulders tried to sag, but she forced them back up, and kept her head high and her tone cool and empty as she said, "Aye. And about you pushing me in front of the horse and cart. They all know."

She saw panic flash over his face, and hopelessness, and asked, "Why, Simon? I trusted you. My father was good to you. Our families have been friends for years. You were like a member of the family. Why would you work for de Buci against your king?"

"I don't have a choice." Simon ran a hand over his scalp, his eyes darting this way and that as if seeking escape.

"You always have a choice," she said firmly.

Simon stilled then, and closed his eyes briefly. When he opened them again they were steady and sad. "Not this time," he said, and started forward, pulling his sword from his belt.

"At least tell me why first," Elysande demanded, and much to her relief he stopped again.

"You know why," he said grimly.

Her expression must have been as bewildered as she felt at that statement, because he frowned and said, "My father?"

Elysande shook her head slightly. "Your father what?"

"His name is in Wykeman's message to de Buci. He is one of the conspirators," Simon said as if that should be obvious, and then he shook his head with disgust. "The stupid bastard. I never would have imagined he'd do something so foolish, and I'd let him hang for it, but it wouldn't just be him. My whole family would be shamed, our title and lands stripped from us. My sisters' betrotheds would probably refuse to fulfill the marriage contracts. My mother would die in ruin and—" He shook his head miserably. "You've been like family to me for years, m'lady. But they *are* my family, and much as I loathe the doing, it has to be done."

When he started forward again, Elysande stood her ground and said sharply, "Your father's name is not on the scroll from Wykeman, Simon. Whoever told you that lied to you."

Stopping again, he frowned with uncertainty. "But Capshaw said . . ."

"Who is Capshaw?" Elysande asked quietly when he hesitated. "How do you know him?"

Simon glanced down at the slats, his expression troubled. "I do not know him," he said unhappily. "I met him for the first time the night we arrived in Ayr. When I went back out to get your bags, he was waiting in the stables. He said his name was Capshaw, that he was Wykeman's man and was surprised that I would champion you when it would see my own father hanged and my family ruined. He said Father's name was in the scrolls as a co-conspirator, and unless I wished to see him swing and lose my title and inheritance, I'd best be sure you never got to Sinclair or the king with those letters." His mouth tightened. "I have been reporting to him ever since."

"I see," Elysande murmured. "Well, Mr. Capshaw lied," she assured him, and when he looked unsure whether to believe her or not, she asked, "Do you really think my mother would have sent me with you had your father's name been in Wykeman's message? I promise you, it is nowhere in those letters."

For one minute she thought he would lay down his sword and

beg her forgiveness, but then he frowned. "Or mayhap you're lying to save yourself."

Now that was just insulting, Elysande thought with irritation, and glared at him as she began to pat at her skirts in search of the messages. "I do not lie, and I can show you the messages to prove it. I—" Pausing, she scowled with vexation and started using both hands to find the messages that should be in a pocket sewn into her skirts, and then she stilled as she realized the last time she'd seen the scroll to Sinclair had been when she'd put it into the gown she'd been stabbed in. She had never transferred it to this gown when she'd donned it. She hadn't even seen the old one since the attack. Dear God, she'd lost the messages and the warning to the king!

"Tom has it."

Elysande's head jerked up at those words to see Rory stepping down into the heads, his sword drawn. His appearance made Simon cross the last few steps to Elysande and grasp her upper arm.

"Or perhaps the king does now," Rory added, his gaze narrowing on Simon even as he asked her, "Are ye all right, love?"

"Aye," Elysande answered, and ignoring Simon, she asked, "What does Tom have?"

"The scrolls," he explained, looking ridiculously relaxed despite the sword in his hand. "Your mother's message to Sinclair with the other messages inside. I took it from your dress after the stabbing and gave it to Tom, then I put him and Fearghas and Donnghail on the *Marie Levieux*, another cog, one heading south to Bristol. I would guess they have put ashore by now, and are on their way to court, or, if the wind was with them for their journey, they may have already arrived at court and the king may even now have your mother's warning."

Elysande gaped at him and then snapped her mouth closed and asked, "Why did you not tell me? I thought my heart would stop when I could not find it. I feared I had lost it."

"I could no' risk anyone overhearing, love. I did no' ken who was or was no' working for de Buci, and who might listen at doors for him for a coin. If he caught wind of the fact that the boys were headed for court with Wykeman's letter, he would have dropped everything and cast a net over the whole of South England to try to capture the men and stop the message. And aside from no' wanting to see Tom or me men killed, I kenned it was important to ye that the king get his warning." He smiled slightly. "But I planned to tell ye today or tomorrow. I just wanted to wait until it was too late for de Buci to stop them before I did." His gaze slid to Simon as he added, "In case some other scurvy bastard traitor who worked for de Buci overheard."

Elysande saw the slight wincing motion around Simon's eyes, and felt his hand tighten on her arm and knew Rory had struck a blow. Simon was young, and newly knighted with all the grand notions of honor and chivalry that a knight was said to have, and he had betrayed them. She knew he would not be able to reconcile himself with what he'd done, even if it had been for his family.

"Simon," she said gently. "You need to put your sword down now."

His head turned very slowly toward her, and he closed his eyes briefly, before opening them to ask, "Do you promise me my father is not named as a conspirator in the plot?"

"I promise you," she said solemnly.

Simon nodded wearily, and glanced past her to the icy water spreading out around the ship, and then lifted his gaze to the steep cliffs they could just make out in the distance. The shores of Scotland, though she had no idea where. Somewhere far north, she supposed, if they were only a day away from Thurso.

"Simon, no," she said, her voice low and urgent. "You would never make it. You will freeze to death or drown."

"And hanging is better?" he asked softly, keeping his voice low so that Rory couldn't hear. "I am sorry for trying to kill you, m'lady. It was a terrible struggle for me even to attempt it each time. Mayhap that is why I failed," he added wryly, but then shrugged and said, "But while I know I should give myself up and let them hang me for it, I find I have a great desire to live . . . if only long enough to have a word with Capshaw."

"Simon," she began, but it was too late. Releasing her arm, he dropped his sword, stepped past her and disappeared over the side of the ship.

Chapter 17

ELYSANDE RUSHED TO THE RAILING AND LEANED FORWARD TO peer anxiously down at the water below. It seemed to take a long time, but finally she saw Simon's dark head bob to the surface, and then he struck out, swimming for the distant cliffs.

"Do you think he will make it?" she asked when she felt Rory's heat at her back and his hands at her waist.

"I do no' ken," Rory said solemnly. "But if he does, I hope he heads to France or somewhere else on the Continent."

"Why?" Elysande asked, glancing around at him with surprise.

"Because do we meet again I would have to kill him," Rory admitted solemnly. "And I suspect ye would no' like that."

"Nay, I would not," she agreed, turning back to watch the man struggle through the frigid water. "He was only trying to save his family."

"By killing you," Rory said grimly.

"Would you not kill for your family?" Elysande asked quietly, and when he scowled at the question, she said, "I would have killed de Buci in a heartbeat to save mine."

Rory let his breath out on a sigh and slid an arm around her, drawing her into his side. "Ye're a fierce lass. Have I mentioned I like that about ye?"

"Nay," she said, leaning into him.

"Well, I do," he assured her, and laid a kiss on her forehead before releasing her. "Now go away."

"What?" Elysande turned on him with surprise, but stilled when she noted the green tinge to his skin, and the sweat above his upper lip. "Your stomach is churning again," she realized, and then muttered, "Of course 'tis. The tincture I gave you yesterday will have worn off."

"Aye," he groaned, and moved to lean over the railing. "Now go away. Ye do no' need to see this unpleasantness."

"Oh, aye, but watching me on the plank is so much more pleasant," she said dryly, moving to his side, and pulling his hair back from his face to hold it out of the way for him.

Her words startled a half chuckle out of Rory that ended on a groan as he clutched his stomach. "Dear God, I hate boats."

"And yet traveling to Sinclair by boat was your idea," she said softly, pressing a kiss to his arm.

"Aye. It was the best way I could think o' to keep ye safe," Rory admitted. "I'd ride into hell to keep ye safe, lass."

Elysande felt her heart swell, and pressed a kiss quickly to his cheek. "I love you. I will be back directly."

Rory merely groaned as she released his hair and hurried out of the heads.

"Oh, good. I was starting to worry, lass."

Elysande's steps slowed, and she smiled at the captain as he approached. "Worry about what, sir?"

"Well, I saw that Englishman follow ye out to the heads," he explained. "Looked to me like he was up to no good, so I thought I'd best warn yer husband. He hied himself out there, but the three o' ye were down there so long I worried the Buchanan was tossing the bastard overboard."

"Oh, nay," Elysande assured him quickly, and then explained, "Simon jumped overboard."

"What?" he squawked with alarm.

"Aye. He was planning to kill me until Rory arrived, and then he dropped his sword and jumped when he knew he was caught," she explained. "And thank you for waking and warning my husband, Captain. Now I hope you will forgive me, but I have to go. Rory has a touch of tummy upset from the motion of the ship. I need to fetch him his tincture."

Giving the man a bright smile, she rushed off to the cargo hold and made her way down. The men were taking care of the horses when she got below: feeding them, cleaning up after them and brushing them down to soothe them. Elysande smiled and waved as she passed, but didn't stop to talk.

"Simon's missing," Alick announced, approaching as she quickly mixed up more of the tincture for Rory's stomach. "So is Rory."

"Rory is on the head deck, spewing," Elysande told him as he worked. She didn't tell him about Simon though. She just didn't want to talk about him at the moment. Her feelings about the man were conflicted. She knew he'd tried to kill her, but it had been out of fear for his family, and she found she felt sorry for him.

"Making him more tincture?" Alick asked, and she nodded as she stirred the mixture she'd made. "Is there anything I can do to help?"

Elysande started to shake her head and then changed her mind. "Mayhap you could lay out the fur again. It looks as if Rory rolled it up when he woke and he'll probably want to lie down until the tincture starts to work."

When Alick nodded and moved to do what she asked, Elysande thanked him and headed for the cargo doors with the tincture.

Rory was hanging over the railing, looking exhausted and pale when she got back to him. But he straightened and took the tincture when she offered it. He paused a moment though, swallowing several times before he drank it, and then he stood absolutely still as if afraid any movement might lead to it coming back up. Elysande took the chalice from him and simply stood rubbing his back as they waited for the mix to take effect. A smile claimed her lips though when he began to stretch and press into her caress like a cat being petted.

A few minutes later, they left the heads—much to the relief of a sailor who had apparently been waiting. They returned to the cargo bay and sat down together on the fur Alick had laid out, then Elysande urged him to rest his head in her lap.

Rory smiled faintly when she immediately began to run her fingers through his long hair, then rub them gently over his forehead. The touch was almost as soothing as the tincture she made, and he eventually opened his eyes to look up at her face.

Rory then stared at her for a long moment, taking in the shape of her eyes, and the fullness of her lips. Now that the bruising was gone, he could see she was a fine-looking woman. But even when her looks had been marred by the bruises, he'd been attracted to her. She had a strength and calm that had drawn him, a steely determination that had impressed him, and he only wished he could have impressed her as well.

"That is an odd look, m'laird," Elysande said suddenly. "What are you thinking about?"

Rory recalled asking her the same question not long ago and answered it the same way she had at the time, saying, "You," and they smiled at each other.

"Ye ken ye've rendered me useless," he said suddenly.

Elysande's eyebrows rose. "I have?"

"Aye," he assured her on a sigh, and then closed his eyes and admitted, "From the minute I saw the bruising on yer face on that first day when I dragged ye off yer horse, I wanted nothing more than to help in some way, to use me healing skills to ease yer pain."

"You pitied me," she said sadly.

"Nay," he said at once, his eyes shooting open. "Lass, there was no pity. Ye were so magnificent. Until that moment I had no idea ye were wounded, but when I saw the bruising I kenned the pain ye must be in, and yet ye had no' complained, or even shown that ye were hurting, and ye kept up with us though I'd set a grueling pace fer the ride." He shook his head with remembered awe. "And then, when I saw yer back . . . My God," he murmured at the memory. "I did no' ken where ye got the strength to carry on, but ye did. I was impressed," he admitted. "And I wanted to impress ye too. I wanted to show off me so-called skills and heal all yer pains. But I was no' able to help ye at all in the end."

"Of course you helped me, husband," Elysande argued at once, and blushed when the word *husband* made him smile.

"How did I help ye?" he asked with amusement.

"You put liniment on my back," she reminded him, but he snorted in response.

"Lass, it was liniment ye made yerself, and that the alewife put on ye several times ere I ever did," he pointed out dryly. "It did no' take much skill. Just hands."

Elysande frowned, but said, "Well, you also wrapped my ankle when I twisted it."

"Alick could have done that, or any one o' the men," he scoffed.

"You also sewed up my chest wound, and bandaged my head wound."

"Aye, I was so desperate to do something that I put two stitches in yer chest that ye probably did no' even need," he admitted with disgust. "As fer yer head wound, all I did was wash and bandage it, and again, the bandage was no' really necessary. Anyone could ha'e done that. Ye did no' need a healer."

"You gave me those tinctures to ease my pain when I woke up with my head pounding so vilely after the attack," Elysande pointed out.

"'Twas a sleeping tincture. I made ye sleep through the pain, lass. I could no' ease it," he said sadly. "While ye've made a tincture that I did no' even ken existed, one that eased my sickness from the motion o' the boat."

She frowned briefly, and then said, "You have kept me safe since Monmouth, seeing me safely out of Carlisle, and on to Ayr."

"Lass, I did no' keep ye safe. Mildrede saved us all in Carlisle, and you led me out o' the city blindfolded," Rory pointed out dryly. "Nor did I keep ye safe in Ayr. Ye saved yerself by cleverly tucking yer coins between yer beautiful breasts and falling as ye were stabbed so the blade barely scratched ye."

Elysande bit her lip to keep from smiling. He'd called her breasts beautiful. Forcing the smile away, she said, "You are getting me to Sinclair and you sent Tom, Fearghas and Donnghail to court with the warning for the king. You are a hero, husband."

"Let's hope," he said wearily. "We will no' ken fer a while if they made it or were stopped and slaughtered by de Buci's men."

Elysande stiffened at the suggestion. "I hope not. I am quite fond of all three men."

Rory grunted, his eyes closing. But they popped open again when she said his name softly.

Meeting his gaze then, she said, "'Tis true I have some skill at healing. But that only means I can help you when you need assistance healing others. And," she added firmly when he would have interrupted, "you have impressed me time and again since our first meeting. You have given freely of your time, your own coin and your caring to help a lass you had never even heard of before that day in the clearing. You also made me feel safe, and gave me hope." She met his gaze solemnly. "Those are not things one can learn in a book. They are . . ." She paused briefly, searching for the right word, and then said simply, "They are you. You are a good man, Rory, a man who shows kindness to an English alewife even though she treated you badly at first, and who saves a king who is your enemy just because it is right." She smiled. "You are a man worthy of love." Tilting her head, she added, "People may need a healer, but they do not love them. They love the man."

Rory stared at her blankly for a minute, her words rolling around inside his head, and then shifted to tug her down to lie with him on the fur. Once he had her arranged in his arms in the morning position he liked so much, he then kissed the top of her head and said, "Thank God yer mother sent ye to me. She called ye her treasure, and she was right. Fer that's what ye are to me."

Epilogue

"I WANT YE ALL TO BE READY," RORY GROWLED IN AN UNDER-tone. "Does the king try to have our marriage annulled and take Elysande away, we'll need to act quickly. I'll no'—"

"What are you men whispering about?"

Rory snapped his mouth closed and glanced around at his wife's exasperated voice, and then hurried over to take her arm when she pushed herself up off the chair the king's guards had rushed to get for her when they'd realized her condition.

"Ye should stay seated until we're called, lass," he reprimanded with a scowl, trying to urge her back into the chair. "Ye should really have yer legs up too. They've been swelling o' late." Scowling at her, he added, "I canno' believe ye agreed to travel to the English court in yer condition."

"I am only just over five months along, husband," Elysande said soothingly. "'Tis fine."

"Five months but looking nine," Alick commented with a grin. "I'm thinking we're about to have more twins in the family."

"Aye," Rory breathed, and swallowed the sheer terror that thought sent through him. God in heaven! They had only just started construction on their castle; it would be five to seven years before it was done. Of course, they could move in once the castle keep itself was done, but that would take at least two years, and then they'd be living with the constant chaos and noise of the wall and remaining buildings being erected. The kitchens, the garrison, the chapel, the towers . . .

In the meantime, they were staying in Aulay and Jetta's hunting lodge. It had seemed a good idea when he'd arranged it with Aulay. They would no longer be underfoot at Buchanan castle, and the lodge was closer to his property and the castle construction he was overseeing. But he was beginning to think it wasn't such a good idea, after all. It wasn't the lodge itself. Rory loved the family hunting lodge. It was full of good memories for him. Hunting parties with friends and family, and the more recent short stays with his brothers and brothers-in-law when the women had wanted time alone to plot marrying off the remaining single Buchanan men.

Aye, Rory loved the hunting lodge . . . for a getaway. He was not enjoying living there so much though. It was just too damned small for his growing family, and he didn't just mean Elysande and the coming bairns. That would have been fine. But Tom, as Elysande's man, was there as well, as were Conn, Inan, Fearghas and Donnghail, whom Aulay had released to him as a wedding gift—after asking if they were willing, of course.

Rory was grateful for his brother releasing the men to him. They would be his head men at the castle he was building. Until then though, the men, Tom included, were all sleeping on the floor of the main room on ground level, while he and Elysande had the bedroom above. And then there was the maid Jetta had sent with them for Elysande after the wedding. She slept on a pallet in the hall outside their room. But soon there would be more members of their family. Once this interview with the English king was over, they were taking a boat north to Carlisle where they would stay a day or two to visit Mildrede and the others before taking another boat home. Rory had arranged that to avoid Elysande suffering the strain of riding in her condition. The men were not sailing with them, however. They were traveling by horseback, and he had agreed to his wife's request for them to stop at Kynardersley on the way back to check on her people and she hoped to bring back Betty, and the boy Eldon, if they had survived de Buci and were willing.

Rory hadn't been able to refuse the request; the pair had helped save Elysande's life, after all. He also hadn't been able to refuse allowing Tom to look for and invite back an older maid named Ethelfreda, who had been Elysande's nursemaid when she was a lass, and whom she hoped would be willing to move to Scotland and act as nursemaid for their child.

Children, Rory corrected himself because he was damned sure his wife was carrying twins. Which meant soon they would have five soldiers, three maids, a lad, two bairns and he and Elysande all crammed into the two-room lodge. Thank God winter had finally released the steely grasp it had held on the land this year and the weather had warmed up, because he was quite sure he and the men were going to end up sleeping outside under the stars until he got something built for them all to live in. He'd been hoping to stay at the lodge until the keep was done at least, but that could take two years and there was no way he and the men could sleep outside through the next winter.

"It was not as if I had a choice, husband," Elysande said now, drawing him from his thoughts. "He is my king. He commanded my presence here and so I had to come."

"Ye're a Scot now, lass. David is yer king," he growled.

"So he is," she agreed soothingly, patting his arm. "I have two kings and one husband. Goodness, has a woman ever had more men to boss her about?"

"Ye—" Rory broke off when the door opened beside them and Elysande's name was called. Well, her old name. Elysande de Valance. She was Elysande Buchanan now, and had been since they'd been married good and proper by a priest, a month after their arrival at Sinclair. It would have been sooner had they been able to arrange it, but it had taken that long to get everyone there for the wedding, including Tom, Fearghas and Donnghail. Elysande had refused to hold it until the three men returned from their mission and she knew they were well and the king had been warned.

"Stop scowling, husband, everything will be fine," Elysande whispered as they followed two soldiers armed with lances to the door. Tom, Fearghas and Donnghail were following close behind them. But Alick, Conn and Inan were waiting in the woods outside the city with a small army in case they had to steal Elysande back from the king.

Rory considered that, and sighed at his wife's reassuring words, not sure even she believed them. That was something he had learned about Elysande. She wasn't always as confident or calm as her serene demeanor suggested. She just was not the type of woman to have hysterics or start screaming and shouting in panic. She rarely lost control, except when he was loving her. Only then did she let go of that fine control of hers and give him all of herself. The rest of the time, she kept herself in check, and thought before she did anything. He liked that about her.

"Ah, Lady Elysande. How delightful to finally meet the woman who saved the lives of both myself and my son."

Rory eyed the King of England a bit leerily as they were led to stand several feet in front of where he sat on the throne. Edward III was young, in his mid-twenties. Rory had known that, but even so, it was startling to actually see. The man looked more a boy than he'd expected.

"Your Majesty." Elysande's soft voice drew Rory's attention and he frowned when he noted that she had dropped into a deep curtsy. One he was quite sure she would not be able to get out of on her own at this stage in her pregnancy. He was startled from his concern when she glared to the side at him and mouthed, "Bow."

Rory scowled in response, but he did bow as requested. It was best not to upset a woman so large with child, and that was the only reason why he would bow to the English king, he assured himself. He was positive that was the only reason that Fearghas and Donnghail bowed as well. None of them liked to disappoint Elysande. Of course, Tom bowed because he was English. But they forgave him that.

"Please, Lady Elysande, rise," King Edward III said, actually sounding concerned. "In fact, come, sit here next to me. I suspect you should not be kept standing around like this. Had I realized your condition, I would have delayed having you come."

"Oh, 'tis fine, Your Majesty," Elysande said breathlessly as Rory caught her under the arms and raised her back to her feet so she would not strain herself. She gave him a grateful smile, and then waddled forward to plop into the chair that was quickly produced and set next to the king.

Rory tried to follow, wanting to stick close to Elysande, but the guards that had escorted them in and stood on either side of their small group suddenly thrust their lances out, crossing them in front of him. He supposed that meant he was to wait right where he was. He also supposed he didn't have much choice in the matter. He didn't like it though.

"I must thank you, Lady Elysande, for your part in revealing the plot de Buci and his cohorts had planned against us. And I, of course, offer my condolences on the loss of your parents and their soldiers. I liked your father. He was a good man."

"Yes, he was," Elysande murmured, and Rory frowned when he heard the husky tone to her voice and saw the glassy look to her eyes. Elysande did not cry. Or at least she hadn't used to. But she had become most sensitive this past month of her pregnancy. He didn't like to see her cry. It made his heart hurt. Fortunately, she regained control of herself, cleared her throat and said, "And thank you for your condolences. I am just glad to see that you are healthy and well and de Buci's plan did not succeed. My parents' sacrifice was not in vain."

King Edward nodded, and then glanced around when a man standing beside and a little behind him suddenly bent to whisper in his ear, gesturing toward Rory and the men as he did. The king followed his gesture to Rory as he listened and then sighed and nodded before turning back to Elysande.

"I understand that you have married?" he said gently, and then added solemnly, "Without gaining my permission first?"

Rory felt his hands clench into fists as he braced himself for trouble. He was sure he'd been right. The man was going to demand an annulment.

"Aye," Elysande murmured, and then smiled crookedly at the king. "And I do feel awful about that. For while I knew you would surely approve of my marrying the man who saved your life, I was most distressed that he felt forced to offer marriage simply to save my reputation. Especially when it was only ruined in my efforts to save you."

When she stopped speaking and offered him a sweet smile, the king sat blinking briefly before saying, "The man who . . ."

"Saved your life, aye," she supplied gently, and then asked, "Did you not know?"

King Edward turned to glance at Rory standing behind the crossed lances in his finest plaid, and then turned back to Elysande. "I understood that you— That is, the letter is from your mother . . ."

"Aye. But I fear I should never have got it to you, Your Majesty. I did my best, but in the end it was my husband, Rory Buchanan, who found a way to get the warning to you. While I lay unconscious after an attack by one of de Buci's agents, he took the messages that I had hidden away and gave them to my man, Tom, then arranged passage for him on a ship heading south. He also sent two of his best men with him, to help keep him safe on the journey to court: Fearghas and Donnghail," she informed him, and then pointed toward Rory and the men, saying, "That is them there. The two tall men standing on either side of Tom in the back are Fearghas and Donnghail."

"Good Christ, she's pointing at us," Rory heard Fearghas hiss with alarm. "What is she telling him?"

"I do no' ken," Donnghail muttered. "I was no' paying attention. Just pretend they're no' staring rudely and maybe they'll stop."

"Lady Elysande is smiling," Fearghas pointed out. "Do we smile back?"

"I'm no' sure. She's smiling, but the English king's looking a bit vexed and befuddled to me," Donnghail pointed out.

Rory did not comment; he was trying very hard not to laugh. Because his beautiful wife was brilliant, and the king truly did appear vexed and befuddled as he listened to her tell him that he, Rory Buchanan, a Scot, was the hero of the story. No doubt, she did so in the hopes that the king would find it very hard to annul her marriage to a man who had apparently saved his life. And Rory supposed he *had* played a part in that endeavor. But the truth was, he'd only done it for Elysande. He hadn't given a fig whether the English king lived or died.

Before Fearghas and Donnghail could sort out whether to smile or not, Elysande was speaking again and the king's attention had returned to her.

"So you see, my husband is the true hero. Without him, I fear you never would have been warned in time."

"I see," the king murmured, lowering his head. Probably to hide his expression, Rory thought, which was no doubt becoming more vexed by the moment.

"That is why I felt so bad that he felt he had to offer marriage to save my reputation," Elysande murmured with a sad sigh.

The king glanced up. "Your reputation? You mentioned that before."

"Aye. Well, my efforts to get the warning to you necessitated my traveling alone with eight men who were neither husband nor kin. I fear my reputation was quickly in shreds from it. And then he began introducing me as his wife to avoid my suffering the slurs of others and I answered to the title, which as you know, is as good as wed in Scotland."

"Oh. I see." King Edward frowned.

"When he then asked me to wed him good and proper in front of a priest," Elysande went on, "I felt sure you would want me to marry the man who had been so instrumental in saving your life and the life of your son, but I did have qualms about it myself. I felt I was taking advantage of a man of honor and integrity. But I had come to love him." She paused and smiled sweetly again. "How could I not love a man who saved my king?"

She'd left the king blinking again, Rory noted with amusement.

"Fortunately, we do seem to do well together," Elysande went on. Placing a hand over her burgeoning stomach, she added, "And as you can see, the union has borne fruit."

"Aye." King Edward stared at her stomach, his frown returning.

"However," Elysande said, drawing his attention back to her face, "Your Majesty, we are living in Scotland now, and building a keep there."

"What of Kynardersley?" the king asked at once, pouncing on the subject like a cat on a mouse, and Rory knew that was the crux of the problem. The English king would hardly want a Scot as lord over a powerful holding in the south of England.

"That is a dilemma, Your Majesty," Elysande confessed solemnly. "I find I cannot bring myself to return to Kynardersley. The memory of the horrors I witnessed and endured there . . ." She shook her head, her eyes again glassy. "But, of course, I would not deny my child their birthright, so I was hoping that you might consider assigning a guardian to the castle and estates to look after it until my child is old enough to do so."

The king looked so relieved Rory again had a hard time not laughing. Elysande had just taken away the worry of a Scot becoming lord of one of his wealthiest and most powerful holdings. And saved him from having to force an annulment that would make him look like an ungrateful arse.

"Of course, Your Majesty, my husband and his men along with Tom are not the only people we owe a debt of gratitude to for saving your life," Elysande said now.

"Are they not?" King Edward asked warily.

"Nay," she assured him. "There are also the people of Carlisle."

"Carlisle?" he echoed uncertainly.

"Oh, my, yes," she assured him. "I must tell you, Your Majesty, that the people of Carlisle love you dearly, and risked themselves greatly to aid us. You would have been proud to see them work together on your behalf, and would have blushed to hear their love and praise for you. An alewife named Mildrede and her husband, Albert, at the Cock and Bull, as well as the draper's wife, Elizabeth, and a blacksmith named Robbie, went to great lengths to ensure we escaped to get the warning to you when de Buci's men tracked us to their fine city."

Rory felt his lips twitch at Elysande's words. He couldn't wait to tell Mildrede about it when they stopped in Carlisle on the way home. The woman would be pleased as could be to hear she'd been lauded to the king.

"Then we must surely send some special boon to Carlisle, and a personal letter and gift to this alewife, the draper's wife and the blacksmith," the king said solemnly.

"I am sure they would appreciate it, Your Majesty," Elysande assured him.

"And I shall honor your marriage with a gift," the king added.

"That is not necessary, Your Majesty. It is enough that you approve it," Elysande said at once. "You will give us your blessing, Your Majesty, will you not?"

"How could I not bless your marriage to the man who saved my life," King Edward said wryly, and Rory relaxed after that, only half listening to the remainder of the conversation. He caught something about rewards, and then an invitation for her to attend the executions of de Buci and the others, which she refused. But finally, the king stood and helped Elysande to her feet himself, then clasped her shoulders and kissed her cheek, thanking her once again for helping to save him from his enemies.

Much to Rory's surprise, the man, himself, then escorted Elysande to his side.

"He's coming over here," Fearghas murmured behind him.

"Aye," Donnghail rumbled.

"He will probably thank us for our part in saving him," Tom said out of the side of his mouth.

"Huh," Fearghas muttered. "He will no' kiss us too, will he?"

Rory choked on a laugh, tried to hide it with a cough, and then the English king was there, shaking his hand and the hands of the others as he thanked them for their assistance.

Once he had finished, the king turned his attention back to Rory and said, "You have a very beautiful, and intelligent, wife, Buchanan. Take care of her."

Rory's eyebrows rose at the way the man emphasized intelligent. It had been a message. The king had not been taken in completely by Elysande's tale. But he had accepted it because it solved his problems. It seemed the young king was smart at least. Not perhaps a good thing for Scotland if he ever settled his disputes with France and turned his attention on them again, he thought, but Rory merely said, "I will."

Much to his relief, moments later they were back out in the hall, heading for the exit.

"There, I did tell you it would be fine, husband," Elysande said, sounding pleased as they made their way through the crowds of people in the castle.

"Aye, you did," Rory admitted mildly. "I shall surely never doubt you again, wife."

"I notice you did not thank the king for your reward. Were you not pleased by it?"

"Reward?" Rory asked, glancing at her with confusion.

"Well, part wedding gift and part reward for saving his life," Elysande said. "I thought it was most generous."

"Is it?" Rory asked, nodding at the guard who opened the doors for them to leave the castle. "What is it?"

"You truly did not hear?" Elysande asked, eyeing him suspiciously.

"Nay. I may have been distracted," he admitted, but didn't tell her he'd been fretting over how crowded they would soon be at the hunting lodge. "What is this reward?"

Elysande hesitated and then shook her head. "Do you know, I think I might let it be a surprise."

Rory smiled with amusement at the words and shrugged, not really interested in what it might be. He had other issues on his mind at the moment. Not least of which was getting his wife to the docks and onto the boat waiting for them. He did dislike London.

IT WAS A SOFT WARM NUZZLING OF HIS EAR THAT WOKE RORY. Smiling before he was even fully awake, he opened his eyes and slid his arms around his wife where she stood at the side of the bed bent over him. It had been a month since their meeting with the king and their short but surprisingly enjoyable stop in Carlisle. Elysande was even larger now than she had been then, but she was still gorgeous to him and he couldn't resist trying to tug her back into bed with him.

"Nay," she said on a laugh, pressing her hands to his chest. "You have to get up."

"Why are ye up and dressed already?" Rory asked as his hand skimmed over her arisaidh.

"Your bairn was restless and woke me early," she explained. "Now up with ye."

"Nay. Come back to bed, love. Ye canno' wake a man like that and no' expect him to get ideas," he complained, sweeping one hand down her back to her bottom and squeezing gently. "Ye ken I love lovin' ye in the mornings."

"Aye, I know," she laughed. "But you must get up. Our gift from the king is here and you must come and see." Eyes twinkling with excitement, she added, "I just know you will be so pleased."

Rory hesitated briefly, desire warring with curiosity, but when Elysande pulled out of his hold and straightened to head for the door, he allowed curiosity to win and tossed the bed furs aside to get up. He didn't rush after her, however, but took the time to splash his face and tend to personal needs, then donned his plaid and headed out of the room.

Ella, the maid Jetta had sent for Elysande, was the only one on the main floor when Rory made his way downstairs. Before he could ask where his wife was, the woman smiled and pointed to the door, so he continued outside. His eyes widened with surprise when he saw his brothers Alick and Aulay waiting for him on horseback, and he started to smile in greeting, but that smile died under the weight of concern when he spotted Elysande mounted on her mare with his horse saddled beside her.

"What are ye doing, lass. You should no' be riding in yer condition," he said at once, moving to her side with every intention of lifting her back to the ground.

"I am with child, not ill, husband. And I have three months until my time," Elysande said, waving him off with exasperation. "Besides 'twould take too long did we walk. I promise I will go slow and be careful. Now mount up. I cannot wait for you to see our gift."

"Neither can I," Aulay said with a dry amusement that made Rory glance at him in question. His brother did not answer the silent question though, and merely said, "Mount up, brother. There is a boat in my bay that I should like out of it as quickly as possible."

"A boat?" Rory asked, moving to mount up.

"Aye. It brought your gift," Alick told him on a laugh, and then apparently unable to contain himself, he set his horse to trot toward the path to the beach.

Elysande headed out right behind him at a more sedate speed as Rory gained his saddle, and he glanced at his eldest brother as he gathered his reins.

Before he could again ask what it was, Aulay shook his head and said, "There are no words." He then set off after the others, leaving Rory to follow.

It wasn't far to the beach from the lodge, and that's all it was, a beach. There was no dock for boats to tie to.

Or three boats for that matter, Rory thought as he stared at the three large ships presently anchored offshore and the many, many smaller rowboats being paddled to the beach, each one full of men who were apparently coming to join the scores of men already milling about onshore.

"What the hell?" Rory breathed, staring at the men coming from the ships bearing the English king's banner.

"Is it not wonderful?" Elysande asked, her voice filled with excitement.

Rory glanced to his wife to see her attempting to wiggle her way around to dismount and cursed under his breath as he leapt from the saddle to aid her to the ground before she hurt herself.

"Thank you, husband," she said a little breathlessly once on her feet, but then she turned to wave toward the English army growing on the beach and repeated, "But is it not wonderful? The king's gift was to send us workers to help build our castle."

"What?" Rory asked with amazement.

"Aye. He sent a thousand men!" She told him, her mouth spread in a wide grin. "Why, that will double the numbers of our workers and halve the time it will take to build."

"A thousand men," Rory breathed with dismay. "God in heaven, he sent an army."

"They are stonemasons and laborers, husband, not soldiers," Elysande said with an exasperated laugh.

"They are one thousand Englishmen in Scotland, wife," Rory countered. "That's an invasion, not a gift. It'll start a bloody war." Scrubbing a hand wildly through his hair, he shook his head. "We will have the clans marching up here to send the bastards running once news of this gets out."

"What?" Elysande cried with alarm. "But they are a gift from the king. He would be insulted. And they will speed along construction for us. You cannot let the clans chase them off."

Rory frowned at her distress, and moved to slip an arm around her. "Calm yerself. I'll think o' some way to explain this to the neighboring clans so it does no' cause trouble."

"Ye'd best think quickly, brother. It looks like that explaining will be soon," Aulay commented, and Rory glanced around toward him, and then followed his gaze to the path to see that it was filling with men on horseback. He had just recognized the Mac-Gregor, Aulay's neighbor on one side, when Elysande squealed happily.

"'Tis Tom and the boys. Oh, and there is Betty and Eldon." She was off at once, waddling up the beach toward the quickly growing group.

"Did she just call Conn, Inan, Fearghas and Donnghail 'boys'?" Aulay asked with amazement.

Rory waved away his brother's outrage and hurried after his wife. The woman was remarkably quick for her size, and she had nearly reached the group before he caught her up. He was about to take her arm to draw her protectively to his side while he sorted out what was what, when she suddenly squealed again and put on a burst of speed that carried her past Tom and into the crowd where she was enveloped in the arms of an older woman. Her old nursemaid, he realized when she said, "Ethelfreda! You are here! Thank you, I was so worried you would not agree to come."

"Of course I came, love," the old lady murmured, hugging Elysande tightly and rocking her from side to side. "I'd go to hell itself and even come to Scotland for you and those bairns I see you're carrying."

"Oh, Ethel," Elysande sniffled, pulling back to kiss the woman's cheek before her gaze landed on someone else, and she opened her arm to include a younger maid in the hug, crying, "Betty! Thank goodness you are all right. I was so worried for you."

"I am fine, m'lady," the young maid whispered as she stepped into Elysande's arm.

"But she nearly wasn't," a young lad with a fresh scar running down his cheek announced, rushing to the women. "De Buci beat her something awful, m'lady. As bad as he did you. But she didn't tell him nothing. She was ever so brave," he told her, and then bit his lip and admitted, "It was me who told him ye'd headed north, m'lady, and I'm sorry I did. Ever so sorry," he added, tears in his eyes. "I didn't tell him when he was beating me, but I couldn't bear to watch him beat Betty another minute. He was surely gonna kill her and I couldn't bear to watch. But I'm sorry I told. Really, I am. Please don't be angry and send me away."

"Oh, Eldon," Elysande sighed, releasing Betty to hug the boy. "You did the right thing. You saved Betty, and despite your telling, de Buci didn't catch us. I am not angry. All is well."

"Thank you, m'lady," the boy said on a sob, and buried his face against her stomach as she hugged him.

"He's been fretting that she would be angry all the way here," Tom murmured, watching his mistress soothe the boy.

Rory nodded, but then turned to the MacGregor as he dismounted, noticing only then that the man alighting from the horse beside the clan chieftain's was his brother Niels.

"Niels," he greeted with surprise, hugging him and thumping him on the back. "What are you doing here?"

"I was on my way back home from business in Glasgow when I came across your men and their escorts," Niels said with wry amusement as they stepped apart. "I thought I'd best join the party too to make sure they all got here safely."

Rory chuckled at the claim. "Two women and a boy hardly merit . . ." His voice trailed off as he realized what Niels had said. *Your men and their escorts*, not *your men escorting this small group*. His gaze slid to the MacGregor, and then to the other men who had now moved forward to join them. He recognized most of them and each were heads of clans: the Douglas, the Ferguson, the Kennedy, the Wallace, the Stewart, the Erskine and the MacGregor.

"Escorts?" Rory asked uncertainly as Aulay and Alick joined them.

"Ah, m'laird," Tom said suddenly, drawing his gaze around to see that the English soldier was looking extremely uncomfortable and rather nervous. "I know we were really only sent to bring back Betty, Eldon and Ethelfreda, but ye see . . ."

"The others wanted to come too," Donnghail announced when Tom faltered.

"The others?" Rory asked carefully, his gaze moving toward the group surrounding his wife to see that it wasn't all soldiers as he'd first assumed. It was women, and men, and children he had never seen before, all in English dress, and at a rough count he could see at least thirty of them crowding around his wife.

"Aye," the Kennedy said, amusement on his grizzled face as he took in Rory's dismayed expression. "It seems yer wife and her parents were well loved by their people. Not surprising, I suppose. I hear Lady Elysande's mother was a Scot born."

"Aye," Rory said with a frown as he tried to count exactly how many servants there were. It was hard to tell, there were so many soldiers crowding about now.

"'Tis just unfortunate the servants and all are English," the Ferguson said now. "When my man came to tell me there were at least fifty English traipsing through with a passel o' Scots, I had them stopped. O' course, soon as I realized it was yer men and yer wife's people and that they were headed to you, I rounded up me men to help escort them. No telling what trouble could ha'e befallen them their being English and all. Some clans would no' take that well."

"That's about what happened when they reached my land," the Douglas announced. "And I gathered some men to join the escort too."

The others quickly added that it was the way it had been with them too, and Rory nodded and murmured a thank-you, but then turned to Tom and asked, "Fifty? Ye brought fifty o' them back?"

"And more are coming," Fearghas announced. "They're just moving a bit slower because o' the sheep and all, so we left them behind with Conn and Inan to escort them while we brought this group here. I'm guessing the others'll get here in a week or so."

"More?" Rory squawked. "What sheep? What the—"

"Oh, husband!"

Rory snapped his mouth closed as Elysande rushed up beaming happily.

"Is it not wonderful?" she cried, hugging him tightly. "So many more survived than I'd hoped, and they all wanted to come live with us." Pulling back, she told him, "Why, now we have a blacksmith, a cook, a miller, two grooms, the alewife, our own seamstress and maids and—oh, just a whole castle full of people!"

"But no castle to put them in," Rory muttered, reaching up to rub his forehead.

"Not yet, but soon," she said at once. "Why, with the men the king sent to help we should have a castle in no time."

Elysande didn't wait for his response to that, but whirled away to hurry back to the others.

Rory stared after her, noting how happy she looked. He suspected he was seeing the Elysande she had been before de Buci had marched in and raised such havoc in her life. Or as close as she would ever become to that young woman again. She was damned near glowing with joy at being reunited with these people. But then she had grown up with them in her life for so long and they had loved her enough to follow her to Scotland. She was getting her home back without actually having to set foot in the castle that held the terrible memories of her parents' murder. And somehow, he had to figure out a way to let her keep that home, these people, with her.

"They are no' going to all fit in the lodge," Aulay said suddenly as if somehow following his thoughts.

Rory closed his eyes briefly and then speared Fearghas with a gaze and asked, "Sheep?"

"Aye. Sheep, a wagonload o' chickens, a dozen cows and even a few horses, but mostly sheep, about a hundred I'd say," Donng-hail said when Fearghas merely nodded. He then added, "The English king hadn't sent a guardian out to take over watching the land ere we left. I suspect whoever it is won't be happy when he arrives to find the place pretty much empty, but we figured he'd just blame de Buci and it should be all right we brought Lady Ely-sande's people here."

"Dear God," Rory moaned, rubbing his forehead harder. He had sheep. And cows, chickens, servants, and nowhere to put them.

"They are definitely no' going to all fit in the lodge," Aulay repeated as if Rory might have missed it the first time.

"Isn't that the English king's banner?" the Erskine clan chieftain suddenly asked.

"Aye, 'tis," the Stewart chieftain responded. "Why do ye ha'e a bunch o' Englishmen gathering on yer beach? Are we being invaded?"

"'Tis a damned good thing we came if the English are thinking o' invading," the Wallace chieftain said grimly, tugging out his sword. "We'll send the bastards running in a hurry."

"Nay!" Rory said abruptly, and then straightened his shoulders. "We're no' being invaded. And if any one o' ye ever wants the benefit o' me healing skills again, ye'll leave those men be. They're a gift to me wife from the English king for saving his life. He sent them to help construct the castle I'm building so she'd ha'e a home to raise our bairns in, and I damned well need all the help I can get now that I seem to ha'e a castle full o' servants and nowhere to put them."

There was a moment of silence and then one of the chieftains said, "Aye, ye're definitely needing someplace to put all these people. They'll no' fit in that wee hunting lodge o' Aulay's."

"What ye need is a motte and bailey castle to tide ye o'er until the stone one is done," another said thoughtfully, and Rory stared at the man with wonder. That was the answer. An old-fashioned motte and bailey castle. A wooden structure on a raised bit of land, or motte, with a wall around it made from timber. That could be built pretty quick. Why, William the Conqueror had managed to make one in eighty days using only fifty men. With the two thousand he had here, they could have one built in a week easily and it would give them somewhere to live until the men finished the castle proper.

"I hope you are not expecting us to build a motte and bailey for you. The king sent us to build a proper stone edifice. We do not build mottes and baileys."

Rory swung around at that announcement to find that a small contingent of the Englishmen had braved approaching while the other five or six hundred already ashore watched safely from the shoreline. Men were still disembarking from the ship and being shuttled to shore in the smaller boats.

"Now see here," the Ferguson said, stepping up to Rory's side. "If the king sent ye here to build, ye'll build and—"

"Nay, leave off with that," the MacGregor said, interrupting the older man. "They probably have no' the skill to build a proper motte anyway. 'Tis better if the Scottish builders do it. We want a stable motte."

"Do ye think our stonemasons'll know what to do?" Ferguson asked now with a frown. "It's an old skill."

"Do you know how to do it?" the MacGregor asked him.

"Aye," the Ferguson said at once.

"Well, hell, then let's do it ourselves. With all the warriors we have here, and the servants too, we'll have the damned thing up before those English have all their men and their tools ashore."

Rory stood, mouth agape, as everybody but Aulay, Alick, Tom, Fearghas and Donnghail suddenly walked off, discussing what they needed to do to build him a temporary home.

"It looks like you're getting a motte and bailey to tide you over," Aulay said with amusement.

"Aye." Rory sighed the word as he closed his mouth. He should be relieved, but suspected he had a lot of headaches in his future with the three different groups of men. He sincerely doubted that the nearly one thousand Scottish masons and laborers already working on the castle would take kindly to the arrival of the English masons and laborers, and as for the men who had determined to build him a motte and bailey . . . clans had never been known to work well together.

Shaking his head, Rory pushed those worries away for now and went in search of his wife. He wanted to be sure she was safely back at the lodge with her feet up and as many of her people around her as he could arrange for before he left her to lead everyone to the construction site.

It was a thump and a curse that stirred Elysande from sleep. Opening her eyes she listened to her husband's hushed apology and smiled to herself. He'd tripped over Eldon again on his way up the hall. Or perhaps it had been Betty, or Ethelfreda, or one of the other women and children now filling the lodge at night. There were many of them—too many, really—and Rory was forced to tiptoe through them and hope he didn't misstep and tread on anyone when he came to bed at night. But he didn't complain.

She wouldn't blame him if he did. The poor man usually didn't stumble back to the lodge until late at night, and he arrived exhausted from long days overseeing building the castle while helping to build the motte and bailey. Although she suspected he got little actual work done. Most of his time these last two weeks since the king's men had arrived along with the clans and her people, seemed to be taken up with trying to keep the English masons and Scottish masons from killing each other, and trying to stave off all-out war being declared between the various clans as they tried to work together on the motte and bailey.

She heard the faint creak of the door to the bedchamber opening, and waited silently as he entered, closed the door and crossed to the bed. Elysande heard his plaid hit the floor about halfway across the room. His tunic followed a couple of steps later, and then he was crawling into bed behind her. When his arm came around her and he gently rubbed his large hand over her swollen belly, she smiled and covered his fingers with her own.

"Good eve, husband," she whispered, squeezing the back of his hand.

"Good eve, wife. Did I wake you?" he asked with concern as he pressed a kiss to her neck.

"Nay," she lied, knowing he'd feel guilty otherwise and not wanting him to add that burden to the load he was already carrying. She felt him relax and closed her eyes, thinking he would sleep now, when he spoke again.

"The motte and bailey is done."

Elysande's eyes flew open at once and she twisted onto her back to try to look at him, but it was too dark to see his expression. "Really?"

"Aye. We finished tonight," he said, and she could hear the satisfaction in his voice. "We can all move in tomorrow and stop tripping over each other in this place."

"And the clans will leave now," she added, happiest about that. Having them work together was like having a dozen cooks in the kitchen, each of them wanting to lead the meal preparation, each having their own way of doing things and each sure their way was best. She was amazed everyone had made it through the project alive.

"Half of them have already gone, and the other half plan to leave after breaking their fast in the morning," Rory told her.

"And we shall have the place to ourselves," Elysande said on a pleased little sigh, squeezing his arm as she did.

"Ourselves, five soldiers, sixty servants, a hundred sheep, a dozen chickens, two cows, six horses and two thousand masons and laborers banging away nearby every day," Rory said dryly.

Elysande chuckled at the complaint and turned onto her side facing him. "We could always slip away back here on occasion when you wish a break. Aulay did give us use of the lodge until the castle is built."

"Aye, he did, didn't he?" Rory murmured, drawing her closer and rubbing his hand up and down her back. Pressing a kiss to her cheek, he sighed, "I love you, Elysande. I'm so glad your mother sent you to me."

"So am I," she whispered back. "And I love you too."

When his response was a light snore, a smile slid over Elysande's lips. She wasn't upset that he'd fallen asleep and missed her declaration. She had told him that before and would tell him again. In fact, she planned to tell him that at least once a day for the rest of her life. Because she did love him, and she too was grateful she had been sent to him. Elysande's mother might have called her a treasure in the letter she'd sent to Rory, but the truth was her brave handsome Highlander husband was the treasure, and he was all hers.

"I love you too, my highland treasure," she whispered softly and closed her eyes.

Turn the page for a sneak peek of
Lynsay Sands's

MEANT TO BE IMMORTAL

Available May 2021

Prologue

*M*AC HAD JUST FINISHED SETTING UP HIS CENTRIFUGE WHEN he caught a whiff of what smelled like smoke. He lifted his head and inhaled deeply; there was the astringent cleaner he'd used on the counter surfaces, various chemical and other scents he couldn't readily identify that were coming from the boxes he had yet to unpack, and—yes—smoke.

A frisson of alarm immediately ran up the back of Mac's neck. Where there was smoke there was fire and fire was bad for his kind. It was bad for mortals too, of course, but was even worse for immortals who were incredibly flammable.

Straightening abruptly, Mac stepped over one unopened box and then another, weaving his way out of the maze of unpacking he still had to do and to the stairs leading out of the basement. He took them two at a time, rushing up the steps to the special door he'd had installed several days ago. It blocked sound, germs, and everything else from entering the lab he was turning his basement into. He'd also had the walls sealed and covered with a germ-resistant skin. Apparently, his efforts had been successful. Even at the top of the stairs, he was only able to catch the slightest hint of smoke in the air, yet when he opened the door he found himself standing at the mouth of hell. The kitchen on the other side of the door was engulfed in flames that seemed almost alive and leapt excitedly his way with a roar.

A startled shout of alarm slipped from his lips as heat rushed over him, and Mac slammed the door closed at once. He nearly took a header down the stairs in his rush to get as far away from it as he could and crashed into a box as he stumbled off the last step. Pausing then, he stopped to turn in a circle, a mouse in a blazing maze, searching for a way out.

His gaze slid over the small half windows that ran along the top of the basement wall on the back of the house, skating over the flames waving at him from the burning bushes outside, and then he turned toward the rooms along the front of the house and hurried to the door to the first one. It was a bathroom, its window even smaller than the others in the main room. It was also covered with some kind of glaze that blocked the view. Even so, he could see light from the fire on the other side of it.

Rushing to the next door, he thrust it open. This was an empty room about ten feet deep and fourteen wide, with two half windows that ran along the front of the house. Mac stared with despair at the flames dancing on the other side of the glass. He was trapped, with no way out . . . and no way even to call for help, he realized suddenly. There was no landline in the basement, and he'd left his cell phone upstairs on the kitchen counter to avoid interruptions while he set up down here.

I'm done for, Mac thought with despair, and then glimpsed a flash of red light beyond the flames framing and filling the nearer window. Moving cautiously forward, Mac tried to see what was out there, and felt a bit of hope when he spotted the fire truck parked at the top of the driveway and the men rushing around it, pulling out equipment. If he could get their attention, and let them know where he was . . .

Turning, Mac rushed back into the main room, wading through the sea of boxes until he spotted the one he wanted. He ripped it open and dug through the bubble-wrapped contents until he found his microscope. It was old and heavy, and Mac pulled it out with relief and then tore the bubble wrap off as he moved back to the empty storage room. He didn't even hesitate, but crossed half the room in a couple of swift strides and simply threw the microscope through the nearest of the two little windows. Glass shattered and Mac jumped back as the flames exploded inward as if eager to get in. They were followed by rolling smoke that quickly surrounded him, making him choke as he yelled for help.

He was shouting for the third time when dark figures appeared on the other side of the fire now crowding the window. He thought he could make out two men in bulky gear, what he supposed was the firemen's protective wear, and then someone shouted, "Hello? Is there someone there?"

"Yes!" Mac responded with relief. "I am in the basement."

"We'll get you out! Just hang on, buddy! We'll get you out!"

"Get somewhere where there's less smoke," someone else shouted to him.

"Okay!" Mac backed out of the room, his fascinated gaze watching the fire fan out from the window as the drywall around it caught flame. It would spread quickly now that he'd given the fire a way in, he knew. The smoke was already filling this room and pouring out into the main room, but he could deal with that. Smoke couldn't kill him. Fire would.

Cursing, he turned abruptly and returned to the bathroom next door. There was no fire or smoke in the small room yet, but would be soon enough. Moving to the cast iron claw-foot tub he'd had refinished before moving in, Mac plugged in the stopper and prayed silently as he turned on the taps. Relief slid through him when water began to pour out. The fire hadn't stopped the water from working yet, and the taps and faucet were old enough not to have an aerator to reduce the speed at which the water jetted out. It gushed from the tap at high pressure, filling the tub quickly, or at least more quickly than his tub back in New York would have filled. There it would have taken ten or fifteen minutes to fill the tub; here it took probably half that, but they were the longest minutes of his life and fire was beginning to eat through the wall between the bathroom and the storage room before it was quite finished.

Mac didn't wait for it to finish filling, but stepped into the quickly heating water in his pajama bottoms and T-shirt when it was three-quarters full, and submerged himself up to his nose.

Smoke was coming into the room now, pouring through the air vents, making breathing hard, and the water was hotter than hell, the fire heating it in the pipes on its way to this room and the tub. But it was only going to get hotter. The one wall of the room was now a mass of flames, and the fire was eating its way into the two connecting walls as well. The linoleum tile on the floor was catching flame and curling inward toward the tub. The water he was in would be boiling soon, by his guess. He now knew how lobsters felt when dropped in boiling water. It was one hell of a gruesome way to die . . . But it wouldn't kill him. As long as he didn't catch fire, he would survive, but Mac suspected he'd wish he was dead before this was over.